Praise for
THE DEVIL INSIDE

**Nominated for the 2007 *Romantic Times* Reviewer's
Choice Award for Best Urban Fantasy
Finalist for Love Romances and More Café's Best
of 2007 Awards for Best Book All Around**

"An exorcist with an attitude, Morgan Kingsley is sure
to win Black a legion of fans."   —Kelley Armstrong

"A sassy heroine who's not afraid to do what it takes to get
the job done or to save a loved one's life. Add to that a sexy
hero, great secondary characters, and a story line that
keeps you reading, and this one is definitely a keeper."
—Keri Arthur

"[Black's] got a winning heroine, a well-crafted contem-
porary world where demonic possession is just a part of
life, and a nice balance of mystery, action and sex, making this light but engaging novel an urban fantasy series
kickoff full of promise."   —*Publishers Weekly*

"Talk about your odd couples! The delicious irony of
trapping a sexy demon and a cranky exorcist in the same
body gives rising star Black lots of room for conflict and
action. It's inventive in the extreme! 4½ stars. Top pick!"
—*Romantic Times*

"The plot is nonstop from the first page and the romance is sprinkled throughout.... A wonderful new addition to the genre, *The Devil Inside* is an intriguing
story and Morgan Kingsley an engaging heroine. I can't
wait to see what the next book, *The Devil You Know*,
has to offer."   —*Romance Reviews Today*

"With characters you can't help but love, and those you love to hate, Ms. Black begins her new series with a story line that's full of action and surprises. It's sometimes dark, often loving and completely sexy."

—*Darque Reviews*

"5 Ribbons. *The Devil Inside* is nail-biting, powerful and passionate all in one...a fast-paced, nonstop adventure that I'm sure everyone will love as much as I do." —RomanceJunkies.com

"A dark, edgy, and erotic paranormal. [Black's] writing is intense and she really makes her world come to life. I was hooked from the beginning....A truly sinister tale that reaches out and grabs your attention. Ms. Black has created a spine-chilling new series." —FreshFiction.com

"An outstanding beginning to a new supernatural series! The book starts out with action and only gets faster. I never noticed the story to slow down at all. The plot slowly unfolds to reveal that more is going on than anyone can possibly guess. I sincerely believe the author to have a major winner on her hands with Morgan Kingsley. Five stars." —*Huntress Reviews*

Praise for
THE DEVIL YOU KNOW

"A gritty and gutsy tale....Wonderfully written with complex characters, an intricate plot, and intense demon encounters, this book will keep readers enthralled. For an intense thrill ride, pick up a copy of *The Devil You Know*." —*Romance Reviews Today*

"A suspenseful, sexy paranormal that you will love!"

—FreshFiction.com

SPEAK OF
THE DEVIL

JENNA BLACK

A DELL SPECTRA BOOK

A Dell Mass Market Original

Copyright © 2009 by Jenna Black

Published in the United States by Dell, an imprint of The Random House Publishing Group, a division of Random House, Inc., New York.

DELL is a registered trademark of Random House, Inc., and the colophon is a trademark of Random House, Inc.

ISBN 978-0-440-24493-6

Cover design: Jaime S. Warren
Cover illustration: Craig White

Printed in the United States of America

www.bantamdell.com

2 4 6 8 9 7 5 3 1

To Dan, for . . . everything.

Acknowledgments

My thanks to Wendy Rome, who helped me figure out how to make up laws—and lawsuits—to govern exorcists. Morgan hates you for getting her into so much trouble, but I'm very grateful! Thanks also to my wonderful agent, Miriam Kriss. And a special thanks to all the fabulous people at Bantam Dell who've made working on the Morgan Kingsley series such a joy: publicist Alison Masciovecchio; editorial assistant (and sender of all things good) David Pomerico; and most especially Anne Groell, editor extraordinaire!

SPEAK OF
THE DEVIL

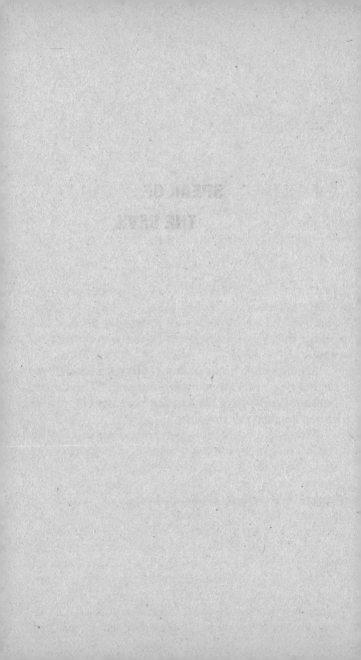

Chapter 1

"**I don't** need a lawyer," I told Brian once again.

He looked more mulish each time I said it. "Yes, you do!" His voice had risen a tad, but he was still calmer than I was. I suspected I was red in the face by now.

Arguing with Brian is almost always a losing battle, but that never stops me from trying. "This case is bullshit. People have tried to sue exorcists before and gotten laughed out of court."

That was a bit of an exaggeration, but still... The general public doesn't know why most hosts are catatonic after their demons have been exorcized, or why a small percentage are actually brain-dead. And there was absolutely zero evidence that the exorcist's performance had anything to do with it. But that hadn't deterred Jordan Maguire Sr. from filing suit against me when my exorcism on his son didn't go quite the way he'd have liked.

"I don't think you understand lawyers," Brian said with a sardonic grin. "The fact that no one's been successful in a suit so far is more of a plus than a minus for some of them. If they happen to succeed where everyone else has failed, they make a big splash. If the suit fizzles, there's no harm done—but it'll still be a major pain in the ass for you."

"Yes, but—"

"It's not just going to go away, Morgan."

I think I was beginning to believe that, but that didn't stop me from hoping. I had more than enough problems in my life without dealing with a lawsuit. I felt a whopper of a headache coming on. "Why can't you just defend me yourself?" I'm afraid I sounded a little whiny, but I couldn't help it. What's the good of dating a lawyer if he can't defend you when some asshole decides to sue?

"Because you need a tort defense attorney, not a corporate attorney."

I plopped down on Brian's couch and rested my head against the back, staring at the ceiling. If Maguire's goal was to make me miserable, he'd succeeded. But there was a reason I was violently opposed to hiring a lawyer, and it wasn't anything I'd said out loud—yet. See, a couple of months ago, my house and all my worldly possessions had burned to the ground. It was going to take me approximately forever and a day to recover from the financial devastation, even when the insurance company finally coughed up every cent they owed me. There was no question it was arson, and the official investigation had ruled that I was not the guilty party. However, since the fire had been started *inside* my house while I was still in it, the insurance company had launched its own investigation. My theory was that they were looking for excuses to delay paying me, but it turned out that mentioning this to the insurance investigator wasn't the way to win friends and influence people.

Add to that the fact that the U.S. Exorcism Board had suspended me when the lawsuit was filed, and I was already on a strict diet of ramen noodles and peanut butter sandwiches. I didn't want to think about how much I'd have to pay a lawyer to defend this suit.

"Look," I said, "I know this isn't your area of expertise, but I'd feel a hell of a lot more comfortable with you defending me than some stranger."

Brian sighed as he took a seat on the couch beside me. "You wouldn't find it so comfortable if I bungled the case."

"You wouldn't!" I protested, raising my head to give him an indignant look. Brian is competence personified, and I'm not just saying that because I'm in love with him.

He frowned at me. "Yeah, I would. Not because I'm an idiot, but because I'm not an expert. Believe me, this thing could get ugly fast, and I'd be out of my league."

"But—"

"What percentage of hosts end up catatonic after an exorcism?"

It was my turn to frown. "I don't know, about eighty percent. Why?"

"Okay, how many end up brain-dead?"

I could tell from the intense way he was looking at me that he wasn't going to answer my question until I answered his. "Maybe about two percent? I don't have the exact figure."

"Let's say you've got the figures exactly right. What percentage of the hosts that you personally have performed exorcisms on are catatonic, and what percentage are brain-dead?"

I didn't feel like sitting still anymore, so I jumped to my feet and started pacing. "How should I know? You think I keep a tally or something?"

Brian stayed seated and watched me pace. "I bet the U.S. Exorcism Board does."

"Well, I'm probably right around the average."

"What if you're not? What if it turns out three percent of your exorcisms end in brain death?"

"I—"

"You're the most successful exorcist in the U.S.," he interrupted, in full lawyer mode now. "You get called in to exorcize demons other exorcists have failed to cast out. Is it possible these demons who are extra powerful do more damage to their hosts' brains?"

My chest felt kind of hollow all of a sudden. Because I myself was possessed by Lugh, the king of the demons, I knew a lot of things that your average human being didn't know. Like that the reason most hosts are catatonic or brain-dead is that illegal or rogue demons—those who possess unwilling hosts or commit violent crimes—are much more likely to abuse their hosts than legal ones. Brian knew this, too, but most humans thought it was a total mystery why most hosts were fried, and that was just the way the demons liked it. It was certainly within the realm of possibility that I'd exorcized demons who'd been extra abusive.

"You know Maguire's attorney is going to look into those statistics right off the bat," Brian continued. "And if your numbers don't exactly match the national average, he's immediately going to have fuel to attack you."

Yup. Definitely getting a headache. I pinched the bridge of my nose. But Brian wasn't finished hammering home his point.

"What about your exorcism ritual?" he asked.

I crossed my arms over my chest. "What about it?"

"Is it *exactly* like everyone else's?"

"Of course not," I said through gritted teeth. "There's no standard procedure. Each exorcist has their own ritual." Brian already knew this, so I wasn't expecting my answer to satisfy him.

"But there are some things most exorcisms have in common, aren't there? For example, isn't it common practice to create a circle of protection around the person to be exorcized?"

I rolled my eyes. "A lot of people do that," I admitted, "but it doesn't actually *do* anything. It's just something that helps put the exorcist into the trance state."

"Did you create a circle of protection around Jordan Maguire?"

Oh shit! It didn't take a genius to figure out where he was going with this. I'd always had a more nononsense style than most of my fellow exorcists. My ritual is very simple, relying only on lighting a few vanilla-scented candles. For me, that's all it takes to induce the trance state I need to be in to perform an exorcism. Sometimes, when I'm really stressed out or upset, I'd set up the candles in a circle just for the reassurance of the more traditional ritual, but I usually just put them wherever it's convenient.

"Like I said, the circle is just symbolic." But even I could imagine how this could sound to a layman when delivered with proper flourish from a sharklike attorney.

"And what were you wearing when you performed the exorcism?"

"What?" I cried, giving him an are-you-crazy look. "What the hell does that have to do with anything?"

"Were you wearing a suit? Or at least dressed in business casual?"

"No! That's not my style, and you know it." I didn't specifically remember what I had worn that day, but the outfit had likely included low-rise jeans. I was pretty sure I hadn't gone with my leather look. But whatever I'd worn, it would be captured for posterity on a digital recording of the procedures.

Brian frowned theatrically. "Then you don't really take these exorcisms seriously, do you?"

"Of course I do!" I could tell from the heat in my cheeks that my face had flushed nice and red. And my voice had grown steadily louder.

"You expect me to think you take an exorcism seriously when you don't bother to create a circle of protection and you show up wearing jeans?"

It was all I could do not to kick the coffee table. Or Brian's shin. "That's just ridiculous. I told you, the circle is just for show. And what does it matter what I wear?"

Brian nodded sagely. "You'll make a wonderful impression at your deposition when you start shouting like that."

Okay, now I *really* wanted to go after his shins.

"You wouldn't be getting so worked up if you didn't see my point," Brian said. "Like I said, this isn't my specialty. Imagine what an expert can do. You need someone who can anticipate questions like these—and worse—so you can be prepared to answer them reasonably. I'm not the man for the job."

My palms were sweating, so I wiped them on my pants legs. Yeah, he'd definitely made his point.

I blew out a deep breath, then sat beside him on the couch again. I clasped my hands between my knees and stared at them. "I don't even want to ask how much this will cost me," I said.

"No, you probably don't."

I swallowed hard and forced myself to look at him. "How much is this going to cost me?"

"Depends on how ugly it gets and how long it

goes on. Your attorney will probably charge somewhere around two-fifty to three-fifty an hour, and then there will be all kinds of other expenses, like hiring expert witnesses and—"

"Just give me some kind of ballpark estimate."

The sympathy in his eyes told me more than I wanted to know, but he verbalized it anyway. "It could easily run fifty to a hundred grand, and that's kind of on the low side."

I'm pretty sure my face went completely white. I'd known it was going to be bad, but not *that* bad. I couldn't possibly afford that kind of money. Not even close. I was real grateful Brian didn't start in on me about having let my liability insurance lapse. It wasn't something I'd done on purpose. It was just that with my house burning down and various people trying to kill me and my loved ones, I'd been a little slack on the day-to-day stuff. I was lucky if I remembered to pay my rent.

"You know I'll help you," Brian said softly.

The gentleness in his voice made my eyes burn. I suck at accepting help of any kind, and Brian knows it. To accept that kind of money from him was absolutely out of the question.

"I don't think you're going to have much of a choice," he continued, as if he'd heard my thoughts.

I really hated that he was right. Again.

I felt like complete crap after my conversation with Brian. I'd been hoping for a little action when I went to his place, but talk of the impending lawsuit had spoiled the mood.

Brian had given me the names of a couple of attorneys he thought would do a good job for me. This being Sunday, I'd have to wait until tomorrow to call one. I'd promised Brian I wouldn't wait any longer than that, but I'm an expert at procrastination, and I was betting something would come up and give me an excuse not to.

After giving up all hope of a roll in the hay, I left Brian's and went back to my apartment, where I busied myself with such exciting tasks as cleaning the toilet.

About the only time I'll act all housewifey is when I'm under a lot of strain. The fact that my apartment was already spotless was a testament to what my life had been like lately.

At around three o'clock, the front desk called to let me know I had a visitor: Adam White. Adam's the Director of Special Forces, the branch of the Philly police department that's responsible for demon-related crime. He's also a demon who's into S&M, heavy on the S, and one of Lugh's chief supporters. Too bad he and I get along about as well as your typical snake and mongoose.

The last thing I wanted to deal with was another verbal sparring session with Adam, but he wouldn't have stopped by just for a social call. He had something important to talk to me about, and hearing him out was the only responsible option.

Because I'm completely paranoid—with good reason, I might add—I checked the peephole to make sure it really was Adam before I opened the door to let him in.

Despite the fact that I disliked Adam and that the feeling was mutual, I couldn't help noticing how scrumptious he looked. All legal demon hosts are good-looking—the Spirit Society thinks it's beneath a demon's dignity to reside in someone unattractive—but Adam's looks definitely pushed my buttons. He was the classic tall, dark, and handsome, with a super-sized serving of bad boy on top. He was obviously off duty today, wearing a pair of heavily faded blue jeans and a white oxford shirt with the sleeves rolled up past his elbows. My inventory of his appearance came to a screeching halt when I saw the manila folder tucked under his right arm.

The last time he'd shown up at my place with a manila folder, he'd blithely shown me some of the most gruesome crime scene photos you could imagine. It had slipped his mind that as a civilian, I wasn't used to looking at images of people whose insides weren't inside anymore, and it had been all I could do not to hurl.

Adam chuckled softly when he saw me staring at the folder. "No, these aren't more crime scene photos," he assured me.

I hated that my train of thought had been that obvious, but by now I was beginning to believe I'd never learn to keep everything I'm thinking from flashing across my face like the CNN crawl.

"Glad to hear it," I said, trying to sound casual as I gestured him in.

He nodded his thanks and headed for my dining room table, laying the folder down and flipping it open. Despite his assurances, my subconscious clearly didn't trust him, because I had to fight my instinct to look away.

The first thing I saw was an eight-by-ten photo of a pretty, perky blond woman. I recognized her immediately as Barbara Paige, aka Reporter Barbie. Actually, I was going to have to stop calling her Reporter Barbie, because we'd established beyond a shadow of a doubt that she wasn't a reporter, despite her claims.

She'd started following me around and asking questions shortly after the Maguire exorcism. I hadn't seen her in the weeks since then, though I often felt like I was being watched. But again, that could just be my paranoia speaking.

Adam picked up the photo and handed it to me. "Her real name is Barbara Paget. And it turns out she's a private investigator."

I groaned and sank into one of the chairs. A reporter was bad enough, but a PI? "Let me guess. Hired by Jordan Maguire Sr.?"

"I don't know for sure, but that's a good guess. And there's more."

"Great."

He pushed another couple of photos across the table to me. One of them was a family shot—mom, dad, and two beautiful teenage girls, maybe about sixteen years old. The girls looked so much alike that they had to be twins, although they didn't go for the cutesy matching clothes some twins favored.

The second photo was of what had once been a pair of cars. They'd both been smashed, and it was obvious from the photo that one car had hit the other square in the passenger door. One of the cars had been burned almost black, but the other car apparently had not caught fire.

It didn't look to me like the kind of accident that left any survivors.

Adam pointed at the picture of the family. "The girl on the left is Barbara, and those are her parents and her twin sister, Blair." He then pointed at the accident photo. "Barbara was staying overnight at a friend's house when the accident happened. Both parents were killed, and Blair was horribly burned. She had to be resuscitated twice on the way to the hospital. The doctors say it's a miracle she survived, but I'm not sure she'd agree. She's paralyzed from the neck down and suffers from severe brain damage."

I couldn't help wincing, seeing the picture of her

looking so young and vibrant and happy. I knew what it was like to lose family members, both to death and to what I considered worse. Even though Barbie had been a major pain in my ass and was looking to continue in that role, I couldn't help feeling a bit sorry for her.

"Barbara, as Blair's only living relative, is paying for her stay at the long-term care facility." The grimness in Adam's face told me just which facility he was talking about.

"The Healing Circle."

Adam nodded to confirm my guess. The Healing Circle is possibly the best and biggest hospital-cum-long-term-care facility in the city. It's also run by demons who tend to be loyal to Dougal, the would-be usurper of the demon throne.

"Is it a coincidence, do you think?" I asked Adam, not sure what to think myself.

"Hard to tell. On the one hand, it does seem like a pretty major coincidence that the PI hired to investigate you has any kind of tie to The Healing Circle. On the other hand, anyone who has a relative in the condition Blair is in would want that relative at The Healing Circle if they could afford it."

That was true. My own brother had spent a chunk of time there, catatonic after his demon had left his body. He was one of the lucky few who recovered.

I frowned. "I don't know what kind of money private investigators make, but is it enough to pay for that kind of care?"

"I'd say that's pretty iffy. Of course, if all her clients are like Maguire..."

I nodded, not needing him to finish the thought. Maguire had more money than some small countries, and I doubted he would spare any expense in his little witch hunt. And that's all this lawsuit was. Obviously, Maguire didn't need more money, even if I'd had any.

"So, have you had one of your little chats with Ms. Paget?" I asked. Adam is a real pro at the intimidation game. Not to mention other kinds of games that I don't want to think about.

To my surprise, he shook his head. "Considering that Maguire must be a real cash cow, I doubt I'd be able to get her to back off. And the fact that I'd tried would probably set off all kinds of warning bells in her head."

"So what you're telling me is there's basically nothing we can do about her?"

"Pretty much."

Great. I was broke. I was unemployed. I was being sued. I was being followed and otherwise investigated. And through all this, I was supposed to help restore Lugh to his throne while his enemies made repeated attempts to kill us.

I really needed to get a new life. Mine, frankly, sucked.

Chapter 2

I offered to make a pot of coffee, because caffeine is my drug of choice. I expected Adam to decline. We weren't exactly bosom buddies, so when he accepted my offer, I knew there was something else he wanted to talk about. Knowing him, I wouldn't like the subject, but I hoped it would be better than brooding about the lawsuit.

My financial situation had reduced me to el-cheapo store-brand coffee instead of the freshly ground beans I much preferred. At least it still smelled good and packed the caffeine punch I needed. I brought two mugs of coffee to the table and handed one to Adam before taking my seat once more. I suppose it would have been more hostesslike to move this party into the living room, but somehow that seemed too . . . cozy.

Adam regarded his mug suspiciously, then grimaced when he took a tentative sip. I took my own sip and had to admit, it was pretty bad. I'd made it extra strong, and that only served to enhance the bitterness.

I shrugged as casually as I could manage. "You want gourmet coffee, stick with Dominic."

Dominic is Adam's boyfriend. The two of them had been involved even before the court ordered Dominic's demon, Saul, to be exorcized, but the relationship had only grown stronger since then. Dominic's a really nice guy, and he's also the best cook I've ever known. He'd been thinking of opening his own restaurant lately, and I really hoped he'd do it. I was sure the place would be the talk of the town.

One corner of Adam's mouth lifted in a grin. "I have every intention of sticking with Dominic, and it's not because of the coffee. Or the food."

As usual, my cheeks heated with a blush. Like I said, Adam is into S&M, and Dominic is the M part of the equation. I wasn't quite as horrified by it now as I had been when I'd first found out, but I wasn't exactly comfortable with my knowledge, either. Adam loved watching me squirm when he made references to the kinkier side of his relationship with Dom.

But apparently today he wanted more than just to see me squirm. "I have a proposition for you," he said. "It won't help you afford the gourmet stuff, but it might help you upgrade from this swill to bad coffee."

I had no idea what Adam was talking about, but I already knew my answer. "I'm not interested."

He laughed. "Nothing indecent," he assured me. "I was just thinking that, considering your current situation, you might benefit from having someone to split the rent and groceries with."

I was so surprised I practically sloshed my coffee out of my cup. "You mean Saul, don't you?"

Saul had originally been Dominic's demon. He'd been attacked by God's Wrath, the most militant of the anti-demon hate groups, and although he's one of those demons who finds pain fascinating enough to be pleasurable, the attack had been too much for him.

He'd struck back. One of his attackers had died on the spot, and another had died in the hospital a few days later. The law is very strict where demon conduct is concerned. If a demon commits a violent crime, even in self-defense, he's going to be exorcized. Adam had asked me to perform the exorcism, and it was the first time I'd ever felt bad about exorcizing a demon.

Saul was also one of Lugh's lieutenants, so when Lugh decided to set up his court on the Mortal Plain, he'd wanted to summon Saul back from the Demon Realm, where he'd been banished after the exorcism. Lugh had wanted Dominic to host Saul again, but Dom had refused the "privilege." Although he and Saul had been close, Dom hadn't been willing to give up what he had with Adam to host Saul once more.

We'd found another host for Saul—Dick, a mentally challenged product of Dougal's human breeding program. The poor guy had been raised since infancy to believe his only purpose in life was to host a demon, and so when I'd exorcized the bad-ass demon who'd possessed him, the majority of Lugh's council agreed he'd be the perfect host for Saul. After all, he wouldn't have much of a life on his own, what with his complete lack of social skills and his limited intelligence.

Brian and I had been the sole holdouts. We both thought it immoral to take advantage of Dick's childlike naiveté, but we'd been overruled.

Adam's jerky nod confirmed the identity of my would-be roommate.

"Trouble in paradise?" I asked, and I couldn't help the nasty edge that had slipped into my voice. I don't think I was ever going to get over my disgust at Saul's possession of poor Dick.

Anger glinted in Adam's eyes, but he answered

mildly enough. "The three of us cannot continue living together indefinitely, and I'd be happy to foot the bill for his rent."

Saul had been staying with Adam and Dom ever since his return to the Mortal Plain, but I supposed it was an awkward arrangement. After all, Adam and Saul had been lovers once, but Adam had clearly chosen Dom over Saul.

I shook my head. "You can't seriously believe I'm willing to share my apartment with Saul." True, Saul wasn't to blame for the council's decision to summon him into Dick, but far be it from me to be rational. I couldn't help holding it against Saul, whether it was his fault or not.

"You need the money, don't you? Besides, it wouldn't hurt for you and Lugh to have a bodyguard, and this would be a way to arrange it without it looking suspicious."

"I don't need a bodyguard!" I protested, and felt a sense of déjà vu. This was beginning to sound like my argument with Brian.

"Are you sure about that?"

I didn't answer, because, of course, I *wasn't* sure. Unlike most demon hosts, I've retained full control of my body while being possessed. With some practice, and with the help of extenuating circumstances, I'd learned how to let Lugh take control, letting him use his demon strength and healing ability to defend me when necessary. However, now that I'd finally learned to do it at will, I'd discovered that nothing comes without a price.

I'd been sick as a dog for about three days after the last time I'd let Lugh take over. The experience left me less than anxious to let him in again, so in reality, a demon bodyguard wasn't a bad idea at all. But talk about cramping my style!

"Have you forgotten you're not the only one who has a boyfriend?" I asked.

Adam rolled his eyes. "I'm sure you could work something out if you wanted to." The muscles in his jaw twitched, and his lips pressed tightly together. He was keeping his temper under control, but just barely.

"You're probably right, but I don't want to." Okay, I bought into both of Adam's arguments—that I needed the money and that a bodyguard could be useful. But Saul was pretty much a complete stranger to me, and whether it was fair of me or not, I already had a pretty bad impression of him. How could I share my small, cramped apartment with the guy?

I expected Adam to let go of the reins of his temper and yell at me. I'm a pro at bringing out the worst in him. But instead, he bowed his head and his shoulders slumped.

"So you won't do it for yourself," he said, speaking to the tabletop instead of me, "and I *know* you won't do it for *me*." He raised his eyes to mine, and I could see how much this conversation was costing him. "Would you do it for Dominic?"

I blinked in surprise. "For *Dominic*? Why is *he* having a problem with Saul? I thought the two of them were great friends."

Adam let out a mournful sigh. "As far as Dom's concerned, they are. But I've known Saul a long time. I told you, we've been friends since we came to the Mortal Plain. And I can clearly see that what he feels for Dom is more than just friendship."

"Oh." I couldn't think of anything more to add.

"Dom doesn't seem to have picked up on it yet, but he will eventually. And when he does, things are going to get even more . . . awkward than they are now."

I shook my head. "So why doesn't Saul get his own place?"

"He will, but it's going to take time. Remember, he's a man with no identity. No Social Security number, no driver's license, no ID . . . You get the idea. I'm working on fixing that, but in case you've forgotten, I'm a cop. If I don't tread carefully, I'll get myself into a hell of a lot of trouble."

I snorted. "Since when do you 'tread carefully'? I can't even begin to count the number of laws you've broken since I've known you."

He nodded. "In controlled circumstances, where I'm taking action myself. Not in circumstances where I have to rely on others to keep their mouths shut. I can't manufacture an identity for Saul all by myself, but I have to be very, very careful who I approach. So it's taking longer than I'd hoped."

I might not like Adam much, but I *did* like Dom, and I certainly didn't want him to get stuck in the middle when he figured out that Saul wanted more than friendship. But despite all the rational arguments for why I should take him in, I just couldn't do it.

"Ask Andy," I said, shaking my head. "He's got a spare room in his apartment, and he's not exactly raking in the bucks, either."

Andy is my brother. He has twice been the host for the demon Raphael, Lugh's youngest brother—once voluntarily, and once very much not so. Recently, Raphael had released Andy by taking a new host. Both Andy and I were struggling with guilt, since we'd allowed Raphael to take over another, very much unwilling host. Andy had been reclusive and sullen ever since Raphael took his new host, so I wasn't surprised when Adam told me he'd already asked and been refused.

"I suppose I could ask Brian," Adam said doubtfully. "But there'd be nothing in it for him, and he's not as...involved as you are."

I sighed. "Give me a couple of days to think about it, okay?" I couldn't believe those words were leaving my mouth, but it was too late to take them back.

Adam echoed my sigh. "Thanks."

I opened my mouth to protest, but Adam held up his hand to stop me.

"I know you haven't agreed to anything," he said. "I'm just thanking you for at least thinking about it." He smiled, making the laugh lines around his eyes crinkle. "Why don't you come over for dinner tonight? You can get acquainted with Saul a bit and get a good meal in your belly." He pushed his mug away, having drunk at most two sips of the coffee. "And get some decent coffee in your system."

I had never yet found the will to refuse a home-cooked meal from Dominic, and today was no exception. My mouth started watering at the offer, and there was no way I could settle for ramen noodles with that kind of temptation.

I hadn't seen Saul since we'd summoned him to the Mortal Plain, a little more than a week ago. His host was a successful product of Dougal's eugenics program in Houston—Dougal's idea of success being a host with superhuman capabilities and the mental capacity of a turnip. The Houston facility had managed to breed an amazing ability into its lab-created hosts: the ability to shape-shift.

No, I don't mean these Houston hosts can turn into werewolves. But when a demon possesses one of these hosts, it can rearrange and restructure the host's appearance. The bad guys had used this ability to change Dick into a replica of a human being they had murdered.

I knew Saul had been working on changing his host's appearance. It wouldn't do for him to continue looking like Devon Brewster III, who, as far as the authorities knew, was on the loose somewhere with a rogue demon in residence. So when I knocked on Adam's door and a complete stranger answered, my mind knew this had to be Saul. But my instinctive paranoia made me back hastily away anyway.

Saul hadn't gone for the stereotypical drop-dead gorgeous look of your standard demon host, but he wasn't painful to look at, either. He had made himself both taller and leaner than Brewster, and banished the signs of middle age. If I hadn't known better, I'd have put him somewhere in his late twenties. He'd squared off Brewster's jaw, changed the color of his eyes from blue to hazel, accentuated his cheekbones, and given him a substantially larger nose. He'd also changed the salt-and-pepper hair to pure pepper, though that might have come from a bottle. All in all, I'd say there was nothing about him that even remotely resembled the previous appearance of his host.

When I got over my moment of surprise, I blurted the first thing that came to mind. "Wow, that must have hurt." When Raphael had moved out of my brother's body, he, too, had taken one of the Houston superhosts who, not coincidentally, was Devon Brewster's adopted son, Tommy. To demonstrate the abilities of this strain of superhost, Raphael had temporarily changed the shape of Tommy's nose, and he'd made it clear just how much that small change had hurt.

Saul grinned, an expression that reminded me of

Adam. "Yes, it did," he agreed, and I belatedly remembered that Saul really liked pain.

Great. It looked like Saul had Adam's taste for making me squirm. I willed myself not to blush, but my body never seems to obey my commands. I decided then and there that there was no way I was sharing my apartment with Saul.

I pushed past him into Adam's house, then frowned as I realized I still thought of this as Adam's house when Dom lived here, too. But I had to admit that, except for in the kitchen, Dom hadn't left much of a mark on the place. Of course, considering what his rat hole of a house in South Philly had looked like, that was probably a good thing.

I breathed deeply, expecting to catch the scent of Dominic's cooking, which usually filled the house. Instead, I caught a noseful of way-too-strong aftershave and sneezed three times in rapid succession.

I glanced at Saul through watering eyes. "What did you do, bathe in the stuff?"

His nostrils flared as he sniffed the air. He frowned, as if just noticing the overpowering fumes. "Too strong?"

I rolled my eyes. "Uh, yeah." I tried breathing through my mouth, but ended up tasting it in the back of my throat instead.

Saul shrugged. "I've been without my human senses for a while. I suppose I'm overcompensating."

We must have been taking longer than expected to make our way into the kitchen, because Adam came looking for us. As soon as he got within about five feet of Saul, he recoiled.

"Agh!" he said, his nose wrinkled in disgust. "Remind me never to let you borrow my aftershave again. Did you leave any for me, or did you use the whole bottle?"

The stuff was so strong, I hadn't even recognized it as Adam's scent until he spoke. I'd always found the scent sexy on Adam, but Saul might have just ruined it for me forever.

Saul gave him a chagrined look. "Morgan was just pointing out that I'd overdone it." He sighed. "Guess I'll go take another shower."

I saw that the ends of his hair were still damp. If the aftershave were even mildly bearable, I'd have told him I'd live with it. As it was, I couldn't wait to get rid of him. Adam made a shooing motion with his hand, and Saul trudged to the stairs.

The scent lingered after he was gone. I met Adam's eyes, and he had no trouble reading my thoughts.

"He'll tone it down soon," he said. "You can't imagine what it's like to experience physical sensations, even tastes and scents, when you first set foot on the Mortal Plain. He'll overdo it for a little while, then he'll start acting more like a normal person."

I regarded Adam skeptically. "Did *you* bathe in perfume when you first came to the Mortal Plain?"

Adam's frown told me the answer was no. He hastened to explain. "Okay, so Saul's a bit of a hedonist. But once he gets reacclimated, it won't be so bad."

"Uh-huh."

"Where is everybody?" Dominic called from the kitchen. "Dinner's almost ready."

Adam made a sweeping gesture toward the kitchen. "I don't know about you, but I have no inclination to wait for Saul before we start eating."

My nose was starting to recover from the shock, so I could take in the cooking smells, and my stomach grumbled its opinion. I was halfway to the kitchen before Adam finished talking.

Saul joined us at the kitchen table about five minutes into the meal. Apparently, showering at superhuman speed was one of his talents.

As soon as Saul entered the room, I felt the tension that Adam had mentioned. Maybe only because Adam had warned me, but I think even someone as dense as me would have noticed it—though it was a subtle brand of tension.

The three of them joked and laughed amiably, and Dominic practically glowed when anyone praised his cooking. But there was still something slightly...off. Perhaps it was in the way Saul looked at Dom, with a hint of wistfulness in his expression. Or perhaps Adam was making more possessive little gestures than usual. He did seem to go out of his way to touch Dom. Dom had told me once that Adam was insecure. I had a hard time seeing Adam that way. To me, he always seemed a pillar of self-confidence. Arrogance, actually. But I had to admit, he did rather resemble a man afraid he was going to lose his lover.

Call me a cynic, but I suspected the reason Adam wanted Saul out was more for his own sake than Dom's.

You could never get out of Dom's kitchen without eating dessert, and tonight was no exception. It was a simple cheesecake, no fancy toppings, no froufrou flavors, but it was the best I'd ever eaten.

The conversation came to a bit of a lull as we were sipping the dark, bold Italian roast coffee that topped off the meal. I suck at small talk—ask anyone, they'll agree—but unfortunately that didn't always stop my gums from flapping at inopportune moments.

So as some light, pleasant after-dinner conversation, I looked at Saul and blurted, "What's the deal with you and Raphael, anyway?"

There was a lot I still didn't know about Saul, and I had to admit I was curious. It wasn't until we'd summoned him to the Mortal Plain that I'd learned his true identity: He was Raphael's son. Raphael's *estranged* son. I didn't know anyone who actually *liked* Raphael—Andy and I both hated him—but I think even we didn't hate him as much as Saul did.

My words were about as welcome as a cockroach parade. All three men turned to look at me with varying degrees of disapproval.

I'll admit, I knew I was in the wrong. This wasn't the right time to discuss Saul's relationship with Raphael. But once I'd hurled the question out there, I wasn't willing to take it back.

I shrugged as if unconcerned by the glares the guys were shooting at me. "Come on. It's a fair question, and I've waited more than a week to ask it. I'm not usually that patient." I could have asked Lugh about it, but we hadn't been communicating a whole lot lately. I was having a lot of trouble sleeping, and Lugh didn't want to disturb those hours I managed with our lucid dream conversations.

"It's none of your business why Raphael and I don't get along," Saul finally said, breaking the tense silence.

It didn't escape my notice that Saul had said "Raphael" rather than "my father." Whatever it was that lay between them, it was deep-seated.

"You're both part of Lugh's council, and I'm Lugh's host," I retorted. "If there's a problem between you and Raphael, I need to know about it." I tried to sound like the voice of authority, but I'm not sure I succeeded.

"You know there's a problem. There's no reason to go into the specifics."

To my surprise, Dominic cut in before I could formulate my reply. "There's also no reason not to," he said. "Why should it be a secret?"

I glanced at Dom, wondering if he knew the answer himself. But I was pretty sure he wouldn't tell me even if he did. It was Saul's story to tell—or not to tell, as the case may be.

Saul's mouth pursed like he'd just eaten something nasty, but he caved under Dominic's persuasion.

"Fine. I'll tell you all about my relationship with my *sire*." His eyes narrowed, and I could see the muscles in his jaw working. "I refuse to call him my father when the only reason he sired me was to piss off Lugh."

I felt my eyebrows arch in mingled surprise and curiosity. I was never much into gossip—you have to have girlfriends for that, and I'd always related better to guys—but this definitely piqued my interest.

"Back up one moment," I said, despite my curiosity. "There's something I don't understand. You guys are incorporeal in the Demon Realm. So how do you, er, reproduce?" I wondered if that was a rude question, and I also wondered if the answer would embarrass me, but Saul answered matter-of-factly enough.

"We don't have bodies as you would understand them, but we are still distinct entities. It might help if you think of us as collections of energy. It's not a very accurate description, but it works as an analogy. When we mate, the child we create draws energy from both parents. The more powerful the parents, the more energy the child draws. If the parents are of unequal power, then the more powerful parent has to contribute more energy to protect the less powerful one. Otherwise, the less powerful one can be drained completely and die.

"My mother was a . . . friend of Lugh's, although she was of a much lesser rank and was much less powerful. Lugh is egalitarian enough to care about the lower-ranked demons as much as about the royals and elite, and he and Raphael fought about it. Raphael thought Lugh should 'stick to his own kind.' When Lugh didn't agree, Raphael struck out at him through my mother. He convinced her to have a child with him. He promised to contribute the lion's share of the energy and to protect her from the drain. But, as usual, he lied. He put in as little as possible and let my mother pour her . . . life force into me.

"My mother was destroyed, and I was born a royal without a royal's power." He swallowed hard, his Adam's apple bobbing.

"It's not unheard-of for demons of such wildly disparate power to have children," Adam said softly when it seemed that was all Saul had to say. "But it is unusual. When it happens, it is usually the more powerful parent who is most . . . depleted. They return to full strength eventually, but it can take centuries for them to regenerate all the energy they lost. If Delilah had known Raphael better, she'd have realized he'd never put himself in such a position. But she didn't, and the lure of having a royal child was too much for her to resist.

"We are something of an elitist society, I'm afraid, and had Raphael followed through on his promise, her rank would have been greatly elevated."

I rolled all that information around inside my head, wondering what to make of it. I'd never really speculated on demon reproduction before, but I guessed I understood Saul's explanation—except for one thing.

"Why did Raphael do it?" I asked. Yes, I hated him. Yes, he was ruthless, and selfish, and at least borderline evil. He was even capable of being petty. But for all of that, there was a reason behind everything he did. Not a *good* reason, mind you, at least not from my point of view, but a reason nonetheless.

"I told you," Saul said with a little snarl. "To piss Lugh off. And because he could."

My every instinct told me there was more to it than that. I glanced at Adam and raised an eyebrow. He shrugged and shook his head, which I took to mean he shared my opinion but didn't know Raphael's motivation, either.

I wasn't about to approach Raphael to ask him about it. But surely Lugh knew exactly what his brother had been up to. I sent him a mental message to talk to me in my dreams tonight. I was pretty sure he'd grant my request.

Chapter 3

I was in quite the pensive mood when I left Adam's place. I could clearly see that the current housing arrangements weren't optimal, but I felt no more inclined to offer Saul my spare room than I had before. I like to think I'm a pretty decent human being, but I'm not all that altruistic by nature.

I decided that instead of brooding on my inadequacies, I'd brood on what Adam had told me this afternoon about Reporter Barbie. Although I'd known I hadn't seen the last of her, I'd sort of allowed myself to forget about her for a while. Out of sight, out of mind, you know? But now that she was back in the forefront...

I was halfway to my car, which I'd parked by the curb a little more than a block from Adam's house, when it occurred to me that if Barbie really was bent on investigating me, she might well be following me around, trying to dig up dirt. So instead of just getting in my car and driving away, I took a moment to regard my surroundings.

When you grow up female in a big city like Philadelphia, you learn to always be aware of who's around you. But you also learn to ignore people who don't register on your threat radar. Sometimes when you see people walking down the street, it looks almost as if each one believes he or she is the only human being around.

No one had tweaked my threat radar, but then, Barbie wouldn't. Scanning the pedestrians who were within my line of sight, I searched for any sign of her. No dice. I almost convinced myself to just forget it, but my paranoia was in high gear, so I began examining the parked cars by the sides of the street.

There were enough streetlights to more than illuminate the streets and sidewalks, but car roofs made great shadows, and if I hadn't been looking so closely, I never would have seen her. She was nothing more than a patch of deeper darkness in the shadowed interior of a nondescript little sedan, and I might almost have missed her even in my careful sweep if the headlights of another car hadn't momentarily shone on her face.

Clenching my teeth, I strode toward the car. I wasn't sure what I was going to do—after all, as far as I knew, she wasn't doing anything illegal—but I was determined to get her off my back one way or another.

It didn't take her long to realize she'd been made, and I halfway expected her to start her car and zoom on out of there. Instead, she opened the door and stepped out to wait for me.

I thought of her as "Barbie" because she was petite, blond, and curvy, and her sweetly pretty face still reminded me of some stereotypical vapid cheerleader. However, today she seemed to be going for the Cat-burglar Barbie look: tight black pants, a snug black T-shirt that clung in a way that would make guys' tongues hang out, and a light black jacket. Her usually ostentatious blond hair was pulled back into a pony-tail at the nape of her neck, the stray wisps held back from her face by a black velvet headband. All the better to hide in the shadows, I guess, though with her pale skin she probably needed camouflage makeup—or a ski mask—to stay truly hidden.

I came to a stop in front of her, close enough to make the most of our disparate heights. Of course, this was a woman who'd been willing to go toe-to-toe with a demon, so I wasn't surprised that she wasn't intimidated. She was also probably armed—it was a little warm for that jacket tonight, unless she was wearing it to hide her shoulder holster.

"You look like an extra from *Mission Impossible*," I informed her, but instead of being insulted, she smiled and shrugged.

"So it's a bit of a clichéd outfit. But black works best for nighttime surveillance."

"I guess that means you're not pretending to be a reporter anymore."

"I'm sure you've already shot that cover story full of holes, so I see no need to insult your intelligence by keeping it up."

"Considerate of you," I said, then wondered what to say next. What did I hope to accomplish by confronting her? I didn't know, and now I wished I'd thought it out beforehand.

"For an exorcist, you seem to spend an awful lot of time in the company of demons," she commented.

I didn't know what to say to that, so I decided to keep my mouth shut.

"Especially Adam White," she continued. "I've canvased the neighbors, and I know you've spent the night there at least once."

I've never been any good at keeping a poker face, and I'm sure my shock and dismay were obvious.

This was the city! People weren't supposed to pay any attention to their neighbors here. I couldn't think of any reason why my spending time with Adam would be harmful to me in the lawsuit, but Barbie could definitely make my life ... uncomfortable if she decided to share that information.

Brian knew, of course, that I spent a lot of time with Adam. We were, after all, both members of Lugh's council. But he *didn't* know about my overnight stays. Not that I'd stayed overnight anytime recently, and I'd been a prisoner both times, but I didn't want Brian to know anything about that. I had made a pretty sickening sacrifice, allowing Adam to "play" with me in return for his help in rescuing Brian when he'd been kidnapped by Dougal's supporters. Adam's idea of "playing" was to whip me until my back was reduced to bloody shreds—damage that Lugh was able to heal over the course of a few hours. And that Brian would never know about, because knowing would damage him.

Since my face had already told Barbie she'd hit a nerve, I decided not to try to hide it. "The time I spend with Adam is none of your business," I snarled. "I can't blame you for doing your job." Actually, yes, I could, and I'm sure she heard that in my voice. "But my personal life has nothing to do with my professional life, so keep your nose out of it."

It would have been nice if Barbie had looked chastened and repentant, then apologized profusely and driven away, never to be seen again. But I wasn't exactly shocked that it didn't go that way.

Barbie flashed me a sardonic smile, very much at odds with her innocently pretty face. "I know you're not as naive as that. Anything and everything can be used as evidence against you in the suit. It may not affect the final outcome, but it can certainly make your life difficult for months, maybe even years."

I reminded myself that Barbie was just doing her job and probably didn't deserve to have her bright white teeth knocked out of her jaw. "I don't understand. I don't have any money, and Maguire wouldn't need it even if I had it. Between his lawyers and you, he's spending way more than he can ever hope to get back. What's the point?"

I thought I saw a hint of sympathy in Barbie's expression, though it might have been wishful thinking on my part. "I think the point has already been amply demonstrated." She opened her car door. "It's going to get worse before it gets better." Her face actually looked a bit grim. "I'm very good at my job."

Her words sent a very definite chill down my spine, and I couldn't think of a good retort as she climbed into her car and drove away. Instinct told me she wouldn't go far, and I'd better scrutinize my every move for the duration of the suit.

Have I mentioned that my life sucks?

I'm not big on medically enhanced sleep, but that night I couldn't resist the lure of a sleeping pill. But even with the drug, my mind was reluctant to drift away into unconsciousness, and I lay in my bed tossing and turning, despite my heavy eyelids, for well over an hour.

Eventually, I succumbed, but I doubt I'd gotten more than a few minutes of blissful oblivion in before I "awoke" in Lugh's living room.

He didn't really have a living room, of course. But he had complete control of my dreams, and he could set those dreams in any environment he pleased. This living room was the environment he chose most fre-

quently, but in the past he'd also conjured an intimidating throne room and a sexy bedroom, depending
on what effect he wanted to have on me.

Apparently, he wanted to be comforting tonight,
because in addition to the usual decor of his living
room, there was a crackling wood fire. I was sitting—
reclining, actually—on the world's softest leather
couch, my bare feet propped on a matching ottoman,
facing the fire. Without raising my head from the
back of the couch, I turned to face Lugh, who was sitting just close enough to invade my personal space.
I'd given up on trying to get him to respect my boundaries, so I didn't bother scooching away.

Just like the living room, Lugh's body was an illusion—a construct created specifically to appeal to me.
But let me tell you, he sure knows how to appeal. Tall
and golden-skinned, with long black hair, warm amber eyes, and a body to die for—hopefully, not literally—he pushed every one of my buttons. Hard. If it
weren't for the fact that I was in love with Brian, I
don't know that I could have kept myself from jumping Lugh's bones.

To make matters worse, Lugh didn't think Brian
should be any impediment to my enjoyment of his...
charms. As far as he was concerned, since I could
only be with him when I was asleep, and I could only
be with Brian when I was awake, there was no competition between them—and therefore, no reason for
me to choose one over the other. But we were never
going to see eye-to-eye on that issue. And while
tonight Lugh looked as yummy as ever, he didn't seem
to be putting the moves on me. Yet.

"I gathered you wished to speak to me?" he asked
with an elegant arch of his brows.

Gathered my ass. He lived in my body, and in my
mind. He knew all my thoughts and feelings, even the

ones I kept under lock and key. Even the ones I didn't want to acknowledge. If I allowed myself to think about it, I could bring on a panic attack, so I stopped thinking and answered him instead.

"Care to give me your version of the Raphael and Delilah story? I'm not sure Saul's version is reliable."

"My version won't be completely unbiased, either," he warned with a self-deprecating smile. But behind that smile, there was something else in his expression, something...angry? Bitter? I wasn't sure. All I knew was that it wasn't a happy emotion.

"I'm not expecting it to be," I assured him. Though I must admit, I was expecting it to be less biased than Saul's. Lugh had the enviable ability to regard people and events with a certain degree of distance. It wasn't a lack of emotion, it was...

"An ability to temporarily set those emotions aside."

I scowled at Lugh. Not that I didn't know he could "hear" my internal conversations, but sometimes it would be nice if he would just pretend he couldn't.

He smiled apologetically. "Saul's description of the actual events was basically accurate. His assessment of my brother's motivation was not."

"So Raphael didn't do it just to piss you off?"

A muscle ticked in Lugh's jaw. "Oh, I'm sure he considered that one of the fringe benefits. And it wasn't until very recently that I realized how much more there was to it than that. At the time, I took it at face value. I believed he was striking out at me through the woman I loved, and that was when I formally severed our relationship."

The woman he loved? Somehow, that idea took me by surprise, though of course it was silly in the extreme. Demons may be very different from humans, but I'd seen plenty of evidence that they were capable of love. And, while I didn't know exactly how old Lugh was, I knew he was ancient. The chances of him living that long a life without having loved a woman...

Of course, I wasn't about to question him about his love life, though the subtle twitching of his lips reminded me he knew what I was thinking.

"What do you mean you formally severed your relationship?"

The hint of a smile disappeared as if it had never existed. "I mean from that day until I ascended to the throne, I refused to see or speak to him. And the only reason I spoke to him when I ascended was to try to get him to give me his True Name."

As king of the demons, Lugh was entitled to know the True Name of all his subjects who had earned one. If he knew a demon's True Name, he could summon that demon to him from anywhere in the Demon Realm. That humans could use True Names to summon demons to the Mortal Plain was merely a...side effect. Lugh could have forced his brothers to reveal their True Names, but, in a moment of naiveté, he'd chosen not to, hoping his act of trust would repair their fraternal relationship. Instead, it had given Dougal the power he needed to launch his palace coup.

"So what is it you've figured out now that you didn't know then?" I prompted when Lugh fell silent.

He shook his head, and I got the feeling he was shaking off memories. "You were right to think that Raphael always has some way to justify his actions, at least to himself. I don't think he would have killed Delilah like that for the sole purpose of angering me. But since, at the time, we were practically at war with one another, it never occurred to me that he might have done it for my sake."

My eyebrows shot up, and I sat up straight, turning my body to fully face Lugh on the couch. "How the hell could that possibly have been for *your* sake?" I asked, my outrage clear in my voice.

Lugh's head dipped, his eyes now focused on his knee. He must have been really uncomfortable; it wasn't like him to avoid eye contact.

"Demons don't marry like humans do," he said. "We do form lasting relationships—it's just that there's no formal acknowledgment of them. So, while we don't actually marry, it would be accurate in human terms to think of Delilah as my wife."

"Okay," I said, giving him a keep talking gesture, which he probably didn't see, since he still wasn't looking at me.

His voice dropped until it was so low I had to lean forward to hear him. "What usually happens eventually when a man and a woman marry?"

It shows the frame of mind I was in that I didn't even consider some kind of smart-ass quip. "They have children," I answered, and Lugh nodded. I continued the thought. "But if you had a child with Delilah, you would have contributed a hell of a lot more energy than Raphael did."

He nodded again. "It would have been the only honorable thing to do. Besides, I wouldn't have wanted to risk hurting her."

And now the lightbulb finally turned on over my head. "And how long would you have been... depleted?" I remembered Adam saying something about centuries, but it was hard to believe.

"Believe it," Lugh said. "If Delilah and I had had a child, I would still be... very weak. It's virtually impossible for demons to kill one another in the Demon Realm—unless there's a huge disparity in power. I'd have handed Dougal the opportunity he needed to destroy me, and he would now be sitting on the demon throne as king, rather than regent."

I chewed that over for a while. "So you think even back then, Raphael knew that Dougal was going to make a try for the throne?"

Lugh nodded. "He even warned me of it, though of course I didn't listen. I thought he was just trying to stir up trouble. As much as Dougal and I have disagreed on political issues, I never believed he would try to take the throne."

As you may have gathered by now, I am not the most sensitive, compassionate woman in the world. But even *I* could tell that Lugh was hurt and bewildered by it. For all that we'd talked about defensive strategies and plans to right the wrong, we'd never talked about how Lugh felt when his brother betrayed him. I knew how awful it had felt when my best friend had betrayed me and tried to have me killed. How much worse would it be if it had been my brother?

Once again, Lugh didn't bother to pretend he didn't know my thoughts. "I am more disillusioned than hurt," he said. "Dougal and I have never been close, so I don't take his attack personally."

"Huh. You know how you always get on my case for lying to myself? Well, I don't have to be a demon in control of your body to recognize it when I see it."

Lugh actually winced. "I am a king. My feelings are irrelevant."

I wasn't sure I followed his logic, but I didn't much care. I did the unthinkable and moved a little closer to him on the couch, laying a sympathetic hand on his arm. "Your feelings aren't irrelevant to me."

As soon as I said it, I wished I could suck the words back in. What kind of an idiot says something like that to a man she's trying to hold at arm's length? Never mind that with him in my body, I couldn't actually do it.

I moved away from him with a little groan, and I covered my eyes with my hand as I cursed myself. Maybe I should take lying lessons from Raphael. I was pretty sure that part of being a good liar was knowing when to keep your mouth shut. And, of course, the poker face I didn't have.

Lugh chuckled. "Lying to me would do you no good." He drew my hand away from my eyes. I made the mistake of meeting his gaze and found I couldn't look away.

"You can't hold me at arm's length, Morgan. And you can't lead me on. What you choose to say doesn't matter." His voice gentled even further. "You can't choose what to feel, either. Life would be very much easier if we could direct our feelings, but even demons can't do that."

My pulse quickened, and there was a pleasant fluttery feeling in my belly. He hadn't let go of my hand, and I was suddenly intensely aware of the warmth of his skin against mine. I swallowed hard.

In the World According to Morgan Kingsley, the fact that I was in love with Brian should have deadened my sexual attraction to every other male of the species. Sure, I could find them pleasing to look at. I could even entertain a fantasy or two. But I shouldn't *want* them, not the way I wanted Lugh.

"Feelings don't respond to 'should' and 'shouldn't,'" Lugh reminded me.

"God damn it!" I said, finding the will to yank my hand from his grip. "Stop responding to my thoughts! Can't you at least give me the *illusion* of privacy?"

He raised one shoulder in a delicate shrug. "That would be a form of deception."

I snorted. As far as I could tell, Lugh had never outright lied to me, but he was perfectly capable of deceiving me. "So what?"

"So that deception would serve no purpose except to anger you when you find yourself believing the illusion."

Against my better judgment, I liked Lugh. But at times like these, I'd have happily strangled him.

"Has it ever occurred to you," he continued, "that the reason you're so attracted to me is precisely *because* your mind is completely open to me? I know your thoughts, your feelings, your fantasies, your secrets. And knowing all that, I still want you."

I jerked awake. It was the first time in a long while I had woken up from one of Lugh's dreams without making a conscious effort. I sat up abruptly in bed, my skin clammy as I shivered in the air-conditioned chill of my apartment. I pulled my knees up to my chest and wrapped my arms around my legs. Lugh's words echoed in my mind, repeating endlessly. I wanted to shut the words out, to force my mind away from them. Because Lugh, damn him to hell, had struck at what he knew was a weakness in my emotional armor.

To the outside world, I came off as bold, confident, even cocky. But I carry around a hell of a lot of baggage, and it's stuffed to bursting with insecurity and self-doubt. That baggage kept me from fully committing to—or opening up to—Brian. I couldn't help being terrified of what Brian would think of me if he *really* knew me, couldn't help fearing that he would eventually wise up and discover that he was too good for me.

"That was a low blow, Lugh," I muttered to the empty room. Yeah, maybe Lugh knew what was in all that baggage I carried around, and yeah, in some ways that made him "safer" than any human being could ever be. But it was *Brian* I loved, *Brian* I needed. And to prove this to myself—or maybe to Lugh—I picked up the phone and dialed Brian's number, even though it was the middle of the night. I begged him to come over and fuck me senseless, and, being a guy, this was an offer he couldn't refuse.

My only excuse for not thinking this decision through was . . . Well, that I wasn't thinking at all.

Brian was deliciously tousled when he came over, and I jumped him practically the moment he walked in the door. He was happy to oblige me, and soon his jeans and my pajama bottoms had been tossed aside and I was pinned to the wall.

Our physical chemistry has always been one of the best facets of our relationship. The bliss of his body pressed against mine, of his cock deep inside me, of his tongue thrusting into my mouth, banished all thoughts of Lugh. I was reduced to a collection of nerve endings, losing myself in the physical pleasure, and in the feeling of *rightness* that always pervaded me when Brian and I were locked together.

Ever the gentleman, Brian waited until I came before he let his own pleasure explode. When it was over, we were both breathing hard, our bodies slick with sweat. My legs were wrapped around his hips, my arms around his neck, and I allowed my head to sag to his shoulder.

He recovered faster than I did, and, with me still wrapped around him like a clinging monkey, he carried me to my bedroom. I was on the verge of starting to think again, but Brian saved me from that horror by pulling my pajama top up over my head and then removing his own T-shirt. His naked bod put all thoughts other than "I want" out of my head.

Unfortunately, we couldn't make love forever. And even more unfortunately, Brian didn't succumb to his usual habit of falling asleep afterward. Instead, he asked the question that I would have anticipated if only I'd stopped for a moment to consider the consequences of calling him in the middle of the night for sex.

"What's wrong?" he asked, tucking me firmly into his arms, his front to my back, his lips brushing my sweaty shoulder.

I had never mentioned to Brian that Lugh was putting the moves on me in my dreams. In many ways, Brian is the quintessential modern, sensitive guy— always understanding, and far more willing than I am to talk about how he felt. But no matter how sensitive he was, he was still a guy, and he would *not* like the idea that another man was trying to trespass in his "territory."

Having never been possessed himself, I'm sure he had no true understanding of just how real Lugh was to me, or how real my dreams of him were. It therefore wouldn't have occurred to him that the demon who possessed me could be a rival. But I felt sure that's how he'd see it if I told him what was wrong, and I felt equally sure he would take it badly. Especially if he thought I was tempted by Lugh.

"I just . . . needed that," I said, knowing he'd never in a thousand years settle for something so lame.

I felt his body stiffen against my back, and not in a good way. Probably the number one cause of our fights was my unwillingness to fully open up to him.

I know your thoughts, your feelings, your fantasies, your secrets. The memory of Lugh's words taunted me, and I wished putting my hands over my ears would shut them out.

Brian was silent for a long time. I might have hoped he'd fallen asleep, except I could still feel the tension in his body. I prayed he'd drop the subject, but it did me no good.

"You called me at two A.M.," he said tightly. "Scaring the shit out of me, I might add, since phone calls at that hour are rarely good news. When you asked me to come over, I dragged myself out of bed and hurried here as fast as humanly possible. And now you're going to give me the 'there's nothing wrong' story?"

Once upon a time, Brian had been one of the most even-tempered men I'd ever known. He was still pretty even-tempered compared to most people, but I could piss him off in five seconds flat. It was not a skill I was proud of.

Usually in situations like this, I get mad right back. Pretty much every time Brian has scolded me for keeping my emotional distance, I've thrown some version of a tantrum and ordered him to back off. The temptation to do the same thing now was almost overwhelming, but I managed to squelch it.

I rolled over in Brian's arms so that I was facing him. His jaw was set, his eyes narrowed, and I knew there was anger as well as pain in that expression. I reached up to brush back a lock of hair that had stuck to the sweat on his brow. I was going to put our relationship at risk whether I chose to speak or to keep quiet. My gut instinct told me to keep quiet, but, as I've mentioned, I often flap my gums when I shouldn't.

"Lugh's trying to seduce me," I blurted. Lugh also had a temper, so he sent a sharp pain arrowing through my head. I hissed and winced. Luckily, he let up after that one, quick spike. He could have made me feel much, much worse.

I risked a glance up at Brian's face and saw that he was frowning. I could almost see the gears turning in his head as he processed what I'd said. I'd told him I communicated with Lugh in my dreams, but I'd never actually gone into detail about it. Brian probably assumed that I just heard Lugh's voice in my head, or something benign like that. Which would explain how puzzled he looked now.

"When I dream of Lugh, it's a full sensory experience," I said. "While it's going on, he feels as real to me as you do right now." I closed my eyes and rolled over onto my back. "If it were some other guy making a pass at me, I could avoid him—or beat the shit out of him, if necessary—but I can't avoid Lugh. He's . . . relentless."

I didn't open my eyes when I felt Brian sit up. I didn't want to see the expression on his face.

"And so what set you running for the phone tonight?" he asked. He was trying to do neutral lawyer voice, but I heard the suspicion underneath.

I forced my eyes open. His neutral lawyer face wasn't much more convincing than his voice. I reached up to stroke his chest, and felt the tightness in his muscles.

"I didn't sleep with him or anything," I assured him. I wanted to avert my eyes, but that would make it look like I was lying.

"That's not an answer."

It was an answer to the question in his eyes, but, of course, he wanted to know more. I swallowed hard. And despite my best efforts, I couldn't hold Brian's gaze any longer. Once again, I closed my eyes. This time, I laid my forearm over them for good measure.

"He just scared me tonight is all," I whispered, afraid my voice would shake. "Do you have any idea how manipulative a guy can be when he has access to every one of your hidden thoughts and feelings?"

The silence in the room was deafening. I waited for a beat or two, then lowered my arm and opened my eyes. Pain stabbed through my heart at the stricken look on Brian's face.

If anyone teaches a Relationships 101 class, I really need to go to it. Maybe even a remedial version, because I was obviously a moron. The number one source of conflict in my relationship with Brian is my unwillingness to share my thoughts and feelings. So what made me think it was a good idea to rub Brian's face in the fact that Lugh knew *everything*? Never mind that I had no way of keeping that information from Lugh, and that I wouldn't share any of it with him if I had the choice.

Lugh had accused me in the past of subconsciously sabotaging my relationship with Brian. Maybe he had a point.

Ya think? I had no idea if the voice in my head was actually Lugh's, or just a product of my own self-loathing. But it was time for some damage control.

I sat up and sidled closer to Brian on the bed, slipping my arm around his waist and laying my head on his shoulder. For all that he was clearly upset, he didn't push me away. He even put his arms around me.

"I called you because you're the antidote to all Lugh's machinations," I murmured. "I know you actually love me, and that you're not trying to manipulate me. And I trust you."

I trust Lugh most of the time, too, but I also know what he's capable of. And I know that his duties as a king will always come first, and that he would violate my trust in a heartbeat if he thought he had to.

Brian sighed heavily. The tension faded from his body, but in a defeated way, not a relaxed way.

"If you *really* trusted me, you would have told me what was going on long before now."

He pulled away from me then, slipping out of bed and groping for his shirt. His pants and shoes were still in the foyer somewhere.

"That's not true!" I protested.

Brian shook his head. "You didn't tell me because you assumed I'd think you were having some kind of affair with him. You're always on guard, waiting for me to hurt you if you take a false step. That's not trust, Morgan."

My chest ached as I watched him and tried to think of what to say. But since everything I'd said so far had only dug the hole deeper, I decided I'd better shut up.

It would have served me right if Brian had left my apartment without another word, leaving me to stew in my fear that he was leaving me for good. But Brian's just too damn nice.

"I need some time to think," he said after he pulled his T-shirt back on. "We'll talk again tomorrow."

He headed for the bedroom door, and I said the only thing I could think of that seemed safe.

"I love you."

Brian looked at me for a long, excruciating moment, and I swear my heart stopped beating. "I love you, too," he finally said. But I wasn't going to forget that hesitation, and I agonized about it for the rest of the night.

Chapter 4

The next day, I felt lousy—naturally. This was a really sucky time to be suspended by the U.S. Exorcism Board. It meant I couldn't burn any hours doing work. Not that I'd done all that many exorcisms since Lugh had joined me. I'd had to turn down some pretty attractive contracts, but when half the world is trying to kill you, the day job has to take a backseat.

My apartment was so clean Martha Stewart would have bowed at my feet in admiration, so I couldn't kill time by cleaning. Not if I didn't want to qualify as OCD, that is. But twiddling my thumbs while sitting alone with my thoughts didn't seem like such a hot idea, either.

I looked at the list of recommended attorneys Brian had given me. I got as far as picking up the phone to dial one before I balked. I didn't think last night's fiasco would make Brian dump me, but the last thing I wanted to do now was ask him for money to help pay the attorney. I decided to try to wriggle my way out from under the lawsuit instead. It couldn't hurt to pay a visit to Maguire and see if I could convince him his son's death wasn't my fault. Yeah, it was a long shot, but I figured it was worth trying.

People as wealthy as Maguire tend not to be listed in the phone book, so it took me half the morning—and all of my admittedly limited patience—to get a number for him. When I finally got it, I put it aside as I made myself a gourmet lunch of store-brand corn-flakes. Maybe I was overdoing the economizing, but I had never felt this financially vulnerable before, and it was damned uncomfortable.

While I munched my corn flakes, I pondered what I could possibly say to Maguire to convince him of my innocence. If he was as grief-crazed as I thought, it was probably a hopeless cause. Especially since I'm not known for my silver-tongued eloquence. But maybe he was just confused. Maybe he just needed to hear how terribly sorry I was.

I hand-washed my bowl and spoon, taking my time about it. Stalling, if you must know. But then I dug my courage out of hiding and picked up the phone. At this point, I had nothing to lose by calling.

The phone rang three times before it was picked up and a woman's voice said, "Hello?"

My own voice tried to flee in panic, but I sternly ordered myself to stay calm.

"Hello," I said. "May I speak to Mr. Maguire, please?"

"Who may I say is calling?"

It would have made things easier if Maguire himself had answered the phone. Then I might be able to slip in a few words in self-defense before he figured out who I was and hung up on me. If this woman—wife? maid? daughter?—told him I was on the phone, he might well refuse the call.

"Morgan Kingsley," I said reluctantly.

There was a long silence on the other end of the line. "The exorcist?" she finally asked, and I couldn't tell from her tone of voice what she thought of me.

I sighed. "Yeah. I just wanted a chance to tell Mr. Maguire how sorry I am about what happened."

She snorted. "I'll bet. You might as well save your breath. Daddy's just . . . Well, he's not in his right mind these days."

She sounded surprisingly apologetic. "I gather I'm speaking to Laura?" When I'd first had an inkling that the Maguire exorcism would end in trouble for me, I'd Googled his name and found out that in addition to Jordan Junior, Maguire also had a daughter named Laura. She was a couple of years older than Jordan Junior, and was an artist of some sort.

"Yes, this is Laura. And I'm sure this doesn't help you any, but I don't think what happened to my brother is your fault."

Surprisingly, this admission made my throat tighten. I *knew* it was Jordan's demon's fault, not mine. But I guess the relentlessness of Maguire's grief was wearing on me.

"Thank you," I said.

"I think, in his heart of hearts, Daddy knows that, too," she continued, her voice now low and furtive. "It's Jack Hillerman who's so all-fired eager to sue."

Hillerman was Maguire's attorney. I hadn't yet met the man, but of course I'd been well on my way toward despising him even before hearing this.

"Why?" I asked.

I could almost hear Laura shrug. "He's been a friend of the family for as long as I can remember, and I guess he took Jordan's death hard. At least, that's what he implies." Her voice dropped even lower. "I suspect he just wants to win a high-profile case so he can make partner at his firm. He's kind of a weasel."

I was really beginning to like Laura Maguire. "May I talk to your father anyway? Maybe I don't have much chance of convincing him to cut me some slack, but I feel like I should at least try."

"Hillerman's with him at the moment, so I'd say that's a big no. But if you'll leave me your number, I'll do my best to convince Daddy to call you when Hillerman's gone."

That was the best deal I could hope for, so I gave her my number and then hung up. Then it was back to trying to find a way to while away the long, boring hours.

At three o'clock, the front desk called to let me know I had a package. I wasn't expecting anything, but I headed right down to pick it up anyway. Anything to distract me from my brooding.

The package was the size of a small shoe box and was wrapped in brown paper. The return address was Adam's, which definitely threw me for a loop. What the hell would Adam be sending me in the mail? I couldn't even come up with a guess. I took the package—along with my latest pile of bills, which I'd be hard-pressed to pay—up to my apartment, then dropped everything on my dining room table.

I stared at the package, still unable to make a guess at what it might contain. Of course, unless I was on the verge of developing X-ray vision, staring at the package wasn't going to tell me much of anything.

Still feeling weirded out, I picked up the package and tore the paper away. Inside was a plain white box, the lid held closed by a couple strips of Scotch tape. Like a child at Christmas—only a lot more suspicious—I shook the box. Nothing rattled inside, though what a rattle would have told me was anyone's guess.

With a shrug, I picked open the tape and lifted the lid. Whatever was inside was packed in tons of bubble wrap, which would explain why nothing rattled.

I patiently worked my way through the bubble wrap until I found the object at its center, an irregularly shaped lump wrapped in baby blue tissue paper. This was just getting stranger and stranger.

I picked up the bundle, frowning at the...odd texture. It was kind of hard, but also had a bit of give to it. I unwrapped the tissue paper and finally saw what was inside.

It was a rubber hand, closed in a fist, except for the extended middle finger. What the fuck? I turned it this way and that, and my gorge started to rise. I guess my body figured out exactly what I was holding before my mind did. It was only when I saw the severed bone at the wrist, surrounded by ragged, pale, bloodless flesh, that I realized this wasn't a rubber hand at all.

I'm not much of a screamer, but if ever there's an occasion for screaming, finding out you're holding a severed human hand is it. I dropped the hand and the tissue paper, taking several steps back as if expecting it to attack. I stared at it in horror for a second, then ran to the bathroom.

After I finished puking, I scrubbed my hands frantically, trying to erase the feeling of that dead flesh against my skin, but of course I couldn't. I gripped the sides of the sink and stared at myself in the mirror.

My face was ghost pale, my eyes red and swollen from crying, though I hadn't even noticed the tears. I was easily stressed out enough now to break down the subconscious barrier that usually kept Lugh from speaking to me when I was awake, and right now I desperately wanted to hear his voice, just to know I wasn't alone.

You're not alone, his voice whispered in my head. *I wish I could say or do something to make you feel better, but I'm afraid I can't.*

"No," I said. "Not unless you can erase the last ten minutes or so from reality."

I would if I could, he assured me.

"I know."

I stood there a little while longer, staring at myself in the mirror, trying not to think. But there's only so long I could get away with that.

When I finally managed to shake off the worst of my shock, I slipped out of the bathroom and into my bedroom, averting my eyes so that I couldn't see into the dining room where the hand still sat on the floor like some discarded movie prop. An image flashed into my mind of those fingers uncurling, beginning to drag themselves across the floor toward me.

Can you tell I was a bit spooked?

One thing was for sure: it wasn't Adam who'd sent me that package. Right after the Maguire exorcism, I'd gotten a series of death threats on my answering machine. I hadn't received one in at least a week, and it sure looked like my admirer had decided to raise the stakes. Like I didn't have enough other problems in my life at the moment.

Instead of calling 911, which I suppose is the proper protocol at times like this, I decided to call Adam himself. I don't suppose this scare tactic was in his official jurisdiction, but he had enough status within the department to get away with occasionally stepping on other people's toes. Besides, with his name on the package, he definitely qualified as an interested party.

He was on duty today, which meant I had to call

his office to reach him. Never fun. The staff at the Special Forces office seemed to have been hired specifically for their unpleasant personalities. The first time I called, I got put on hold and then dropped after listening to elevator music for about five minutes. Elevator music is about as soothing to me as nails on a blackboard, and in my present state of mind it had me practically climbing the walls.

The next time I called, I was put through to Adam's voice mail even though I specifically requested not to be. The third time I called, I ranted like a lunatic, claiming it was a matter of life and death that I reach Adam immediately. I'm not sure the guy who answered the phone actually believed me, but maybe he was just sick of answering my calls. Whatever the reason, he transferred my call.

The call must have gone to Adam's work cell phone—a number he had never given me, though I was pretty sure Dom had it. Hmm, maybe next time I needed to reach Adam at work, I should call Dom instead of the damn office.

I swear I could actually *feel* Adam's annoyance at my call through the phone. "I'm in the middle of something," he said curtly. "Unless—"

"I just received a severed hand in the mail."

That shut him up in a hurry. He was quiet for a moment, then I heard him mutter something, the sound muffled. I think he was holding his hand over the phone.

When he spoke to me again, there was a lot less background noise. I guess he'd moved to somewhere more private. "I'm on my way to interrogate a suspect," he told me. "I can't get away just now."

"Don't you have flunkies to do that kind of thing?" I think there was an edge of hysteria in my voice.

Adam sighed. "Sorry. Not this time. You need to call 911."

"The return address on the package is yours."

"Fuck," Adam said after a moment of shocked silence.

"Yeah, that about sums it up."

Another long silence. "All right. I'll see what I can do about getting free to come over. I'll be there as soon as I can."

"Thanks."

Adam was never big on saying hello or good-bye, so he just hung up.

There was nothing I could do now but wait. Shivering in a phantom chill, I fluffed up the pillows on my bed and made a nice backrest out of them. Then I sat and tried my hardest not to think.

Chapter 5

It took Adam more than an hour to get to my place. Lugh did his best to keep me calm while I waited, but I was seriously rattled, and I was lucky I didn't spend the whole hour bent over the toilet. I was so creeped out that when the front desk called to announce that Adam had arrived, I jumped so high I almost hit my head on the ceiling.

I was glad he was finally here. But my front door was locked, which meant I had to walk by... *it*... on my way to let Adam in. Feeling like a little girl in a haunted house, I held a hand up to my eyes to shield my vision. I didn't even take my usual precautions to confirm the identity of my visitor. Luckily, it really was Adam, and not some homicidal maniac out to kill me.

"Where—" he started to ask, but I just pointed in the general direction, still trying not to look.

He nodded briskly and took a couple of steps toward the dining room. Out of the corner of my eye, I saw him take in the scene and frown.

"I see you took good care of the evidence," he said dryly as he pulled on some gloves.

"When I first opened it, I thought it was rubber," I said, and my voice hardly sounded like my own. I liked to think of myself as a tough chick, but I wasn't feeling so tough right now.

Adam must have finally noticed what bad shape I was in. He gestured to the living room. "Why don't you go sit down? You look like you're about to pass out."

I'd have liked to argue with him, but I was afraid he was right. I made my way rather unsteadily toward the couch. Adam squatted to examine the hand, his body thankfully hiding it from view. I was pretty sure that was deliberate, and I felt absurdly grateful to him. He studied it in silence for what felt like forever, looking at it from every angle without touching it.

"It's embalmed," he informed me. "And from the looks of it, I'd say it was already embalmed when it was cut off."

I crossed my arms over my chest, still feeling the chill that had descended on me the moment I'd realized what was in the package.

"Don't you need a lab tech or something to make a determination like that?"

He glanced at me over his shoulder. "I've been a cop for fourteen years, and I've seen a lot of corpses. I can make an educated guess, though yeah, the lab guys will have to confirm it. I'm thinking there's a funeral parlor somewhere that's misplaced a hand."

That was better than thinking someone had been killed specifically for the purpose of sending me this love note. But I still wasn't exactly basking in relaxation.

"I'm going to have to call in a team," Adam said.

"This bubble wrap should hold a print nicely, though if this is from the same guy who's been leaving you the phone messages, I doubt he'd be so accommodating as to leave prints."

I doubted it, too. My anonymous caller used some kind of voice-altering device when he called, and he seemed to be quite a pro. I couldn't even say for sure whether it was a man or a woman, though I had automatically assumed man. I'm not sure why.

"Um, Adam?"

"Yeah?"

"If you call in a team, how am I supposed to explain that I didn't call the police about the death threats?" I'd talked it over with Adam when I'd first started getting the threats, and he'd agreed with me that there wouldn't be much the police could do. He'd also agreed with me that I was better off keeping a low profile as far as the police were concerned. There'd been a lot of seriously bad shit happening around me in the last couple of months, and more police attention was *not* something I needed.

"Tell them the truth: that you didn't think there was anything they could do about the calls." Adam covered up the hand with the sheet of tissue paper, then tore off his rubber gloves and came to sit on the love seat next to the couch.

"This isn't something I can sweep under the rug for you," he said. "We need to figure out who that hand belongs to and confirm my guess that the victim was already dead and embalmed before the hand was severed. Otherwise, we could have an actual murder here."

I leaned back into the cushions of the couch and groaned. He was right, of course. The police weren't going to be happy with me for not having reported the death threats, but I was just going to have to suck it up.

"You still convinced you wouldn't be better off with a bodyguard?" Adam asked me.

For half a second, I wondered if Adam really *had* sent me that hand, hoping to scare me into letting Saul stay in my spare room. But no, that wasn't Adam's style. He'd always been remarkably straightforward.

I guess I was quiet long enough that Adam assumed I hadn't changed my mind—which I hadn't.

"Maybe you should consider staying at Brian's for a while," he said. "And no, I'm not saying that because I hope you'll let Saul stay in your apartment while you're gone. It's just that whoever's threatening you is obviously escalating, and I suspect it's going to get worse."

Great. Just what I needed.

"I'll deal with it," I told Adam. I wasn't any more likely to ask Brian to let me stay with him than I was to ask him for money at the moment.

Adam shook his head in disgust. "What is it with you? Why do you have to do every fucking thing on your own? Why can't you accept help when it's offered?"

I'd usually have bitten his head off for a comment like that, but I guess I was feeling rather vulnerable right then, so I answered him.

"I've learned from long, hard experience that the only person I can ever truly count on is myself. I just...don't dare lean on anyone."

He regarded me with cocked head and furrowed brow. I think he was genuinely concerned about my well-being, which was kind of a nice change. Usually, I had the feeling he only cared about Lugh and that he despised me.

"Is there some reason you can't accept help and count on yourself at the same time?" he asked. "Just because you went to stay with Brian for a little while wouldn't mean you were putting your entire life in his hands. You can still defend yourself even if you're with him."

"You wouldn't understand," I said, and it was true. Adam couldn't know the utterly devastating feeling of trusting someone and having them fail you. It was easier just not to trust, to rely only on myself.

I expected Adam to get mad at my obvious brush-off, but he didn't.

"How do you know I wouldn't understand?"

"Because you've never..." I let my voice trail off, realizing how foolish it was to make any kind of sweeping generalization about Adam. The fact was, I knew almost nothing about him other than what had happened since Lugh had joined me.

"Remember for a moment that there are basically two people in this body," he said. "I suspect my host has dealt with more betrayals and disillusionment than you can possibly imagine."

I knew next to nothing about Adam's host, although I had met him briefly when Adam had—highly illegally—transferred to Dom's body to heal what would have been a fatal gunshot wound. I'd decided from that brief meeting that Adam and his host were more alike than not, but I had no good way to justify that conclusion.

"What happened to your host?" I asked.

Adam was silent for a moment, perhaps consulting with his host to confirm it was all right for him to share.

"He came out when he was eighteen," Adam said, "though by that time he'd already experimented with both men and women. He likes women just fine, but he prefers men. His entire family disowned him—mom, dad, two brothers, and a sister. His dad gave him a bunch of money, in exchange for which he was never to call or otherwise contact any member of the family again."

I'd always wondered how Adam could afford his impressive house on a cop's salary—even on the salary of a high-ranked cop. I guess this explained it. I swallowed hard, regretting that I'd insinuated he'd always had it easy. Adam and his host were obviously fond of one another, and assuming Adam had as much ability to read and understand his host as Lugh did, then he probably did understand exactly what it was like to be betrayed by the ones you counted on.

"I'm sorry," I said, even though it was a lame, generic thing to say. Seriously, though, what else can you say to a confession like that?

"I'm sure in the end that my host is better off having no contact with his family. Such a toxic environment would have turned him inside out. But believe me, that doesn't make it easy."

I'm not sure if it was because I was so shaken up by the hand, or if it was because Adam and I were suddenly so in sympathy with one another, but I said, "I'll see what I can do about staying with Brian for a while. And Saul can house-sit while I'm away if it works out."

"It will."

I shook my head. "Don't be too sure."

"Don't tell me you two are fighting again."

I winced. "Not exactly. We just had...an awkward moment, let's say. We're going to talk again today, and we'll probably get it all hashed out and settled." Wishful thinking, perhaps, but what else could I do? "I'll let you know what happens."

Adam nodded his agreement, then proceeded to call in his brothers-in-arms to investigate the hand.

Chapter 6

After the men in blue were called in, I no longer had to worry about how to while away the hours of the day. If I'd called them about the death threats, they might have brushed me off, but it seemed like a hand in the mail made a definite impression.

At this point in my life, I had *way* too much experience being interviewed by the police. I knew that the questions would get repetitive, and that the repetition would irritate the crap out of me. I would then proceed to irritate the crap out of whoever was interviewing me, which would make the whole thing last longer.

Color me shocked, but the process went just about like I expected. As an extra giggle in this already fun-filled afternoon, I was lectured by some pimple-faced rookie with Dumbo ears about how I should have called the police sooner. I managed to refrain from lecturing *him* about the wonders of Clearasil.

The cops found a bunch of fingerprints on the bubble wrap, but I had a hunch they would all turn out to be mine. Adam was right—whoever was after me wasn't stupid or careless enough to leave fingerprints. The cops would check the fingerprints they found anyway. Conveniently, my prints were already on file from when I'd been arrested for illegal exorcism. Lucky me.

It was well past my usual dinnertime, and the cops were just packing up to leave, when Brian showed up. This, of course, meant I couldn't get away with any delay tactics—I had to tell him right away about the lovely gift I'd received. At least the police were gone by the time I finished giving Brian the details, though they had left plenty of fingerprint powder behind. Yay, an excuse to do some more cleaning!

When I'd finished telling Brian about my day, he leaned back into the cushions of the sofa and let out a heartfelt sigh.

"You're just unbelievable," he muttered.

"Hey!" I said, punching him in the shoulder. "It's not my fault some wacko decided to send me a hand in the mail."

He smiled faintly as he rubbed his shoulder. "I'm just saying that your life is too eventful to believe. I'm not saying it's your fault."

I couldn't disagree with his assessment.

Since my day was already shot to hell anyway, I decided to add a little more stress and misery to my plate and forge ahead with the conversation I usually would have done my best to put off.

"So, are you still pissed at me?"

Another sigh. "I'm not pissed at you. I never was."

"Your nose is growing, Pinocchio."

He propped his elbow on the back of the couch and half turned to face me. "I wish you had told me what was going on before last night. I wish you could be a quarter, or even an eighth as open with me as you are with Lugh."

I started to say something indignant, but Brian cut me off.

"I know you don't have a choice with Lugh. But you *do* have a choice with me."

"Brian—"

"Let me finish." He took my hand, giving it a firm squeeze. "You're probably the most frustrating person I've ever met, but I've known that for a long time, and I still love you." His lips quirked in a half smile. "Even though you drive me crazy." The smile faded. "But I need you to trust me every once in a while."

"I do!" I responded instantly. I'd loved Brian from the first moment I'd met him, even though logic had insisted—and still continued to insist—that we were all wrong for each other. And I trusted him more than I'd ever trusted anyone else in my life—not that that's a ringing endorsement.

He quirked an eyebrow at me and looked skeptical.

"Look, I'm sorry I didn't tell you about what Lugh was up to earlier. I just thought things between us were complicated enough without adding that to the mix."

"And that's the perfect example of what I mean when I say you don't trust me enough. What bad thing would have happened if you'd told me as soon as you knew Lugh was interested?"

I crossed my arms and gritted my teeth. "You'd have gone all macho-man on me and gotten jealous." I had to admit, I was surprised he seemed so much more upset about my failure to communicate than about the thought of Lugh trying to seduce me.

"Okay. I'm a normal guy. I don't like finding out that some other guy is making moves on my woman." He suddenly looked me straight in the eye while seeming to look right through me. "You hear me, Lugh? Morgan's taken, and I'm not willing to share!" His eyes focused on me once more. "So I'm annoyed at Lugh. Big deal. You don't think I'm going to dump you just because someone else wants you, do you?"

Reluctantly, I shook my head, because he was making way more sense than I liked.

"As long as you didn't actually sleep with him, there's only so upset I can get," he concluded.

There he went with his impeccable logic again. "I still didn't want to upset you."

"So you're never going to tell me anything that might upset me?" He was starting to get all pissed again. "You're going to keep me in the dark, packed in cotton like some fragile glass ornament you only bring out at Christmas? How would you feel if I treated *you* that way?"

Once again, he had a point. My internal defense mechanisms wanted me to attack right back—I'm one of those "offense is the best defense" people—but I fought that instinct, taking a deep breath to calm myself down before I spoke.

"You're right," I admitted.

Brian looked startled.

"I'd hate it if you did that to me. And I'll try my best not to do it again."

His look was one of classic skepticism. "You're going to stop hiding things from me 'for my own good'?"

I grimaced. "I'll try," I promised. I thought of the big secret I was *still* keeping about what I'd let Adam do to me. But that was an *old* secret, and I was only promising not to keep *new* ones, right? "I'm probably going to screw up now and again, because it's second nature to me. But I'll try *hard*. Can you live with that?"

He regarded me for a long time before he answered, and I got the feeling he was searching every nuance of my expression for hidden clues. Finally, he sighed.

"I can live with that," he said guardedly, "as long as your attempts meet with some success. Consider yourself on romantic probation and be on your best behavior for a while, okay?"

I didn't like the way he'd phrased that—it sounded suspiciously like an ultimatum—but he was being pretty reasonable under the circumstances, so I nodded my acceptance.

I was still trying to figure out whether I should ask Brian about staying with him for a little while, just until we discovered who my secret admirer was, when the phone rang. I grabbed the phone and glanced at the caller ID. Jack Hillerman.

The name sounded vaguely familiar, but it took me a moment to place it. Then I remembered that Hillerman was Maguire's attorney, the one Laura thought was trying to make a name for himself at my expense. Just who I wanted to talk to right now.

"Who is it?" Brian asked as I sat there stupidly staring at the phone.

"Maguire's lawyer." The phone rang for a fourth time, and my answering machine picked up. I was pretty sure I didn't want to hear whatever Hillerman had to say. I noticed Brian wasn't bugging me to answer it, so I figured I was making the right decision.

The answering machine beeped, then started to record.

"Ms. Kingsley," said a deep male voice with an upper-crust accent that immediately made me think "pretentious snob." "This is Jack Hillerman. I am

Jordan Maguire's attorney. It is my understanding that you made an attempt to contact my client this afternoon."

Brian raised an eyebrow at me. I held up a hand in a "wait a minute" gesture.

"From now on," Hillerman continued, "I must insist that any attempts to speak to my client be made through me. If you call him or speak to him again, I will have a restraining order put on you. My client has been through enough trauma without having to be harrassed by the author of his troubles."

The answering machine beeped again, and I realized Hillerman had hung up. Brian was still giving me the eyebrow arch, so I answered his unspoken question.

"I thought maybe if I talked to Maguire, we could work something out without having to go through all this lawsuit bullshit. I knew it was a long shot, but I figured it couldn't hurt to try. I just left a message with his daughter asking him to call. I certainly didn't *harass* him."

"Have you hired an attorney yet?"

I didn't answer, which was answer enough.

"Morgan, hire an attorney. Tomorrow. I mean it."

"Okay, okay."

"These guys are obviously planning to play hardball, and you've never exactly been Miss Congeniality."

I gave him a dirty look.

"Well, you haven't!" he insisted. "It's probably a good thing you didn't reach Maguire or you might have said something he could have used against you."

I crossed my arms over my chest, all my defensive reflexes coming to life at once. "Your faith in me is just overwhelming."

He gave me a pointed look, and I pulled back on the reins of my temper.

"I got the message, okay?" I said. "I'll call a lawyer tomorrow, and I won't try to talk to Maguire again. Promise."

Brian didn't look entirely convinced, but thankfully, he let the subject drop.

Brian stayed the night, so I never got around to asking him if I could stay at his place for a while. Just as well, since I still couldn't decide whether I wanted to. As always, the longer I could put off a decision, the happier I was.

I'm not sure if you could call our discussion of this afternoon a fight, but the sex that night sure had the feeling of make-up sex. Nothing I was going to complain about, that's for sure.

Brian was gone by the time I woke up in the morning. Being currently unemployed gave me the leeway to sleep as late as I wanted. Of course, even when I *was* employed, I pretty much got to make my own hours. I really loved being an exorcist, and I hoped this suspension wouldn't last much longer. But with the lawsuit hanging over my head, I suspected that was a pretty vain hope.

I did my zombie walk to the kitchen and had grabbed the coffee cannister and a filter before it registered in my sleep-addled mind that a full pot of coffee already awaited me. Have I mentioned how much I love Brian?

The coffee sucked as badly as ever, but I still smiled as I drank it, thinking of Brian thoughtfully setting the pot to brew before he headed home to get ready for work. I wandered out of the kitchen and saw that he had left me a note on the dining room table.

My happy little glow dimmed a bit when I saw

that he'd made me an appointment with one of the lawyers he'd recommended. I know I'd been procrastinating about it, but I truly had been planning to make the call today. I guess Brian hadn't believed me. My contrary nature immediately urged me not to show up for the appointment, but good sense prevailed over irritation.

My appointment wasn't until two, so I spent the remaining hours of the morning cleaning up fingerprint dust and trying not to speculate too much about the package and its origins.

After a lunch of PB&J with a bad coffee chaser, I headed out to meet with my new lawyer.

As a general rule, I have a pretty low opinion of lawyers, Brian being a big exception. So I was prepared to despise Brandon Cook, Esq., long before I set foot in the offices of Beacham, Carrey, and Cook. And when I stepped into the ritzy, stuffy-looking lobby with its mahogany furniture and cigar-club decor, I mentally docked him another point. You may have noticed I'm not much for pomp and circumstance, and there was a hell of a lot of pomp on display. I was tempted to do an about-face and march right back out, but I resisted the impulse. I needed a lawyer, and this guy was someone Brian respected. The least I could do was give him a test drive.

Being me, I hadn't dressed up for the occasion. The receptionist tried to be subtle as she took inventory of my outfit—low-rise jeans, my uniform of choice, along with a sleeveless cropped sweater that left my navel and the tattoo on my back on display. No doubt about it, I was underdressed. Ask me if I cared.

Despite her thinly veiled disapproval of my attire, the receptionist told me Mr. Cook would be right with me and asked me to take a seat in the waiting room.

Cook didn't keep me waiting long, which was a good thing, or I might have bolted. I was relieved to see he wasn't quite as stodgy as I expected. Yes, like everyone else in my field of vision, he was wearing a suit, but his tie was a cheery red with white polka dots instead of the ultraconservative brown, blue, and gray that everyone else wore. Then again, Cook was a partner, so he could get away with a little eccentricity.

He smiled when he saw me, holding out his hand for me to shake and greeting me without once seeming to notice my outfit. I'd guess his age at around forty-five, though he wore his years well. His salt and pepper hair was neatly cropped, and his gray-blue eyes looked disproportionately large behind his thick glasses.

"Come on back to my office," he said, gesturing me to follow him as he headed down a long hallway to an impressive corner office.

"Nice view," I said when I stepped inside, though I was thinking something more along the lines of "So this is the kind of office you get when you charge more than three hundred dollars for an hour of your time."

The twinkle in his eye suggested he'd read my thought, but he refrained from commenting. I sat in one of the twin mahogany chairs that faced his desk and clasped my hands in my lap, not knowing where to begin.

"Brian has given me the basics about your case," Cook said, "but I'd like to hear it all in your own words."

I frowned. "So you and Brian know each other

personally? I thought he was just making a recommendation based on your reputation."

Cook shrugged. "I can't say we know each other well, but you're hardly the first client he's sent my way."

The fact that Brian knew him personally made me feel a little better, though I don't know why. "Before I start telling you about my case, can we talk money? As in, I haven't got any, but according to Brian I desperately need an attorney anyway."

It was Cook's turn to look surprised. "Brian instructed me to send the bills to him. I suppose he neglected to mention the fact to you?"

I wasn't sure whether to feel amused, annoyed, or absurdly grateful. I settled for a mix of all three and spent the next hour explaining my situation and answering a dizzying array of questions. At least, I tried to answer them. Sometimes, all I could say was "I don't know," though I felt like I was failing some kind of test every time I did.

Most of the questions I couldn't answer had something to do with statistical averages on exorcisms—the same kinds of questions Brian had asked when he'd browbeaten me into admitting I needed a lawyer. By the end of the hour, I was exhausted and well past the point of being ready to leave.

"I took the liberty of researching some of the questions I asked you before I met with you today," Cook said just when I was starting to hope he was planning to let me go.

"Huh?"

"Brian told me he'd asked about exorcism statistics, so I went ahead and looked them up."

I glared at him. "If you looked them up, then why did you bother asking me?"

"I was curious to see whether *you'd* looked them up after Brian asked you, but apparently not."

Any suggestion of warm, fuzzy feelings I'd started to get over this guy vanished, and I seriously considered doing a Donald Trump "You're fired!" Luckily, my temper isn't quite that bad. And I *did* get the "You're not taking this seriously enough" message.

"On average, twenty-one percent of exorcisms result positively with the host in full possession of his or her faculties," Cook said. "Fifty-eight percent result in permanent catatonia, twenty percent result in temporary catatonia, and one percent in brain-death."

From the tone of his voice and the expression on his face, I knew my statistics weren't going to compare favorably. I gritted my teeth.

"And *my* averages?" I asked, even though I didn't want to.

Cook glanced down at a piece of paper. "According to the U.S. Exorcism Board, they are seventeen, sixty, twenty-one, and two." He glanced back up at me. "I haven't had a chance to have a statistician look at the numbers yet to tell me whether the variation is statistically significant, but even if it isn't, it's not going to sound very good in court."

A depressing thought, to be sure, but there wasn't anything I could do about it now. Maybe I should start leaning on Dom to open his own restaurant so I could get a job waiting tables for him when I lost everything.

"It's not a cause for despair," Cook assured me. "It just means that there could be hard times to come. I'll contact Mr. Maguire's attorney and see if there's any hope of convincing them to drop the suit. Considering your financial situation, Mr. Maguire will no doubt spend far more money pursuing the case than he can ever hope to recoup by winning it."

"Good luck with that," I murmured. I'd have liked to believe there was an easy way out, but I thought it was about as likely as me winning the lottery without buying a ticket.

Cook was escorting me down the hall toward the front door when something struck me, and I came to a halt with a frown.

"You work fast," I said as a suspicion took form in my head. "You found out all those statistics in the time since Brian made the appointment?"

Cook looked surprised. "Four days was more than enough time. I certainly don't consider that to be working particularly fast."

I bit down on my tongue to stop myself from saying something I would regret. I'd save that for when I next saw Brian. I'd been somewhat annoyed to discover he'd made the appointment for me this morning. Finding out he'd made it four days ago and only got around to telling me about it this morning did not sit well at all.

Preferring to think about being angry with Brian than about what the outcome of this lawsuit might be, I left Cook's office and began plotting my verbal smack-down.

Chapter 7

I didn't get home until a little after six, having run some errands and stopped for groceries along the way. I'd calmed down a bit by then, realizing that everything Brian had done, he'd done for my own good. That didn't mean I would let him get away with it without a tongue-lashing, but there wouldn't be a great deal of heat behind it.

I was lost in my thoughts when I stepped through the door into the lobby of my apartment building, and I walked to the elevators without looking around me. In fact, it wasn't until I'd actually stepped into the elevator and turned to push the button for my floor that I realized Brian was there.

I jumped like a startled cat as he joined me in the elevator.

"Jesus, you scared me!" I said, putting my hand to my chest and feeling the frantic beat of my heart. "Why didn't you say something?"

The doors slid closed, and the elevator started to rise. Brian didn't look at me, instead staring at the lighted numbers above the door. Tension radiated from him in almost palpable waves, and though I was pretty sure his face was supposed to be neutrally blank, he looked like he was majorly pissed off. I put a hand on his arm, and he actually jerked out of my grip.

"Brian, what's wrong?" I asked. I'd never seen him anything like this before.

"Wait until we get into the apartment," he said, and it sounded like he was speaking through gritted teeth.

I was mystified. It wasn't like Brian had never been angry with me before, but I couldn't think of a time when he'd been angry and I hadn't known the reason why. Swallowing a lump of fear, I joined him in staring at the lighted numbers. It was one of the longest elevator rides in the history of mankind.

Eventually, the doors opened, and I made my way to my apartment, not at all sure I wanted to know what was going on. Ignorance is supposed to be bliss, but I wasn't feeling so blissful at the moment.

I unlocked the door and stepped into my apartment, gesturing for Brian to come in. It was then that I noticed the manila envelope he held in his right hand. I gathered it was something about that envelope that had made him so mad, but I hadn't the foggiest idea what it could be. I put the bag of groceries in the kitchen, but didn't bother to put them away. Brian hadn't followed, so I went back to the entryway.

"Would you like me to make some coffee?" I asked, trying to sound normal.

"No." Brian's voice was brusque and curt. No pretense of normalcy here.

"Then should we sit down?"

"No," he said in that same tone of voice.

I shook my head, starting to get pissed off myself.

"Enough with the caveman grunts already! Just tell me what's the matter."

He met my eyes, and for the first time ever, I saw genuine coldness in his gaze. It was almost enough to make me take a step backward, but then I decided it was ridiculous to be scared of Brian, no matter how upset he was.

Still giving me that marrow-freezing look, he reached into the manila envelope and pulled out a sheet of paper. Without another word, he shoved it in my face.

With a sigh, I took the paper from Brian's hand. It was a short letter, printed out on plain white copy paper. I started to read.

> *Mr. Tyndale, I thought you might be interested to know that your girlfriend has spent the night with Adam White on more than one occasion.*

I gasped, and the paper jerked in my hand. My jaw dropped open, and I looked at Brian in horror. But the note wasn't finished yet, and I forced myself to read the rest.

> *Lest you think these overnight stays were somehow innocent, I must tell you that I have attained some concrete information about what took place while she was there. I presume Ms. Kingsley has mentioned to you Mr. White's distasteful proclivity toward sadistic sexual practices. Would you be interested to know that in Mr. White's house there is a bullwhip that bears traces of Ms. Kingsley's blood?*

The note was signed "An Interested Observer."

My face lost all color, and for a moment, the room

seemed to swim before my eyes. My hands shook hard enough that I dropped the sheet of paper. I couldn't have looked more guilty if I'd tried. Why, oh why, hadn't I told Brian the truth when I'd had the chance? I wished he didn't have to know at all, but at least if he'd gotten it from me, this damn note wouldn't be so devastating—or hard to explain.

"It's not what you think," I stuttered, then wanted to slap myself upside the head for uttering the most guilty-sounding phrase in the English language.

"The hell it isn't," Brian growled at me. He wasn't giving me the icy stare anymore. In fact, he couldn't even bear to look at me. "This is why you were so touchy about Lugh, isn't it? Because you already had a guilty conscience!"

I tried to reach out to him, but he jerked away before I made contact. "Don't touch me!"

I took a deep, quavering breath. I had vowed to myself never to tell him what Adam had done to me, what I had *let* Adam do to me in exchange for his help rescuing Brian. If I didn't have Lugh around to keep my dreams under control, I'd have had recurring nightmares about the hell I'd gone through in Adam's black room. I'd never wanted Brian to find out, and, most of all, never wanted him to feel guilty about the sacrifice I'd made to save him.

I wasn't even sure if it would be better for Brian to think I had cheated on him than to know the truth. But I couldn't bear for him to think that.

I sucked in a deep breath, trying to calm myself, knowing that my next words were crucial to whether our relationship could survive this blow. "What happened between me and Adam wasn't in the least bit sexual," I said carefully.

Brian laughed bitterly, and he allowed himself to look at me once more. I almost wished he hadn't, because the combination of pain and fury in his eyes was more than I could bear.

"Don't bother lying to me," he said. "Your face is an open book, remember?"

"Yes, and I'm telling you the truth. Adam did whip me, but it wasn't sexual. It was about as far from sexual as it's possible to get." For me, at least. I still remembered how the thought of what he was about to do to me had aroused Adam, though he'd told me the arousal didn't mean he wanted to have sex with me, and I'd believed him.

"Save it!"

"But Brian—"

"If you'd told me the truth about it from the beginning, I might have been able to find a way to forgive you. I assume it happened while we were broken up." He shook his head. "But no, you made a point of assuring me the two of you weren't lovers."

"We weren't. We *aren't*." Once again, I reached for him, and once again, he evaded me.

"It's over, Morgan. I could put up with your bitchiness and your unwillingness to open up to me, but I can't deal with you cheating on me."

"I didn't cheat on you!" I cried, knowing I sounded desperate. "Just let me—"

"Stop lying!" he bellowed, and his face turned red with his rage. This time when I reached for him, he actually shoved me away. Not hard enough to hurt me, but easily hard enough to shock me into temporary silence.

He reached into the manila envelope one more time, pulled out an eight-by-ten photo, and shoved it at me. I felt like an elephant had just sat on my chest, and it was all I could do to breathe.

The photo was of a couple locked in a passionate kiss. The man's hands were on the woman's ass, and her arms were wrapped around his neck, one hand buried in his black hair. Their faces were obscured because they were kissing, but the woman had my hair color and style, as well as my telltale sword tattoo on her lower back, and the man certainly had Adam's height and build. Worse, they were standing on the doorstep of Adam's house.

I shook my head, barely able to find enough voice to muster a weak protest. "This is a fake. I never—"

Brian didn't even let me finish. He dropped the envelope and the photo on the floor, then turned away and stormed out my front door, slamming it behind him so hard my teeth rattled.

I fell to my knees, clutching my abdomen, unable to absorb the enormity of what had just happened. I wanted to cry, *needed* to cry, maybe even to scream and break things. But all I could do was kneel in my foyer, trying to remember to breathe as I stared at the faked photo that had just destroyed something precious.

Chapter 8

I don't know how long I knelt there, swimming in misery. Long enough for my knees to ache and my feet to fall asleep. Eventually, I staggered to my feet, pins and needles jabbing fiercely at me, and moved the pity party to the sofa, where I could be more comfortable in my despair.

I knew who had to have sent Brian that envelope, of course: Barbara Paget, PI to the rich, famous, and vindictive. She'd even warned me, in a way, that time I'd spotted her snooping outside Adam's. She'd said it was going to get worse, and that she was good at her job. Of course, what she'd done had been well over and above her job, and surely against the law. I don't suppose it's against the law to falsify an incriminating photo as long as you're not using it in court, but it was clearly unethical. And the note had said she'd found traces of my blood on a whip in Adam's house. I didn't imagine she'd come by that evidence legally. What kind of moron would break into the house of the Director of Special Forces, especially when he was a demon?

A desperate moron, Lugh's voice whispered in my head. *Remember the sister at The Healing Circle?*

I remembered, all right. I remembered speculating on how Barbie could afford to keep her sister in such an expensive facility in her line of work. She must have been well paid for tearing my heart out of my chest. I wanted to track her down and beat her into an oozing puddle of goo, but getting arrested for assault probably wasn't in my best interests.

Of course, if Barbie had broken into Adam's house to acquire evidence of our supposed affair, she might have left some evidence behind herself. Wouldn't it be lovely if Adam searched the room and found a hair that could be matched to Barbie's? It probably wouldn't mean a whole lot of jail time or anything satisfying like that, but it could put her reputation in the toilet, where it belonged.

I forced myself to my feet and trudged to the foyer, picking up the envelope that Brian had dropped. I shoved the note and photo in the envelope; then, without giving myself time to think about what I was doing or whether it was wise, I headed out to Adam's place.

There were lights on in the house, and both Adam and Dom's cars were in the small private lot across the street, so I knew someone was home. However, it took about ten rings of the doorbell, which Adam had finally gotten around to fixing, before anyone came to the door. The small part of my brain that was still working told me the delay in answering the door meant I'd come at a bad time, but that didn't keep me from hitting the buzzer over and over again.

The door swung partially open to reveal Adam, his hair mussed, his feet bare, and his shirt misbuttoned. Yup, I'd interrupted something all right. And I didn't give a shit.

"This had better be good," he growled at me. His glare should have reduced me to a pile of ashes.

I couldn't meet his eyes, unable to bear that look when I was about one wrong word away from shattering into a thousand tiny pieces that could never be put back together again. I tried to think of something to say, some way to broach the subject of what Barbie had done, but I couldn't seem to form words.

"Shit," Adam muttered. "I guess it's not anything good." He sighed heavily, then opened the door all the way. "Come on in."

I stepped inside and saw Dominic leaning against the wall in the foyer. He didn't look quite as disheveled as Adam, but he'd obviously dressed in a hurry, and his face was flushed. For half a second, I worried that Dom might react as badly to the falsified photo as Brian had, but I shook the idea off. For one, Dominic knew *exactly* what had transpired between Adam and myself. For another, his relationship with Adam was a lot more solid—and, let's face it, more healthy—than mine with Brian.

"What's wrong?" he asked.

I had a childish urge to throw myself into his arms and bawl my eyes out. Dom is probably one of the nicest human beings I've ever met, the kind of guy who would always know the right things to say. I felt the sting of tears in my eyes and blinked rapidly.

Instead of answering Dom, I invited myself into the living room, taking a seat on the couch and hugging a throw pillow to my chest. The guys followed me, Adam sitting on the opposite end of the couch, Dom once again leaning a shoulder against the wall. I glanced up at him.

"Why don't you come sit down?" I asked. I could hear the strain in my voice. I tried clearing my throat, but it didn't help. "This might take a while."

The flush in Dom's face deepened, and one corner

of his mouth rose in a grin. "I think I'll stand, thanks."

I was a little slow on the uptake—as usual when it came to these two—so I stared at him cluelessly for an awkward moment before I figured out what he meant.

"Oh," I said, and felt the heat rising in my own cheeks. I must admit, I was a bit surprised. Obviously, I knew the two of them were into S&M, but I'd been under the impression that Adam didn't inflict any serious pain on his partner. Then I remembered the time Adam had been forced to "perform" for Shae, the owner of a demon sex club. I'd gotten a front-row seat, so to speak, as Adam took a paddle to Dom's ass. Those had not been little love taps. Of course, Shae wouldn't have been satisfied with little love taps.

I must have looked more uncomfortable than usual, because Dom hastened to reassure me.

"I'll be fine in a little bit," he said. "You just caught us at a, um, awkward moment."

"Sorry," I mumbled, squeezing the throw pillow tighter and dropping my gaze to the floor.

"Come on, Morgan," Adam prompted. "Tell us what's wrong."

I took a deep breath, doing my best to shove my rioting emotions into a closet and close the door on them. I glanced up at Dominic once more.

"I know you'll figure this out on your own, but let me tell you anyway that it's complete bullshit."

He blinked at me. "Okay."

I let go of the throw pillow and dug the envelope with the incriminating evidence out of my purse. I handed the note and the photograph to Adam.

"Someone sent these to Brian," I said.

Adam's eyebrows shot up when he saw the picture. Dominic came over to look, and his expression mirrored his lover's. He reached for the photo, and Adam handed it over without any hesitation. I guess he didn't suffer a moment's worry that Dom might think it was the real thing. Dom frowned at the photo while Adam read the note.

I looked up at Dom. "Like I said, total bullshit."

He waved his hand dismissively and handed the picture back to Adam. "I know." He put a hand on Adam's shoulder in a silent show of solidarity. "I'm guessing from how awful you look that Brian took it at face value. Frankly, I'm a bit surprised at him."

Adam shook his head and handed Dom the note. "Read this and you'll understand," Adam said. He looked at me. "Let me guess: Brian asked you about the blood, and you gave him your usual poker face."

I nodded. "He showed me the note, and I just..." I shrugged. How could I describe what I'd felt when I read it? But I didn't really need to describe it. Adam and Dom both understood.

Dom dropped the note on the coffee table then came and sat beside me on the couch, a brief wince the only evidence that sitting down was uncomfortable. He grabbed both my hands and gave them a squeeze.

"It'll be okay," he said, and the tears I'd been fighting since I stepped through the door rose closer to the surface. "I'm sure he's not thinking straight right now, but when he's had a little time to calm down, he'll listen to reason."

I wished I could believe that. Maybe if there hadn't been so many other problems in our relationship, I would have. But honestly, we'd been fighting an uphill battle to stay together anyway, and I wasn't sure our love could survive a blow like this. Right now, I was the walking wounded, my heart bleeding all over the floor and my soul bathed in pain. But when that first wave of pain and shock began to ebb, I knew what would follow: fury.

Yes, I understood that the evidence looked damning. If there'd been nothing but the photo, or if there'd been nothing but the note, I probably could have convinced Brian that it wasn't true. I knew the two together had been a devastating one-two punch, especially when I'd acted so guilty over the note. So in many ways, Brian's reaction had been perfectly reasonable, and it should have been hard for me to blame him.

But it wasn't.

How could he know me as well as he did and still believe I would cheat on him? I wasn't even willing to cheat on him in my *dreams,* despite the constant temptation Lugh threw my way. I'm the first to admit I have plenty of flaws, but fooling around on the man I love wasn't one of them.

How could he have believed it of me? And even if he could somehow come to see the truth, even if he could somehow come to forgive me, the question remained—how could *I* ever forgive *him*?

I gently extracted my hands from Dom's grip and leaned back into the cushions of the sofa. The elephant was still sitting on my chest, and holding my head up was more trouble than it was worth.

"I assume our faux-reporter friend is the source," Adam mused.

"Why don't you leave your investigation hat in the closet for a while," Dominic suggested softly.

I shook my head. "Thanks, Dom," I said, forcing what I'm sure was a pathetic imitation of a smile. "I appreciate the thought, but I need to keep my mind occupied. From the content of that note, it sure sounds like she broke into this house. If she conveniently left some evidence behind . . ."

"Did you tell anyone about what happened that day?" Adam asked me.

I shuddered. "No." I couldn't look at him, fearing I would remember the terror that had shaken me as I waited for the lash.

"Dom?" Adam asked, and I saw Dom's eyebrows shoot up.

"Why would *I* tell anyone?"

Adam shook his head. "Just asking. I'd have an easier time believing Barbara found out because someone let something slip in a conversation than that she broke into the house and found the whip."

I winced. Adam could talk about this so calmly, not the least bit troubled by the hell he'd put me through. I had for the most part managed to suppress the memories, but clearly Barbie's little fishing expedition had dredged it all up.

"Besides," Adam continued, "only an amateur doesn't clean his whips when—"

"Adam, shut up," Dom interrupted as he slipped his arm around my shoulders protectively.

The corners of Adam's mouth tightened, but he stopped talking. I found myself leaning into Dominic's body. Since he wasn't into women, Dom was probably the only man—other than my brother, who seemed to have checked out of the human race— I could accept a hug from right now without having to worry about what signals I was sending. And I badly needed that hug.

Without another word, Adam stood up and left the room. Great. Now *he* was pissed off, too.

"I'm sorry," I murmured, and Dom gave me another squeeze.

"Nothing to be sorry about."

I groaned. "If only that were true." A little self-pity, anyone? But I had ample justification for it.

Dom ignored my whining. "You look like a woman badly in need of a drink," he said.

I had to bite my tongue to quell the protest I wanted to utter when he let go of me.

"I don't want a drink," I said instead. I've never been much of a drinker, and I was upset enough that my stomach threatened to toss anything I put in it back up.

"I'll get you one anyway. You don't have to drink it if you don't want to, but it'll be here if you want it." He flashed me a sad little smile, and I nodded in acquiescence. Dom stood up and reached his hand out to me.

"I'll wait here."

He rolled his eyes. "No, you won't. Come on."

It would have taken more energy than I had to argue, so I took his hand and let him drag me to my feet. I followed him into the kitchen and took a seat at the table.

Dom knew my tastes well enough not to try to convince me to drink anything too hard and manly. Instead, he made a perfect, frothy cappuccino and then added a generous shot of Frangelico. Adam's host had made that drink for me once, and it had been damn good. And despite my misery, the smell of first-class coffee was more than I could resist. When he put the cup in front of me, I immediately picked it up and took a sip.

I couldn't help smiling a little in wonder. "You are an absolute genius in the kitchen," I said, savoring the smooth, sweet aftertaste.

"Thanks."

I took another sip, trying to focus all my attention on how delicious the drink was. Dom sat next to me at the head of the table, and his presence was a balm on my wounded soul. I realized he was the one man I knew who was just an uncomplicated friend, not someone who wanted something out of me. That realization threatened to bring on the tears, so I shoved it aside and drank more coffee.

My devastated mental state left most of my barriers and shields down, and I found myself asking Dom something that under ordinary circumstances I'd never have even considered asking.

"How can you like it when Adam hurts you?" I immediately regretted the question, but Dom didn't look offended.

"I like it because when he hurts me, it doesn't really hurt."

"Huh?"

He smiled at me. "I can't believe you're actually asking me about this. You usually look like you're going to die of embarrassment if we even vaguely allude to anything you might consider kinky."

I stared at the foam in my coffee cup. "I guess I'm hoping you'll say the magic words that will somehow help me deal with what Adam did to me. I've never really dealt with it, you know? I just kind of...pretended it didn't happen."

"The only thing that happened is you got beat up," Dom said. I gave him an indignant look, but he went on before I could put my thoughts into words. "The fact that he used a tool that can be a BDSM toy to do it is irrelevant. It wasn't about BDSM, it was about a seriously pissed-off demon getting his pound of flesh. You know there's a big difference, don't you?"

I heaved a sigh. "Yeah." I wouldn't say I came close to understanding the dynamics of Adam's relationship with Dom, but I knew what Dom was saying was true. "Can we just forget I started this conversation?"

Dom was silent for a moment, but I wasn't surprised when he ignored my request.

"When Adam plays with me," he said, "I'm in something like an altered state. Some people describe it as 'subspace.' When I'm in that subspace, pain doesn't really register as pain. It's just a very strong physical sensation." One corner of his mouth lifted, though I think he was trying to suppress his smile. "One I happen to like." The half-smile faded. "But the point is, I have to be in that subspace to like it. I'm not really a masochist. Under ordinary circumstances, I'm as anxious to avoid pain as anyone else.

"It's Adam's job as my dominant to help me find my way into that subspace." Dom grinned. "He's very good at it, though he's not a natural. Demons don't need to be in subspace to enjoy pain. For them, it's all about the novelty of physical sensation. When I was hosting Saul, there was almost no dominance and submission going on between him and Adam—it was all about sensation play.

"The point is that demons are interested in SM for different reasons than humans. I've kind of trained Adam to treat it in a human way, but what he did to you was pure demon. Don't confuse it with BDSM. They're not the same at all."

I chewed that over for a bit, knowing that if I ever broke free of my own altered state, brought about by shock and emotional pain, I was going to be mortified about this conversation. But then again, if I was having this conversation with Dom, then I wasn't thinking about Brian or about my session in the black room.

"I guess that makes sense," I finally said. "I'm not sure I really *understand* it, but it makes sense." I frowned. "Of course, that *sentence* doesn't make sense." Hmm, maybe the Frangelico was starting to get to me. Since I wasn't a big drinker, it didn't take much to make me loopy.

I was saved from making any more silly, incoherent statements—and from asking any more questions that would embarrass me later—when Adam joined us in the kitchen. I was staring into my cup again, but I still managed to catch the warning look that Dom gave Adam.

Adam sat at the table across from me. "I'm sorry if talking about this makes me insensitive," he said.

"Adam..." Dominic said.

"I think it's important we establish just what we're dealing with in Barbara Paget," Adam said. "And it's now obvious that she did, in fact, break in and snoop around."

I found my courage somewhere and lifted my gaze from the depths of my coffee cup. "How is that obvious?"

"Like I was saying before, I clean my whips. At least, I did when I had need."

Meaning back when Dominic was possessed, and their "play" involved bloodshed. I knew that was not the case anymore, that Adam was very careful with his lover. I still shuddered at the thought.

"But that time with you," Adam continued, "I put the whip back in its box for a little bit before I got around to cleaning it. I hadn't opened the box since, but when I did just now, I saw that all the padding inside had been removed."

I blinked a couple of times, my thoughts feeling sluggish, either from stress or from booze. "So Barbie broke into your house and stole the padding from the box."

Adam nodded. "Along with a few other things that I'd probably never have noticed if she hadn't sent that stuff to Brian. But here's the part that's really disturbing—not only did she steal the stuff, but she also had access to someone who was able to analyze the blood and identify it as yours."

That didn't sound good at all. "I guess I need to go have a chat with Private Eye Barbie tomorrow."

"No, I think *we* need to go have a chat with her," Adam countered.

And, realizing that my mental faculties probably wouldn't be much sharper tomorrow than they were today, I had to agree.

Chapter 9

I left Dom and Adam's place at around eight, when Saul got back from wherever he'd been. I'd pretended not to notice the pointed looks Adam was giving me. There was no way in hell I was inviting Saul to stay at my place tonight. I could hardly stand my own company, much less Saul's.

When I got home, I went directly to bed, even though it was way too early for that. I put on my comfiest PJs and pulled the covers up over my head, wishing myself into a deep and oblivious sleep.

The sleep itself came with surprising ease. Amazing how much having the love of your life accuse you of cheating on him can take out of a girl. I should have known better than to hope for oblivion, however.

Once again, there was a merry fire crackling in the fireplace in Lugh's living room, and the air held just enough chill to make the warmth welcome. However, this time I was lying down on the butter-soft sofa, my head pillowed against the armrest. A cashmere-soft blanket was tucked snugly around me. My feet were propped on Lugh's lap, and under the blanket, he was running his thumbs up and down their soles with just the right amount of pressure to make my toes curl pleasantly.

For just a moment, I felt warm, and comfortable, and cherished. Then my mind clicked back into gear and I remembered my disastrous evening. I closed my eyes and then covered them with my forearm. Lugh continued to massage my feet, and though I could only describe the touch as sensual, I knew that he didn't have seduction on his mind, that he was merely trying to comfort me.

Silence stretched for what seemed like an eternity, and I think I would have fallen asleep, if I hadn't been asleep already. I kept waiting for Lugh to say something, but he didn't. He just kept rubbing my feet soothingly.

Eventually, the silence got to me, and I had to break it.

"Aren't you going to reassure me that everything's going to be okay?" I asked, and I'm afraid my voice sounded a little plaintive and childlike.

I heard him draw in a deep breath and let it out slowly. "Demons are capable of many things that humans are not, but seeing the future isn't one of them."

I dragged my arm away from my eyes and forced them open. Lugh was watching my face, his amber eyes serious, and intense, and hard to read. I frowned.

"That's a pretty noncommittal answer."

His hands stilled on my feet, though he didn't withdraw his touch. "One thing I have never done is tell you soothing lies. I don't plan to start now."

My throat tightened and my eyes burned. "In other words, you think it's over between me and Brian. For good."

He shook his head. "I didn't say that." He regarded me gravely. "But I suspect this rift is going to be hard to repair. And if it's going to be repaired, you're going to have to put a lot of effort into it."

I swallowed past my tight throat. "I bet Adam can get some expert somewhere to verify that the photo was doctored. I mean, any idiot with PhotoShop could have done it, but surely there's some way you can tell. And once Brian knows the photo is fake, he'll listen to me about the rest."

Lugh raised an eyebrow at me. "And if Brian is persuaded that you didn't have an affair with Adam, will that make things all better between you?"

I had to suppress a groan, because I'd already realized earlier this evening that it wouldn't. He was far from the only injured party in this mess.

"Don't rub it in, okay? I feel shitty enough already."

"It was not my intention to rub it in. I'm just explaining why I haven't said what you wanted to hear."

I nodded. "Okay, fine. If you're not going to whisper sweet nothings, is there any particular reason we need to talk right now? Can't you just let me sleep?" Talking wasn't going to make anything better, so I'd just as soon have done without.

"It has always been my impression that humans appreciate having a shoulder to cry on when they are having romantic difficulties."

I snorted. "You know perfectly well I'm not the crying-on-shoulders type. Try again." There was something he wanted from me. He just hadn't gotten around to telling me what yet. Whatever it was, I wasn't in the mood to give it to him. I just wanted to crawl into my little hidey-hole and disappear until the pain went away. Too bad life didn't work that way.

"Maybe I just wanted to remind you that you weren't alone," he said softly, looking at the fire, not at me. He smiled faintly, but it looked forced. "Or maybe I figured if I *didn't* talk to you tonight, you'd be angry with me for my perceived desertion."

Despite my less-than-alert state of mind, I was beginning to hear the faint ringing of warning bells in my brain. It wasn't like Lugh to be this cagey. It took a considerable amount of willpower to move, but I forced myself to sit up and slide my feet off of his lap. I wrapped the sinfully soft blanket tightly around me, not sure what Lugh had dressed me in for this dream and not wanting to find out.

I suspected everything he'd just said was true. I also suspected there was more going on than met the eye.

"Will you stop with the tap dancing and just tell me what this is about?"

He gave me an assessing look that made my stomach do a back flip. Suddenly, I wasn't sure I wanted to know what he was up to after all. I had more than my fair share of turmoil already, and the last thing I wanted was to add more to my plate.

Lugh smiled at me ruefully. "Take it easy, Morgan. It's nothing as devious or as worrisome as you're making it out to be."

"Then what is it?"

"I just wanted to make some arrangements that I knew you weren't going to get around to making in your state of mind."

The warning bells were now so loud I was almost surprised Lugh didn't hear them.

"In other words, you've been keeping my mind busy here in la-la land while you've driven my body around." It wouldn't be the first time Lugh had taken control of my body during my sleep, and, of course, he generally used such opportunities to do things I very much didn't want him to.

"What did you do?" I demanded, meanwhile trying to muster my mental defenses enough to wake myself up and kick Lugh out of the driver's seat. It always required some effort, but right now I felt so weighed down by the circumstances that I wasn't sure I could do it at all.

"No need to try to shake me off," Lugh said. "I've done what I set out to do, and I've put you back to bed."

"Why doesn't that make me feel any better?" I muttered, but my struggles to break through his control were weak and halfhearted. Somehow, it just didn't seem worth the energy.

"I talked to Adam. I thought it best for you to have a bodyguard, at least until we find out what the story is behind that hand you received in the mail."

I groaned. "Don't tell me you invited Saul over."

"All right, I won't tell you that." He smiled at me, a teasing glint in his eye.

I shook my head. "I don't need a bodyguard!"

"I know," Lugh said, nipping my incipient tirade in the bud. "But it made for a good excuse to move Saul out of Adam and Dominic's house. There is enough tension already between various members of my council. I don't need Saul and Adam in a romantic rivalry."

I met his eyes. "If there's a romantic rivalry going on, then just moving Saul out of the house isn't going to stop it."

Lugh shrugged. "Maybe not. But I'm sure it's better for all involved, and it should at least slow things down."

"Maybe you should have put more thought into it before you insisted on summoning Saul to the Mortal Plain!"

He gave me a quelling look. "There's no point in

arguing about that. Saul's here—both on the Mortal Plain and in your apartment. Let's just move on from there."

My eyes widened. "You mean there's more?"

He nodded. "I suspect that in his current state of mind, Brian isn't going to be overly anxious to pay your legal bills."

The blood drained from my face. The thought hadn't even occurred to me, but of course Lugh was right.

He patted the air reassuringly. "Don't worry. I've made other arrangements."

I was anything but reassured. I lowered my head into my hands. "Adam again?"

"Yes. He has the financial resources to help you."

I raised my head and glared at him, my hands trembling with rage. "And what if I tell you that I absolutely refuse to accept money from Adam?"

"Then I'll call you a mule-headed fool and I will continue to take matters into my own hands as often as necessary."

My jaw dropped. Lugh usually tried to be so gentle and patient about everything. I would have thought now, of all times, he'd treat me like a porcelain doll.

"My apologies," he said, though he didn't sound particularly apologetic. "You need money to defend yourself, and Adam has money. Getting through the lawsuit is going to be difficult enough without financial strain loaded on top. And don't forget, the rest of your problems aren't going to magically disappear while you're being sued."

I crossed my arms over my chest and scowled. "I haven't forgotten."

"Also don't forget that you're my host, and that I need you. I can't afford to leave you undefended, and as Adam's king, I have every right to demand that he pay for your defense."

I was too tired and beaten down to argue, though I wanted to. "Adam paying for my defense is just going to reinforce Brian's assumption that he's my lover."

"That can't be helped." He looked genuinely sorry this time, but I wasn't sure I cared anymore.

"Let me go back to sleep now," I said, my voice flat and hopeless-sounding.

Lugh slid across the couch until he was right by my side, then he slipped his arm around my shoulders and gave me a firm squeeze. "It will be all right," he murmured in my ear.

Tears stung my eyes, and I felt the elephant weight on my chest again. I was going to humiliate myself by crying on his shoulder, after all.

But Lugh knew me too well to let that happen. Just when I thought I couldn't hold the tears back another moment, the room began to dissolve around me, and I drifted into the peaceful oblivion I'd longed for.

The next morning, I woke up feeling like my head was stuffed with cotton. I remembered what had happened, and knew I should be very upset, but my emotions were stuffed in cotton, too. That was probably a good thing, since I needed to function today.

I took a long, steamy shower, moving by rote, not thinking about much of anything. Distantly, I thought perhaps I was a little *too* spaced out for my own good. But when I considered the alternative . . .

I was afraid coffee might wake some of my still blissfully sleeping brain cells. However, there was no way I was getting through the day without coffee, so I was just going to have to take a chance.

Luckily, I pulled on some yoga pants and a T-shirt before I headed for the kitchen, because I'd forgotten that Lugh had invited Saul to stay here. I came to a screeching halt in my bedroom doorway when I saw him sitting on my living room sofa sipping from a travel mug that hadn't come from my kitchen. Considerate of him to bring his own dishes. I grabbed the door frame, my mind reorienting itself to my new reality.

"I brought some of Dom's coffee," Saul said when I just stood there like an idiot. "I hope you don't mind." He tried a grin that didn't look terribly convincing. Oh, good. He wasn't any more comfortable being here than I was having him here. "Adam told me your coffee sucks."

"He didn't lie." I shambled toward the kitchen, hoping Saul had made enough coffee for both of us. When I saw he had made a full pot, my opinion of him softened considerably. I poured a cup and inhaled deeply. It smelled heavenly, so I took a big sip, not bothering with my usual cream and sugar.

It was a good thing it was such high-quality java, because Saul had made it strong enough to make espresso seem mild and diluted by comparison. I felt like pounding my chest with my fist after I swallowed. I turned to stare at Saul with watery eyes.

"Have you ever heard of the concept of moderation?" It was a good thing he'd brought the coffee himself or he'd probably have used my entire week's ration in that one pot.

He frowned and took a sip from his mug. He made a show of rolling it around his mouth then swallowing. "Too strong?" he asked, and it sounded like he was just guessing.

I rolled my eyes and poured half the contents of my mug back into the pot. I then filled the mug to the brim with hot water, added cream and sugar, and tried again. It tasted just about right. I wrapped both hands around the mug. Not that it was cold in my apartment, but this was just so damn awkward.

"I don't suppose there's any chance I can convince you to go back to Dom and Adam's place," I said.

He took another swig from his travel mug. "Not when my king has ordered me to stay here and keep an eye on you." He stood up and came toward the kitchen.

I didn't think the kitchen was big enough for the both of us, so I moved to my dining room. I probably moved a little too quickly, because Saul gave me a funny look. I pretended not to notice as I sat down at the table and paid more attention to my coffee than it was worth. Out of the corner of my eye, I saw Saul refill his mug. Unfortunately, he didn't take my subtle "Leave me alone" hint and came to join me at the table.

"You don't like me," he said.

I can't deal with drama before my morning coffee on the best of days. I fixed him with a steady look.

"I don't know you well enough not to like you. I just don't want a baby-sitter. Now can you let me drink my coffee in peace?"

"You're upset that I've taken this particular host."

So much for drinking my coffee in peace. I shrugged, trying to act as casual as possible in the hopes he'd just drop it and shut up. "You didn't have a choice, so I can hardly blame you."

"But you do anyway."

I seriously considered splashing my coffee in his face. Of course, being a demon, he'd probably like it. "Look, Saul. I'll tolerate having you here because it's not worth the energy to fight with Lugh about it. But that doesn't mean I have to have heart-to-heart talks with you. It's nothing personal, but I need you to shut up right now."

He opened his mouth as if to argue, then seemed to think better of it. I nodded my approval, and that was the end of our breakfast conversation.

Afterward, I took him downstairs and introduced him to the front desk clerk—though I said he was my guest, not my roommate. I saw his disapproving glance, but pretended not to. I had his name officially recorded on my "okay to let into the elevators without calling me first" list. His was the only name on it. And then, with the utmost reluctance, I had the front desk issue him his very own key.

Chapter **10**

Adam saved Saul and me from a morning of prolonged awkwardness by showing up at ten, just as
we were finishing off the last of the way-too-strong
coffee.

"Ready to go have a word with our dear friend
Barbara?" Adam asked me with a fierce grin.

The grin made me shudder. Adam could be one
scary dude when he wanted to be, and however much
I hated PI Barbie right now, I wasn't sure she deserved
to have Adam sicced on her.

"I don't suppose there's any chance you'll let me
go chat with her by myself?" I asked.

"It's *my* house she broke into." His grin became
even more ferocious. "Besides, I can put the fear
of prison into her. She did commit a crime, you
know."

Knowing Adam, I didn't think prison was going to
be the scariest thing he'd threaten Barbie with. It was
kind of amazing how many laws Adam managed to
break while being a police officer. And that he always
seemed to get away with it. The Philly PD had never
been the poster child for incorruptibility, but I could

scare myself thinking about how much leeway the officers apparently had.

The good news was that Saul didn't get to accompany us for this interview. He would remain in my apartment "keeping watch." I think that basically meant "keeping out of the way." And for just a moment as Adam and I were leaving, I met Saul's eyes and got the feeling he thought the same thing. I might even have felt a bit bad for him if I weren't still in so much pain myself.

Adam didn't disturb my silence as we took the elevator down to the garage level and then made our way to the visitors' parking area in an unpleasantly secluded corner. When I climbed into his unmarked, I put on my seat belt and let my head fall back against the headrest as I closed my eyes. I'd gotten plenty of sleep last night, but I still felt like I could sleep another week.

I swore I could feel Adam's eyes on me for a long moment before he started the car and pulled out of the parking space. I knew I wasn't acting like my normal self, but I couldn't help it. Eventually, I'd dredge up some anger, and with that anger would come energy. But for now, all I felt was... depression, I suppose.

I must have totally spaced out for a bit, because when next I was aware of my surroundings, we were parallel parked on one of the seedier sections of Broad Street and Adam was staring at me. We could have driven five minutes or five hours—my senses were so scrambled I doubt I'd have known the difference.

Trying to shake the fog out of my brain, I unhooked my seat belt and gave Adam an annoyed glance. "What?"

He pursed his lips, and I had the impression he

was trying to decide what to say. I hoped he'd decide on nothing, but I wasn't that lucky.

"Are you up to this?"

I looked for the surge of indignation a question like that would usually inspire, but I couldn't seem to muster it. Instead, I shrugged. "Probably not, but let's do it anyway." I started to get out, but Adam grabbed my arm. Again, I thought I should object but couldn't be bothered.

"There's no point in you coming with me if you're just planning to sit there and pout."

I tried a glare, but I didn't think there was much heat behind it. "I've just had my heart broken. Forgive me if I'm a little down."

His glare was much more effective. "Down is one thing. Dead is another. And dead is what you'll end up if you don't snap out of it and fast!"

I searched my brain for a good retort, but none came to mind. My vision blurred for a moment, and the next thing I knew, I wasn't in control of my body anymore.

"Morgan needs some time," Lugh said through my own mouth. "I'll fill in for her until she's ready to participate again."

If I needed proof positive that I was in bad shape, I now had it. I hadn't made any attempt to lower my mental barriers, and yet Lugh had been able to take control without the faintest hint of resistance on my part. And though I should have felt alarmed—I was too much of a control freak at heart to appreciate being a passenger in my own body—I merely felt . . . relieved. Adam was right: I wasn't up to interviewing PI Barbie.

Adam didn't look much happier than he had a moment ago. "Should we be . . . worried?" he asked.

Lugh shook his head. "I feel confident she'll make a full recovery."

That makes one of us, I thought at him, but he didn't bother to answer the thought.

We got out of the car and entered a small office building that might have been a bail bonds office in a past life. Barbie's office was toward the back, down a dismal hallway that had needed new carpet about twenty years ago. One of the ceiling tiles sported an impressive rust brown water stain, and the paint on the walls had so many scuffs you could almost mistake them for stripes. To enhance that aura of genteel respectability, the letters on Barbie's door proclaimed *ARBARA PA ET, RIVATE INVE TIGAT ON.*

I couldn't help wondering how the hell Barbie could afford to keep her sister at The Healing Circle if this was the best she could do for an office.

How the hell did an old money tycoon like Maguire end up hiring a bargain-basement PI? I thought at Lugh.

Good question, he answered.

Adam knocked on the door, and Barbie told him to come in. She had her back to us when we walked in, her nose buried in a battered metal filing cabinet. Her office itself looked a little better than the hallway, though it didn't exactly scream of astounding financial success. At least it was neat, and the furniture, though no doubt secondhand, didn't look like it had been stolen from a Dumpster.

Barbie stopped messing with the filing cabinet, shoving the drawer closed with a good bit of muscle. Even so, it got stuck about six inches short of fully closed. She gave it a bang with the heel of her hand, but it didn't budge.

"Damn thing," she muttered under her breath, then finally turned and saw Adam and me.

Her baby blue eyes widened in surprise as she looked back and forth between the two of us. "Ms. Kingsley, Mr. White. What a surprise."

"I'll bet," Lugh said, adopting my hostile conversational style.

She blinked innocently. "To what do I owe the pleasure?" she asked.

Her poker face was a hell of a lot better than mine. If I hadn't known better, I might have believed she had no idea why we were here.

"I'm sure you're aware, Ms. Paget, that breaking and entering is against the law," Adam said.

Adam has an uncanny ability to intimidate, and it looked like his juju was working overtime with Barbie. Her face paled and her mouth dropped partway open. So much for the poker face.

Adam laughed. "Come now," he chided. "How can you act so surprised? If you're going to brag about evidence you found in my house, it should come as no great shock that I know you broke in."

With a shudder, she moved to the chair behind her desk and slowly sat. Her face had not regained its color. She glanced up at Adam's face, but couldn't seem to hold his gaze for more than half a second. She shook her head.

"How exactly did I brag about the evidence?" she asked, her voice shaky.

Maybe she was a really great actress, but it sure seemed to me she was genuinely surprised and distressed by Adam's accusation. Lugh and Adam shared a look, and I remembered that I wasn't currently in control of my body. I wanted to peer into Barbie's face, looking for evidence of a lie. Not that I'm that great at telling when someone's lying to me, but still . . .

Lugh reached into my pocketbook and pulled out the letter Brian had received, handing it to Adam, who handed it to Barbie. Annoyingly, Lugh still didn't look at Barbie, so I couldn't see her reaction. He seemed inordinately fascinated by the potted fern that languished in one corner of the office.

"Where did you get this?" Barbie asked.

Lugh was still examining the fern, and I felt the first stirrings of real irritation. *What's so fascinating about the damn plant?* I asked.

Lugh didn't answer.

"Are you sure you don't know?" Adam asked Barbie.

Damn it, Lugh, turn your head!

"I didn't write it, if that's what you're asking."

It finally occurred to me that Lugh was studiously refusing to look in Barbie's direction for the sole purpose of pissing me off. It was working, too. Sometimes, his ability to push just the right buttons is downright scary. I didn't particularly *want* to be roused from my funk, but Lugh knew just how to goad me out of the soothing numbness.

I hated the fact that Lugh had manipulated me into this move, but I started to rally my mental forces to kick him out.

"But you know who did," Adam said, and Barbie didn't answer.

I wasn't shocked that Lugh resisted my attempt to wrest back control. Damn him, he was going to make me *fight* for it. Feeling a bit like a marionette on his strings, I struggled harder to shut him out of my mind.

"Ms. Paget," Adam said, "I found a long blond hair lying on the floor near the whip mentioned in the letter. What do you suppose the chances are it'll match yours and help convict you?"

I was sure Adam was bluffing about that; otherwise, he would have mentioned it to me earlier. However,

Barbie couldn't know that, and Adam sounded pretty damn sure of himself.

Still, Lugh wasn't letting me take control back, and a little of my habitual panic was seeping into my efforts. I wanted Lugh out of the driver's seat, and I wanted him out *now*. Trying to still the panic while drawing energy from my anger, I visualized slamming the doors of my mind shut, then double-locking them to keep Lugh out.

His resistance faded as if it had never existed, and I was back in my own body, my pulse beating frantically in my throat. My stomach lurched unhappily with my now habitual post-control-change nausea. *Thanks a lot, Lugh,* I thought as I struggled not to toss my cookies.

I turned to look at Barbie, and she looked as panicked as I had felt a moment ago. Her hands had clenched in white-knuckled fists around the letter, and she was panting like she'd just finished doing push-ups.

"You'll go to prison, Ms. Paget," Adam said. I saw that he had taken a seat in front of her desk and was lounging in it casually, his long legs stretched out in front of him, a smug expression on his face. "Probably not for long, but you'll still lose your PI license, and you won't get it back. Ex-cons have a lot of trouble finding work, you know. You'll be lucky to get a job flipping burgers." He made a mock-regretful face. "And you can forget about keeping Blair at The Healing Circle. But don't worry. There are some excellent nursing homes for the indigent."

Barbie's eyes closed in pain, and when she opened them again, I saw the glimmer of tears. If she hadn't just ruined my life, I'd feel a lot sorrier for her. Still, it wasn't just *her* we were threatening, it was her helpless, innocent sister.

I was all ready to step into the "good cop" role, but before I figured out what to say, Barbie spoke up again.

"What do you want?" she asked, and I could hear the tears in her voice even though she hadn't let any fall. "If you were planning to arrest me, you would have done it already." She glanced briefly up at me. "And you wouldn't have brought Ms. Kingsley with you."

Adam shrugged. "That wasn't my initial plan, but don't fool yourself into thinking I won't arrest you if you don't cooperate."

She drew in a deep breath and sat up straighter in her chair. The tears had vanished, and she looked grim and determined. "Tell me what you want."

"I'd like you to tell me how you ended up working for Jordan Maguire—because, frankly, this doesn't look like his kind of place—and what, exactly, he's hired you to do."

Barbie shook her head. "I don't work for Jordan Maguire. I was hired by Jack Hillerman, Mr. Maguire's attorney."

"A technicality. My question still stands."

She squirmed, then looked up at me. "I'm very sorry," she said, and she sounded sincere. "When I first took the job, I had no idea..." Her voice trailed off, and her gaze dropped to her scarred desktop.

I should have hated this woman, but either my emotions were still muted, or I recognized Barbie as a victim. I took the seat beside Adam, and we both waited in silence for Barbie to continue. She took another deep breath, then folded her hands on the desk and looked up.

"Mr. Hillerman originally hired me to dig up dirt on Ms. Kingsley," she said, addressing her answer to Adam. "I was to follow her and try to find incriminating information for the lawsuit. He offered me a more than generous retainer." She grimaced. "I should have known something was fishy, but I just couldn't turn down the kind of money he was offering."

"And how did Hillerman end up hiring a second-rate PI to investigate for a client of Maguire's stature?" Adam asked.

Her eyes narrowed in a glare. "I'm *not* a second-rate PI! I happen to be very good at my job."

Adam swept the office with a contemptuous look. "Yeah, I can see you're the pinnacle of success."

Her cheeks flushed. "Appearances can be deceiving. I could rent a fancy office in a better part of town, or I could give my sister the best care money can buy. I decided my sister was more important than my office."

I could tell from Adam's expression that he was going to continue growling at her. I didn't think that was going to get us what we wanted, so I interrupted.

"You may be real successful," I said, "but it still seems unusual for a guy like Hillerman to hire you. He'd have taken one look at this place and turned right back around. Assuming he'd even bother to come after finding your address." Like I said, this was one of the seedier sections of Broad Street, and Hillerman would have known that.

"He said I'd been recommended by one of my former clients."

Adam and I gave her twin skeptical looks.

She raised her chin. "Yes, I wondered why he was hiring someone like me when I'm sure he has investigators he uses regularly. But I couldn't afford to turn down the kind of money he was offering." Her shoulders slumped. "I should have known it was too good to be true."

"It must have been quite some paycheck to inspire you to break into the house of the Director of Special Forces," I commented.

"That's not how it started," Barbie said. "At first, it was just ordinary, tedious investigation. Then Mr. Hillerman convinced me to follow some leads in rather, er, unconventional ways. I managed to get some financial and medical information through less-than-legitimate sources. I didn't think it was anything very helpful to the case, but my client asked for it and was willing to pay a premium for it, so I did what he wanted.

"When I learned that Ms. Kingsley had spent a couple of nights at your house, and I shared that information with my client, he asked me to search the house for any kind of proof of an affair. I refused."

"Oh, really?" Adam asked, his voice laced with sarcasm.

Barbie returned his gaze calmly. "Really. I'd been willing to bend the law a bit for the kind of money he was paying, but I drew the line at breaking and entering." She sighed heavily. "But he'd been setting me up all along. I don't think he really cared about that financial or medical information—he just wanted me to do something illegal so he could use it against me. He said if I didn't search the house, he'd turn me in."

I frowned. "But since he's the one who paid you for the information, wouldn't he incriminate himself if he turned you in?"

"Yes. But, as he pointed out, I had a lot more to lose. All he had to do was disrupt my ability to work, and I wouldn't be able to afford to keep Blair at The Healing Circle. He's got enough money he could retire right now if he wanted to, so even in the worst-case scenario, he'd come out all right. It wasn't anything he would go to prison over.

"Besides, how could I *prove* he ordered me to do it? He wasn't stupid enough to give me written instructions. Hell, he wouldn't even give me instructions over the phone."

"But now that he sent the letter to Brian, he's blown everything out of the water!" I said.

"Has he?" Adam asked. "We can't prove he sent the letter."

I motioned at Barbie. "She can testify that she gave him the information."

"And he'll deny it. Right now, we have her word against his. And he's a very respectable attorney who has nothing to gain by sending information like that to Brian."

That made me frown. "Neither does she," I said, once again motioning at Barbie. If she objected to being talked about in the third person, she didn't say anything about it. "But let's back up a step. You said Hillerman had nothing to gain by sending that shit to Brian, and you're right. So why did he?"

Adam looked as puzzled as I felt. When we'd been assuming it was Maguire himself behind the letter, it had made a twisted sort of sense. But for it to be Hillerman...

"If things go south for him, he could ruin his whole career over this," I mused. "Why the hell would he bother?"

We both turned to look at Barbie, who shrugged.

"I don't know what it's all about," she said. "I didn't ask very many questions. What I do know is that he has some kind of personal grudge against you."

That knocked me for a loop. "I don't even know the guy! How can he have a personal grudge?"

"I don't know. He tried to pretend he was just looking out for Mr. Maguire's interests, but I could tell it was personal. He'd get this look in his eyes when he talked about you…" She flashed me an apologetic smile. "I don't know what you did to piss him off, but it was something."

"But I've never met him!" I said again. "The closest I've come to having contact with him was when he left a message on my answering machine telling me not to try to contact Maguire."

Adam gave me a meaningful look, but I had no idea what he was trying to tell me. I tried to convey my cluelessness with my own meaningful look.

"We'll talk about this later," he said firmly. "Right now, we have something else to discuss." He turned toward Barbie, a feral glint in his eye.

She swallowed hard. "So you're going to arrest me, after all."

"Give me one good reason not to."

I could tell she was thinking furiously. And I could also tell she was too worried about her fate and that of her sister to figure out what Adam was getting at.

"Maybe you'd like to do some pro bono work for us," I suggested.

Relief washed over her face. "I'd be happy to. I know I've made some terrible mistakes, but this," she grabbed the letter and tossed it back across the desk to us, "is not something I ever thought I'd be a part of. If there's something I can do to make up for it, all you have to do is ask."

"There's no way you can undo the damage you've caused," Adam said. He pulled the photo out of the envelope and handed it to Barbie. Her eyes widened.

"I didn't take this!" she said immediately.

"I know," Adam answered. "It's been doctored

somehow, because that never happened. How about you start by trying to find out who created the photo and get them to admit it's fake?"

Barbie looked at him steadily. "Is it really fake? Or are you asking me to find someone to lie about it?"

"It's fake!" I said, my voice near a shout. I took a deep breath to calm myself. "Adam and I don't have that kind of relationship and we never did. Forget what you think you know, because you don't know jack shit."

She held up the picture and gave it a thorough once-over. Then she nodded. "All right. I'll see what I can do. I'm presuming if I find the party who made the photo, you'd like me to get evidence to link them to Hillerman."

"Naturally," Adam said.

I had a few other assignments I wanted to put her on, stat, but Adam gave me another of those damn meaningful looks. I still didn't know what he was trying to tell me. Except for the "shut up" part. That, I got.

"Did *you* arrange to have those blood samples analyzed?" Adam asked Barbie.

She shook her head. "I just gave the stuff I found at your house to Mr. Hillerman. But considering the faked photo, he could have just lied about matching the blood. He knew he could make plenty of trouble without having genuine evidence."

"True," Adam conceded. "Just focus on the photo right now. I don't suppose I need to tell you that Morgan and I were never here."

She nodded briskly. "No, you don't."

"And, of course, you'll let us know if Mr. Hillerman has any other assignments for you."

She didn't look too happy about that suggestion,

but she nodded again anyway. "I suppose it would be hypocritical of me to worry about client confidentiality at this point."

I couldn't help but agree. Leaving Barbie to her work, Adam and I headed back out.

Chapter 11

I held my questions until we got into the car, but the moment Adam closed the door behind himself, I turned to him.

"So, what were you trying to convey to me with all those pointed glances?"

He buckled up and pulled out into traffic. "You seem to have come back to life."

"Leave my mental state out of it and just answer the question."

"Of course, you're obviously not at the top of your game yet, or you'd have figured this out already."

I reminded myself it would be a bad idea to smack Adam while he was driving. "Are you going to answer the question, or are you just going to kick me while I'm down?" I'm not usually one to play the guilt card, but sometimes you've just got to play the hand you're dealt. From the corner of my eye, I saw Adam's lips tug down in a mild frown. I guess he didn't feel all that guilty.

"You're forgetting that there's more than one person in your body," he said, eyes on the road. "If a man you don't know suddenly seems to have it in for you, chances are good it's not *you* he's after."

Adam slammed on the brakes suddenly and just avoided crashing into a guy who apparently forgot you're supposed to look to see if someone's coming before you pull out of a parking space. Adam cursed and leaned on his horn.

"Lucky for him I don't feel like being a traffic cop today," he muttered under his breath.

"And lucky for all involved you have a demon's reflexes," I said, my heart thumping from yet another near-death experience.

We resumed our normal pace, and I rolled Adam's suggestion around in my brain for a bit. I understood where he was coming from, but still...

"The people who are after Lugh want him dead, not stuck in a heartbroken host. If gathering dirt on my supposed relationship with you is meant to be a strike against Lugh, then it's pretty feeble. Besides, if the bad guys knew I still had Lugh, we'd be fending off assassins right and left."

As far as Dougal and his people knew, I had transferred Lugh to another host when the shit hit the fan. I still had a target on my back, seeing as I might be a bread crumb in the trail leading to whoever was hosting Lugh right this moment, but so far, Dougal didn't seem to think questioning me was a high priority.

He knows I'm not stupid enough to stay in whoever you transferred me to, Lugh's voice said in my head. *I'm sure he figures I've gotten far away from you by now and it's not worth his effort to question you. Besides, we've already established that time is on his side.*

Yeah, because eventually, I would die of natural causes—if I was lucky—and send Lugh back to the

Demon Realm so he could be trapped in a new host and killed. I could have done without the reminder.

"Thanks for the update," I muttered under my breath. Adam raised his eyebrow at me, but I got the feeling he knew I wasn't talking to him.

"It does seem to be a strange way to attack Lugh," Adam conceded. "But I don't think we should dismiss the possibility. I'll check and see if Hillerman has any known ties to the Spirit Society. And don't forget the little gift you got in the mail."

The fact that I actually *had* forgotten all about that showed just what my life had been like lately. "You have any updates about that?" I asked, trying to act like it had been preying on my mind all morning. I doubt I fooled Adam, but he didn't call me on it.

"Nothing that's going to lead us to who sent it, unfortunately. The only fingerprints on the bubble wrap were yours."

I swallowed my gorge as I remembered feeling that dead flesh against my skin. "And did you find out where the hand came from?"

He nodded. "My guess was right: it was embalmed. When we polled the local funeral parlors, one of them came up with a corpse missing a hand."

At least no one had been killed specifically to spook me. "Do you think Barbie had anything to do with that?"

He thought about that a moment, but quickly dismissed it. "Nah. If she'd done something that dangerous, she'd have been a lot twitchier when we talked to her. Breaking and entering is one thing, but grave-robbing and then sending something like that through the U.S. mail . . . That's a whole different league."

"But Hillerman could still be behind it."

"I don't know. It seems too violent to fit his MO. I wouldn't rule it out, but I'd say it's unlikely."

"Are we going to confront him?" I asked.

"Hillerman?"

I rolled my eyes. "No, Elvis Presley."

Usually, my smart-ass comments seemed to piss Adam off, but this time I could have sworn he was suppressing a smile.

"We don't have enough information to confront him yet," he said. "The only evidence we have to tie him to any of this is Barbie, and that's just not enough."

I knew he was right, but that didn't mean I had to like it. "So we just wait to see what else he's going to do to make my life miserable and hope he screws up enough that we can prove he's involved?"

"Basically, yes."

I felt like punching the glove compartment, but this was a sturdy car, and with the way my life was going, I'd probably end up with a broken hand.

"Remember, Barbie's looking into the origins of the photo, and I'm going to check for Spirit Society connections. It's not like we're doing nothing."

"It's like *I'm* doing nothing," I countered. "I can't do my job because of the damn suspension, and I can't work on rebuilding my house because the insurance company's got its thumb up its ass. I can't look into what Hillerman has against me..." I shook my head violently. "If I have to sit around and do nothing, I'm going to go crazy." And sink into a black pit of depression, but I didn't feel like mentioning that.

"You can work with your attorney to try to defend yourself against the lawsuit. That ought to take plenty of time and energy."

I turned to look out the side window. I don't know what my face must have looked like at the reminder that I was now beholden to Adam for my legal fees. I think the only person in the world I'd be *less* happy to take money from was Raphael. But Lugh had ordered him to do it, and he would always follow Lugh's orders to the letter.

We didn't say anything else for the remainder of the drive back to my apartment building. I refrained from pointing out to Adam that, although I could, indeed, spend a lot of time and energy working out my legal problems, I wasn't scheduled to see my lawyer again until the day after tomorrow. Which meant that as soon as Adam drove away, I officially had nothing to do.

I had once again forgotten about my "bodyguard," so when I stepped into my apartment and saw Saul sitting at my dining room table chowing down on some Chinese takeout, I nearly had heart failure. He raised his eyebrows, his only indication that he'd noticed my gasp of terror, then shoveled another bite of food into his mouth. I could have sworn I saw one of those sadistic dried red peppers they used to spice up Chinese food on his fork—you know, the kind of peppers you're not supposed to eat if you know what's good for you?

When I approached the table, trying to figure out how to act around my unwanted guest, I took a closer look at his plate and another sniff of the air. I decided it wasn't Chinese food after all; it was Thai. And if there's any culture in the world that makes hotter food than the Thais, I don't want to know about it. But Saul was putting away those dried red peppers like they were candy.

He grinned at me through a mouthful of food. "I'd offer to share, but I think you might find this a little too spicy."

I shook my head. "Isn't that going to give you

an ulcer or something?" Stupid question, of course. Demons don't get ulcers—or, at least, if they do, they can heal them so fast they don't matter.

"There's another carton of Thai green curry in the fridge," he said. "I wasn't sure whether you'd be home for lunch or not, but it'll probably still be hot enough to eat. It's only been in there about five minutes."

"And is this green curry going to eat a hole through my stomach lining?"

He shook his head. "I asked for it extra mild. I didn't know if you liked spicy food or not."

I shifted uncomfortably from foot to foot. The smell of food was making my stomach rumble, and all I'd had for breakfast was coffee. But still . . .

"You don't have to feed me, you know," I said.

Saul shrugged and put his fork down, leaning back in his chair. "I know I don't have to. I also know you want me here even less than Adam wants me at his place, so I figured I'd make myself useful."

I pulled out a chair and sat down at the table, not sure what to say. I'm sure my face showed my surprise at his bald statement.

Saul picked up his fork again, but he merely used it to stir the food around his plate. "It's kind of funny, if you think about it. Adam, Dom, and me, all acting like we have no idea there's anything wrong, when we all know perfectly well what's going on."

I didn't know Saul well enough to figure out whether that sound in his voice was bitterness, or just resignation. "Are you okay?" I asked, my current heartache making me more sensitive to romantic troubles than usual.

Saul dismissed the question with a wave of his hand. "I'm fine. Nothing's really changed since I last walked the Mortal Plain. Remember, Dom and I were in the same body for a long time. I've always known that he loves Adam. And I've always known that if he had to choose between the two of us, he'd choose Adam." Saul's smile was wan. "But when Dom was my host, he didn't have to choose."

"You mean he didn't have a choice." Since Dom's personality had been buried beneath Saul's, he could never communicate with anyone except Saul. So if he was to have a romantic relationship, it would have to be with Saul—or with an illusion Saul created for him. I wondered if Saul had played the role of Adam in Dominic's dreams. Then I shook my head at myself and reminded myself it was none of my business.

My bitchy comment seemed to have ended the conversation. Saul resumed picking at his food, and I decided that if I had food in my mouth, I'd be much less likely to say things I would later regret.

I dumped the curry Saul had brought me onto a plate, nuked it for thirty seconds, and brought it to the table. Thirty seconds was too long, and now I didn't dare take a bite unless I wanted third-degree burns on my tongue. I stirred my food around the plate, sending up a cloud of fragrant steam.

"I'm sorry," I said, still looking at my plate. "I have a tendency to blurt out whatever comes to my mind without thinking about it. I've been getting better about it lately, but I feel so shitty right now I guess I'm backsliding."

A brief nod was the only indication he gave that he heard my apology. I'm not sure if that meant he accepted it or not, but since we'd already determined I had a tendency to stick my foot in my mouth, I decided to keep my mouth closed.

The curry was finally cool enough to eat, as long as I blew on it first, so I took a tentative taste. Despite Saul's assurance, I was afraid it would be Thai-spicy, but it turned out to be just perfect. A bit of a kick, but not so much it was painful to eat.

There was a long silence as I ate, and Saul stirred the remains of his food around his plate, taking an occasional nibble as if he weren't sure if he was done or not.

"My host isn't mentally challenged, you know," Saul said out of nowhere.

It wasn't a topic I felt like discussing at the moment, but I didn't have it in me not to argue. "I met him before you took him. I know mentally challenged when I see it, and Dick fit the description."

"He isn't brilliant, but his intelligence is normal. It's the way he was raised that made him seem challenged. Amazing what a total lack of socialization and stimulation of the mind will do to a child."

I flinched. "Now you sound like your father, objectifying Dick like he's some kind of lab rat."

He leveled me with an unnerving, level gaze. "*Never* compare me to Raphael. In any way. Understand?"

"Don't sound like him, and I won't compare you."

His fists clenched on the table. "I was commenting on what was done to my host to make him seem mentally challenged when in fact his intelligence is perfectly normal. I'm not the one who did it to him, and I'd never condone doing that to anyone!"

I backed off. "Fine. I'm touchy about the subject is all. If you'd heard some of the cavalier things Raphael has said about the 'test subjects'..." I let my voice trail off. Raphael was on Lugh's side in the demon war, and he was our ally whether I wanted him to be or not. But it seemed obvious he'd never accepted the idea that there was anything wrong in Dougal's damn breeding program.

"He's getting better," Saul said.

My mouth dropped open.

"Dick, not Raphael," Saul amended quickly. "I'm not sure how much of the damage I can repair. A child's brain is much more malleable than an adult's. But the point is, I can make him more functional over time."

"And what good does that do him, when he doesn't get to function anyway?"

He gave me an annoyed look. "Do you cease to exist when Lugh takes control?"

"No, but—"

"Dick is still alive and well within me. And whether he can personally interact with the outside world or not, he's still a person with a life. A life that will be fuller and richer if I can undo some of the damage he's taken from lifelong abuse and neglect."

I forced myself to take a moment to think before I blurted out something else aggressive and potentially offensive. Saul had been right in his accusation this morning—I didn't like him. But it made no sense, even to me. He'd done absolutely nothing to justify my opinion of him.

"So you really care that much about Dick's well-being?" I asked, trying not to sound skeptical. "Lugh said you'd had trouble getting along with hosts in the past and that your hosts had suffered. Why is Dick so different?"

He frowned. "It was just one host, and the problem was that he was a sanctimonious son of a bitch. He had no trouble inviting a demon into his body, but he thought once he invited me in, he would convert me to his way of thinking. Which was that sex should only occur between a man and a woman, that it was an abomination for the woman to enjoy it, and that anything but straight missionary position was a sin.

And that foreplay was unnecessary." He gave a little snort. "You can imagine what he thought of SM practices. Any time I wanted to partake of any 'pleasures of the flesh,' he let his objections be known. So no, we did not get along. And since I was in the dominant position, I did what I wanted. If he was offended, I shut him out."

I bit my tongue to keep a retort from flying out of my mouth. I knew what it was like when a demon shut a host off from his own body. In my opinion, it was a fate worse than death.

"I'm not proud of what I did," Saul said, "but possession is a risk, both for the demon and the host. We have no way of knowing how compatible we will be with our hosts. We are more adaptable than humans, so we're able to bridge some pretty big gaps. But that one was way too big and the relationship was doomed from the beginning."

"So Lugh was just being paranoid when he said a host other than Dominic would suffer with you?"

I never said that, Lugh protested.

Damn. My mental barriers were still weak enough that he could speak to me. It made me feel like a crazy person when I heard voices in my head.

"If I understand correctly," Saul said, "Lugh wanted to summon me into Dominic because, at the time, there was no other host available. I'm not surprised he would bring up such a possibility if he was trying to get his way. And it's true that I've never had another host I was as compatible with as I was with Dominic. But whether you believe me or not, Dick and I are doing just fine together."

I was working on a diplomatic but noncommittal reply but was interrupted by the phone ringing. I hoped I didn't look like I was running for my life when I dashed to get it.

It was the front desk calling to tell me I had a visitor—Dominic, of all people. I told the clerk to send him up, then chewed my fingernails as I waited for him to arrive. A little evil voice in my brain said that Dominic wouldn't have shown up on my doorstep with good news. And from the look on Saul's face when I told him who was coming, it seemed he had the same suspicion.

Chapter **12**

My assumption that Dominic wasn't coming with good news was confirmed the moment I opened the door and got a look at him. I was getting pretty good at reading him—unlike Adam, Dom actually has an expressive face. My first impression was that he was uncomfortable and perhaps a bit embarrassed. Nothing good, but at least it wasn't a "somebody died" face. With my life, that could be considered a positive.

"Come on in," I said, gesturing him toward the living room. He and Saul exchanged nods of greeting.

"Do you mind if I talk to Morgan in private for a bit?" Dom asked Saul.

Saul looked as startled as I felt. "Anything wrong?" he asked.

Dom managed a rueful smile but didn't answer the question. "If you hear any sounds of violence, please come running to my rescue, okay?"

Saul laughed at that and gave Dom a pat on the shoulder. "Sure thing, buddy." He must not have been as amused as he sounded, though, because he gave me what I can only describe as a warning look before he retreated to the guest bedroom.

That almost made *me* laugh. I'm tall and strong for a woman, but Dom is more than six feet and two hundred pounds of muscle. If Saul thought I was capable of physically hurting Dom, he had an exaggerated opinion of my abilities.

Dom and I sat on opposite ends of my hard-as-a-rock sofa. Between his facial expressions and his little interchange with Saul, I was afraid I had a pretty good idea what had happened.

I fixed him with my fiercest stare. "Tell me you didn't do what I think you did!"

He tried a sheepish smile. His shoulders were hunched a bit, making him look like a turtle seriously considering retreating into its shell. "That depends on what you think I did."

"Dominic..."

"I talked to Brian."

I groaned. Sometimes being right really sucks. I covered my eyes with my hand and shook my head.

"I figured he might listen to me when he wouldn't listen to you," Dom said. "And I also figured you'd be too stubborn to try to talk to him yourself."

I wasn't sure if I wanted to hit him or hug him. Maybe he was just too nice for my own good. "I'm sure your heart was in the right place," I said through gritted teeth, "but that really wasn't your call to make."

He shrugged. "I know that. But since I was in the house when Adam..." He let his voice trail off. I didn't think he was much more comfortable with what Adam had done to me than I was. "I could tell Brian what really happened, and he'd have no reason not to believe me."

My eyes stung with the tears I still hadn't allowed myself to shed. "I repeat: That wasn't your call to make." And since it was Dom here talking to me right now, not Brian, I figured it hadn't gone as well as Dom had hoped.

"Doesn't matter. I did it anyway." He gave me a piercing look of his own. "Are you going to tell me you've never stuck your nose where it didn't belong with Adam and me?"

I grimaced. He had a point, unfortunately. I'd been very judgmental about their relationship when I first knew them. I'd even urged Dom to "get help" because I thought he was a "sick puppy" to stay with Adam. Since then, I'd come to the startling realization that theirs was the healthiest romantic relationship I'd ever known.

"Sorry," I mumbled. "I was a real bitch to the two of you."

"*Was?*" he asked with an ironic lift of his brow.

I leaned over and smacked him on the shoulder, though I couldn't help smiling a little.

"Ow!" he teased, rubbing his shoulder as if I'd punched him with brass knuckles.

Half a second later, Saul poked his head out of his room. Running to Dom's rescue as requested. Dom and I both looked at him and then at each other. We burst into laughter, and Saul withdrew.

When the laughter threatened to morph into tears, I bit the inside of my cheek and sucked in air for all I was worth. Control was hard to find, especially since Dom kept laughing. I guess he was kind of tense and needed the release. I didn't dare look at him, or I really would cry.

So I stared at the coffee table when I said, "I appreciate the thought."

My serious words killed the laughter, and I kind of wished I'd kept them to myself, at least for a little while. Tension and discomfort crept over both of us almost immediately, and the air felt heavy.

A waiting silence descended. I knew Dom was waiting for me to ask what Brian had said. I also knew I wasn't going to ask. I'd already deduced that it hadn't gone well. And really, even if it had, I wasn't ready to face the question of whether the relationship was worth repairing.

Eventually, Dom got the hint that I wasn't going to ask. He sighed, and I could see him shaking his head in my peripheral vision.

"You're really going to hold it against him that he believed the story, given the evidence?" Dom asked, sounding incredulous.

I glared at him. "Imagine how you would feel if Adam believed you'd cheated on him."

He thought about that a moment, then nodded. "I'd feel like shit. And I'm sure I'd be pretty pissed at him. But I'd also understand."

"Well, you're a nicer person than I am," I snarled, even as I told myself not to take my anger out on Dominic. Yeah, I thought he should have kept his nose out of it, but he'd meant well.

To my shock, Dominic grabbed both my arms in a firm grip and turned me to face him on the sofa. I was startled enough that I met his gaze. His eyes were narrowed almost to slits.

"I'm not as nice as you think I am," he said, and he sounded really pissed. "And Adam's not as mean as you think he is. And Brian isn't as saintly as you think he is. And even Raphael isn't as evil as you think he is. Why do you always have to slap some neat little label on everyone? And then refuse to see anything that doesn't fit under the label?"

Being yelled at by Dominic was kind of like being bitten by an adorable, fluffy kitten. It was shocking enough to really get my attention, that's for sure. I didn't know what to say.

He let go of my arms and slumped back into the cushions of the sofa, crossing his arms over his chest. He was still fuming, and I shook my head.

"I don't get it," I said. "Why do you care so much if Brian and I are together or not?"

He caught my gaze and didn't let go. "Why do you care if Adam and I are together or not?" he countered.

"I don't!" I snapped, but we both knew it was a lie.

I cared about them being together because they were my friends—yes, even Adam, in his own bizarre way—and I knew they were happy with each other. A lump formed in my throat.

Did Brian and I make each other happy? Sure, we had our moments. But we had a lot more moments of fighting. Didn't there come a time when a wise person admits defeat?

Dominic rose to his feet. "I've never met anyone who makes being miserable such a point of pride."

The lump still ached in my throat, so I couldn't muster a snappy comeback. I didn't look up as Dominic crossed the floor. He hesitated a moment on the doorstep. I don't know if he was trying to find the magic words to make me see things his way, or if he was hoping I'd ask him to stay. But I didn't ask him to stay, and he didn't find those magic words, so he stepped out into the hall and closed the door behind him.

When Dominic left, I was still in the unpleasant situation of having nothing to do. Except brood, that is. I don't do well with inactivity in the best of times, which these weren't, so I decided to go shopping. Window shopping, really, because I could barely afford to buy food, much less anything fun. But at least it got me moving for a while.

One of the good things about living in Center City as opposed to the suburbs is that just about everything is in walking distance. That allowed me to chew up some of the hours of the long afternoon just by getting from place to place.

I tried to amuse myself by trying on clothes and shoes in various fashionable Walnut Street shops, but it wasn't much fun when I couldn't afford to buy. Still, it was better than sitting in the apartment gazing at my navel. Or talking to Saul.

When I got home, I ate the remainder of the Thai food for dinner, while Saul tried to stay unobtrusive and watched TV. In my now habitual attempts to win the Good Housekeeping award, I hand-washed the dishes when I was finished, then put everything away. By that time, my feet were aching pretty bad from all the walking I'd done earlier, and I decided I'd have to spend the rest of the evening vegging in front of the TV, even with Saul there.

I had just sat down on the love seat—declining to sit beside Saul on the sofa—when my phone rang. Saul had an old *Seinfeld* rerun on, and someone cued the laugh track immediately after the first ring. If I didn't know better, I'd swear my TV was mocking me.

Saul was obviously still trying to win me over with his world's-best-roommate act, because before I mustered the energy to haul myself to my feet to answer the phone, he picked it up and tossed it to me. I caught it easily and checked the caller ID. It was the front desk. I'd been hearing from them way too much lately.

"Hello?" I said wearily. If anyone was hoping to pay me a visit right now, I fully intended to send them away.

"Ms. Kingsley?" the clerk asked. He had a raspy smoker's voice, and I realized it was Carl, one of the nicest of the building staff. Too nice, sometimes. Engaging him in conversation could kill an hour of your time, easy.

"Yes." Keeping responses to monosyllables was always wise when talking to Carl.

"Is your car a blue Civic with license plate EXY 1902?"

I closed my eyes and pinched the bridge of my nose. What now? "Yes," I responded reluctantly.

"I'm sorry, Ms. Kingsley, but one of the other residents reported it had been vandalized. Do you want me to call the police for you?"

Great. Just great. I'd ask him how bad the damage was, but since he wasn't the one who saw it, I assumed he wouldn't know. "No, thanks, Carl. I'll take care of it myself."

"I'm sorry," he said again, sounding genuinely distressed on my behalf.

I heard him take a breath, and instinct told me he was about to sympathize with me some more. Knowing him, about fifteen minutes more. So I cut him off before he got started.

"Thanks for letting me know," I said. "I'd better go check and see how bad it is." Then I hung up without saying good-bye.

I fought an urge to fling the phone against the wall. Maybe it was time for me to consider taking up residence in some remote little shack in Tibet. A life of peaceful seclusion might be just the thing. But knowing my life, trouble would follow me all the way there.

"What's up?" Saul asked me, turning off the TV without having to be told. I gave him a reluctant brownie point for that.

"Apparently, someone's vandalized my car." I dragged myself to my feet. "I'm going to go see how bad it is."

He stood up. "I'll come with you."

My usual inclination would be to tell him to stay here, but I was feeling beaten down enough not to bother tonight.

We rode the elevator in silence down to the parking level. It was about eight o'clock in the evening, which wasn't a busy time for garage traffic, so we had the place to ourselves. Saul's sneakers made squeaky new-shoes sounds as we climbed the ramp up toward where I'd parked. I couldn't see my car yet because the vehicle next to it was one of those super-sized SUVs that made cars like mine look like toys in comparison.

When we got a little closer, I saw crumbles of broken glass, both red and clear, littering the floor. Great. I'd tried to hope that the vandalism had entailed only some damage to the paint job or some nasty messages written in soap on the windows. You know—the kind of stuff you don't have to pay to fix. But it looked like I'd be forking out money for new taillights, if nothing else.

I closed my eyes for a moment. *Please let it be nothing else,* I prayed. Then we got around the SUV, and I stopped in my tracks.

"Holy shit!" I said with what little voice I could muster.

To say my car had been "vandalized" was the understatement of the century. It looked like an army of gorillas armed with baseball bats and tire irons had attacked it.

Every window was shattered. The tires had all been shredded to ribbons. There were so many dents in the doors, they resembled that "hammered copper" look that was popular in decorative plates and vases. Inside, the dashboard had been smashed, and stuffing oozed out of huge rents in each of the seats.

But bad as all that was, it wasn't half so disturbing as the message that had been painted in what looked suspiciously like blood on the car's hood. It was short, simple, and to the point.

Die, bitch.

I hugged myself and tried to keep my teeth from chattering as Saul pulled his cell phone off his belt and dialed 911.

Chapter 13

As soon as Saul got off the phone with 911, he called Adam, which meant that even after I'd answered five thousand thirteen questions and been given the hairy eyeball by what seemed like thirty cops, the ordeal wasn't over.

I recognized Adam's car when he drove by, but he didn't stop to talk with his fellow men in blue. Instead, he parked in the visitors' area and waited for all the excitement to die down. I was very aware of him sitting there in the dark, watching, and I'm sure Saul was, too. The officers never noticed. That would have really sucked if Adam had been the homicidal maniac who'd been making my life just that much brighter lately.

Okay, it's true, we weren't sure the guy was a homicidal maniac. As far as we knew, he hadn't killed anyone. Yet. But it sure did look like he was escalating, and I didn't want to know what his next move would be.

When the last police cruiser's taillights disappeared down the ramp, Adam finally got out of his car and headed in our direction. He was wearing heavy black motorcycle boots with sinfully tight black jeans, a faded blue T-shirt, and a black sport coat. Ah, the off-duty look. Gotta love it. Out of the corner of my eye, I caught Saul giving him a similar once-over. Adam had the grace to pretend not to notice either of us ogling him, but I didn't believe for a second it had escaped his attention.

Without saying anything, he examined the car, which the police had kindly left for me to dispose of. They'd have towed it away if the love note had actually been written in blood like I'd first thought. Turned out it was just paint, which was a relief.

Adam circled the car, looking at it from every possible angle while Saul and I watched. What he thought he'd see that the others had missed, I don't know. Bored with watching Adam and his scrupulous examination, I let my eyes wander. Beside me, Saul was grinning faintly, a look of mingled lust and amusement in his eyes. I followed his gaze and saw the mouthwatering back view Adam was giving us as he bent over to scrutinize the broken taillights. If he'd wiggle his ass a bit, he'd look like he was auditioning for Chippendales in that pose. And he'd probably be hired in a heartbeat.

"Would you like me to get you a pole?" I asked Adam. Then I slapped myself on the forehead like a character in one of those V8 commercials. "Oh, wait, you already have one."

Saul snickered, and Adam straightened up to look at us. He seemed genuinely puzzled, though I could have sworn he was purposely teasing Saul and me. I guess he'd been looking for evidence after all.

He figured out my comment after a brief glance at Saul's face, and he rolled his eyes. "Get your minds out of the gutter."

I decided to just pretend I hadn't said anything. "Did you find anything interesting?"

"Let's go upstairs to talk about it, shall we?" he suggested.

"Good idea," I agreed. I was sick to death of looking at the ruin that had once been my car. I had a feeling my car insurance company was going to drop me. My last car had been destroyed by the fire at my house, and now here was another one ruined in less than two months.

The elevators in my building are ancient and slow. I sagged against the back wall as we inched upward toward my apartment. As if we were strangers, we were all staring at the glowing numbers above the door.

"I'm thinking of moving to Tibet," I commented in a vain hope that it would break the tension. No one answered. Worse, no one even cracked a smile. So much for my comic relief.

When we got back to my apartment, I flopped onto the couch and propped my feet up on the coffee table. I didn't feel too freaked out. I was just...tired. The numbness that Lugh had helped me shake off this morning was threatening to come back. And really, would that be such a bad thing? Because if I let myself feel everything, it might be time to call in the boys with the white coats.

Adam sat on the other end of the couch, and Saul took the love seat. I didn't look at either of them.

"So, *did* you find anything?" Saul asked when I failed to repeat my earlier question.

"Nothing the regular cops wouldn't have found," Adam replied. "But I have been putting some thought into the big picture."

I felt his eyes on me. Probably I was supposed to show some interest. "And what did you come up with?" I asked, because if I didn't, he'd probably start psychoanalyzing me or something.

"Based on our conversation with Barbie earlier, it seems like Jack Hillerman has something against you personally for some unknown reason. It seems like he's using Maguire's death as an excuse to take up his personal grudge with you."

I huffed out a frustrated breath. "It doesn't make sense for him to have anything against me personally! Remember, I've never met the guy."

Adam pulled a four-by-six photograph from his back pocket and handed it to me. A slightly overweight forty-something guy with a pathetic combover smiled out at me. I shook my head and gave Adam a blank look. He took the picture back.

"It was worth a shot," he said. "It was possible you really had met him and just hadn't known his name."

"Sorry, but I don't recognize him. Did you have a chance to find out if he has any Spirit Society affiliations?"

"Yeah. No connections that I can find."

I threw up my hands. "Then what's his problem?"

"I don't know," Adam said. "But I'm beginning to rethink my position on whether Hillerman is behind the threats or not. What are the chances two separate people would a) hold you personally responsible for what happened to Maguire, and b) be crazy enough to start this kind of vendetta? I mean, I'd think if *anyone* would take the heat for this, it would be Maguire's ex-girlfriend."

Adam was referring to the ex-girlfriend who'd pressed charges on Maguire for apparently having beaten her up. He'd always proclaimed his innocence, and it was her testimony that put him in the hot seat.

"Or how about the judge who ordered the exorcism?" Adam continued. "No one seems to be targeting *her*. Even if you swallow the idea that it's two different people, you'd think at least one of them would have chosen a different scapegoat."

It made sense, if anything could be said to make sense these days. "Okay, I get your point," I said. "But seriously, can you imagine someone like Hillerman breaking into a funeral parlor and chopping off a corpse's hand? And hell, he looks like he'd die of a heart attack before he could do that kind of damage to my car!"

"He hired Barbie. Maybe he hired someone else to do the less subtle work. If it's okay with you, I'd like to ask Barbie to do some surveillance on Hillerman, see if we can find any other shady characters he's hanging out with."

Since when had Adam cared if something was all right with me? I'd have liked to object in this rare instance when he was actually giving me a choice—or at least *appearing* to give me a choice—about something, but I couldn't see a good reason to.

"Go for it." I frowned. "But why Barbie? Can't you use your resources?"

He raised one shoulder in a shrug. "We don't have enough evidence against him to launch anything official." He met my eyes. "Besides, it's possible this investigation could lead us to something we'd rather keep off the books."

Once again, I had to agree with him, though I didn't like it. If this all blew up in our faces, the fact that we hadn't told the police the full story would come back to bite us in the ass.

"I *am* going to drop by to visit Maguire's girlfriend tomorrow," Adam said. "If she was shacked up with Maguire, and if Hillerman really did launch his little terror campaign out of some weird, overblown grief at the death of a client's son, I might be able to suss out a reason."

"And my assignment is still to sit around doing nothing?" I asked sourly.

Adam had no sympathy. "Considering the damage this guy did to your car, I think keeping your head down would be a good idea. He's escalating, and it seems logical that the next strike will be actual violence against you."

"Hold on a sec," I said, thinking furiously. "We're beginning to think Hillerman is behind *everything,* right? I mean the lawsuit, the letter to Brian, the psycho stalker—they're all supposed to be him."

"Right," Adam agreed.

"If he's planning to kill me, why the hell would he waste the time and energy to talk Maguire into suing me? And why would he bother ruining my relationship with Brian?"

"Part of his escalation pattern," Adam said, but he didn't sound as sure of himself as usual.

I let the subject drop, but I had my own theory now: Hillerman didn't want me dead. He wanted me alive and miserable. I still had no idea why, but I felt pretty sure my psycho stalker wasn't going to be escalating any further.

When I woke up the next morning, I felt marginally better than I'd felt yesterday. Saul had made coffee again. It was still strong enough to put hair on my chest, but with a little extra cream and sugar, it was drinkable. We sipped our coffee in what felt almost like a companionable silence.

During the night, I'd come to the conclusion that I was sick and tired of sitting on the sidelines of my own life. I was confident—to a point—that I wasn't going to get myself killed if I nosed around a bit, and I knew I'd feel better if I was out doing something than if I was sitting around the apartment playing house with Saul.

I also knew that after last night's brutal attack on my car, Saul wasn't about to let me leave my apartment without an escort. One thing all the demon-possessed men in my life had in common was a protective streak the size of Texas, and I doubted Saul was any different from the rest. Not that it was unjustified—I was hosting their king, after all, and if I died, he'd be forced back into the Demon Realm, where Dougal and his supporters could get their metaphorical hands on him. But for what I wanted to do today, I had to forego the pleasure of Saul's company.

My first plan was to slip out while Saul was in the bathroom, but with my building's slow and cranky elevators, I'd probably still be standing in the hallway pushing the elevator button repeatedly by the time Saul caught up with me. My second plan was to make my getaway when I went down to the front desk to pick up my mail, but my unwanted bodyguard came with me even for that small task. Plan C was to send him to the deli around the corner to pick up some sandwiches for lunch, during which time I would "wait for him" in my apartment. I think he saw through that one, though, because he insisted on ordering delivery.

That was when I decided subtlety just wasn't going to work. It was the frontal assault or nothing. Anyone surprised I chose the frontal assault?

While Saul was finishing up the enormous hoagie he'd ordered for lunch, I casually picked up my purse, rooting through it as though looking for something. As I shuffled junk around, I armed the Taser that was my constant companion and made a surreptitious check of its charge level. It was good to go, so I drew the Taser out of the purse and pointed it at Saul.

He was too busy stuffing his face to notice at first, but when he did, he froze in the middle of biting off a big, drippy mouthful of hoagie. His eyes widened with alarm, and even after the first moment of surprise passed, he didn't move, barely even seemed to breathe.

"Go on and finish that bite," I told him pleasantly. "I don't particularly want to get hoagie innards all over my dining room."

He bent over the paper wrapper that lay unfurled on the table, then carefully released the hoagie from his mouth. Shredded lettuce, diced tomatoes, and mustard spilled out all over the paper, but at least it wasn't on my carpet.

"Let me finish chewing," he said with his mouth full. Apparently he hadn't finished his previous bite before he'd tried to stuff another one in. I reminded myself to give him a lesson in table manners later.

I was worried his request might be some kind of trick, so I put some extra distance between us, making sure I had time to fire off a shot if he came after me. But he just sat at the table and chewed, watching me with wary eyes. Maybe he was trying to make sure his host didn't choke to death while he was disabled. Electricity mucks with a demon's control so badly that I wasn't sure he'd be able to swallow once I shot him.

His face had paled a bit, and if I didn't know better, I would have sworn he was scared. There was even a sheen of sweat on his upper lip. I told myself he had to be faking it, trying to think of some way to keep me from shooting, but I hesitated anyway.

"Why are you looking at me like that?" I demanded. "You *like* pain, remember?"

His Adam's apple bobbed as he swallowed. "Yeah, but I don't like being completely helpless."

I sympathized. So I pulled the trigger before I had a chance to think about it any more, or I might have changed my mind.

Saul went rigid when the probes latched onto him, a strangled sound escaping his throat. His muscles were no longer in control enough to keep him in the chair, so he tilted sideways and hit the floor with a thud. This was the first time I could remember Tasering a demon and actually feeling guilty about it.

I ejected the spent cartridge and shoved the Taser back in my purse. Then I turned Saul over onto his back so his arm wasn't trapped in an awkward position. He was sweating all over, and my guilt spiked.

"Sorry," I said, and I meant it. "You'll be back in control in ten minutes. Fifteen, tops." Enough time for me to get far enough away he couldn't stop me.

He tried to talk, but since he wasn't in control of his tongue, all that came out was a garbled groaning sound.

"Sorry," I said again, then forced myself to my feet and headed for the door.

Chapter 14

Jack Hillerman's office was on Broad Street, within spitting distance of City Hall. A much nicer part of Broad Street than Barbie's office inhabited, I might add. The building had probably been around since the turn of the twentieth century, and the lobby was dismal and depressing. The elevators were new, though, so they shot me up to the fifteenth floor fast enough to make my stomach have to run to catch up. The doors opened onto a very conservative, genteel reception area.

Despite the age of the building, the reception area was decidedly modern in decor, with spare, clean furnishings, good lighting, and abstract art on the walls. Three hallways led away into the depths of the firm. I saw a cubicle farm at the far end of one hallway, but the other two were lined with real, honest-to-God offices.

The receptionist was an older woman with tastefully gray hair arranged in a picture-perfect pageboy. A pair of chic red-framed glasses perched on her nose, adding a modern touch to her otherwise old-fogyish dark gray suit. She flashed me a practiced smile as I approached her desk, and she didn't even give my so-phisticated jeans-and-T-shirt outfit a second glance.

"May I help you?" she asked, and she managed to convey the impression that she genuinely wanted to help.

I returned the smile. "I'm here to see Jack Hillerman," I said, knowing things were about to get dicey. I was pretty sure that talking to me wasn't high on Hillerman's list of preferred activities—not to mention that it was probably against the rules for him to do so without my attorney present.

The receptionist frowned ever so slightly. "Do you have an appointment?" she asked, in a voice that told me she already knew I didn't.

I tried to look sheepish. "I'm afraid not. I'm here for personal reasons, not for a business meeting. Can you let him know I'm here? It'll only take five minutes, I promise."

"He's in a meeting just now," she said, and in-stinct told me she was lying. "Would you care to leave a message?"

"I just have a quick question for him, and it's not something I can leave in a message." I gave her my most pitiful pleading look.

Her gaze darted uncertainly toward the hallway on her left—one of the two lined with real offices. "I can let him know you're here, but I'm not sure..."

I smiled brightly at her. "Thanks so much!"

She still looked pretty uncertain. "May I have your name?" she asked, picking up the phone.

I'd considered going the phony-name route, but I'd dismissed it almost instantly. I'm probably the world's worst liar, so I didn't think I'd fool anyone.

"Morgan Kingsley," I said, hoping against hope that the firm had so many clients she wouldn't recog-nize my name. But things never go that well for me.

Regarding me carefully, she hung the phone up once more. "I'm very sorry, Ms. Kingsley," she said, "but unless you have your attorney with you, there is no chance Mr. Hillerman will agree to see you."

"But this isn't about the case!" Okay, maybe it kind of *was* about the case, but it was pretty obvious Hillerman had not only misplaced his ethics, he'd buried them in some deep, dark pit and built a parking lot on the site.

The receptionist shook her head. "It's just out of the question, I'm afraid. I'll let him know you stopped by, and he and your attorney can schedule a meeting."

So far, this was all going about as I expected, with the added bonus that the receptionist's nervous little glances let me know which hallway to go down to find Hillerman's office. Without another word, I headed down that hallway.

I heard the receptionist say my name sharply a couple of times, but she didn't follow me or physically try to stop me. I glanced at the name plates on the offices I passed. The doors were closed on most of them, and they didn't have any convenient little windows I could look in. The name plates were discreet enough that I was almost past Hillerman's office before I realized it was his. Inside, I heard the phone ringing—probably the receptionist letting him know I was storming his fortress. I pushed open the door.

Hillerman was sitting at his desk, phone to his ear. In front of him lay an enormous, greasy calzone, oozing cheese and tomato sauce into a Styrofoam take-out box. He smiled at me, but the smile didn't come close to reaching his eyes.

"That's all right, Marta," he said into the phone. "No need to call security. I'll talk to her." Apparently, Marta had something to say about that. Hillerman listened politely to whatever it was, then said, "Yes, I'm sure."

I think Marta was adding yet another protest to the list when Hillerman hung up.

"Please come in," he said, gesturing me forward.

I closed the door behind me and remained standing. I hadn't expected him to be willing to talk to me. I'd just hoped he'd let something slip as he was trying to kick me out. Or that somehow, looking at him would trigger a memory in my brain, give me some idea who he was and why he had it in for me.

"You're not worried about your professional ethics?" I asked, stalling while I tried to figure out what his game was.

He pushed aside the calzone. "Not particularly." He smiled again, and the expression gave me the creeps.

I shook my head. "Why not?"

"I have my reasons."

Maybe I should have listened to my common sense and stayed home. He was looking way too happy about me being here. And way too cavalier about his career. Yeah, okay, he was obviously dirty, but it wasn't like the whole world knew about it. Yet.

"Please," Hillerman continued, dabbing grease off his fingers with a paper napkin, "come have a seat. I'd offer you something to eat, but all I have is the calzone."

How hospitable of him! "Why are you eating a crappy takeout calzone at your desk?" I asked. "Aren't you supposed to take two-hour lunches with lots of martinis?"

"What can I say? I'm a workaholic."

I didn't feel like sitting down, but I did come to stand closer to the desk, resting my hands on the back of one of the dark green leather visitor chairs that sat in front of it.

"Do I know you?" I asked bluntly.

He gave me a look of faux innocence. "I hardly think you would have come to visit if you didn't know me."

Oh, great. A smart-ass. "I meant before the case. Is there something you have against me personally?"

He didn't even try to pretend he didn't know what I was talking about. "Funny you should mention it, but yes." The creepy smile was back. This guy was freakin' weird!

"Care to elaborate?" I prompted. "Because, frankly, I have no idea who you are or what you have against me."

He giggled. Actually *giggled*. "I know. That's part of the fun."

I'd known he had to be some kind of psycho to carry out this incredible vendetta against me, but I'd assumed it was a subtle kind of psycho, the kind that would be hidden under a polished, professional veneer. Right now, he was looking like a good candidate for the psych ward.

I'm beginning to suspect Jack Hillerman isn't the only one in that body, Lugh's voice whispered in my head, and suddenly things made a lot more sense.

I hadn't kept an exact count, but over my years working as an exorcist, I must have sent hundreds of demons back to the Demon Realm before they were ready to go. Because I'm stronger than the average exorcist, I get called in on cases where the local exorcist has failed to cast out the demon, which meant I'd worked far more cases than other exorcists my age.

In the good old days before Lugh had entered my life, I thought demons died when they were exorcized. Up until right this moment, I hadn't put much thought into what the fact that they just returned to the Demon Realm meant for me.

Hundreds of demons, floating around the Demon Realm, blaming me for their banishment. Since these were all illegal or rogue demons we were talking about—meaning demons who had the morals of cockroaches—I guess it shouldn't come as any great shock that one of them had made his way back to the Mortal Plain and decided to get revenge.

Don't let on that you've figured it out, Lugh warned. *You're not supposed to know the demons you've exorcized aren't dead, so you should still have no idea why he's after you.*

Damn it, Lugh was right. Hillerman was looking really pleased with himself. I had about a million legitimate questions to ask—like when did the demon move in? Did the vendetta have anything at all to do with Jordan Maguire, or was that just an excuse to come after me? Why would even a psycho demon be this determined to get revenge on his exorcist? It wasn't like sending him back to the Demon Realm had hurt him!

But I couldn't afford to ask any of those questions, couldn't allow myself to tip my hand. So what I said instead was, "Did you forget your meds for the last several weeks or something? Because you are making about zero sense."

Some of the manic humor faded from his eyes, and I got a glimpse of the malice that lay hidden beneath. It was enough to send a serious chill down my spine.

"I don't like to be thwarted, Ms. Kingsley," he said, his voice now arctic-cold, the humor deeply buried. "I will make sure the remainder of your life is a living hell."

I had to clamp my jaws together to contain my retort, which would have been something about how much I looked forward to exorcizing him a second time.

Perhaps now would be a good time for a tactical retreat, Lugh suggested.

Once again, he was right, though I was loath to admit it. Sitting right here in front of me was the man who was responsible for all the hell I'd gone through since Jordan Maguire Jr. died. He could call off the goons with the baseball bats and the severed hands. He could probably convince Jordan Maguire Sr. to drop the lawsuit. There was nothing he could do to heal the damage he'd done to my relationship with Brian, but I would have loved nothing more than to make him suffer for it.

But there wasn't a thing I could do, at least not right now. When I left the office, I could contact Adam and let him know Lugh's and my theory that Hillerman was possessed. I'm not sure if we had enough evidence to convince the court to order an examination by an exorcist, but Adam would know for sure what it took, and he'd find a way to produce the evidence.

"Won't you at least tell me what I did to piss you off?" I asked, because that's what I would have asked if Lugh hadn't guessed about the demon. "Were you and Jordan, er, *close*?" I said that with just the right inflection and facial expression to get my meaning across. I have a feeling the real Jack Hillerman would have objected strenuously to the implication. It would be nice if the demon would tip his hand by attacking me, giving me an excuse to sic Adam on him— assuming I survived the attack, that is—but he just laughed.

"I think it's time for you to leave now, Ms. Kingsley."

I wondered if it was possible to die of frustration.

If so, I was on the verge of doing it. Two things I really hated: sitting around doing nothing while my life went to hell around me, and retreating—even when I knew it was the right thing to do.

"This isn't over," I said. It sounded like a line from some bad action flick, but it's hard to be witty and clever when you're so pissed you're trying to talk yourself out of punching someone's lights out.

Hillerman looked absolutely delighted. "No, indeed it isn't."

Before I could say anything else to amuse him, I hightailed it out of his office, slamming the door behind me for the sheer satisfaction of it.

Chapter **15**

I tried to call Adam as soon as I left Hillerman's office, but he was on duty today. I didn't feel like going through the hassle of trying to get his office to put me through to him, so I just left an urgent message for him to call me. Then I bought an extra-salty, mustard-coated soft pretzel from a street vendor for lunch. What can I say, I like to eat healthy. Besides, the pretzel didn't break my bank.

Afterward, I went to my own much-neglected office. I didn't have anything terribly interesting to do, not when I was under suspension, but at least I could sort through the mail and make sure there weren't any bills I'd forgotten to pay.

For once, there weren't. I threw away approximately ten acres' worth of junk mail, then cleared my work e-mail of the penis enlargement and debt consolidation ads. Do I know how to live it up or what?

I'd run out of time killers and was on my way home when my cell phone rang. As usual, it was at the bottom of my purse, and it seemed to consider ringing an invitation to play hide-and-seek. I finally got a grip on it and pulled it out, dislodging a used tissue and a pair of tampons at the same time. I answered the phone while I dove after the tampons, which naturally rolled to a rest right at the feet of a stuffy-looking middle-aged man in a three-piece suit. He started to bend to help me retrieve the dropped items. Then he saw what they were and gave me a look like I'd just flashed him.

"Hello!" I barked into the phone as I grabbed the tampons and shoved them back into my purse.

"Where are you?" Adam asked. His voice wasn't quite a bark, but there was no missing the tension in it.

"About three blocks from my apartment," I said, standing up now that I had everything stuffed back in my purse. "Why? What's wrong?"

"I'll be at your apartment in about fifteen minutes."

"You know, you could at least acknowledge that I spoke, even if you're not planning to answer me."

"Just be there. This isn't something we want to talk about on the phone."

Of course, I objected to being ordered around. I guess Adam knew that, because he hung up after making his will known.

I'd have loved to say "to hell with him" and gone on about my day. However, that probably wasn't a good idea, and right now, going on about my day entailed going home anyway.

I made it home before Adam arrived. Saul had gotten a cryptic call from Adam, too, but he didn't know any more than I did. Neither one of us had been terribly comforted by the tone of Adam's voice, so the wait for Adam was a tense one. It didn't help that Saul was still ticked at me about the whole Taser thing.

I'd told the front desk Adam was coming, so they didn't bother to call and let me know he was there. I was so tense I actually jumped when he rang the doorbell.

His face when I opened the door suggested that whatever was wrong, it was serious. Not that I'd doubted that, but a girl can always hope. I wanted to curse out the universe for piling even more shit on my shoulders, but that wouldn't be terribly productive.

"Do I need to sit down for this?" I asked. I was trying for a tone of nonchalance. *Trying* being the operative word.

"Not a bad idea," Adam said, gesturing me toward the couch.

Shit. I was beginning to hate my couch. Nothing good ever seemed to happen when I was sitting on it. But I sat anyway, with Saul on the other end of the sofa and Adam in the love seat. I tried to brace myself for whatever was coming, but it's hard to brace for the unknown.

"Jack Hillerman is dead," Adam said, and the words detonated like a bomb.

There was a moment of shocked silence afterward. I replayed the words in my head, hoping I'd misheard. But no, he'd said what I'd thought he'd said.

"What?" I finally managed to yelp. "When? How?"

Adam gave me one of those chilling glares of his—he's really good at that. "How was with a silenced 9mm. When is somewhat under debate, but it's around the time *you left his office.*"

Gee, he sounded kind of ticked about that. I refused to bow my head in shame. "I was hoping I could get a read on his motive."

He was still glaring at me. "You realize that 'around the time you left his office' can very easily be 'while you were *in* his office,' right?"

I swallowed hard. No, I hadn't realized. I'd been too focused on the accusation in his voice.

"As of now," he continued, "you're officially a 'person of interest,' not a suspect. So far, the police don't know you have a motive, so it's hard to pin it on you just because you were there sometime around the time he was killed. The receptionist doesn't remember seeing anyone else go into his office after you left, nor does she remember seeing Hillerman after you left. Luckily for you, she's not *sure* no one went in."

I shot him a glare of my own. "You make it sound like you think I did it."

"It doesn't matter what I think. It matters what the evidence suggests. And if the police discover you have a motive, the evidence is going to point to you. More than it does already, that is."

"That's crazy!" I protested. "If I were going to kill him, you can bet I wouldn't show up at his office and announce my presence to the world beforehand. And obviously—" I cut myself off, remembering with a start that Lugh and I had determined with a fair amount of certainty that Jack Hillerman wasn't himself.

How badly did he have it in for me? Based on our conversation, pretty bad. Bad enough to kill his own host in an attempt to make my life even more miserable.

"Whoever 'discovered' the body," I said, making the requisite air quotes, "is the real killer. And he or she is now possessed."

Adam did a double take. "Come again?"

I told him about my chat with Hillerman and about how bizarre he'd acted. It was hard to argue Lugh's diagnosis. And it was hard to imagine someone just happened to sneak into Hillerman's office and shoot him to death shortly after I left.

"That's why he was so happy to see me this afternoon," I concluded. "I'd come at the perfect time for him to frame me for his own murder."

Adam looked grim. "He was discovered by an intern. If you're right and the intern is now possessed, you can bet he's going to produce evidence that you have a motive."

"You mean evidence like Barbie?"

He cursed, and I had to agree. It was looking bad for the home team.

While we were chewing over this latest disaster, the phone rang. I didn't feel like talking to anyone, but I guess Saul was feeling like he lived here—which he did for the moment, in a manner of speaking—because he picked up the phone. His side of the conversation consisted of a couple of uh-huhs and a very unhappy face.

"That was the front desk," he said when he hung up. "The police are here and want to talk to you."

A bolt of panic shot through me, and I looked at Adam with wild eyes. "Can't you take care of this?" He'd intervened for me with the police numerous times already, taking my statements—sometimes making up my statements and informing me later of what I'd said.

"I've already gone out on a limb for you enough times to raise a few eyebrows. I can't interfere this time. I'd do you more harm than good."

"But—"

"As long as you're just a person of interest, you're not legally required to answer their questions. I'd advise you to admit to nothing more than when you arrived at the office and when you left."

"And if Barbie's already told them about the letter?"

He looked almost as unhappy as I felt. "Then say nothing without the advice of your attorney."

I was getting far too accustomed to being interviewed by the police. I didn't like it when I was the victim. I liked it even less when I was the suspect. Oh, excuse me, "person of interest." Based on the intensity of the questioning, I didn't think there was a whole lot of difference between the two in the cops' minds. They were pretty grumpy with me when I refused to tell them what Hillerman and I were talking about. The receptionist had told them I'd said it was personal, and that's the generic answer I stuck to.

Adam had abandoned me, though with good reason: he wanted to have a word with Barbie before the police tracked her down. I knew he was taking a big risk on my account. If Barbie felt like it, she could probably accuse him of obstructing justice, and the charges might stick. After all, for a cop, he played pretty fast and loose with the law on a regular basis.

Despite my lack of cooperation—or perhaps because of it—the interview with the cops went on forever. They wanted to take our little discussion downtown, but I declined their offer of hospitality. It made me even more popular. I was on the verge of calling my lawyer to see if he could scrape them off my back when they finally wrapped it up with instructions that I shouldn't leave town. Gee, just like in the movies!

As soon as the cops were gone, I went ahead and called the lawyer who had represented me when I'd been accused of illegal exorcism. I wasn't sure if Adam would be footing her bills as well, but at this point I was just asking her to be on standby anyway.

By the time I got off the phone, I had an unexpected visitor: my brother, Andy. Apparently, Adam had taken it on himself to call a meeting of Lugh's council, so I could expect to have quite a collection of testosterone gathered in my apartment before the evening was out.

Andy looked terrible. He'd never fully regained the weight he'd lost while he'd been catatonic. In fact, he might have even lost a little since I'd seen him last. His cheekbones stood out in stark contrast on his face, his eyes shadowed by dark circles. My heart clenched with pity, and I wished there were something I could do to make him feel better. Problem was, I wasn't sure what was wrong with him. He still insisted it was "nothing," but I don't think he expected me to believe it.

He gave me a hug in greeting, but though I appreciated the gesture, I couldn't help noticing how bony he felt. Damn it, the last thing I needed to do at a time like this was worry about someone else's problems!

To take the situation from uncomfortable to nearly unbearable, Raphael was the next of Lugh's council members to arrive. I think Saul is the only person in the universe who hates Raphael more than Andy does, and that's saying a lot. The air in the room fairly crackled with tension as the three men sized each other up.

"Is a fight going to break out, or can you behave like civilized beings during a time of crisis?" I asked.

Raphael held up his hands in a gesture of innocence. "I'm on my best behavior. I have no quarrel with anyone here."

Saul opened his mouth like he was going to make a cutting remark, but I pointed at him sternly. "You be quiet. I know you and Daddy Dearest have issues, but I'm not in the mood to referee."

Saul's mouth closed with an audible click, and I

could see the muscles working in his cheeks as he ground his teeth. But he didn't say anything, so it was a moral victory for me.

Andy didn't look inclined to start anything. On the one hand, that was good, because I didn't want to deal with it. On the other hand, if he'd started something, it would have given me some evidence that he was still alive inside.

But I forgot all about my brother and my worries when Adam arrived. Because, you see, he'd brought the rest of Lugh's council with him—including Brian.

Chapter 16

I sat there in silent, dumbfounded amazement. Adam and Dominic dragged a pair of dining room chairs into the living room and sat down, pretending they didn't see my shell-shocked expression. Brian stayed where he was, only a few steps past the door.

He met my eyes when I stared at him, and I didn't see anything I expected to see in them. Not anger, not hurt, not contrition. Instead, his expression was one of cool neutrality. It was almost his lawyer face, but with an added chill.

My hands clenched into fists in my lap. He had no right to look at me like that. Not when Dominic had gone and told him the truth!

I turned to Adam. "What is he doing here?" I asked. My heart thudded against my breastbone, and I couldn't make sense of what I was feeling. All I knew was it wasn't good.

"He's part of Lugh's council," Adam said simply.

I glared at him. "He's only part of Lugh's council because of me! And, as you can see, we're not together at the moment."

Adam was unmoved by my quite reasonable

argument. "I already had this conversation with Brian. It doesn't matter whether you're dating anymore or not. Once a member of Lugh's council, *always* a member of Lugh's council. He lost his option to fade into the background as an innocent bystander long ago."

Impatiently, Adam waved for Brian to join our cozy little circle. Brian didn't look happy about it, but he grabbed a chair and dragged it into the living room.

My nerves buzzed with tension, and my jaw ached from clenching my teeth. I wanted to run away, lock myself in my bedroom, hide.

"I don't want you here," I said to Brian in a voice that shook. I don't know if it was from anger or from pain.

"I don't want to be here," he responded. "But I wasn't given an option."

I had something else pithy to say, but Raphael shocked me into silence by grabbing my arm in a firm grip. I turned to snarl at him, but of course he didn't let go.

"If Saul can tolerate my presence, then you can tolerate Brian's," he told me, and there was none of his usual sarcasm or mockery in his voice. "I agree with Adam: Brian knows too much already. He's a member of this council whether we want him or not, and whether he wants to be or not."

Again, I started to argue, but Raphael squeezed my arm hard enough to make me gasp.

"Who here in this room do you think has an option to walk away?" he demanded.

I swallowed my protests. There was no way I could argue Raphael's point, though I wished I could. We had all been dragged into this at least somewhat unwillingly. Even Lugh, for that matter. I wasn't the only one whose choices were limited, and I wasn't the only one suffering.

I glanced at Andy, with his hollow cheeks and haunted eyes, and it put things in perspective for me. My pain was nothing compared to what he'd gone through, what he was *still* going through, but though he wanted nothing to do with demons ever again, he had never protested his inclusion in Lugh's inner circle.

I nodded to indicate my agreement, but I couldn't find my voice. For a long moment, it seemed like no one else could, either. The silence in the room was thick with tension, dense enough to make the air feel heavy and hard to breathe. If ever there was a group of people as unsuited to working together as this one, I'd never heard of it. But not one of us could live with the consequences of letting Dougal usurp the demon throne. Between Lugh and Raphael, we all had a pretty good picture of what the Mortal Plain would be like if Dougal had his way. Humans would be nothing more than slaves, available to any demon to possess and discard at will.

As long as Dougal sat on the throne only as regent, his powers were severely limited. If he became king, he would have everything he needed to reshape our world into one of his own liking. It was a damn good motivation to keep us all working toward our common goal, no matter how we felt about each other personally.

My thoughts cooled and solidified something inside me, and my emotions stopped rioting. They were still there, buried under the thinnest veneer of calm, but I didn't have to act on them right this moment.

I sat up straighter in my chair and looked at Adam. "I gather this meeting was your idea. Care to tell us why you felt the need to round up the usual suspects?"

He looked at me like I was crazy. "Gee, I don't know. Maybe it's the crazed demon who's out to destroy you? Or maybe it's the fact that you could be arrested for murder any day now? Or maybe—"

I held up a hand for silence. "All right, I get it. I just don't know what we can do about any of it."

"First off," said Raphael, "you can bring those of us who aren't quite in the know up to speed on everything that's going on."

I didn't feel up to that, and I was insanely grateful to Adam for taking on the responsibility himself. I let my eyes glaze over as he talked. This morning's numbness was seeping back into my system, shutting down my emotions—and a lot of my reasoning power.

Do you need me to take over for a while? Lugh asked.

For the briefest moment, the offer actually tempted me. I could let Lugh send me to some secluded place, where I didn't have to interact with anyone, where I didn't have to think, where I didn't have to *feel.*

The fact that the offer tempted me was enough to shock me out of the creeping numbness. I was a fighter, damn it! I wasn't going to crawl away and hide.

When I focused my mind on my surroundings once more, it was to find everyone staring at me expectantly.

Adam asked if you have any idea who the demon who's after you could be, Lugh said.

Thanks for clueing me in, I responded. At least *one* of us had been paying attention.

"I've exorcized probably hundreds of demons. I

don't know why any one of them would hold more of a grudge than any other one."

"Is there someone who was in a particularly sweet situation when you came around to kick him out?" Raphael asked.

I shook my head. "Keep in mind that by the time I'm called in, the demon is already toast. If I or another exorcist can't cast him out, he's either dead or imprisoned for the life of his host. I can't see any reason why they'd hold *me* responsible." I looked up at Saul. "Did you blame me when I exorcized you?"

He didn't answer immediately.

"Let me rephrase that," I said, strangely stung by his silence.

"No, don't bother," Saul said. "I did blame you in a way, but that's just because I was angry at the world in general. If I were out for revenge, I'd be hunting down the God's Wrath fanatics who beat me, not you."

"The ones who are still alive, you mean," Raphael needled. It was a low blow. Saul hadn't meant to kill any of his attackers, had just been trying to escape.

Saul's eyes blazed, his demon shining through. I was the only one who seemed to notice this, but then, I was the only one in our circle who could read auras. Usually I had to be in a trance to do it, but I'd seen this demon eye-shine more than once, and I knew it wasn't my imagination. I tensed, afraid there was about to be a fight, one it would be beyond my power to stop.

To my shock, however, Raphael didn't respond to the flare of aggression, instead lowering his gaze.

"I'm sorry," he said. "I shouldn't have said that."

Saul looked at him with all the trust he'd give an angry cobra. "You're *apologizing*? You *never* apologize."

"That's because no one ever accepts my apologies." Ah, now that was more like the usual Raphael—whiny self-pity.

Though considering my current state of mind, I wasn't in a position to throw stones.

Tell my brother it's because it's hard to tell if his apologies are sincere.

Oh, yeah. This was *so* something I wanted to get in the middle of. Not!

"Let's just move on, shall we?" I suggested.

Saul leaned back in his chair, looking stubborn and angry. But at least he refrained from stirring the hornets' nest.

"I'm still sorry," Raphael said softly, before he, too, sat back and subsided.

"The point was that it's really weird for a demon to hold this kind of a grudge against an exorcist," I said. "I don't know how to begin guessing who it could be."

"We're pretty sure he's currently residing in the intern who supposedly found the body, right?" Saul inquired.

"Yeah." I got the feeling there was supposed to be a follow-up, but Saul grimaced and stared at his feet instead of continuing.

"Since everyone already thinks I'm the world's worst bastard," Raphael said, wearing a mocking smirk that I was beginning to think was a mask for some inner pain, "I'll finish my son's thought. The obvious solution is to send the son of a bitch back to the Demon Realm again."

"I didn't mean it the way you're making it sound!" Saul protested. "I wasn't ever going to suggest we kill anyone."

Raphael raised an eyebrow. "Then why did you suddenly become so shy?"

The glow was back in Saul's eyes. "I just started thinking about all the logistical issues with capturing a hostile demon and holding it still long enough for an illegal exorcism."

Raphael nodded. "And following that thought to its logical conclusion—which is it would be a hell of a lot easier to just kill the host."

"No!" Saul shouted. He leapt to his feet and lunged after Raphael, who remained seated.

Adam had apparently been on the lookout for such an eventuality, for he managed to grab hold of Saul before he reached Raphael. Saul then whirled on Adam with a snarl, which Adam didn't seem to appreciate. They grabbed each other's shirts, both sets of eyes blazing now. I flinched, sure one of them was about to hit the other and then all hell would break loose.

Moving slowly and carefully, Dominic sidled up to them and put one hand on each man's shoulder. "Let's take it down a notch, shall we?" he said, his voice low and gentle.

They both turned to look at him. If it had been me, I'd have let go and backpedaled. Saul and Adam were both scary-looking when they were mad. But Dom wasn't intimidated by either of them, and he didn't back down.

"It's not each other you're mad at," Dom reminded them.

Raphael still hadn't risen from his chair, and now he released a little breath of air that may have been a choked-off laugh. "Gee, thanks, Dominic. Sic them both on me."

By now, I'd had enough. "Everyone sit down and shut up! I'm not in the mood to deal with all this macho chest-pounding bullshit."

Dominic smiled at me. "Always the diplomat."

I shrugged. "Your way wasn't working."

Adam and Saul let go of each other's shirts and moved apart. Saul seemed to have regained his composure, but Adam bared his teeth at Dominic.

"Don't ever get between two angry demons again!" he snapped.

Dom wasn't any more intimidated now than he had been before. "I wasn't between you," he said mildly.

"Listen to Adam, bud," Saul said as he returned to his seat. "We couldn't have hurt each other if we'd tried. Not really. You, on the other hand..."

Dom dismissed that with a wave of his hand. "You wouldn't have hurt me."

"Not on purpose," Saul agreed.

I suppose Dom got the point, because he didn't argue anymore.

Saul grinned. "I'm sure Adam will 'explain' the error of your ways later," he said with a waggle of his brows. Then he looked at Adam. "Give him a few lines of 'explanation' for me while you're at it."

Dominic blushed and returned to his seat.

Ick. Maybe it was better when they were fighting. I didn't voice that opinion, and I breathed a sigh of relief when everyone was again peacefully seated.

"For the record," I said, "we're not killing anyone. Got it?" I let my eyes roam over all of them, though I skipped right over Brian. I saw various expressions of acquiescence or annoyance, but no one contradicted me. I let my gaze rest a little extra long on Raphael. He was the loose cannon among us, the one who might disregard orders. But he just shrugged.

"So," Adam said, "the plan is to grab the intern and do an illegal exorcism, right?"

He was looking at me, so I nodded. Then I

frowned. "But if we send him back to the Demon Realm, what's to stop him from coming right back?"

It was Raphael who answered. "The only way to stop him for sure is to kill him."

"No!" I said. "Killing the intern is already off the table as an option. And I sure as hell am not sitting by and letting you guys burn him alive." Which was what it took to actually kill a demon on the Mortal Plain. I had more than one gruesome death on my conscience already. I refused to entertain the idea of adding another.

"That's the only sure thing," Raphael repeated, then cut me off before I could light into him. "Our second-best option is to put the fear of God into him, so to speak." He grinned and let his demon shine through his eyes.

Just the mention of Raphael's name was enough to make most demons piss themselves in terror.

"We don't even have to let on who's hosting me," Raphael continued. "You just tell him I'm your close personal friend, that you had to work hard to convince me to let you handle him this time, and that if he ever shows up on the Mortal Plain again you'll let me have him. That ought to be some pretty strong incentive for him to butt out."

And it was probably the only hope I had of keeping the poor intern alive. I hoped Raphael wasn't just blowing smoke up my ass and planning to take things into his own hands no matter what I said. I was going to have to keep a very close eye on him.

"That's as good a plan as any," I said. "Now, if we could grab the intern before he manufactures some evidence linking me to the murder, that would be a nice bonus."

"That could be the tricky part," Adam agreed. "I can't afford to be too closely involved at this point, although I can get you the name and address of the intern. We need to tread carefully. This demon obviously has some power and clout, or he wouldn't have been able to make it back to the Mortal Plain within Morgan's lifetime."

I raised my eyebrows at that.

"There are a lot more demons who want to visit the Mortal Plain than there are available hosts," Adam explained. "The waiting list is decades' long for rank-and-file demons. The fact that he's back so soon means he was powerful enough to pull strings and move his name way up the list."

"A very powerful demon who has a grudge against Morgan," Brian said, looking worried. "Is there any chance it's Dougal?"

Raphael snorted and gave Brian a disdainful look. "Gee, wouldn't *that* be convenient. Leave the safety and power of the Demon Realm to take a jaunt to the Mortal Plain where we can get our hands on him and eliminate his threat permanently." He shook his head. "Neither of my brothers is an idiot."

Brian's face turned red, and in the past, I'd have jumped in to defend him. I felt no compulsion to do so now.

"Since we know the demon isn't rank and file," Adam continued as if his speech had never been interrupted, "we should send two demons after him."

Raphael laughed. "Hmm. Two demons, and one of them isn't you." He looked at Saul and cocked an eyebrow. "Just you and me, son?"

"No," I said emphatically. "Considering you two were about to rip each others' throats out, I'm not sending you out together." *Listen to me,* I thought, *talking about this as if I were actually in charge of anything.* I managed not to laugh at the idea.

"I beg to differ," Raphael said with exaggerated

politeness. "If you'll remember, I did not leave my seat. My temper is under better control than that."

"Enough with the needling!" I said.

"You misunderstand. My point is that, although my son and I do not get along, we aren't in any real danger of killing each other. I can hold my temper even if Saul loses his."

Saul looked like he was on the brink of losing his temper right this minute. However, everyone seemed to be responding to my Master of the Universe impersonation, so I fixed Saul with my most imperious look. "No encores. Stay in your seat and keep your mouth shut."

I thought for a moment I might have a mutiny on my hands, but Saul managed to get himself back under control. None of this was exactly building my confidence that they could work together. Maybe they couldn't actually hurt each other, but they *could* kill each other's hosts if they decided to fight, and I don't think I'd be able to survive the guilt if they did.

"Like I said," Adam piped in, "we don't know how powerful this demon is."

Raphael shrugged. "He's unlikely to be more powerful than me."

This wasn't arrogance speaking—as part of the royal family, Raphael was one of the most powerful demons in existence.

"True, but are you powerful enough to subdue him by yourself without killing his host?"

Raphael's face told me everything I needed to know. He couldn't care less if the hapless intern died. In fact, he might *prefer* it, since that would eliminate a witness.

"You're not going anywhere near him," I decided. Even if he and Saul were working together, and working together well, there was no guarantee Raphael wouldn't take matters into his own hands. And Saul wasn't powerful enough to stop him.

"But—" Adam started to protest.

I cut him off with a slashing gesture. "I agree we need two demons. But it's going to be Saul and Lugh." I shivered at the idea, not exactly excited about letting Lugh take control for any length of time. It wasn't something that would ever come easily to me.

"No," Raphael said. "We can't involve Lugh in something that involves risk to your person."

I glared at him. "Having a psycho demon constantly on my ass very definitely involves risk to my person. Besides, however powerful this asshole might be, he's just one demon. And I do have a Taser."

Raphael crossed his arms over his chest. "Absolutely not. It's too dangerous."

"You're not in charge here," I retorted.

"Neither are you! Why don't you ask Lugh what *he* thinks?"

I didn't need to ask, because Lugh took that moment to make his opinion known.

Raphael has a point.

"But—"

But so do you. I suggest a compromise. Raphael and I together should have no trouble subduing this demon, no matter who he is. I assure you, Raphael won't kill the host while I'm there to stop him.

I didn't like the idea of having Raphael anywhere near the intern. He had always been a ruthless son of a bitch, and if he thought Lugh would be safer with the intern dead, I doubted he'd hesitate to make it so. Then again, there were plenty of problems with the other alternatives.

Lugh, will you promise *me you won't let him kill the intern?* Lugh was a hell of a lot nicer and more compassionate than Raphael, but that didn't mean he was an old softie. He was perfectly capable of killing if he felt the situation warranted it.

I give you my word.

I thought about it a little while, aware of the others watching me, waiting for the verdict.

"His Majesty has decided that he and Raphael will go after the intern," I finally said.

No one looked happy with the decision, but no one was going to argue with Lugh, either.

"Adam, how long will it take you to get us a name and address?"

"The time it takes me to make one phone call."

That didn't leave much time for stalling, but that was probably a good thing. "Make the call."

He didn't seem to object to me giving orders, although he did excuse himself and duck out into the hallway to make the call. I'm not sure why. Perhaps his informant was confidential.

"I guess this meeting is adjourned," I said, eager to get the lot of them out of my house, even if it would leave me with Raphael on my hands.

Chapter **17**

I stared at the piece of paper Adam had handed me with the intern's name and address scrawled on it. It was near Penn, not surprisingly. If I'd had a working automobile, we'd have driven there. As it was, I had to call a cab.

I was still trying my hardest not to think too much. If I did, I'd keep replaying the moment right before Brian walked out the door.

I hadn't been able to resist reaching out to him, wishing that he would give me some reason to hope that the damage could be repaired.

"Brian, we need to—" I'd started.

"Not now," he'd answered. "Maybe not ever." And then he'd walked away from me once again.

I was sure Raphael was going to give me a hard time about it, poking at my open wounds. I was more relieved than I could describe when he didn't.

We had twenty minutes to wait before the cab was due to arrive. I wasn't all that eager to have a conversation with Raphael, but I started one anyway, with my usual tact and diplomacy.

"What did you do to my brother?" I asked, remembering once again the gaunt, haunted look on Andy's face. He hadn't said a single word throughout the meeting. That wasn't like him at all.

"I didn't do anything to him," Raphael said.

I wanted to hit him. "You sure as hell did! Don't lie to me."

He let out a dramatic sigh. "Why bother to ask the question if you're not going to believe the answer?"

Raphael had told so many lies, sometimes I wondered whether he even knew what the truth was anymore. I'd rarely, if ever, managed to get him to spit out the truth when I didn't have him backed into some kind of corner, but that didn't stop me from trying now.

"I'm supposed to believe it's just a coincidence that he was fine before you took him, and now he's a wreck since you left?" Actually, Andy hadn't really been "fine" beforehand, but he'd been in a lot better shape than he was in now.

Raphael gave me one of his infuriating mocking smiles. "What can I say? He misses me."

I leaned back into the cushions of my sofa and crossed my arms over my chest. If I kept my arms crossed, I wouldn't be able to deck the son of a bitch. "If you're going to keep pulling shit like this, then stop getting your panties in a twist when we treat you with a certain amount of..."

"Hostility?"

"That works."

"I'm telling the truth, though I know it's my own fault you don't believe me. But I promised you I'd take better care of Andrew this time, and I kept my word."

"Then why does he look like he's the walking wounded all the time?" Andy had originally volunteered to host a demon out of the misguided desire to be a hero. He'd been a firefighter, and I know that he and Raphael together had saved many lives, even if that hadn't been Raphael's primary purpose, and even if they'd hated each other's guts. Now my hero-wannabe brother barely seemed to acknowledge the existence of the rest of the human race.

I expected Raphael to make another one of his caustic remarks, but instead he looked thoughtful. Choosing which lie would entertain him most?

"Andrew's not as strong as you are," he finally said.

"Huh?" The words were so unexpected, I didn't know what to make of them.

Raphael turned to face me on the sofa, his expression uncommonly grave. "You've had to make some really tough decisions in the last couple of months."

"Yeah, so?"

"So you're doing a lot better than your brother at dealing with the consequences."

Maybe I was being dense, but I still didn't know what he was talking about. Maybe his alternative to lying or telling the truth was just to spout nonsense.

"When you were trying to decide whether to let me take Tommy, you asked me if that's what Andrew wanted."

I remembered. Tommy was a violent, fanatical member of God's Wrath and was probably one of the least willing hosts on the face of the planet. I'd had to choose between Tommy and my brother. I'd chosen my brother, though I still suffered from the guilt of that decision.

"I told you that Andrew did, indeed, want me to move into Tommy," Raphael continued. "It was true. I was treating him better, but we still weren't exactly best friends. He wanted me out of there desperately."

"I can't blame him."

"No, but he's pretty good at blaming himself. You've said it yourself—he wants to be a hero." A little self-deprecating grin. "He wants to be as little like *me* as possible. But when it came right down to it, he was willing to let me move into someone he knew couldn't cope with me in order to save his own hide."

"Now wait just a minute!" I said indignantly.

"I'm not blaming him," Raphael said before I could really work up a head of steam. "It was perfectly understandable and very human. But he's blaming himself, and it's eating him up inside. He didn't live up to his own expectations, and he's not dealing well with the reality."

I regarded Raphael skeptically. He was, after all, Raphael, and even when what he said sounded logical, I felt compelled to examine it for lies and deceptions.

"Remember, Morgan, whether he likes it or not, I know Andrew better than anyone in the world. Beating himself to death with guilt is one of his favorite pastimes—and it's one of the reasons he and I clashed so badly from the very beginning."

My lip curled even though I didn't mean for it to. "You mean because it's never occurred to you that you should feel guilty for anything you've done?"

He didn't rise to my bait. "I feel remorse for some of my bad decisions. But no, I don't feel guilty. There's nothing I can do now to change what I did in the past, and there's no point in dwelling on my inadequacies. Andrew dwells."

I still wasn't sure I believed he was telling me the truth. It was just so hard to know with Raphael. But it did make a kind of sense, and I did know that Andy felt guilty about what had happened.

"Is there any way I can help him?" I asked, but I think I already knew the answer.

"Not really," Raphael said, sounding mildly regretful. "Therapy and drugs might help—if he could actually tell the therapist what was wrong, which he can't. It's up to him to figure out life is still worth living even if he's not as perfect as he wants to be."

I had to bite my tongue to restrain the retort that wanted to leap out of my throat. Raphael made it sound like it was Andy's own fault he was miserable, proving once again how unwilling Raphael was to take responsibility for his own actions.

"It's almost time for the cab to get here," I said instead. Raphael took the hint, and refrained from offering any further psychoanalysis as we headed out to capture our possessed intern.

It would have been a quiet ride out to David Keller's apartment if it weren't for the cabbie. He was one of those garrulous, overly friendly drivers who make me want to bash their teeth in. With no encouragement from either me or Raphael, he shared his entire life history and each of the shining moments in his kids' childhoods over the course of a fifteen-block drive. With my nerves already stretched taut by stress, it was all I could do not to commit murder before we arrived at our destination.

The driver was still chattering when we got out of the cab. Raphael handed him a twenty and told him to keep the change. It was a ridiculously big tip, but it seemed Raphael was as anxious to get away from him as I was.

Raphael and I had agreed that I would remain in control and in the background unless he needed help in containing our rogue demon. No one outside of Lugh's council knew I was possessed, and it was better for everyone if it stayed that way. But Lugh would be available if I needed him.

Keller's apartment was on the third floor of an old but well-maintained brownstone. There was no real lobby in this building, just a foyer with a row of mailboxes and intercom buttons on one side. We found Keller's name, and Raphael rang the buzzer. There was no answer.

I'd been primed for action, and my heart sank as Raphael rang the buzzer a second time. I hadn't allowed myself to consider the possibility that Keller might not be home.

Raphael tried the buzzer a third time, but the result was the same. Then he headed for the stairs.

"Where are you going?" I asked as I followed.

He gave me a look. "Up to Keller's apartment. Where else?"

"But he's not home."

"So we'll wait for him."

Raphael didn't bother with any further information. I had a feeling we were about to do something I was going to regret, but I followed him anyway.

This was a small building, and there were only three apartments on each floor. The bulb at one end of the third-floor hallway was burned out, which made it easy to see the light that shone under the door of David Keller's apartment. Of course, this was the city, and it was generally a good idea to leave a light or two on when you were gone, to discourage certain segments of the population from paying a visit.

When we got closer, I could hear the faint sound of music coming from behind the door. It sounded like something classically romantic, and I suddenly wondered if Keller hadn't answered the doorbell because he was otherwise occupied.

Raphael didn't seem to care if he was interrupting.

He knocked on the door, but there was still no response. Then he put his hand on the doorknob and gave it a turn.

The hair on the back of my neck stood up when I realized the door wasn't locked. Raphael gave me a stern look. "Don't touch anything, just in case."

I could have asked "Just in case what?" But I didn't, because I had a pretty good idea what he meant.

Raphael went in first, beckoning me to follow and stay behind him. I didn't like taking orders from him, but I did it anyway. He closed the door softly once I was in.

The apartment was tiny and cramped, and every flat surface was covered in books and papers. The room we were in was a combination living room and kitchenette, though it looked like Keller used the kitchenette for book storage rather than cooking. There was only one doorway visible other than the front door. I couldn't imagine living in an apartment that didn't even have a coat closet, but it looked like a straight-backed chair tucked into one corner was an unofficial coat rack.

The music was a little louder now, and it was clearly coming from behind the closed door. If Keller had a girl in there—or a boy, for that matter—this was going to be very embarrassing. But somehow, I didn't think that was going to be the case. Raphael put a finger to his lips, and I rolled my eyes. I wasn't about to make conversation while we were breaking into someone's apartment.

I followed Raphael through the piles of books that were strewn carelessly on the floor. He paused in front of the door, which could only lead to the bedroom. We both listened intently, but there was no sound from inside other than the music.

His face grim, Raphael pushed open the door and peeked inside. I held my breath.

Raphael's head and shoulders drooped, and he let out a sigh of resignation. I tried to peek around his shoulder, but he blocked me with one arm and pushed me back.

"You don't want to see this," he warned.

No, of course I didn't. But I ducked under Raphael's arm anyway.

David Keller lay naked on the bed. Duct tape sealed his mouth and circled his wrists and ankles. His eyes were wide and staring, and the bloody circular wound in the center of his forehead looked almost like a third eye. The pillow and mattress beneath him were soaked in blood, and I belatedly noticed the nasty, coppery odor.

Suddenly light-headed, I swayed and reached out to grab the door frame to keep from falling. Raphael snatched my hand away before I made contact.

"Don't touch anything!" he snapped. "Do you really want your fingerprints here?"

That thought didn't do much for my light-headedness. For a moment, I seriously thought I was about to faint. Raphael kept me on my feet, his arm wrapped around my shoulders. With his free hand, he used the bottom of his T-shirt to wipe off the door-knob, then dragged me through the cluttered room back to the front door.

"Get a grip on yourself," he said sharply, giving me a little shake for emphasis. "We need to get out of here before anyone sees us."

I blinked, hoping that would make the dizziness go away. It didn't, but I gritted my teeth and pushed away from Raphael. I was pleasantly surprised to find I could stand on my own power, and I took a deep breath to further steady myself.

Raphael peered out of the peephole, making sure the coast was clear. Then he opened the door and once again used his T-shirt to wipe down the knob, both inside and out.

"Keep your head down," Raphael said, "and if we run into anyone, try to keep me between you and them. You're more easily identifiable than I am."

Unfortunately true. Just for tonight, I wished my hair were some sedate, nondescript color. Maybe I needed to rethink my flamboyant look now that I was constantly running from trouble.

We made it all the way to the first floor without being spotted, but we had the bad luck of opening the front door at the exact same time someone was coming in. I lowered my head and hunched my shoulders, trying to look smaller than I really was, and I slid my arm through Raphael's, using his body for cover. My mouth was bone dry, and I had to remind myself to breathe or I might have passed out.

Because I was hiding behind Raphael, I didn't get a good look at the young couple who came in, but from what I could tell, they seemed to be in too much of a hurry to find the nearest bedroom to pay much attention to Raphael and me.

My nerves still on red alert, I allowed Raphael to lead me out into the street and put a few blocks between us and Keller's apartment before calling a cab to take us home.

Chapter **18**

We hadn't gotten more than two blocks before Raphael suddenly, and without consulting me, told the cabbie there was a change in plans and gave him his own address. The cabbie, much quieter than our previous one, barely gave a grunt of acknowledgment as he changed course. I gave Raphael a furious look— I didn't want to spend more time in his company than was absolutely necessary—but of course I didn't dare question him in front of a witness.

I fumed in silence as we drove past the university and into a residential area that was too rich for the average student's blood. At a guess, I'd say it was a popular area for faculty.

Tommy Brewster had been living in student housing, sharing his apartment with a slimy roommate, but that situation hadn't been to Raphael's liking. As soon as he'd moved into Tommy's body, he'd ditched the roommate and relocated to a town house. I didn't know where he got the money to afford the nice town house, and I didn't ask. Sometimes, ignorance really is bliss.

As soon as we stepped out of the cab, Raphael whipped out his cell phone.

"Oh, no, you don't," I said, grabbing his wrist. "First, you tell me why the change of plans."

He broke my grip easily. His face looked uncommonly grim as he held the phone between his cheek and his shoulder and unlocked his front door. "Just give me a minute," he said.

I crossed my arms over my chest and narrowed my eyes. "Tell me what the hell you're up to!" I demanded, but he ignored me.

The tension visibly eased from his shoulders when someone answered his call. I couldn't hear the other side of the conversation at all, but Raphael considerately clued me in as to whom he was calling.

"Saul," he said, sounding relieved. "You need to get out of Morgan's apartment ASAP. Come to my place, and I'll explain."

I didn't need to hear the other end of the conversation to know Saul's reaction. Raphael's jaw tightened. He pushed open his front door, then shoved me over the threshold when I stubbornly refused to move.

The door slammed behind us, and Raphael threw the deadbolt while glaring at me. I was too used to being glared at to be terribly bothered by it.

"Please, just get out of there," Raphael said. "The police may be paying a visit soon, and if they find you there, they might start asking questions. Unless Adam has made more progress than I think in creating an identity for you, you can't hold up to much scrutiny."

He listened intently for a moment; then the tension in his body language dwindled, and I knew Saul had agreed to get out of my apartment. I was beginning to think through the ramifications of Keller's death, and I wasn't liking them one bit.

First off, it meant that we had no idea whose body my demon enemy was in now. Second, it meant there was another mysterious death that I could be a suspect in. And last, but certainly not least, it hinted that the demon had no more use for Keller, which meant that if he'd been planning to plant incriminating evidence, he'd likely done so already.

Raphael hung up the phone, finally turning his attention back to me. "Saul is on his way here. Have you caught up with me yet?"

"You want me to hide from the police," I said in an accusatory voice.

"At least for the moment," he agreed. "If anyone saw us go in there tonight and they tell the police, I'm betting you'll get promoted from 'person of interest' to 'suspect' in no time flat. We can't afford to have you locked up."

"Running away is just going to make me look guilty!" I protested, but I wasn't surprised that Raphael didn't budge.

"Better to look guilty than get thrown in jail," he said. "We need Adam's input. Do you want to call him, or shall I?"

Control freak that I am, I should have insisted on making the call myself. But I just couldn't psych myself up to do it. I was too tired, too stressed, to deal with Adam, who would probably find some reason why this fiasco was all my fault.

"You do it," I said flatly.

To my surprise, Raphael reached out and gave my arm a squeeze, and it didn't feel like he was trying to crush my bones into powder.

"We've gotten through worse situations," he said. "We'll get through this, too."

I wanted to object to the word "we," didn't want to admit that Raphael and I were in any way in this together, but for once I managed to keep my opinion to myself. I gave a brisk nod that Raphael took as agreement of some kind. Then he parked me in his living room with a strong rum and Coke by my side and called Adam for advice.

Despite my desire to retreat into my personal cone of silence, Adam demanded to speak to me after Raphael finished briefing him on the situation. There was nothing in the world that could *force* me to give in to Adam's demand, except for the knowledge that not talking to him would be a form of cowardice.

"Please don't tell me the situation is any worse than we already know," I begged him.

"Sorry, love," he answered, and he did actually sound sorry. "The late Mr. Keller 'found' a thumb drive belonging to Hillerman, and when the police looked at it, they found the letter Hillerman had sent to Brian, as well as the doctored photo."

"Shit." There wasn't anything else I could add.

"Yeah. My esteemed colleagues have had some questions for me now that they've seen the photo. I told them it was a fake, but they're starting to wonder about the times I've taken statements from you."

"Shit." A good, all-purpose cuss word always comes in handy.

"I don't think they're going to find anything that would hurt me too badly, but it does mean I have to step back even further in this case."

Once upon a time, I'd been a bit shocked by

Adam's casual disregard for the law, but right now, I'd have loved to have that back. He'd kept me out of more trouble than I could believe, and I couldn't help being terrified that I'd end up in prison without his help.

"I tried to talk to Maguire's ex-girlfriend earlier today," Adam said in what seemed like a non sequitur, "but I never managed to reach her, and now that I'm under a microscope, I don't think it would be a good idea for me to be seen talking to her."

Great. Now that the demon had fled his second murdered host, we needed information to help identify him more than ever. I doubted, however, that anyone in our merry band other than Adam had the requisite skills to question the girlfriend with any success. I glanced at Raphael and amended my thought: No one but Adam could question the girlfriend without getting us into even worse trouble.

Adam read my mind. "We need to get answers from her, see if she knows anything that could help us identify our rogue."

"Are you suggesting *I* go talk to her?" I asked doubtfully.

His snort of derision would have hurt my feelings—or pissed me off—if I didn't know how badly suited I was for the job, and how conspicuous I would be if I tried to approach the girlfriend.

"No, I'm suggesting we get *Barbie* to go talk to her."

"What? Are you crazy?"

"Just hear me out. It's very important to her to keep her nose clean. If she loses her license for some reason and can't keep up her payments to The Healing Circle, Blair's going straight to whatever crappy nursing home has an open bed. Barbie knows it's in her best interests to keep you out of jail, since you can so easily take her down with you."

"And just how does she know that?" I growled, although I knew Adam far too well not to guess the answer.

"Because I drew a picture for her."

"In other words, you've already sent her on a mission to interview the ex."

I could almost hear the smug grin on his face. "I didn't think asking your permission would be in our best interests."

"Asshole," I muttered. "You know you're just handing her rope she can hang us all with."

"I don't get the impression she's anxious to hang us, even if it wouldn't have such serious repercussions for her."

I wasn't sure how good a judge of character Adam was, but since he'd already had his little talk with Barbie, it wasn't looking too likely that I'd be able to undo whatever damage he may have done.

"You'd better hope you're right," I said, resigned.

"I do indeed," he answered, then hung up—as usual—without saying good-bye.

The evening was already majorly sucky even before Saul arrived at Raphael's place, but the minute he stepped through the doorway, the tension that filled the air quadrupled in intensity. Raphael acted like he didn't notice, calmly filling Saul in, telling him about the murder of David Keller.

Saul was quiet for a couple of minutes as he absorbed the story, then he nodded briskly.

"All right," he said, "I guess I'll go back to Adam's place."

"No, you won't," Raphael said, and that was all it took to get Saul's eyes glowing.

I considered attempting to take on the role of peacekeeper, but I didn't have Dominic's bravery or tact. Instead, I took a couple of steps backward to put some space between me and them, and I scouted out my escape route should the fur begin to fly.

Raphael's voice remained calm, and there was no outward sign that he was preparing to defend himself. "Adam's now under some scrutiny himself. If you go stay there, they may become curious about your identity, and that would be bad."

"I'll take my chances," Saul said, then tried to duck around his father to reach the front door.

Raphael stepped between Saul and the door. "Use your brain. If they can't identify you, they're going to be even more curious, and they'll start asking Adam and Dominic some difficult questions. If they aren't satisfied with the answers, they might even bring in an exorcist to examine your aura."

For the first time, a hint of alarm entered Saul's face. I clamped my teeth together to keep from blurting out a stream of expletives, because Raphael was right. If Saul acted like he was hiding something, it was certainly possible they'd call in an exorcist. Pennsylvania is one of the least demon-friendly states, and it was fairly routine to submit suspects to an examination by an exorcist. After all, if you locked someone up thinking he was just your average, everyday human, and he turned out to be possessed, you were pretty likely to find yourself with an escaped prisoner and a bunch of dead guards. All it would take was the slightest pretext for the court to order an examination—which was generally considered a minor inconvenience rather than a violation of privacy—and when the exorcist found Saul was possessed and he didn't have any paperwork to prove it was legal...

"You don't want to be declared an illegal demon in this state," Raphael said, hammering home his point.

I'd exorcized Saul once before, and I hadn't had any real difficulty doing so, but Lugh contended it was only because Saul hadn't resisted, and because I'm a particularly powerful exorcist. But if the court were to order Saul exorcized now, when I was under suspension, would another exorcist be able to cast him out? Like I said, Pennsylvania is not demon-friendly, and we're one of only ten states that executes illegal demons that can't be exorcized.

Saul looked indecisive.

"Whatever you think of me," Raphael continued, "I wouldn't want you to be killed."

Saul gave him an unfathomable look. "It's too late to pretend fatherly affection."

Raphael shrugged casually. "Does it require a great deal of affection not to want to see someone burned alive? At the moment, I can't think of a single person I hate enough to wish that fate on. Even Dougal, who would not hesitate to do it to me if he ever catches me.

"Morgan can have my guest bedroom, and you can have the couch," Raphael continued, as if everything were settled. "I'll stay out of the way as much as possible so you don't have to suffer my presence."

Saul glanced at me. "Do you have an opinion, or are you just window dressing?"

"If you're trying to get a rise out of me," I answered, "then give it up. I'm tired, I'm scared, and the love of my life rejected me again. I don't have any energy left for petty quarrels." I turned to Raphael.

"Point me toward the guest bedroom so I can go collapse. You two work out your differences without me. Or don't. I honestly don't care."

I must have looked as bad as I felt, because neither Saul nor Raphael argued.

Chapter **19**

That night, I slept like the dead. I half expected Lugh to interrupt my sleep for a little strategy meeting or a seduction attempt, but he didn't. I should have been well rested when I woke up the next morning at around ten, but I still felt almost as exhausted as I had when I'd turned in.

"Lugh, please tell me you weren't driving my body around during my sleep," I muttered to the empty air.

My defenses were obviously still down, for I had no trouble hearing his response: *I wasn't driving your body around during your sleep. The exhaustion isn't physical.*

Great. At least physical exhaustion I knew how to fix. This emotional breakdown, or whatever it was, I had no idea what to do with.

I'd slept in my clothes, so I was looking less than my best when I dragged myself out of bed. I took a quick shower, which failed to make me feel any more lively, then pulled on the same outfit and wandered out into the main room.

There was a plaid blanket neatly folded over one

arm of the sofa, but that was the only visible evidence that Saul had ever been here. I wondered where he'd gone, but I wasn't interested enough to call him and find out.

There was also no sign of Raphael, which I couldn't see as anything but a positive. In the kitchen, a pot of coffee at least an hour old languished on the burner. I helped myself to a cup anyway. Even stale coffee is better than no coffee, and I was too lazy to brew a fresh pot.

I sat on Raphael's couch for I don't know how long, sipping coffee and staring off into space, trying not to brood. I was surprisingly successful at it, unless sitting around doing nothing while white noise filled my head could be considered brooding. I might have been able to sit there all day, but the sound of a ringing phone snapped me out of it.

It was my cell phone, which, of course, was in my purse, which was in the bedroom. I had to sprint to get to it in time. Considering the stupor I'd been in, I moved remarkably fast. I hate to admit it, but the only reason I moved so fast was the faint hope that it might be Brian, that he might be ready to talk. I wondered if that spike of hope meant that I'd be able to get over my own irrational anger if Brian would only come back to me.

If my brain had been even marginally functional, I'd have known it wasn't Brian. I'd assigned him a special ring tone on my cell, and this wasn't it. When I answered the phone and heard a female voice on the other end of the line, I was so disappointed I felt almost dizzy with it.

"Morgan? Hello?" It was PI Barbie—just the person I wanted to talk to first thing in the morning.

I frowned. First thing in the morning was long

gone. It could be afternoon for all I knew. I glanced at my watch and saw that it was eleven-thirty.

"Hello?" Barbie queried again. "Can you hear me?"

I sighed. "Yeah, I can hear you."

"This is Barbara Paget. I talked to Maguire's ex-girlfriend, Jessica Miles, this morning, and I found out something very interesting."

She sounded kind of excited. I couldn't muster any excitement myself, but I managed to make an encouraging noise that prompted her to continue.

"Your whole...situation started when Jessica accused Maguire of beating her up. But it turns out that wasn't what really happened."

This was what she was getting all excited about? "So what? Maguire always claimed it was the new guy in her life who hit her, not him." I'd even felt sorry for him for a while, until after I'd exorcized the demon and seen the wreckage that was his host. The demon might not have hurt Jessica Miles, but he'd sure done a job on Jordan Maguire Jr.

"Turns out Maguire was right, and it was her new guy who hit her. But get this: It was a setup, on both their parts. The new guy, Tim Simms— great name, huh?—convinced her Maguire had been cheating on her. He even produced photographs for proof."

Okay, I had to admit my interest was piqued now.

"Simms whipped Jessica into a frenzy about Maguire, the two-timing jerk, and they came up with a plan to get revenge. They waited until after she'd argued with Maguire, then she called Simms over and he gave her a couple of showy bruises. And that was all it took to get Maguire's demon exorcized."

I shuddered. The general public thinks demons die when they're exorcized, which meant Jessica and her boyfriend had committed what they thought was cold-blooded murder.

"And here's the *really* weird part," Barbie said. "Simms disappeared on the day you exorcized Maguire's demon. He didn't pack up a bag or anything, and his car's still in his apartment's parking lot. But no one has seen or heard from him since."

I had a sneaking suspicion that Simms would eventually be found, and that he wouldn't be breathing. Psycho Demon—as I'd now dubbed the demon who had it in for me—seemed to have no qualms about using "disposable" hosts. I frowned, wishing all the information I had would line up and add up to a clear and tangible threat.

It sure seemed like Psycho Demon had possessed Tim Simms. His method of fabricating evidence was too familiar to be coincidence. Then he'd moved to Jack Hillerman after the exorcism, and he'd come after me with every gun in his arsenal. He'd then burned through both Hillerman and the hapless David Keller and was now in yet another host, still aiming to up my misery quotient.

But *why*? And why would he choose such a bizarre, elaborate scheme for his revenge? Why did he have to induce Jessica to frame Maguire? He couldn't have known Maguire would be brain-dead at the end, could he?

Too many questions, too few answers.

I settled for asking a question I thought Barbie *would* be capable of answering. "How the hell did you get Jessica to basically confess to murder?" Barbie had said she was good at her job, but that was downright miraculous.

"I pretended to be Simms's little sister, desperate to locate him. As Simms had discovered, Jessica's biggest asset is definitely not her brain. She was pretty easy to, um, mislead."

"I'll bet," I muttered under my breath.

"Does any of this mean anything to you?"

"No," I lied, but no amount of practice was going to turn me into a good liar. I should have followed that monosyllabic answer with a little speculation about what the real story was, but my mind went completely blank.

Neither Barbie nor I spoke for what felt like about five minutes but was probably only thirty seconds or so.

"You know," Barbie said when she finally deigned to break the awkward silence, "at this point, I'm in this up to my neck. It really wouldn't hurt you to level with me."

I made a sound between a snort and a laugh. "I'm not as easy to mislead as Jessica Miles."

"Think about it a minute, Morgan. I knew before the police did that you had an excellent motive to kill Jack Hillerman. I could have gone to the police with that, but I didn't."

"Yeah, because Adam put the fear of God into you, so to speak."

"I wasn't going to talk to them anyway, but that's beside the point. My career is history if my recent activities come to light. I'm in this with you till the end, and I'll be able to do better work if you tell me what you and Adam think is going on."

"So you have no problem helping out someone who may have murdered your former employer?"

It was her turn to snort. "I'm confident you didn't kill him."

I raised my eyebrows, though of course she couldn't see that. "What makes you so sure?"

"Gut instinct, for one. But it's also that I can't see

you being stupid enough to openly waltz into his office during regular business hours and shoot him. The fact that the shooter used a gun with a silencer is pretty clear evidence that it was premeditated murder, but if it was premeditated, it hardly made sense for you to do it in such a way as to make yourself the prime suspect."

Very true. I wondered how the prosecutor would explain my reasoning. But I was getting ahead of myself. Perhaps I'd never be formally charged with Hillerman's death. Yeah, and perhaps even now, pigs were flying over the frozen plains of Hell.

Barbie's reasoning made perfect sense, and she was probably telling the truth about her current commitment to the cause. However, there was no way in hell I was going to level with her. I'd have to reveal too much of my hard-earned, forbidden knowledge to even begin to explain.

"Have you had any success finding out who created the photographs?" I asked. I wasn't going to tell Barbie the whole story, but I decided not to rub her face in the fact, either.

She paused, and I felt sure she was going to press me to give her the juicy details. But she didn't, and I let go of a breath I hadn't realized I'd been holding.

"Not yet. But I'm going to work on the assumption that Hillerman and Simms used the same source, and that gives me a few more bread crumbs to follow."

"Great. Let me know if you find anything." I meant that to be a dismissal, but Barbie either didn't get it, or she chose to ignore it.

"So I hear Hillerman's intern met with an untimely end sometime last night."

Internally, I cringed. Considering Psycho Demon

was gunning for *me*, there were sure a lot of other people getting hurt in his wake.

"Yeah, I heard that, too."

"And is it a coincidence that I haven't been able to reach you at your home number?"

"Is there a point you're trying to make, or are you just jabbing pins in me for shits and grins?"

"My point is you can use all the help you can get."

"Oh, we're back on that, are we?"

"I don't give up easily. I'll figure out whatever it is you're hiding, and then I'll help you whether you want me to or not."

The sound that left my throat now was almost a growl. "What the fuck do you care? I'm not even a paying client, and if I *were* a paying client, I'd fire you for sticking your nose where it doesn't belong."

Barbie was silent so long I thought she might have hung up. But she'd been telling nothing but the truth when she said she didn't give up easily.

"The things I did for Jack Hillerman..." She sighed. "It wasn't the first time I'd compromised my professional ethics on a case, but always before, it was for a good cause. I did more than just compromise my ethics this time, and I did it for money. I can't even hide behind a good cause. That's not the kind of person I want to be. So if I can help you, it'll help me feel a little less like a scum-sucking bottom feeder."

"You were just trying to protect your sister," I said, then was surprised at myself for coming to Barbie's defense. By all rights, I should hate this woman.

"That's what I told myself," Barbie agreed. "But now I think I was looking for an easy way out. For years, I've busted my ass to keep Blair at The Healing

Circle, and I couldn't resist the lure of easy money. I should have just kept busting my ass like always."

Maybe if I hadn't sacrificed Tommy Brewster to save my brother, I wouldn't have been able to identify with Barbie at all. I'm certain I wouldn't have been able to forgive her. I'm not the most forgiving of people under the best of circumstances. But honestly, I'm not sure I wouldn't have done the same thing had our roles been reversed, so I was having a hard time throwing stones.

"Believe me, Barbie, I know exactly what it's like to make bad decisions when people you love are involved."

"Very intriguing, but I'll resist my urge to pry. One thing, though: please don't call me Barbie. My name's Barbara."

I couldn't help laughing. "If you don't want me calling you Barbie, then you need to either change your name, or gain twenty pounds and dye your hair."

"Fine. But remember, two can play that game, Morgie."

We both laughed at that. It felt kind of surreal, trading quips with the woman who'd wreaked such havoc on my life. But it also felt kind of...good. Once upon a time, before Lugh came into my life, I'd had a friend I could banter with. I'd never been big on the whole "girl talk" thing, but Val and I had on occasion indulged, discussing our romantic woes over pints of chocolate chip ice cream. I missed those days. I missed *Val,* at least the woman I'd thought Val was.

I think Barbie caught the vibe of my thoughts even over the phone line, because she followed up with, "If you ever decide you need to spill those secrets of yours, just give me a call. I think you might find me a useful asset, especially now that you can't lean on Adam as much."

It was my turn to sigh. "Don't get your hopes up," I warned. "But thanks. I appreciate the offer."

There was nothing more to say after that, so we hung up.

Chapter **20**

I **was** supposed to meet with my lawyer that afternoon, but I was afraid the police might know that and would be waiting for me there, so I called and canceled. I wondered if the lawsuit was still in the works now that Hillerman was dead. It hardly seemed to matter, not when I had possible murder charges hanging over my head.

Raphael made an appearance shortly after I hung up with Barbie. He brought takeout Chinese food for lunch and gave me first choice, pretending to be a gentleman. I took the chicken lo mein, leaving him with the fishy-smelling shrimp fried rice. We didn't bother with plates or silverware, instead opening the takeout cartons and digging in with our cheap disposable chopsticks.

I told Raphael what Barbie had told me, but he couldn't figure out what it meant, either. I was more convinced than ever that I had to unmask Psycho Demon, though God only knows what I was going to do when I found out his identity. The chances that it would help me figure out who was hosting him right this moment were pretty slim, but maybe it would help me get a step ahead of him.

I didn't like the idea that was forming in my head, but once it took root, it was pretty much impossible to ignore it. There was one obvious place to go when looking for information about illegal demons who inhabit our fair city; one person who would know more about the demon underworld than anyone else.

I'd spoken with Shae, the owner of The Seven Deadlies, more times than I would have believed possible, considering how much I loathed her. The Seven Deadlies was a demon sex club, and its basement, aptly named Hell, was a haven for demons who were into hard-core S&M. I shuddered and tried to block out my memories of my one and only visit there.

Shae was a mercenary, and as far as I could tell, she was willing to do just about anything as long as she was paid enough—though the payments were not necessarily monetary in nature. She was also an illegal demon herself, allowed to remain on the Mortal Plain only because she served as Adam's snitch.

I had bargained with Shae for information once before, and lived to tell about it. In exchange, I'd had to give her some information I'd have preferred to keep to myself, but all in all I felt like the interview had gone well. Perhaps trying a second time would be tempting fate, but I wasn't just going to sit around on my ass and wait for either the police or Psycho Demon to find me. The question then became, would I be able to shake my demon bodyguards?

I spent too much time pondering the question as I slurped up greasy lo mein noodles. If my brain had been firing on all cylinders, I would have Tasered Raphael and made my escape while I still had only one demon to get through, but as it was, Saul returned to the house before I'd come up with the idea.

Raphael and I were both eating standing up, leaning against the kitchen counter. Raphael put down his carton of fried rice and laughed when Saul came in the front door.

"What's so funny?" I asked, frowning.

"Your face," Raphael said, and laughed again. Even Saul's lips were twitching.

"What?" I wondered if Raphael would mind me sticking my chopsticks through his eye.

Raphael took a deep breath and contained his mirth, though his eyes still sparkled with it. "Your face is such an open book. I've never seen anything like it."

I was beginning to suspect what had so amused Raphael and Saul, but damned if I was going to admit anything, so I just scowled and shoved a heap of lo mein into my mouth.

"It wouldn't have worked anyway," Raphael said. "The only reason Saul wasn't in the house when you woke up was that he was taking a break from my company. If you'd set foot outside the house without me, he'd have herded you back in."

I turned my scowl toward Saul, though I'd stuffed too much greasy lo mein into my mouth to tell him what I thought of him. He shrugged.

"You Tasered me yesterday," he reminded me. "If you think you're going to get away with the same trick twice, you're delusional."

I swallowed my mouthful of noodles and resisted the urge to throw the carton at Saul. Not trusting my impulse control, I decided I was best off putting the carton down.

"So you guys are going to keep me prisoner here?" I asked, crossing my arms over my chest, and, I'm sure, looking pretty damn belligerent.

"It would be safest for you to stay inside and out

of sight," Raphael said. "No one is going to figure out you're taking refuge *here,* of all places."

That was true. As far as the outside world was concerned, I was right now hanging out at the house of Tommy Brewster, a legal, registered demon host whom I hardly knew. The police wouldn't find me here, and neither would Psycho Demon. Of course, I wouldn't be able to do jack shit to clear my name or identify my enemy while living under house arrest, either.

A little help, Lugh? I thought at him, though I already knew he wasn't going to be on my side in this battle.

I'm always on your side, his voice chided gently in my mind. *But you've got nowhere to go right now. I agree that talking to Shae may yield some results, but the club won't open until nine tonight.*

So you'd actually let me go? I asked, somewhat incredulously.

Not by yourself, of course. But you can take Saul and Raphael with you.

I bristled at the idea. *I can take care of myself! If I get caught by the police, the last thing any of us needs is for Saul or Raphael to interfere. And if I run into Psycho Demon, I can let you take control.*

I could almost see him in my mind, his face taking on that familiar, patient expression as he explained the facts of life to me. *Remember, we're trying not to kill the host. I'm not at all sure I'd be able to restrain him without killing him all by myself. That's why we sent* two *demons after David Keller.*

"I gather from that distracted look on your face that you're having a conversation with my brother," Raphael said.

I blinked, momentarily disoriented. I'd gotten so

absorbed in my mental discussion that I'd almost forgotten about the outside world. Something about that creeped me out—it was like I'd checked out of reality for a minute or two. I shook my head to clear it.

"Yeah," I said. "We've got a plan for tonight." I explained what I had in mind.

Saul and Raphael both listened without interruption, but I could see suspicion in both their expressions.

"What?" I finally asked, throwing my hands up in disgust, hating the way they were looking at me.

"Are you *sure* Lugh is okay with this?" Raphael asked in a voice steeped with skepticism.

I swear I could feel my blood pressure rising. I had to fight a mighty battle not to say something about how I didn't need Lugh's permission, because, in a way, I did. I took a couple of slow, calming breaths before I answered.

"Yes, I'm sure. You've said it yourself many times: I'm a shitty liar. So decide for yourself: Am I lying?"

Raphael accepted that argument with a reluctant shake of his head, but Saul still looked doubtful. He didn't know me well enough to understand how badly I sucked at lying, and the fact that Raphael was now taking my word for it probably was more of a hindrance than a help, considering their relationship. I was trying to figure out how to convince Saul, when suddenly I wasn't in control of my body anymore.

Lugh reached out and grabbed Raphael around the throat, then lifted him off the ground with one hand. Raphael's eyes bugged, but he didn't struggle.

"Morgan has my seal of approval," Lugh said, then lowered Raphael to the floor and flowed back into the background where he belonged.

As soon as Lugh ceded control back to me, a

headache slammed behind my eyes and my stomach gave a lurch. I considered dashing to the sink to hurl, but I thought maybe I could keep the nausea in check.

"Are you all right?" Raphael asked as he rubbed his throat. There was no mark there, and I doubted Lugh had actually hurt him, though I supposed it had been a disconcerting experience.

"Yeah," I said, closing my eyes and trying to steady myself. "Apparently, I can't even let Lugh in for a few seconds anymore without suffering the consequences."

Sorry about that, Lugh said. *Saul wasn't going to believe you unless I told him it was okay, and I had to prove it was really me talking.*

Raphael was giving me a curious look. "How much has he been in control lately?"

"Not enough that I expected to get sick," I muttered. We knew my body seemed to object to repeated control changes, but we hadn't exactly determined how much was too much. Still, there'd been times when he'd been in control much longer and we'd exchanged more often without my suffering ill effects. "Maybe I react more strongly when he takes control without asking first." Or maybe the idea that he now seemed able to do so at will was belatedly triggering my mental alarms and making me sick.

My stomach heaved, and I just barely managed to keep my lo mein from making a return appearance.

"I think I'd better go lie down," I said, and neither Saul nor Raphael argued.

I'd felt about a thousand times worse the last time I'd had such an adverse reaction to the control changes, but I found that wasn't comforting at all right now as I lay on my bed with a pillow over my face, my head throbbing in time to my pulse. I thought about taking some aspirin, but Lugh didn't think it would help, since he couldn't figure out exactly what was causing the reaction. Besides, it wasn't like Raphael would have aspirin sitting around the house. Demons don't get headaches or colds or any of the other annoying physical ailments that plague mankind.

Apparently, I fell asleep, because the next thing I knew, I was in Lugh's living room. Even asleep, I could feel the pounding in my head. I winced, and Lugh frowned.

"I wish I could figure out what's causing that," he said.

"Yeah, me, too," I responded, closing my eyes even though I knew that wouldn't make the pain go away.

I jumped a little when I felt Lugh's hands on my face. When I'd closed my eyes, he'd been sitting on the other end of the sofa, but now we seemed to have changed locations. Instead of the living room, we were in the bedroom, on the sinfully soft king-sized bed. Lugh had a fondness for red silk sheets, but he must have known they would instantly put me on seduction-alert, so he'd settled for ivory-colored silk instead.

He was behind me, his back probably resting against the headboard, though I didn't turn to see. His warm, large hands cupped my cheeks.

"Lie down," he urged me. "Let's see if I can make it any better."

If I'd realized my head was going to end up on his lap, I probably would have resisted his suggestion. But the hands on my face were so soothing, and his voice was so hypnotic, that I complied without thinking.

A hint of alarm surged when my head made contact with his crotch. His legs were spread, and I was cradled between them. Not a safe position to be in with Lugh, but before I managed a protest, his thumbs drew exquisite circles on my temples, and my whole body went limp. The pressure was just right, and the headache instantly eased.

I couldn't help the little groan of relief that escaped me. I suspected it made Lugh smile smugly, but I didn't want to open my eyes and see.

His hands were so big, he could massage me from chin to forehead all at the same time, which he proceeded to do. His skillful, dextrous fingers found every knot of tension and gently but firmly erased them. I relaxed even further, abandoning myself to hedonistic pleasure, shutting down my worries and cares so I could better concentrate on the physical sensation.

I don't know how long I lay like that, basking in a warm glow, feeling safe and comfortable for the first time in ages. I think it was a long time, because my every muscle felt like heated candle wax, soft and malleable, when I started noticing sensations other than Lugh's hands on my face. His fingers were still at work, still drawing circles on my skin, but there was no more tension left to find. The headache had disappeared entirely.

Which was all very nice, but now that I wasn't drifting anymore, I couldn't help noticing that my, er, pillow was very, very hard. I kept my eyes closed and tried not to tense, but of course there was no corner of my mind Lugh couldn't see into, so he knew how aware I was of his arousal. He was also aware that it didn't exactly repulse me.

Considering how many times Lugh had made advances, you'd have thought that by now I'd be ready for it. But no, I had relaxed into his caresses as if he couldn't possibly have any ulterior motives. Worse, I wasn't leaping to my feet and putting as much distance between us as possible.

I could tell Lugh was leaning over me, because the tips of his long black hair tickled my neck and shoulders, which were apparently bare. I didn't think they had been when the dream had started, but then my clothes frequently seemed to morph or downright disappear when I dreamed of Lugh. The tickle moved down the slope of my breasts. Beneath my head, Lugh's arousal pulsed, making my traitorous nipples tighten.

"Don't," I gasped, but I didn't move away or try to close my mental doors. One thing was for sure—if I allowed myself to drown in the pleasure of Lugh's body, no thoughts of my fucked-up life would enter my mind and hurt me. Would it be so wrong to finally stop saying no, to put off for just a while longer the necessity of dealing with everything that was wrong in my life right now? After all, it seemed like Brian and I were history.

"Don't give up yet, Morgan," Lugh said softly just as his hair finally brushed over one of my nipples and caused me to arch my back. "Brian is worth fighting for, and it's high time you put some effort into the fight yourself instead of making him do all the work."

I'm sure I would have had something clever to say to that, except at that moment the hands that had been caressing my face began following the path his hair had taken. Another moan escaped me, and my whole body vibrated with tension as I tried to tell myself I wanted him to stop.

I rallied my mental troops enough to speak, though not nearly enough to make myself avoid his caress. "How can you be trying to fix Brian and me at the same time you're trying to seduce me?"

"As I've said before, I'm not in competition with Brian." He chuckled softly. "I like him, and I enjoy your time with him almost as much as you do." His fingers slid around the outside of my breasts and then under, avoiding my aching nipples. "And I believe I've proven before that I can pleasure you without making love to you, so I'm not sure this counts as a true seduction."

Forbidden arousal tugged at my center as I remembered the erotic fantasy Lugh had created for me. It had been my own hand that brought me to climax, but it had been the visual Lugh had created of Dominic giving Adam a blow job that had made that climax inevitable.

I was still too prudish to be comfortable with the idea that seeing two men together aroused me, but there was no way I could deny that reality. And even the fact that Lugh had been distracting me with sex while he drove my body around without my permission didn't erase the memory of that pleasure.

"Trust me," Lugh murmured, and I don't know whether it was his words or his tone, but the shiver that ripped through me then was equal parts excitement and alarm.

I felt, rather than saw, the change in scenery around me, since I still hadn't gotten around to opening my eyes. The bed disappeared from under me, and suddenly, instead of lying on my back, I was on my feet, hands stretched above my head. My eyes flew open, and I took in my new situation in quick, almost photographic flashes of awareness.

Hands up, wrists circled by decadently soft, fur-lined manacles that attached to a metal bar above my head.

Legs shoulder-width apart, similarly shackled to a pair of metal poles that reached from floor to ceiling.

Body encased in a tight, stretchy black minidress.

Lugh's enormous bed about five yards away, now draped again in his favorite red silk sheets and sporting a footboard that had never been there before.

"Lugh!" I gasped, alarm overtaking the arousal I'd felt before.

"I'm right here," he whispered from behind me, his breath warm against my cheek. His hands rested on my hips.

I tugged at the restraints on my wrists. "I don't like this," I said, my voice coming out in a hoarse croak I barely recognized as mine.

"Shh," he said as he pressed his delicious, warm body up against my back. "Remember, this is just a dream. Nothing bad can happen to you here."

I swallowed on a dry throat, my emotions ping-ponging wildly, moving too fast for me to identify them all. I hated the sensation of the cuffs around my wrists and ankles, hated the fact that I couldn't move, couldn't run away. And yet it was hard to deny the tingle of anticipation that existed beneath it all, the desire to find out what would come next.

"Think of this as a very realistic sexual fantasy," Lugh whispered in my ear, his breath hot upon my skin. "You can enjoy things in fantasy that you know you wouldn't like in real life."

The room was lit by a multitude of candles, which rested on a collection of end tables clustered near the bed. Beyond the reach of the candles' light was an impenetrable darkness. As my heart palpitated in continued confusion, two figures emerged from the darkness.

Considering the events of the last erotic dream Lugh had conjured, I was not entirely surprised to see Adam and Dominic. Adam was fully clothed, but he was clearly dressed for success. His black jeans clung to his every contour, showing off an erection of prodigious size. His black T-shirt was similarly clingy, giving me a mouthwatering view of his well-muscled chest and six-pack abs.

Dominic was stark naked and looked to be very happy about it. His erection was no match for Adam's in sheer size, but it was nothing to be embarrassed about, either. His nipples were so tight they looked almost painful, and the look on his face was one of dazed pleasure. His eyes were almost black with lust, his olive-skinned cheeks flushed with it. The fact that he was wearing a studded leather collar and that his hands were bound together by an intricately knotted length of black satin cord didn't seem to bother him in the least.

Lugh's hands moved on my hips, and I jumped, having almost forgotten he was there. A low, sexy chuckle emerged from his throat, and the sound seemed to vibrate through my every nerve.

Giving me a smoldering, dangerous look, Adam put his hands on Dom's shoulders and roughly jerked him around to face the bed. Dom didn't seem to have any objection to the rough handling; in fact, if it was possible, his erection seemed to gain even more enthusiasm.

I had a feeling I knew why Lugh's bed suddenly had a footboard.

"Bend over!" Adam barked at Dom, who shivered and broke out in goose bumps.

Dom and I moaned in unison as he followed his lover's orders, grabbing the footboard with his bound hands to steady himself. I wanted to rub my thighs together—whether to deny the moisture that was building there or to give my aching flesh some relief, I don't know.

Adam placed his hands on Dom's hips, just the way Lugh's hands rested on mine. And when Adam started to caress up and down Dom's flanks, Lugh's hands mirrored the motion. My skin quivered under his touch as his hands slid down past the hem of my dress and then up again. The dress was still a fragile barrier between us, but I knew that wouldn't last long. Some little part of me thought that maybe I should object, but, of course, I didn't.

When Adam's hands cupped Dom's ass, Lugh pushed the hem of my dress up and out of the way. I wasn't surprised to discover I wasn't wearing any underwear. Feeling Lugh's hands on my naked bottom was practically enough to set me off all by itself, even without the visual of Adam and Dom.

"Don't you dare come yet!" Adam said sternly, and though he was supposed to be talking to Dom, I had a feeling the words were meant equally for me.

Dominic uttered an incoherent protest and pushed himself more firmly into Adam's hands. Adam made a clucking sound with his tongue as he ceased the caress and put his fists on his hips. I no longer felt Lugh's hands on my bottom, and the loss inspired a pitiful mewl of displeasure.

"You should know better than to complain," Adam said, his voice even sterner.

"I'm sorry!" Dominic sobbed, but even an S&M ingenue such as myself could tell there was no genuine remorse or distress in his voice.

"I'm going to have to teach you a lesson."

My brain wasn't functioning at optimal efficiency, but even so, I could put two and two together. Lugh had been mirroring with me what Adam had been doing to Dominic. And Adam was about to do something to Dominic I had no desire to experience for myself.

Lugh sensed my fear before I could even come close to articulating it. "I won't hurt you," he whispered, and I believed him implicitly.

Adam gave Dominic a long, agonizing moment to think about what was going to happen. From my vantage point, I could easily see the way Dom's buttocks tensed as he waited, his thighs quivering with anticipation. If I'd needed any reassurance that he was loving every minute of this, all I had to do was take a look at his cock, flushed and stiff, ready for action.

When Adam pulled back his hand, both Dom and I held our breath. Then when Adam's hand gave him a frighteningly firm smack, we both cried out.

I would have jumped about a mile if my feet weren't so firmly pinioned, because Lugh's hand smacked me at the same time. I was about to make an indignant protest about him breaking his promise, but I realized almost instantly that, despite the loud noise I'd heard, Lugh had given me nothing more than a gentle pat. No pain whatsoever, though that didn't stop me from flinching when he did it again.

It was a distinctly...odd sensation, watching Adam turn Dom's ass red with blow after blow while a shadow of those blows fell on my own flesh. Dom was clearly loving every minute of it, his cock dripping pre-cum despite the fact that it should have hurt like hell. I couldn't at first decide whether my body was enjoying the simultaneous stimulation or not, but as Dominic's cries of pleasure surrounded me and seemed to echo off the invisible walls, my internal censor—the one who told me I was strictly forbidden to enjoy anything about this experience—went on vacation.

I felt like I was both myself and Dominic at the same time, watching the action as well as feeling it, but feeling it only as pleasure. The boundaries of my self blurred and bled, and I was lost in a sea of sensation.

Adam was tearing open the button fly of his jeans now, and Dominic was begging for release, his breath sawing in and out of his lungs, just like mine was. When Adam mounted him, I fully expected Lugh to take me. I was too far gone to stop him, or even to care. I just wanted to come with a desperate urgency that took every ounce of my concentration.

But as Adam began to thrust, it wasn't Lugh's cock I felt between my legs, but his hand. If he hadn't created such a thorough illusion that Dominic and I were one, I doubt it would have been enough to satisfy me. As it was, I could hardly breathe through the pleasure of his touch as his hand stroked me in time to Adam's thrusts.

You know how a tsunami kind of sucks all the water around it into its center and then explodes out from there? That's what this was like. Every ounce of my attention, every sensation in my entire body, seemed to be sucked down into my core. And then Dominic cried out his release, and all that energy, all that sensation that had gathered in my center, exploded outward.

I think I screamed, but honestly, I was too

overwhelmed to remember anything very clearly afterward. All I knew was that I'd never felt anything like that before. And, good as it was, I wasn't sure I could survive ever feeling anything like that again.

Chapter 21

I woke up groggy and disoriented. The image of Adam and Dom seemed burned on my retinas, and I was actually confused to open my eyes and not see Lugh's decadent king-sized bed. Instead, I was sprawled inelegantly on an uncomfortably hard twin bed in a room that could have passed for a closet in some houses.

My skin felt hot and flushed, and my pulse still rushed with the remembrance of pleasure. I wanted to lie back down, to drift back into sleep before I had to think about what had just happened. I wondered if I had screamed as loud in real life as I had in the dream, and that was enough to dispel the last remnants of sleep. I would die of embarrassment if Raphael and Saul had heard anything.

They didn't, Lugh reassured me, but I didn't particularly want to hear his voice right now, and he didn't add any more commentary.

The bedside clock said it was almost five o'clock, and I gaped at it in shock. I'd come to lie down around one. I could hardly believe I'd slept almost four hours. On the plus side, the headache was gone, as was the nausea, so maybe the sleep—and the events that had occurred during that sleep—had been just what the doctor ordered. I shied away from thinking about the dream, unwilling to face the aftermath.

My clothes were getting pretty rancid, so I borrowed some shorts and a T-shirt from Raphael and stuck my own outfit in the wash. I felt a moment of envy as I turned on the washer, which resided in the basement of Raphael's house. I longed for the good old days, when I'd had a house of my own, complete with a washer and dryer I didn't have to share with a hundred other people.

Once again, Saul was nowhere in evidence, though I presumed that, as before, if I made a run for it, he would magically appear to stop me. Not that I actually wanted to make a run for it at this point. I didn't know who was hosting Psycho Demon right now, but I had to assume it was yet another innocent bystander, and if by some coincidence I should run into him at The Seven Deadlies, I'd need help making sure the host and I both survived the encounter.

The only part of the dream with Lugh that I allowed myself to think about just now was the part where he'd told me I had to put some work into my relationship with Brian if I wanted to *have* a relationship with him. It was true that just about any time we had a fight, it was Brian who later came bearing the olive branch. I could hardly argue that it wasn't my turn. But the question remained, would I do more harm than good if I tried to make peace now?

I deliberately poked at my open wound, mentally reliving the moment when I'd realized that Brian believed that I'd cheated on him. The pain stabbed through me with an almost physical force, and I had to fight like hell not to recoil from it and shove it into an imaginary closet where it would never see the light of day again.

The anger came seconds after the hurt, strong and fresh, waving a red flag to let me know it was still ready for action. When I thought about how Brian had snubbed me yesterday, even after he'd found out I hadn't really cheated on him, the anger rose up to overpower the hurt. I felt my teeth grinding and forced myself to relax my jaw.

Okay, no question about it, I was still seething. Not the right state of mind for a conciliatory visit with Brian. I was more likely to further alienate him than to heal the wound.

Or was that just an excuse because the thought of going to him and being rejected again made me sick to my stomach?

When it came to relationships, there was no denying I was an utter coward. That's why it was always Brian who had to make the overtures: because I was too chickenshit to do it myself. True, I was still angry; and true, Brian still was, too, though I didn't understand why. But if I waited for my anger to fade before I approached him, then I'd never do it.

I was still debating my options when Saul made his entrance. Apparently, he hadn't been standing guard outside after all; he'd been on a dinner run. His haul included six burgers and three extra-large servings of fries from McDonald's. I guess when you're a demon, there's no particular need to eat healthy.

We ate gathered around the dining room table in awkward, nerve-wracking silence. The animosity that sparked between Saul and Raphael was so strong that sometimes I could have sworn I heard the crackling buzz of electricity. I wondered if they'd been fighting this afternoon while I...

I shook my head as I bit into a lukewarm, not

terribly appetizing burger. It seemed Saul was doing most of his bodyguard duty at a distance from Raphael, so they probably hadn't had much opportunity to fight. Besides, if they'd fought, one of them would probably be dead.

I looked back and forth between them. Raphael was pretending to be blissfully unaware of Saul's death glares, but I suspected that was nothing but a façade.

If at some point they were called upon to do bodyguard duty, would they have each other's backs? Or were they more likely to shove each other into the line of fire?

Raphael would never hurt Saul, Lugh informed me. *I believe he shocked even himself by coming to love his son.*

As happened now and again, I felt a surge of pity for Raphael. I knew how much it sucked to love someone and have them hate you in return.

I thought for sure Lugh would correct my melodramatic thinking, but he said no more. So I corrected myself instead: Brian didn't hate me. Being angry with someone and hating them were not at all the same.

"I'd like to make a stop on the way to The Seven Deadlies tonight," I said, apropos of nothing. It was so out of the blue I startled even myself. I hadn't realized I'd come to a decision yet.

"Oh?" Raphael said, raising one eyebrow as he finished off his second burger.

My mouthful of burger suddenly seemed dry and chewy, so I took a big gulp from my glass of water before I continued. Nerves made my voice soft, almost breathy.

"I need to talk to Brian."

I was staring at my fries, but I didn't have to look

at my dinner companions to feel their eyes upon me. I didn't even hear any further sounds of chewing.

"Bad idea," Raphael said. I looked up with a snarl, but he met my eyes steadily. "I talked to Adam while you were sleeping, and you are now an official suspect in Hillerman's murder. In all likelihood, the cops will be watching for you to show up there."

"Oh." Shit, I hadn't thought of that. And if the police were watching Brian's apartment, they might have tapped his phone, too, so calling him would be as bad an idea as showing up.

I almost gave up, almost decided the universe was trying to send me a message. But then I thought about the risk I'd be taking the moment I left the sanctuary of Raphael's house. I didn't think I was likely to die at Psycho Demon's hands, not with my demon body-guards in tow, but I certainly ran the risk of being arrested. It would be really hard for me to make my peace offering if I was in jail.

No, I was going to do it now, before circumstances made it impossible—or I chickened out.

I was too nervous to finish my burger, but I did it anyway, hoping Saul and Raphael would think I'd given up on the idea of talking to Brian. If they knew what I was planning, I'm sure they would try to stop me. The return of the hostile silence didn't do anything good for my nerves.

When I was finished with dinner, I asked Saul to find a drugstore and buy some hair color. My bright red hair was way too much of a beacon, and though a change in hair color wasn't much of a disguise, it would have to do. I hadn't made it to the six o'clock news yet, but there had been a picture of me and an article about Hillerman's and Keller's deaths in the paper today. Not on the front page, but still...It was more exposure than I'd liked.

When Saul left, I retired to my room to wait for my clothes to finish drying. And to use the phone.

I was acutely aware of every little sound I made as I dialed Barbie's number, fearing that Raphael would hear and come running to stop me. He didn't.

"Hello?" Barbie said.

"Hi. It's Morgan. I have a huge favor to ask of you."

I had just emerged from the bathroom with my newly dyed jet-black hair when the doorbell rang. Saul and Raphael were sitting at opposite ends of the living room, as far away from one another as possible, but they sprang to their feet in unison, both their heads turning toward the door with identical alarmed expressions. You see, I hadn't warned them we were expecting company, mainly since there'd been no guarantee said company would show up.

"At ease, gentlemen," I said as I headed toward the door.

"What did you do?" Raphael growled the question as he hurried across the room toward me.

"I made a phone call," I responded in a similar growl. "Now back off!"

By the time I'd made it to the door, my bodyguards had converged, each one grabbing one of my arms. I still managed to glance out the peephole to confirm the identity of our visitors.

"Relax," I said, trying to yank my arms free, but when you're a human and a demon's got ahold on you, you'd rip your arm from its socket before you managed to make them let go. "It's Barbie and Brian."

Saul kept his grip on my arm, pulling me back into the living room, while Raphael opened the door.

Barbie and Brian accepted his silent invitation to come in. When Raphael closed the door behind them, it wasn't quite a slam, but it was close.

"Are you crazy?" he asked me. "Are you *trying* to lead the police to my door?"

"Part of my assignment was to make sure we weren't followed," Barbie said. "I lost our tail down in South Philly before I even headed this direction." She smiled her most Barbieish smile and gave Raphael an appraising look. "So, we meet again, Mr. Brewster," she said. "Amazing that you and Morgan are such close friends, under the circumstances."

Okay, maybe having Barbie bring Brian to Raphael's house hadn't been such a hot idea. She knew Tommy Brewster was possessed, but she had no idea he was no longer possessed by his original demon. Nor was there any way it would make sense to her that an exorcist was hanging out with a demon she'd once been hired to exorcize.

Raphael looked like he was about one step short of killing me. His fists were clenched at his sides, his cheeks flushed with rage. "You couldn't have consulted us before inviting her here?" he asked, and he was mad enough that I saw the phantom glow in his eyes.

I shrugged. "You would have said no. Quit crying over spilled milk." I then tried to pretend Raphael didn't exist. "Barbie, this is . . ." I let my voice trail off as I looked at Saul, suddenly realizing I couldn't remember what name he was using. It's customary for demons to adopt their hosts' names on the Mortal Plain—I was going to have to try to remember to call Raphael "Tommy." But though I'd had to give my building staff Saul's name, I was drawing a complete blank. Did I tell them Paul? Or had we stuck with Saul and just made up a last name?

"My name is Saul," he said, striding forward and offering Barbie a smile and a handshake. "Pleased to meet you."

"Likewise," she said, and I could see the questions gathering in her eyes. To her credit, she refrained from asking any. Her beauty-queen smile was getting on my nerves, but she put it to good use, trying to charm my demon bodyguards. "Why don't the three of us get acquainted while Morgan and Brian have a little chat?"

Raphael was still fuming, but Saul's eyes sparked with interest. From the way he was looking at Barbie, I guessed that he, like most demons, swung both ways. I doubted he'd had the chance to do any swinging one way or the other since he'd returned to the Mortal Plain. If hopes of getting laid would keep him distracted, I was all for it.

Heart fluttering in my chest, hands clammy, I finally turned to look at Brian. He was wearing his lawyer face, the one that gave nothing away. It was an improvement over the fury and the coldness, but it wasn't what I'd hoped to see.

I cleared my throat, afraid my voice would come out froggy if I didn't. "Come on back," I said to Brian, jerking my head toward the hallway that led to the guest room I'd appropriated.

He didn't speak, just followed me like a brooding shadow. I had to rub my hands on my pants legs or I might not have been able to get the door open. Again, Brian followed without speaking, closing the door behind himself, then leaning his back against it.

The only place to sit in this room was the bed, and Brian's body language told me not to bother asking. I sat down because I wasn't sure my knees would hold me if I didn't. Brian waited for me to speak. From the living room, I heard the TV turned on. I'd bet anything it was Barbie who'd thought of putting the TV on to give Brian and me some extra privacy.

I took a deep breath in a futile attempt to steady my nerves, then forced myself to meet Brian's eyes. Still nothing.

"You're still mad at me," I said. "Even though you know now that I didn't cheat on you."

"Yes."

I expected him to elaborate, but he didn't. Obviously, he wasn't going to make this easy for me. "Care to tell me why?"

His shoulders drooped, and he shook his head. "The fact that you even have to ask..." His voice faded out, and he wouldn't look at me.

I've always known I'm a bit dense where interpersonal relations are concerned, but once he said that, I knew exactly what I had done wrong. Again. But it was something I was never going to regret.

"Was it so wrong of me not to want to...burden you with what I'd gone through?" I asked softly.

Brian pushed away from the door, but he only took one step closer to me, and his lawyer face was morphing into his mad face. "It was wrong of you to keep secrets, to lie to me! Or had you forgotten you'd just promised not to do that again?"

My knees felt a little steadier, so I stood up to face him. "I didn't lie to you."

He made a grunt of disgust. "A lie by omission is still a lie in my book."

Brian's book had always had a hell of a lot more stringent rules than mine. "So that's it?" I asked, anger making my voice break. "I fail to tell you what I had to do to save your life, and that's the end of us?"

Brian hid his own anger under the lawyer face again. "You still don't get it. If this were an isolated incident, sure, I'd get over it. But it's a pattern of behavior. Would you like me to list all the times you've lied to me or kept me in the dark 'for my own good' in the last couple of months? Because if I start ticking them off on my fingers, I'm going to need another set of hands."

It was true that I'd kept a hell of a lot from him, but I had good cause. "Can you really blame me for trying to protect the man I love?" My voice broke again, but damned if I was going to let myself cry.

"When your idea of protecting me is to treat me as if I'm not able to take care of myself, then yes, I can blame you."

"But, Brian—"

"And you know what? You may tell yourself you're being noble by trying to protect me, but what you're really doing is protecting your own damn self. You didn't tell me about your deal with Adam because you didn't trust me not to act like a caveman and treat you like damaged goods if I knew. How could you possibly believe I'd be *mad* at you for what you did? If there's anyone to be mad at, it's Adam, not you. But did you give me enough credit to believe I'd act rational? No!"

I gasped, appalled in more ways than I could name. I had never even considered that Brian might have interpreted my silence that way. Unfortunately, he wasn't finished.

"Every time you've chosen not to tell me something, it's because you've believed that if you told me, I'd do the worst possible thing. I'd dump you, or fly into a jealous rage, or throw myself in front of a speeding truck. So you've never once trusted me to look out for your best interests, or to agree with your plans, or to act like an intelligent adult. I can't keep living like that."

Despite my best intentions, my eyes were starting

to sting. I blinked frantically, wishing I could tell him he was completely off base, and knowing I couldn't. Time and again, he'd proven that he was someone I could trust. And time and again, I'd failed to fully trust him. How could I blame him for not wanting to be with someone who always expected the worst of him? My throat ached so much I couldn't even talk.

There was no missing the pain in Brian's eyes. There was also no missing the implacability. "I still love you, and probably always will. I wish things could be different between us. But I'm tired of fighting the uphill battle, and I've had enough. I'm sorry."

He didn't wait for me to regain my voice, just turned from me and slipped out the door, closing it behind him. I wanted to run after him, maybe throw myself at his feet and beg. But I knew there was nothing I could say that would change his mind.

The tears came, and I plopped down onto the floor, my back against the bed, my knees drawn up to my chest, and sobbed my heart out.

Chapter **22**

Eventually, I managed to fight off the tears, though it wasn't easy when my heart ached so badly. Even after the flow of tears had stopped, I couldn't seem to find the willpower to get up off the floor.

After a few minutes, there was a soft tap on my door. I didn't feel like talking to anyone, so I didn't answer. I should have known better than to expect anyone in this house to respect my need for time to lick my wounds.

Barbie stuck her head in tentatively; then when she saw me in my little pocket of misery, she invited herself in.

"Why aren't you driving Brian home?" I asked.

Since she apparently didn't need an invitation to make herself right at home, she came to sit beside me on the floor. "He said he'd take a taxi. I'd told him about my role in getting the blood sample, so I'm not his favorite person right now."

I bit my lip, my own misery momentarily forgotten. "That was a bad idea. He's a bit of a...stickler." I'd thought of him as a Goody Two-shoes once, though he'd shown a little more moral flexibility than I'd expected. But I wouldn't put it past him to sic the police on Barbie.

A hint of worry flickered in her eyes, but she dismissed it with a shrug. "It's too late now." She pulled her legs up to her chest, mirroring my pose. "I guess things didn't go so well, huh?"

I laughed bitterly. "That's one way to describe it."

"But he knows all the evidence was phony, right?"

"He knows."

"Then what's the problem?"

I turned to give her a steely look. "That's not really any of your business."

She smiled, not at all intimidated by the obvious "back off" signals I was shooting her. "I'm congenitally nosy. It's part of the reason I became a PI. I can't help noticing your entire circle of friends is male, and it's my experience that even the best male friends are pretty much useless when a woman is having man trouble." She shrugged. "So, if you need someone to talk to..."

My first impulse was to laugh uproariously at the idea. I managed to swallow that impulse, because I was pretty sure she was being sincere. "Thanks, but my inability to talk is one of the reasons—" My voice choked off. I couldn't finish that sentence without a return of the tears.

"Okay, so talk is out. I noticed there was a convenience store about a block away. Is an inability to consume large quantities of ice cream one of your problems?"

This time, I did laugh, but that had been her intention. "A pint of Ben and Jerry's might go down pretty easily right now," I admitted, then sighed. "But I don't have time to wallow at the moment." The clock on the nightstand announced it was eight-thirty, and Raphael and I had planned to arrive at The Seven

Deadlies right around its nine o'clock opening time. We were already running late, thanks to me.

"Going somewhere?" Barbie asked, and the curiosity—or was it cunning?—was back in her eyes.

"Don't even think about following me." Maybe that hadn't been one of her plans, but she'd been on my tail often enough that I wouldn't put it past her. "You know that old saying about curiosity and the cat."

She grinned at me. "As enjoyable a pastime as it is, I only tail people when I'm being paid to do it. But let me give you some professional advice."

My whole body went on red alert. Barbie rolled her eyes.

"Relax, I don't mean anything ominous." She scooted back and regarded me with a critical eye. "The dye job helps, but the best way to avoid unwanted attention is to look inconspicuous."

I gave her a droll look. "I'm five-nine. I don't do inconspicuous well."

"If I promise not to follow you, will you tell me where you're going?"

"Why?"

"So I can decide the best way to make you look *relatively* inconspicuous. I'd pick a different look for, say, South Street, than for around here."

I'm sure my usual poker face made its appearance. "Why would you think I'd be going to South Street?"

She gave me a knowing look. "I told you once that I was good at my job. Well, part of my job is drawing conclusions based on the evidence at hand. The evidence says you have some kind of relationship with Adam White, though I have yet to make sense of what that relationship is."

You and me both, I thought.

"You also have a mysterious relationship with

Tommy Brewster, one that's close enough for you to hide out at his house. This after you'd been hired by Tommy's mother to exorcize him, which would generally create a hostile relationship, if any at all. So why would an exorcist spend so much time with demons? Especially one like Tommy, who any sensible person would suspect is an illegal despite whatever papers he may have signed? Perhaps that exorcist is a demon herself?"

I didn't answer her, too stunned by her conclusion to speak. That probably cemented her assumption, but I was pretty sure anything I said would only make it worse.

"I'm going to go out on a real limb here," Barbie continued, "and speculate that you used to be Jordan Maguire's demon. That somehow during the exorcism, Morgan made the mistake of touching Maguire, and you moved in."

I was painfully conscious of the way her eyes bored into me, studying my responses. I didn't know what she would make of my response to this particular theory.

I tried to imitate Brian's lawyer face. "If you think I'm Jordan Maguire's demon, why are you interested in helping me? I'm a violent rogue who has to be destroyed, remember?"

"And I say that's bullshit. Knowing that beating someone up is an automatic death sentence for a demon in this state, the only way you would have hit Jessica Miles is if you were completely out of control. And if you were out of control, she'd be dead."

I had no idea whether I should try to encourage Barbie to believe this theory of hers or not. So instead of talking about my supposed identity, I nudged the subject back to my original question.

"I still don't get why you'd think I was going to South Street tonight."

"Well, it's something of an open secret that The Seven Deadlies doesn't discriminate against illegal or rogue demons. It's a slightly less open secret that if you want information about the demon underworld, that's the place to get it. With Adam off your case because of the potential conflict of interest, and with the rest of the police force ignorant about the demon angle, if any good investigating is going to be done, you're the one who has to do it. Ergo, you're going to South Street."

Amazing how many facts she could have wrong and still come to the correct conclusion about my destination and purpose tonight. My mind was wheeling around frantically, trying to figure out what I should say. I finally decided that, being such a lousy liar, it wasn't worth the trouble to deny that I was going to The Seven Deadlies.

"I'll neither confirm nor deny any of the guesses you made tonight," I said, hoping I wasn't making a big mistake, "except for the one about The Seven Deadlies. That *is* where I'm going, and if you have any tips on how to make a five-foot-nine woman less conspicuous, bring them on."

There was no full-length mirror in Raphael's house, so I had to make do with the bathroom mirror to examine the end result of Barbie's makeover. She stood leaning against the doorjamb awaiting my verdict. All I could do was shake my head and give her a doubtful look.

"You call *this* inconspicuous?" I asked. My newly black hair was parted to one side—a neat trick, considering how short it was at the top—and plastered to my head with hair gel. And instead of my usual jeans and T-shirt, I was wearing a dark blue pinstriped pantsuit I'd borrowed, reluctantly, from Raphael. Tommy Brewster and I had remarkably similar builds, though we'd had to take in the waistband of the pants with safety pins. Beneath the suit jacket was a crisp white men's shirt, and a conservative striped silk tie. Barbie had even insisted I stuff my feet into Tommy's only pair of respectable dress shoes, which were at least a half size too small for me. I figured this had to have been Tommy's interview outfit, because every other piece of clothing he owned was faded, ragged, and ultracasual. Also, he was an inch taller than me, but the cuffs of his pants were just the right length. He obviously hadn't worn this suit in a while.

"Like you said, you aren't a great candidate for inconspicuous. So instead of really trying to disguise you, we go for a little misdirection."

My mouth was still hanging open. "You don't think a guy wearing a business suit on South Street at this time of night is going to attract attention?"

"Sure. But you don't really look like a guy even in that outfit. So people who look at you are going to be distracted wondering if you're a woman dressed as a man, or a man with effeminate features."

I frowned, looking down at my chest. "The boobs are sort of a dead giveaway, don't you think?"

She laughed. "You've been on South Street before. Have you never seen men with boobs there?"

She had a point, but I still wasn't happy with the idea of drawing eyes toward me. Barbie looked me up and down, tapping her chin. "Maybe we need to make a nice bulge in those pants, just to increase the gender confusion."

"Do you really think this is going to work?" I

asked skeptically. My mind kept conjuring images of cops converging on me with guns drawn.

"Yes. If people are preoccupied wondering if you're a boy or a girl, they won't be thinking to themselves, 'Gee, that woman looks familiar. Maybe she's that fugitive exorcist I'm supposed to be keeping my eye out for.'"

I can't say I was entirely convinced. However, I had to agree I was harder to recognize now than I had been when I'd been wearing my jeans. Besides, I would have Raphael with me for company. If I saw anyone in uniform, I could make sure to put him between me and them.

When Barbie was satisfied with my appearance, she presented her new work of art to Saul and Raphael, who pronounced me unrecognizable.

Because we were all a bit paranoid and disinclined to trust an outsider, we "suggested" that Barbie stay with Saul until Raphael and I returned from our mission. I'm quite sure Barbie understood just what kind of "suggestion" this was, but she didn't look offended. She didn't even object when Saul patted her down for weapons before we left, just to make sure she didn't pull the same trick on him as I had. She had a small gun in an ankle holster, but nothing else. Naturally, Saul confiscated it.

"Good luck," she said as Raphael and I headed to the door. It sounded like she really meant it.

"Thanks," I answered. "And sorry about, er . . ."

She waved the apology off. "No apologies needed. I wouldn't blame you if you left me handcuffed in the closet."

"Now there's a good idea," Raphael muttered, just loud enough for everyone to hear. He, of all of us, was the most concerned about Barbie and her motivations. He motioned Saul forward.

Looking wary and reluctant, Saul approached to within about three feet. Raphael grabbed his arm and pulled him in closer, lowering his voice to a level Saul and I could hear, but Barbie couldn't.

"I've seen the way you've been looking at her, son. Don't fall for the oldest trick in the book. Keep it zipped, at least until we're back."

Not surprisingly, Saul's eyes started to glow.

"Don't you guys start that crap again," I said impatiently. "Ra—" Damn. I really needed to break myself of the habit of calling Raphael by his real name. "Tommy, let go of Saul's arm. Saul, back off and pretend he didn't say a word."

I was pleasantly surprised when they both obeyed. I knew Barbie was now curious as hell, and I also knew she hadn't missed my almost-slip. I wanted to grab Saul and Raphael by the hair and knock their heads together, but I didn't suppose that would solve anything. Instead, I merely grabbed Raphael by the arm and hauled him out the front door before he could start any more trouble.

Chapter **23**

I was nervous enough about poking my head up aboveground—and about going another round with Shae—that I was able to keep myself from thinking about Brian and what my life would be like without him. The Morgan Kingsley solution to postbreakup blues: Do something that risks arrest and a possible life sentence, or even a gruesome death.

We got lucky with the parking situation and didn't have to walk more than half a block before we arrived at Shae's doorstep. I was conscious of the curious glances of various passersby, but I pretended not to be. If I'd had Barbie's confidence, perhaps I would have winked and flirted and given people a "Wouldn't you like to know" smirk. However, acting is a glorified form of lying, and, as we've already established, lying is not one of my strengths. I had to spend most of my concentration pretending not to be as nervous and generally twitchy as I felt.

The demon who had previously inhabited Tommy Brewster's body had been a big fan of The Seven Deadlies, having formed an agreement with Shae to provide him with good breeding stock as he tried to increase the genetic diversity in the lab-bred hosts. The good thing about this was that Tommy/Raphael was a card-carrying member, and was therefore able to bring me in as a guest with no fuss.

When we asked for Shae, we were told she was inside the club, keeping an eye on her domain. That translated into "If you want her, go find her, because I'm too lazy to page her." I would have made an issue out of it—I didn't want to set foot past the safe and tame lobby area—but Raphael slung an arm around my shoulders and directed me to the set of doors that led to the bar and dance floor. I elbowed him in the ribs, and he took the hint and let his arm drop back to his side.

As is typical of nightclubs, the music playing in the heart of The Seven Deadlies was loud enough to do permanent damage to my eardrums. I winced as soon as I stepped through the door and had to resist the urge to cover my ears with my hands. Tonight's theme seemed to be tuneless techno with a heavy enough bass to make the floor vibrate like an earthquake with each beat.

The place was also dark as a cave, giving people an illusion of privacy as they clustered at standing-room-only tables around the dance floor or sat at the bar.

The delay in putting together my disguise meant that we'd arrived considerably later than we'd planned, so the dance floor was already packed with dancers, many of whom had the impossibly good looks of your typical demon host. The only place I could think of that I'd want to be less than here was prison.

Raphael cut a path for us through the crowd toward the bar. It wasn't hard to spot our quarry. Shae probably couldn't manage looking inconspicuous even wearing Goodwill rejects and camouflage paint. However, she obviously had no objection to attracting attention, and she always managed to look drop-dead gorgeous even when wearing the most outrageous outfits.

To my chagrin, her outfit tonight was also a suit and tie. However, that was where the similarity ended. Her suit was of pristine white, the better to show off the night-black color of her skin. And there was plenty of skin showing—the jacket was a flaring, one-button number, and she wore nothing beneath it but the neon blue tie that dangled between her breasts. She had to be using some of that double-stick fashion tape to hold the lapels in place; otherwise she'd be flashing the crowd every time she made the slightest move.

Shae was engaged in a shouted conversation with the bartender when she caught sight of us plowing our way toward her. Her eyes darted quickly between Raphael and me, and I didn't think my disguise fooled her for even a fraction of a second. She said something to the bartender, then came to meet us halfway. The crowd parted for her automatically, even those with their backs to her stepping out of the way as if there were some force field that surrounded her.

"You two make a lovely couple," Shae said when she reached us, flashing us her sharklike smile. Her teeth were as dazzling white as her suit, whiter than teeth had any right to be, and I wondered if that was the effect of tooth whitener or if they were all caps.

As usual, she'd managed to get under my skin almost immediately. It was a unique skill of hers.

"Can we talk in private?" Raphael asked.

She gave us another of those cool, appraising looks, and though she was being coy, I was certain she'd want to talk to us. The last time I'd come to her for information, I'd been asking questions about Tommy Brewster, and she'd told me enough to help me figure out what his demon's mission was on the Mortal Plain. I'm sure she was surprised—and intrigued—to see us together. The plan was to dangle information about our alliance as bait in our attempt to get her to cough up anything she might know about a demon who was out to get me. Raphael, with his superior lying skills, would do most, if not all, of the talking.

"Sounds like fun," she agreed with another shark smile.

Shae took us through a key-carded door marked Employees Only and led us to her office, which was decorated almost entirely in black and silver. If the idea was to make visitors feel cold and unwelcome, the design was perfect. Shae looked perfectly at home there.

"I've missed seeing you at my club, Tommy," Shae said as she took a seat behind her desk. Her smile turned sly. "And I have a number of girls lined up who would meet your requirements perfectly."

I gritted my teeth to keep myself from saying anything scathing. I didn't think Shae was evil, precisely, but she certainly wasn't one of the good guys, and if she had any morals or cared about anyone, I'd yet to see evidence of it. A mercenary to her core.

"That won't be necessary," Raphael said. "I'm not Tommy's original demon."

My jaw dropped, and I turned to gape at him. This had *not* been part of the script. "What are you doing?" I hissed, my hands clutching the cold metal arms of my chair.

Raphael spared me a mocking look. "You know me. I don't have the patience for slow, tactful interrogations." Then he turned back to Shae, who was making a visible effort not to look as interested and eager as she obviously was. For a woman in the information business, this bombshell had to be insanely valuable.

"We're here looking for information about a demon who seems to hold a monumental grudge against Morgan."

I groaned and covered my eyes. This was the problem with carrying out any plan involving Raphael—he had a tendency to ignore the script altogether and do things his way. I tried to comfort myself with the knowledge that, as distasteful as his way often turned out to be, it usually worked.

Shae cocked her head, smiling politely. "And why would I be willing to share this information with you? If I have it."

"Because despite how much you enjoy watching the goings-on in Hell, you yourself are not overly fond of pain."

The smile vanished, and she sat forward, menace flashing in her eyes. "You *dare* to come to my club and *threaten* me?" I got the feeling this was an experience she most definitely was not used to.

Raphael laughed. "Indeed."

"Get out!" she ordered, jumping to her feet and pointing imperiously at the door.

"Oh, sit down," Raphael said with a wave of impatience. "You don't think I'd come in here with threats and not be prepared to back them up, do you?"

Her lips pulled away from her teeth in a snarl. "I don't know who you are, but—"

"Well, let me clear that up for you right now. My name is Raphael. Do you begin to understand?"

"What the hell?" I asked, once again looking at Raphael like he was crazy. His identity was *supposed* to be a state secret.

Shae's indignation had disappeared abruptly, replaced by wariness. "There are many demons named Raphael," she said cautiously.

This time it was Raphael's smile that was shark-like. "I'll give you three guesses just which Raphael I might be. The first two don't count."

The starch went out of Shae's spine, and she sagged back down to her chair. The whites of her eyes were startlingly bright in the dark of her face, and before she hid her hands under the desk, I could see that they were shaking.

Raphael turned to me, still smiling. "As you may know, I've established a certain...reputation for myself among my people."

Yeah, I'd noticed that. But I wasn't about to acknowledge that his reputation as a ruthless bastard might come in handy.

He turned his attention back to Shae, and she cringed. "Let me list all the ways you can earn yourself some quality time alone with me," he said. "You could mention my true identity to anyone, human or demon. I could find anyone, human or demon, tailing me or otherwise paying too much attention to me. Regardless of whether it was you who set them on me or not. My host could die—again, regardless of your responsibility in that death." He leaned forward in his chair, his eyes glinting. "Or you could fail to answer our questions with complete and total honesty."

Shae swallowed hard, and there was a sheen of

sweat on her face. I had never imagined I'd see the day when Shae was actually scared of someone.

"Do you need me to describe what I would do to you before I burned you to death, and how long it would take for me to do it all?" Raphael asked in a pleasant voice as he relaxed back into his chair. "Or are you content to let your imagination fill in the details?"

"What do you want to know?" she asked. Her voice was breathy and shaken, and I almost felt sorry for her.

"You've forgotten my question already?" he mocked with a cluck of his tongue.

She raised her chin. I think she was trying to look defiant, but it wasn't working. "I don't know of anyone in particular who bears that kind of a grudge against Morgan."

"That isn't the answer I was hoping for." Raphael's voice was a menacing purr that made the back of my neck prickle.

Shae swallowed hard. "I'm telling the truth," she said, and I, for one, believed her.

Raphael sighed in mock regret. "I'm disappointed in you, Shae. I was under the impression that you were at least moderately intelligent."

Scared as she obviously was, there was still a glint of anger in Shae's eyes. "I can't give you information that doesn't exist, and I'm not stupid enough to make up a bullshit answer. I know of no demon who has shown any particular interest in harming Morgan. That doesn't mean one doesn't exist, or even that one doesn't spend time in my club, just that whoever it is hasn't spoken about it."

I didn't think Raphael was going to accept Shae's word, and I wondered what I would do if he tried to follow through on his threat. I couldn't just stand aside and watch him torture her—I had no desire to see for myself why he had such a fearsome reputation—but I didn't see how I could stop him. I didn't even have my Taser with me, since we'd known I'd have to check it at the door if I brought it.

"I'm still not pleased with your answer," Raphael said warningly, "but I'll move on to the next question. Has anyone asked you to recommend someone who could falsify photographs convincingly—and discreetly?"

Shae looked almost relieved by the question. "Yeah. But this, uh, client never said anything about being after Morgan. He paid well, so I didn't ask any questions. Besides, it didn't seem like that big a deal."

Raphael snorted. "You know as well as I that if it weren't a big deal, he wouldn't have needed your help. Now tell me everything you know about this demon."

"Sure. He goes by the name Tim Simms, but that's his host's name. The demon's name is Abraham."

"What is it with you demons and the Biblical names?" I muttered under my breath.

Raphael looked at me and raised one eyebrow. "It's not that they're Biblical names, it's that they're *old* names. Most of us are far too old to have names like Tyler or Austin." He turned his attention back to Shae. "Go on. I'm fascinated."

"He hasn't been in for at least a month, but he used to be a regular. He was legal, and his host was tall, blond, and bland."

"While this information is interesting, it's not helpful."

Shae shrugged. "How can I know what's helpful? You haven't told me what you want, other than that you're looking for someone who has a grudge against

Morgan. As far as I know, this guy didn't even know who Morgan was, much less have a grudge..." Her voice trailed off, and her eyebrows drew together in puzzlement.

"You've remembered something important?" Raphael nudged when she didn't say anything.

She looked doubtful. "I don't know if it has any bearing on what you want."

"Let me be the judge of that."

"Okay. Abraham did have one hell of a grudge, but it wasn't against Morgan. The reason he wanted a reference for someone who could doctor the photo was that he planned to use it to get some demon friend of his declared rogue. I don't know how it was supposed to do that, and like I said, I didn't ask too many questions. He did seem really excited by whatever his plan was. I got the impression he'd been building up to this revenge for a long time. And I mean a long time for a demon, which is a lot longer than a long time for a human, if you know what I mean."

Raphael looked grim. "I do, indeed."

The look on his face told me he'd made something more out of this information than I had. How did Abraham's grudge against Maguire's demon translate into a beef with *me*?

"You've been very helpful," Raphael said with a cruel twist of his lips that might have been a smile. "If you should see Abraham again, or if you should hear anything about where he might be—or who his current host might be, since I suspect he's changed—you will let me know."

"Of course."

"And you'll remember all the things that could happen to earn you a date with me."

Shae actually shuddered, and she looked at her

desktop instead of at Raphael. "I'll remember. You'll have no trouble from me."

"No, I didn't think so," he murmured, then gestured for me to stand. "We'll see ourselves out."

Shae, still fascinated by her desk, merely nodded.

Chapter **24**

I let out a massive breath of relief when the door to The Seven Deadlies closed behind us. I really hated that place, and if there was any justice in life, I'd never have to set foot in it again. Of course, I hadn't seen a whole lot of evidence that justice abounded in the world. Call me cynical.

We drove back to Raphael's place in silence. If I were anywhere near my normal self, I'd have been pestering Raphael for theories the moment we got into the car. As it was, I just waited patiently for him to get around to explaining what was on his mind. If I pestered it out of him now, we'd have to repeat it all for Saul anyway.

I'm sure Raphael noticed my abstraction, but he didn't bug me about it, which was a nice change from hanging out with Adam or Brian. Not that I'd be hanging around with Brian anymore. I swear my heart stopped beating for a moment at that thought.

The tableau that greeted us when we entered Raphael's house was...unexpected. From the tension in Raphael's body, I knew he was concerned that somehow Barbie would have managed to betray us even with Saul to keep watch on her. He didn't relax one iota when he saw Saul and Barbie cozied up on the couch together.

They were sitting close enough to give a sense of intimacy, and each had a glass with some kind of amber-colored alcoholic beverage on the rocks. Barbie's body was angled toward Saul, and her smile was practically coquettish. Saul, on the other hand, wore the smile of a big bad wolf. A *hungry* big bad wolf.

They moved apart a little as Raphael and I joined them in the living room. Barbie stared down into her glass, a smile still playing around the corners of her mouth. Saul crossed his legs and—very subtle—rested his hand with the drink in it over his thighs. He and Raphael shared a hostile glare.

"I think it's time for you to leave now, Ms. Paget," Raphael said, his eyes still locked with Saul's.

Barbie's eyes widened, and she looked back and forth between Raphael and Saul. Once again, they were piquing her curiosity, which didn't seem like a good idea to me. However, short of duct-taping both their mouths shut, I wasn't sure what I could do about it.

"I'll walk you to the door," I said, giving Barbie a rueful smile. "I wouldn't want you to perish of testosterone poisoning."

Laughing, she put down her drink and touched her hand lightly to Saul's shoulder. I was impressed to see that that touch was enough to distract Saul from his staring contest.

"It was great to meet you, Saul," she said, a twinkle in her eye.

"The pleasure was all mine," he answered, then took her hand and raised it to his lips like some old-fashioned courtier.

They were both laying it on so thick I wanted to

gag. However, it might make life a lot easier for Dominic and Adam if Saul's attentions were fixed elsewhere, so I had no objection to their flirtation.

"Don't kill each other while my back is turned," I muttered to the guys as I fulfilled my promise and walked Barbie to the door.

"You sure you don't want me to stay where you and your friends could keep an eye on me?" she asked with a grin.

"Nice try," I said, rolling my eyes.

"So you're going to send me home without telling me how things went at The Seven Deadlies?"

"Looks like it," I agreed. I was already putting way more trust in her than was strictly wise, but I was hardly going to tell her all about my demon troubles.

We'd reached the front door, and I politely held it open for her. Of course, I wasn't lucky enough to have her slip out quietly without any parting words. She stopped in the doorway and looked up at me. The smile was gone, as was the sparkle in her eyes.

"Is he an illegal?" she asked quietly. There was no sense of menace or malice in her question, just honest curiosity.

My heart tried to jump up into my throat, though I attempted to make my face look confused. "Huh?"

Her lips twitched. I guess I hadn't hid my shock all that well. "It doesn't matter to me one way or the other," she said. "Even if I were in the position to go blabbing to the police about it, I wouldn't." Her face softened. "Whoever he is, whatever he's doing here, he's a really nice guy."

Oh, brother. "Nice" was not a word I could imagine associating with any of the demons I knew.

I didn't know what to say to her. I wanted to ask how she'd known that Saul was a demon—we certainly hadn't introduced him as such, and I doubted he'd told her. But I was sure she'd make more out of anything I said than I'd want her to. So I ignored the whole topic.

"Thanks for all your help tonight," I said instead.

"Anytime. And you have my number in case you change your mind about the ice cream binge. I'm pretty sure that convenience store is open 24/7."

"I'll keep that in mind." To my surprise, a lump formed in my throat. The image of pigging out on ice cream while pouring out my heartache with an understanding girlfriend was more attractive than I'd ever have imagined. I closed the door and returned to the living room before I said anything stupid.

Raphael and Saul were still glaring at each other, and I would have thought they'd sat there immobile and quiet as statues while I was gone, except that the heightened color in their cheeks suggested an escalation of hostilities. Once again, I had the temptation to bang their bricklike heads together.

"Knock it off, you two," I said.

Raphael was the first to break off the stare, sitting back in his chair and looking over his shoulder at me. "I was merely suggesting that you and Saul relocate to a more secure position, now that Barbie knows where you're hiding."

"And *I* was saying that just because *he's* a traitorous, backstabbing liar doesn't mean everyone is," Saul retorted. "And her name is Barbara."

Irritated as I was with the two of them, I had to swallow a laugh. So much for Saul's undying love for Dominic! It seemed Barbie had wrapped him around her finger in the span of only a couple of hours. Color me impressed.

"Saul and I are staying here," I declared, hoping that would end the argument. "If Barbie is going to screw us, it probably doesn't matter where we are."

And personally, I thought the only person she was interested in screwing was Saul. "Now," I continued without giving Raphael a chance to protest further, "let's talk about next steps."

I briefed Saul on what Raphael and I had learned when we talked to Shae, then turned to Raphael.

"I got the feeling you made more out of the information we learned than I did. Care to share your theory?"

I think he still really wanted to convince me and Saul that Barbie was going to stab us in the back, but he's not an idiot. He had to see that there was no way in hell we were budging. His lips pressed together in a tight line momentarily; then he gave up the fight.

"Let's see if you come to the same conclusion I have when I put all the related facts together in the right order. The story begins when Tim Simms goes to Shae and asks her to recommend someone who can discreetly falsify photographs that make it look like Jordan Maguire is cheating on Jessica. Shae helps him out, he gets the photos, he shows them to Jessica. He then whips Jessica into such a frenzy that in a jealous rage she helps him frame Jordan for hitting her.

"The state of Pennsylvania, with its ever-so-compassionate zero-tolerance policy, orders Jordan's exorcism. Morgan steps up to the plate and performs the exorcism, successfully sending Jordan's demon back to the Demon Realm.

"Then suddenly, she starts getting death threats, is sued for negligence, gets a gruesome package in the mail, and finally is framed for murder."

"You're forgetting the little part about Maguire dying," I said dryly.

"No, I'm not. I said I'd put all the *relevant* facts in order."

Naturally, I bristled. "I think the death of a human being is quite relevant!"

"In an abstract sense, yes, but not necessarily to this case."

"What the hell are you—" My voice choked off as suddenly the facts, as Raphael had recited them, kicked into place. Could it be that we'd had the motive all wrong from the very beginning? "Abraham isn't after me because Jordan Maguire died," I said, probably sounding as stunned as I felt. "He's after me because Jordan Maguire's demon *didn't* die."

Raphael nodded. "We all know you're an extraordinarily powerful exorcist, no doubt because of your unique genetic background." He hurried on before I could make an issue of his part in my "unique genetic background." "You can exorcize demons that ordinary exorcists couldn't handle." Here, he gestured at Saul. "So what if Maguire's demon wasn't just some garden-variety demon? What if he was one of the elite and powerful? The elite are less likely to walk the Mortal Plain than those of lower rank, but it does happen.

"Murder is virtually impossible in the Demon Realm unless there's a huge power imbalance. That's why Dougal had to get Lugh on the Mortal Plain to try to kill him."

Saul laughed bitterly. "You found an effective way to murder my mother."

Raphael didn't rise to the bait. "Delilah didn't have to keep pouring energy into you, so technically it wasn't murder. Besides, I don't think Dougal was going to convince Lugh to have his love child."

"You *dare* to make jokes about it?" Saul cried, and the glow was in his eyes once more. If this was the best he could do at controlling his temper, it was a wonder he hadn't killed someone and gotten himself exorcized within the first week he'd set foot on the Mortal Plain.

"Saul!" I snapped, knowing I had to seize control of this situation. "Raphael's an asshole, and we all know it. Just accept that reality and *deal with it* already!"

For a moment, Saul turned that glowing, furious gaze my way. I felt a strange stirring sensation in my brain, which I sensed was Lugh getting ready to take control if necessary.

Anyone with a modicum of good sense would have been intimidated by the anger of such a dangerous demon, but I found good sense highly overrated. My pulse didn't even ratchet up as I faced him down.

"You're no good to Lugh or to his council if you can't control yourself. Stop the temper tantrums, or I'll send you straight back to the Demon Realm, and not even Lugh will argue to keep you here." *Right?* I added as a mental aside to Lugh. He didn't answer, but I could see from the way that Saul flinched that my reprimand did not fall on deaf ears. He didn't apologize, but he hung his head in defeat and didn't say anything else.

As if he hadn't been interrupted, Raphael continued. "So my theory is that Abraham had some kind of terrible, long-standing grudge against Maguire's demon. He probably had to bide his time for a long while until they were both on the Mortal Plain at the same time, in proximity to each other, and in an execution state.

"His plan seems to work like a charm, and his long-awaited revenge is on the verge of success. He knows Maguire's demon is too powerful to be exorcized, and he's just orchestrated the perfect murder. There's no chance that he will pay the price for it, since no one in the Demon Realm can possibly know what he's done."

I found myself nodding along with the explanation. "And then I came along, and instead of the demon being burned to death in Maguire's body, I sent him back to the Demon Realm."

"Where you can bet he's informed the demon authorities of what Abraham tried to do. And if Abraham ever sets foot in the Demon Realm again, he will be imprisoned for all eternity, since our laws on murder are harsh. So not only did you foil his plan for revenge, you also condemned him to imprisonment—or permanent exile on the Mortal Plain."

I remembered Hillerman's almost manic giggle when he'd faced my confusion over his motive. When I'd thought he was only human, my assumption had been that he was a bit cracked. I don't know why I hadn't allowed for the idea that the demon might be a bit cracked himself.

I was pondering what good our newfound information about motive would do us when Raphael's phone rang. He glanced at the caller ID, then frowned.

"Adam," he informed us as he answered.

I joined him in frowning. Adam was supposedly staying as far away from this case as possible, and since he was at least slightly under suspicion—though it wasn't clear suspicion of what—it didn't seem like calling my hideout was the wisest move.

It didn't take more than about two seconds for me to see that this was an emergency. Raphael's face turned white, and his eyes widened. He dropped the phone and leapt to his feet, crossing the distance between us and grabbing me by the arm.

"Saul, stay here!" he ordered as he dragged me toward the door.

"What?" Saul and I chorused together.

"The police will be here any moment. You can't be seen aiding and abetting, so *stay here!*" The last was a full-fledged bellow.

Saul looked as confused as I felt, but at least for the moment, he didn't move. Raphael hauled me out the front door and slammed it behind him.

"What are you doing?" I gasped. His grip on my arm was so brutal my hand was falling asleep.

He didn't answer, but we hadn't gotten more than about twenty paces from the house before I understood. Three police cars were tearing down the street, sirens wailing. Raphael practically posed us under one of the streetlights, and before I could even blink, we were surrounded by shouting cops with guns.

If we'd stayed in that house even one or two more minutes, the cops would have stormed the place and found Saul as well.

"Still think Barbie's pure as the driven snow?" Raphael inquired, but I didn't get to answer, because I was being wrestled to the ground, even though I wasn't resisting. And moments later, Raphael collapsed to the pavement as the cops Tasered him.

Chapter **25**

Raphael and I were driven to the police station in separate vehicles, and once we got there, we were immediately separated. Luckily, it was Adam who took custody of Raphael. Since the police already knew he was possessed—Tommy was, after all, a legal, registered demon host—he would fall under the jurisdiction of Adam's department.

I, on the other hand, belonged to the regular human homicide squad, and they were eager to book me. However, it appeared my arrest warrant came with a court-ordered examination by an exorcist. Pretty much standard procedure when the police haul someone in. They'd examine me before the whole booking procedure so that they'd know ASAP if they needed to take any extra precautions.

I was handcuffed to the table in a holding room, being watched by guards armed with Tasers, when the exorcist came in. It was something like three in the morning by now, and she looked like she'd been rousted from bed, her eyes heavy and kind of dull. She also looked like she might have graduated from high school approximately yesterday, and she was so new on the scene that I'd never met her before. Of course, cream-of-the-crop exorcists don't get shitty jobs like examining auras at oh-dark-thirty.

Being a newbie, she went with the whole formal ritual, complete with a circle of protection and chanted mumbo jumbo. She wouldn't be able to see Lugh, because as long as I was in control, my aura overwhelmed his, so I wasn't overly worried. I was just tired and depressed and scared, and I wanted this whole ordeal to be over with.

But as the baby exorcist sat down on the floor in front of me with her eyes closed and her palms turned up, Lugh's voice spoke in my mind.

Trust me, he said.

Before I could ask him what I was supposed to trust him about, he gently but inexorably pushed my consciousness aside and took control of my body.

I couldn't give voice to the scream that wanted to erupt from my throat, nor could my pulse shoot up to red-alert speed, but that didn't stop me from mentally screaming in Lugh's ear.

What are you doing? You're going to get us both killed!

I'll explain later, he said, his mental voice annoyingly calm and collected while I spiraled down into panic. *Just trust me.*

The exorcist clearly wasn't expecting to find me possessed. I'm sure your normal illegal demon would be protesting wildly against the examination, trying to wiggle out of it, but I was just sitting there quietly, awaiting her verdict. When she saw Lugh's aura, her eyes practically bulged out of her head, and she scrambled frantically away, her shoes slipping and sliding on the cold tile floor.

She didn't officially pronounce a verdict, but the guards got the message loud and clear, and soon, my body was limp and listing severely sideways, held up only by the handcuffs that attached me to the table. Both guards had shot, so there were four Taser probes sticking out of me. Lugh didn't let me feel the pain of all that electricity running through my body, but that wasn't much of a comfort.

We were up shit's creek, and not only didn't we have a paddle, our boat was taking on water by the gallon. There wasn't an exorcist on the planet who was strong enough to exorcize Lugh. And if they couldn't exorcize him, we were going to burn.

Relax, Morgan, Lugh said, still absurdly calm. The guards were fitting him with a stun belt now, something that would allow them to control him even more easily than the Tasers.

You know how slowly the wheels of justice turn for humans. If we go into the human legal system, we could be in jail for months even if we're eventually found not guilty. And you know how much faster everything works for demons.

A pair of gloved and armored guards—every inch of skin covered so my demon couldn't transfer out of me via skin-to-skin contact—were now dragging us through the hallway toward the demon containment area. There was practically a squadron of them surrounding us, Tasers drawn, ready to react to the slightest movement, though there was no way Lugh could so much as twitch voluntarily for another eight minutes at least.

Yeah, I responded hysterically. *And that means we could be headed to the oven before twenty-four hours have passed!*

Lugh's mental voice was slow and patient, like he was explaining his plan to an idiot. Which maybe he was, but there's nothing like the fear of being burned alive to hamper one's mental processes.

No, we could be headed to an exorcism *before twenty-four hours have passed. And when the exorcist says "abracadabra," I'll transfer you back into control. It will look for all the world like I've been exorcized.* Even though I was only hearing his voice, not seeing his face, I could sense him grinning. *And since I'll confess to murdering Jack Hillerman and David Keller, you'll be a free woman once I've been "exorcized."*

Okay, even in the midst of my panic, I had to admit, that was a pretty clever plan. But panic isn't that easy to beat.

What if the exorcist isn't fooled?

Lugh laughed at me. *What other possible explanation could she have for what happens? One moment, she sees a demon aura, the next, it's gone. Obviously, her exorcism has succeeded.*

It was hard to argue his logic. It was also hard not to be terrified. But the die was well and truly cast, and we'd both better hope like hell his clever plan worked.

This was not the first night I'd ever spent in jail, nor was it the first night I'd spent in a demon containment cell. Containing a creature so strong it could probably juggle cars if they weren't so awkward to grip isn't what you'd call easy. The containment cells are barren white rooms, with vaultlike doors and steel-reinforced walls.

The stun belt was meant to assure my cooperation at all times, especially those times when someone had to open the cell door. I'd be ordered to the far side of the room, and if I didn't comply...zap! But this meant I had to keep the stun belt on, and the only way they could be sure it stayed on was to keep me under twenty-four-hour surveillance. The danger—and expense—of keeping a demon imprisoned was considerable. Do you begin to see why the wheels of justice turn at Daytona 500 speed where demons are concerned?

Lugh tried to give me back control as soon as we were safely locked away in our cell, but I was instantly hit with the delightful headache-and-nausea effect of repeated control changes, and Lugh took over once more.

Great idea, Lugh, I complained. *I needed yet another control shift to make me feel oh-so-much better the next time.*

It would be rather difficult to explain why a demon is puking all over her cell, he countered dryly. *Once I've been "exorcized," you can explain your illness by saying you probably have the flu, but since demons don't get sick...*

I understood his point, but I was not a happy camper. I wasn't sure my mental defenses would stay down long enough to let him be in control for hours on end, for one thing. Like I've said, I'm a control freak, and sitting around in the background of my own body was not at the top of my list of favorite things. It was going to take a massive effort of will for me not to try to fight my way back into the driver's seat.

And I didn't even want to know how sick I was going to feel when I was back in that proverbial driver's seat.

Since I was now officially a prisoner of the Special Forces department, I wasn't surprised to get a visit from Adam, who came to "question" me. He wasn't in on the plan, of course, and Lugh couldn't explain it to him straight out, seeing as we were being recorded on camera for posterity. (Actually, for the judge who would be pronouncing the verdict sometime later in the day. Convicting demons was of such prime importance that even the weekend wouldn't slow it down. There was rarely a doubt as to what the verdict would be in cases like this, anyway.)

Adam looked distinctly worried when he stepped into the cell. Lugh smiled at him.

"Some great demon cop *you* turned out to be." Lugh managed to get a level of mockery into my voice that I probably never could have attained myself. And, I realized, it was a good thing he was in control, because he was a lot better at acting and lying than me. "All the time you spent with me, and you never even noticed when Morgan went bye-bye."

Adam was keeping his distance, though he had the stun belt trigger in his hand and wouldn't need to be particularly cautious even if I had been a hostile demon. He's not exactly a pushover himself. His eyes were narrowed in concentration as he tried to figure out what Lugh was up to.

"And when was that, exactly?" he asked.

"During the exorcism she's been taking so much heat for, of course," Lugh responded, and I figured he'd gotten that idea from Barbie and her guesses.

Adam cocked his head to the side. "You mean she made the mistake of touching Jordan Maguire sometime before his demon—you, I gather—was exorcized?"

Lugh clapped like Adam had just performed a particularly impressive stunt. "Bravo! Give the man a gold star."

"So you're the one who killed Jack Hillerman and David Keller?" Adam asked, and though his change of expression was subtle, I could tell he'd caught on.

Lugh shrugged. "Hillerman was making my new

life…annoying. And Keller was trying to make it even worse. How did you find me, by the way?"

I doubted Adam would have answered that had Lugh been your average, everyday rogue demon, but I'm sure he knew how important that question was to both Lugh and myself. I could only think of two people who could have sent the cops our way: Barbie… and Brian.

I'd shown myself to be a lousy judge of character in the past, but I really hated the thought that I'd started to like Barbie and she might have betrayed me. Of course, I liked the idea of *Brian* doing it even less. And though he was angry with me and was usually a stickler for the letter of the law, I just couldn't see him siccing the cops on me. Even *my* trust issues weren't *that* bad.

"We got an anonymous call from The Seven Deadlies last night," Adam said. "Your friend Tommy Brewster is a regular, so when the report came in that you were seen together, the police came to the natural conclusion that you might be hiding out at Tommy's house."

If I'd been in charge of my body, I'd have heaved a sigh of relief. I hadn't been betrayed after all. I'd merely been recognized. Somewhat surprising, since I hadn't seen a single police officer during Raphael's and my foray. And it was downright odd that someone other than a cop would not only recognize me in disguise and in the dark of the club, but know I was a wanted criminal. The only person I'd seen at the club who actually knew me was Shae, and she'd have to be certifiably insane to risk Raphael's wrath.

There might have been someone else there who recognized you, Lugh suggested. *Someone who's taken a particular interest in your life.*

I cursed—not literally, of course, since my mouth

wasn't my own at the moment. Despite the threats we'd considered, we hadn't taken into account that my good buddy Abraham might be hanging out at The Seven Deadlies in his new body. I hoped like hell he made the mistake of confiding something to Shae while he was there so we could get a bead on whom he'd possessed now.

Lugh twisted my lips into an unpleasant smile. "I *do* hope my dear friend doesn't get into any trouble over this little . . . misunderstanding."

Adam shrugged. "He'll be charged with harboring a fugitive, but it's hard to prove he *knew* you were a fugitive."

And either way, harboring a fugitive was not a violent crime, so there was no danger of Raphael being executed. Which I supposed was a good thing, though I wasn't sure I'd shed a tear if he finally got his just deserts.

"Do you have anything you'd like to say in your own defense?" Adam asked.

Lugh made his laugh sound bitter. "Would it matter?"

The answer, of course, was no, but Adam dutifully spouted the party line about justice being served, yada, yada, yada. He left shortly afterward, but it didn't take more than maybe four hours for the verdict and the sentence to be read. Lugh was declared both an illegal, for possessing me against my will, and a rogue, for the murders of Jack Hillerman and David Keller.

It was another four hours before the court-appointed exorcist arrived. Those were possibly the longest four hours of my life. Despite Lugh's calm assertions that we were in absolutely no danger, and despite my confidence in both his judgment and his logic, it was impossible not to be scared. Not when

the consequences of failure included being incinerated alive in a cremation oven. Of course, if it somehow came to that, they'd anesthetize me first, and
Lugh would block out the pain anyway, but that
didn't take away the primal terror.

Add to that the necessity to leave Lugh in control
of my body, and I thought I might go quietly insane
before this was all over. Lugh did his best to comfort
me, and he tried to give me the illusion that I was under control after all. When I longed to stand up, he
did it. When I felt the need to pace to work off my
nerves, he did that, too. But it wasn't the same, and
we both knew it.

Frightened as I was, it was still a relief when the
exorcist made an appearance. I didn't get the baby exorcist who'd examined me last night, but Ed Rose, a
competent but unspectacular exorcist. He was also
experienced enough to have dispensed with some of
the formalities, so the whole affair didn't take more
than about fifteen minutes.

But maybe it was those fifteen minutes that were
the longest stretch of time in my life, rather than the
previous four hours.

What if Ed wasn't fooled? What if we got the tim-
ing off, and Lugh disappeared from his radar before
he'd even made an effort to exorcize him? What if my
need to be in control suddenly kicked in and I reflexively tossed Lugh out before the ritual even began?
What if Lugh had been in control for too long and
somehow I couldn't get back?

If I'd had control of my stomach, I'd have been
puking with anxiety, never mind the dreaded after-
effects I was about to endure. At least, I *hoped* I was
about to endure, because the alternative was unthinkable.

But despite all the horrors my mind could conjure,

Lugh's ruse worked almost perfectly. I say "almost," because Ed looked slightly puzzled when it was all over, like something about that ritual hadn't been quite right. But whatever it was, Ed shrugged it off. Which was the last thing I noticed before I started vomiting my guts out.

Chapter 26

"**Someone please** kill me now," I moaned as pain hammered at my skull and nausea roiled in my stomach.

I was lying on my very own bed, finally able to return home now that Lugh had been convicted and supposedly punished for my crimes. It wasn't much of a comfort, not the way I felt. Saul, who was playing nursemaid, laid an ice pack on my forehead. It didn't really help, but I couldn't stand just lying there, suffering without trying to make it go away.

"You'll feel better soon," Saul assured me, but he was wrong. The last time I'd gotten this sick, it had lasted a solid three days, though admittedly the intensity had eased over time.

The doorbell rang, sending a spike of agony through my head. For a moment, I thought I'd black out, but no such luck.

"Sorry," Saul murmured, then sprinted out of the room.

I threw the useless ice pack aside, then pulled my pillow out from under me and hugged it to my face, hoping blocking out the light would make the pain go away. The pillow muffled my hearing, but not so much that I couldn't hear Saul greeting Barbie at the door. When he'd invited her to come over—against my wishes, though I was too sick to put up much of an argument—he'd considerately let the front desk know in advance and asked them not to call up to the apartment. I wished he'd told her not to ring the bell, though how he would have known she'd arrived, I don't know.

My nose told me she'd brought dinner, which made my very empty stomach heave again. I couldn't even keep down a couple sips of water, and if I didn't get the vomiting under control, I was going to end up in the hospital so I could get IV fluids. And wouldn't it just be great fun to have the doctors there trying to figure out what was wrong with me? I'd be poked, prodded, and probed for the duration of my stay, and it would all be for nothing.

"Saul!" I yelled, as loudly as I dared. I didn't think my voice carried at all, but the sound still made my head pound.

"Did you call?" Saul asked a few moments later.

"Yeah. Can you please close the door? The smell of food is not doing good things for me."

"Oh. Sorry. Sure."

The door closed, and I was left by myself, fighting the pain, wishing I could fast forward my life. Through the closed door, I heard the soft murmur of Saul's and Barbie's voices, punctuated by the occasional laugh. They were getting along famously. I tried to be glad about that, although I thought it was risky for any of us to hang out with her for any extended period of time. She was just too perceptive, and I feared she would begin poking holes in our story in no time. Hell, considering how she had Saul thinking with his little head instead of his big one, he was probably spewing all our secrets right now. I was in no shape to stop him if he was.

The voices eventually died down, but I knew Barbie was still here. I had a good guess why she and Saul were suddenly being so quiet, and soon, the occasional barely suppressed gasp from the bedroom next door confirmed my guess. At least they were considerate enough not to make a racket.

I think I drifted off for a while, though the pain still reverberated through my head while I was sleeping. The next time I was sure I was conscious, I heard Barbie's voice tentatively calling my name.

"Morgan? Are you awake?"

Maybe I should have just pretended to be asleep, but I decided I'd prefer to have something else, *anything* else to think about than how lousy I felt.

"More or less," I answered, though I'm sure it was hard to understand from beneath the pillow I still held to my face.

I heard her cross the room, then felt the side of my bed dip as she sat.

"I won't bother asking you how you feel," she said, "but is there anything I can get you?"

"A gun so I can put myself out of my misery?"

She laughed weakly. "I really should insist you go to the hospital."

I pulled the pillow off my face and opened my eyes a crack. The light didn't really make my head hurt any worse—it just seemed like it should, so I was cautious with it.

"Not a chance in hell."

One corner of her mouth lifted in a smile. "I didn't think so. But it was worth trying."

Although I was pretty sure she and Saul had been doing the horizontal bop next door, she looked as perfectly put together as always. She was disgustingly pretty, and I reminded myself I didn't like girly-girl cheerleader types.

"Is there something you want?" I asked in my surliest tone of voice.

She was still smiling that half-smile. "Just hoping I could divine the real truth by looking at you."

I groaned. You'd think after we'd confirmed all her suspicions about me and my supposed possession by Jordan Maguire's demon that she'd be satisfied and stop asking questions. Well, no, you wouldn't really think that, not unless you're an idiot.

"Don't do this to me," I pleaded, too sick to pretend. "Not now when I'm practically defenseless."

She shook her head. "I doubt you've been defenseless a day in your life. I'm just telling you that all the pieces of your story don't add up. Remember, we'd already determined that you weren't stupid enough to shoot Hillerman when you were the prime suspect."

"*I'm* not. The demon was."

She snorted. "Right. I just want you to know that I'll help you if you let me. Whatever's going on with you, it's a lot weirder than the pat little explanation I came up with last night."

Geez, had that only been last night? Amazing how time doesn't fly when you're not having fun.

"But I won't bug you with it now," she said. "I just wanted to say to you what I said to the demon: If you ever want to level with me, just give me a call."

"Thanks," I mumbled, then pulled the pillow back over my face in a subtle bid to end the conversation.

Barbie sighed quietly before she left, but she refrained from asking any more questions.

For the next three days, I basically sat on the sidelines of my life. I rarely left my bed, getting up only to go to the bathroom. By the end of the first day, the nausea had eased enough that I could drink small quantities of water without tossing it back up, but clear fluids were the only things I could even get past my lips. My head pounded mercilessly, and I was even grouchier than usual. In retrospect, I feel kind of sorry for Saul, who tried his best to be helpful but probably wished he hadn't.

Dominic stopped by to see me once, letting me know he'd brought some homemade chicken soup for when I was up to eating. It was great incentive to get better soon. Barbie stopped by at least twice, but mostly to see Saul, not me. Adam came to check on me a couple of times, though his visits were brief. Raphael, perhaps being a smart-ass, or perhaps actually meaning to be nice, sent me flowers. There was no word from Brian, of course, though I had hoped he still cared about me enough to send flowers, or at least a card. Andy didn't visit either, which hurt almost as much.

By the end of day three, I was beginning to feel a tiny bit better—meaning I no longer daydreamed about blowing my brains out. That was when Andy finally paid me a visit—with Raphael practically nipping at his heels.

I didn't know what to make of Andy and his former demon showing up together, and I was even more confused when Raphael shoved Andy into the room and then stood blocking the doorway.

I propped myself into a sitting position as Andy approached, his head down, his hands jammed into his pockets. Because of the headache, I was still keeping the room pretty dark, so at first I didn't see the bruises. When I did, I gasped.

"What happened?" I asked. One of his eyes was

blackened, and bruises bloomed all around his throat, like someone had choked him.

He opened his mouth a couple of times, but rejected whatever he'd been thinking of saying. Even in the darkness, I could see Raphael rolling his eyes.

"Oh, for Christ's sake, Andrew!" he barked. "Grow a fucking backbone."

Something sparked in Andy's eyes, a glimmer of anger that made him look more alive than he had in a while. He withdrew his hands from his pockets and clenched them into fists. I couldn't help noticing the knuckles of his right hand were bruised.

"You've been in a fight?" I prompted when he still didn't say anything.

"Not exactly," he answered, and I could tell he was struggling to find words.

"How about if I get the story started for you," Raphael said, speaking slowly so he could get the maximum level of condescension into his voice. "I stopped by your apartment to encourage you to get off your ass and visit your sister..."

I couldn't tell for sure, but it looked like Andy was grinding his teeth. By now, I was, too. I was on the verge of telling them both to get the hell out when Andy finally started talking.

"I'm sorry I didn't visit earlier. I just thought being around me would do you more harm than good."

"Bullshit," Raphael interrupted. "You were just too busy moping to make the effort."

Andy whirled on him. "Did you bring me here so *I* could talk, or so *you* could? Because if you're doing the talking, I don't need to be here."

"Oh, by all means, talk away." Raphael made an expansive hand gesture.

Andy turned back to me, though his eyes didn't quite meet mine. "I'm sorry for ... the way I've been lately. Raphael tells me I've been feeling sorry for myself and need to pull myself up by the bootstraps. I promise I'll try."

My throat tightened, and I reached out to give Andy's hand a squeeze. I was still pretty much mystified by what was going on, but that was the most words I'd heard him string together since Raphael had moved out of him, and that had to be a good sign.

He squeezed my hand back and forced something that vaguely resembled a smile. I wanted to tell him I loved him, but we'd never been real sentimental with each other, and I thought it would come out sounding artificial.

"I'll leave you to get some rest now," he continued. "But I promise I'll come back, and not just for council meetings."

The lump in my throat ached too much for me to talk, so I just nodded and gave him my most encouraging smile. By the time I thought I could speak without bawling, Andy had pushed his way past Raphael and was probably halfway to the front door. Raphael held up one finger in a gesture I took to mean "I'll be right back," and hurried after Andy. I realized I still had no clue what had happened.

Andy and Raphael shared some angry, hostile words—though I couldn't make out exactly what they were saying. Then the front door slammed. My aching head loved that.

Raphael, shaking his head, was back in my room moments later. I figured my raised eyebrows were enough to convey my slew of questions.

"Everyone's treating Andrew with kid gloves," he said. "I prefer the brass knuckles approach. I went to his apartment to drag him over here for a visit. He had a few objections."

I narrowed my eyes at him. "Is that how he got the bruises?"

Raphael nodded, and there was a hint of a feral grin on his lips. "I pissed him off so much the moron took a swing at me. I think he hurt his hand more than he hurt my face."

"And he got the shiner when he tried to head-butt you?" I growled as I glared at Raphael, hating the thought that he'd hurt my brother yet again.

Raphael shrugged. "So I hit him back. He had it coming."

I swallowed the next words that wanted to come out of my mouth, because really, what was the point with Raphael? "What about the bruises around his neck?"

"I told him if he was really ready to check out on life, I'd be happy to put him out of his misery. Funny how being unable to breathe can make someone decide life is worth living."

I could do nothing but gape at him.

"It's not going to fix what's wrong with him," Raphael continued, "but at least I proved to him that he does, indeed, want to live." He grinned savagely, and my headache spiked. "Just think of it as the demon equivalent of tough love."

Someday, I was going to have to let Lugh take control so we could beat the crap out of Raphael. It might almost be worth the pain and nausea that followed.

"Just get out," I said, sinking back down into my bed, hoping to escape into sleep. "I can't deal with you right now."

"You're welcome," he said with a laugh, slipping out the door before I had a chance to respond.

*   *   *

When I woke up on day four of my misery, I felt a little stronger. I was bold enough to try sipping some orange juice, and I even dragged myself out of bed for a while. My head still pounded, and my whole body was weak, no doubt in part because I hadn't eaten anything in days. When the orange juice stayed down, Saul made me some dry toast. My body was starved enough for nourishment that it actually tasted good.

By lunchtime, I was eager to try a real meal, but Saul turned bossy on me and would only let me have broth with Saltines on the side. On the plus side, Dominic had made the broth, so it was rich and flavorful.

"So," I said as I sat at the dining room table with Saul and spooned up some broth, "there was a lot of coming and going while I was, um, convalescing."

Saul gave me a look that would have done Nurse Ratched proud. "Oh, is that what you call it?"

I'm sure I was a lousy patient, and if I'd been in Saul's shoes I'd have been tempted to smother me with the pillow I'd continually clutched. Of course, I hadn't *asked* Saul to play nursemaid.

I decided my best course was to move on without a retort. "Is there any news I need to know?"

"Not a whole lot that's new. The charges against Raphael were dropped, surprise, surprise. He questioned Shae as soon as he got out, but she claims not to have heard anything from our friend, and he believes her. And your lawyer's called every day, hoping you'd be well enough to speak to him."

I frowned. I gathered he meant the attorney Brian had hired for me for the lawsuit, not the criminal attorney I'd had on call.

"If he were calling with good news—like, say, Maguire dropped the lawsuit—I presume he would have left a message," I mused. Damn it, even though I was now cleared of the murder charges, this whole mess wasn't over.

"Yeah," Saul agreed, "I didn't get the feeling he was trying to reach you to celebrate."

"Fabulous." I'd really hoped that with Hillerman dead, Maguire would lose interest in the witch hunt.

"But perhaps not completely unexpected."

I raised an eyebrow. "Oh?"

"Abraham's big scheme to get you convicted of murder has failed spectacularly. Based on what he's done so far, does he seem like the type to just say 'Oh, well' and give up?"

"No," I had to agree. "So he falls back on the original plan until he can think up something even more awful."

"That may not be such a bad thing," Saul said. "It's highly unlikely that he knows everything we've figured out about him, so he's probably not being overly cautious. If he's keeping the lawsuit alive, then that means his host is probably someone close to Jordan Maguire Sr."

"Unless Maguire just decided to continue the case on his own without anyone needing to nudge him." But Laura Maguire had sounded awfully sure that Hillerman was the impetus behind the lawsuit.

"That's possible, I suppose. But it wouldn't hurt to see if we can find out where the burning need to sue is coming from now. Maybe if we do that, we'll find Abraham."

"Okay," I agreed. "I'll give Laura a call. She might be willing to let me know if there's someone other than her father pushing the case." I frowned. "Of course, even if it is Maguire, Abraham could have chosen *him* as his next host."

Saul seemed to roll that one around in his head for a moment. "I think that's unlikely. We've already seen how careless he is with his hosts. If he takes Maguire then ends up forced to abandon him for one reason or another, the case will die. I'm sure he'd rather be on the periphery, where he can afford to move from host to host with ease."

And wasn't that just a cheerful thought? I was really looking forward to consigning the bastard to an eternity of imprisonment in the Demon Realm.

"So," I said, trying to sound casual, "Barbie seems to be coming over a lot." I glanced at Saul from under my lashes as I took a sip of soup.

His lips curled into a half smile. "Yeah," he said, and his voice was dreamy.

"Did you warn her you're on the rebound?"

The smile dimmed, and he didn't answer.

"Sorry," I mumbled, then shoved a cracker into my mouth to keep it occupied.

"I really like her," Saul said quietly.

"I can tell. But speaking as someone who's learned it the hard way, it's hard to keep a relationship going for very long without honesty, and you can never be even close to honest with her."

I'm not sure if I was trying to protect Barbie or Saul. Maybe both. It seemed to me someone was bound to get hurt.

"Maybe a little honesty wouldn't be a bad idea."

Yeah, she had him wrapped around her little finger all right. "Remember, she started out working for the bad guys. It would be stupid to trust her."

"I guess I'm stupid, then."

"Saul—"

"I haven't told her any state secrets," he interrupted. "I'm not going to jeopardize Lugh for a woman I've known for only a handful of days. But my gut tells me she's trustworthy."

I raised my eyebrows. "Are you sure that's your *gut* talking?"

He gave me a dirty look. "Do you realize that when Hillerman died, her paycheck died with him? He was paying her in installments, and she only ever got the down payment. She'll probably get the rest he owed her eventually, but not until the estate gets around to settling his debts, which could take months."

"And this is relevant why?"

"Because she's spending practically all her time doing this pro bono work for you and Adam, which means she doesn't have time for her paying clients. I'd say that's a good indicator that she's dedicated to the cause."

I shrugged. "And *I'd* say it's a good indicator Adam is still threatening her with jail time if she doesn't cooperate."

Saul made an unpleasant growling sound in the back of his throat. He sneered, an expression I'd never seen on his face before. "You sound just like Raphael."

I knew he meant that to be a dire insult, but it fell short of the mark. "Every once in a while, he says something I agree with. This is one of those times. Have your little fling if you must, but keep your mouth shut."

He bristled. "I don't take orders from you, and I certainly don't need your permission to see Barbara."

"But you do take orders from Lugh, don't you?"

His hands were clenched into fists, and his face was dark with anger. "So is Lugh forbidding me to see her?"

"What about it, Lugh?" I asked, and Saul and I both fell silent as we waited for his answer.

I heard Lugh's sigh in my head. *I think it best for*

everyone if he refrains from romantic entanglements for the time being. He sounded regretful, but firm.

I made a sympathetic face at Saul. "Sorry, but he agrees with me."

Saul pushed away from the table. "I don't believe you. You're just saying that because you know I can't check with Lugh directly."

Unfortunately, I had no way to refute his claim. I didn't dare let Lugh into control for even a moment. Just the *thought* made me shudder and made my still-aching head throb harder.

"You're well enough to take care of your own damn self now," he said. "Adam said he should have my new identity all squared away in a couple of days, so I'm going to go apartment hunting. See you later."

He was still mad as hell—though possibly more because he knew he was in the wrong than anything else—but I doubted anything I said to him would make him feel any better. So I bit my tongue as Saul slammed the door behind him on his way out.

Some bodyguard he turned out to be, I thought at Lugh, but he didn't answer.

Chapter 27

After Saul left, I sat on the couch, meaning to call Laura. My head was a little woozy, so I decided I'd better do it lying down. I closed my eyes, intending to gather my strength for the ordeal of dialing.

When I woke up, I don't know how much later, I wasn't alone in the apartment anymore. Saul had returned with Adam and Dominic in tow. The three of them were talking quietly in the kitchen, huddled together. Trying not to wake me, I guess.

My head felt significantly better, so I tried slowly pushing myself up into a sitting position. I didn't puke or pass out. It was almost enough to make me do a little happy dance. My stomach growled noisily, attracting the guys' attention. Adam and Dom hurried to the living room to see how I was doing, while Saul, apparently still sulking, hung back.

"Feeling better, love?" Adam asked. I might almost have thought he cared about me, except he followed up with, "You look like death that still needs more warming over."

Dom punched him in the arm. "Be nice."

Adam made an innocent "Who, me?" face. Instead of being irritated, I actually laughed. The easygoing affection between Adam and Dom always brought a smile to my face, though my smile wilted when I remembered the state of my own love life. I wasn't ready to give up on Brian yet—even if he was ready to give up on me—but I didn't have the mental energy to figure out how to solve that problem in the midst of all the others.

"Saul tells me you've had broth and crackers," Dom said. "Do you think you're up to some more solid food?"

My stomach howled its opinion.

"I'll take that as a yes," Dom said, then headed for the kitchen. "I'll heat up some of that soup I brought for you."

"Thanks," I called after him.

Adam remained in the living room, slouching on the love seat nearby. "I talked to Laura Maguire about an hour ago," he said.

"Oh." So much for my hopes of making myself useful. "Did you find out anything that might be of interest?"

"Maybe. She wasn't sure, but she thought Jessica Miles was starting to bug Maguire about the lawsuit. Something about how he shouldn't abandon the suit, for his granddaughter's sake."

I remembered that Jordan Junior and Jessica had had a child together. Somehow, I'd forgotten all about that. "So you think Abraham has taken Jessica for his host?"

Adam shrugged. "I don't know. Maybe. But based on her history, she's not exactly an angel. She could just be pushing it because she somehow thinks she'll get money out of it."

"Well, it's the best possibility we have, isn't it?"

He huffed out a sigh. "I suppose."

"So when I get a little better, Raphael and I will try to get our hands on Jessica and hope it goes better than when we went after David Keller."

Adam didn't look happy. "What if we're wrong? What if Jessica's just a bitch and Abraham is lurking somewhere else? You can't exorcize a person who's not possessed, and if you've kidnapped her..."

Why was nothing ever easy? "Do you have any better ideas?"

"I'm planning to go have a chat with her later today. Maybe she'll let something slip that will make me positive Abraham's in there."

I frowned. "You can see auras, can't you? More easily than an exorcist, I mean?" He'd examined my aura once in the early days, when I was first discovering that I was possessed.

"Yeah, but I need skin-to-skin contact and maybe thirty seconds or so of quiet concentration. I doubt Jessica would allow that even if she's *not* possessed. But I'll see what I can do."

"And you'll let me know."

"Of course."

The soup was ready now, and Dominic brought it to me on a tray he must have brought with him. I certainly didn't own such a thing. He saw the suspicious look on my face and smiled.

"Consider it a get-well gift. I expect you to eat most of your meals in bed until you've fully regained your strength."

It felt surprisingly good to be taken care of like this. It was an entirely unfamiliar situation, mainly because I usually pushed people away if they tried to pamper me. Hell, I just push people away, period. But just this once, I allowed myself to revel in it. Even Saul's undisguised sulking and Adam's brooding didn't spoil the mood for me. And when all three of the guys left me so I could get some more sleep, I felt strangely bereft.

I dozed on and off for maybe an hour or two. My head no longer hurt at all, though my mind still felt slow and clouded. My stomach seemed to have recovered fully, growling at me to get more food into my system. I dragged myself to my feet and shambled toward the kitchen, hoping there was more of Dominic's chicken soup awaiting me in the fridge. And that was when I noticed the envelope, peeking out from under my door.

Every once in a while, I get a premonition that my life is about to take a turn for the worse. I was getting one of those right now. Unfortunately, my premonitions are usually frighteningly accurate.

My appetite vanished as I stared at that envelope. Nothing good ever seemed to come from mysterious envelopes, and I wondered if the universe would mind if I just pretended it didn't exist.

The envelope was unmarked and unsealed, and inside was a single sheet of white copy paper with a typewritten note. It wasn't hard to guess who had written it.

The note began with a long list of names, all of which were familiar to me: Adam; Dominic; Diane Kingsley, my mother; Raymond and Edna Griffith, my mom's parents, who lived in Florida; Andy; Tommy Brewster; Saul; Barbara Paget; Blair Paget; Carl, the overly friendly clerk at the front desk. Even my lawyer, Brandon Cook, and Laura Maguire, whom I barely knew, were on the list.

The rest of the note was brief and to the point. Abraham "requested the pleasure of my presence" at an abandoned building on the Schuylkill River tonight at midnight for some "fun and games." Failure to show up—alone, of course—would result in the death of one of the people on the list, and a repetition of the invitation until I accepted, or all the people on the list were dead.

My appetite completely forgotten, I trudged back to the couch and closed my eyes. Maybe if I went back to sleep and woke up again, I'd find that the note was just a dream. I sighed. If only!

It seemed that finding my good friend Abraham wasn't going to be much of a problem after all. It was one of those "Be careful what you wish for" deals.

"I have to go," I said, speaking as much to Lugh as to myself. I expected him to argue, to command me to summon the cavalry. Instead, he stayed silent so long I thought I'd somehow miraculously managed to resurrect the mental barriers that had once upon a time existed between me and him. But of course, that wasn't the case.

I agree, Lugh said, right when I'd decided I wasn't going to hear his voice after all. I was actually startled enough to jump.

"You *what?*" I asked, thinking maybe I was starting to hallucinate.

I agree that you have to go. Abraham has already proven how little he minds killing people. I think his threat is genuine.

"So do I, but I still didn't expect you to agree with me that I have to meet him." Lugh was anything but a coward; however, he was very much aware of how crucial his survival was to the human race. If I died, and Lugh returned to the Demon Realm, Dougal's followers would summon him into a sacrificial host who would instantly be burned at the stake. No more Lugh, no more opposition to Dougal's plans.

Even if I were willing to let so many people die in

order to protect myself, the fact remains that every member of my council, including my brother and my nephew, is on that list. I am as useless on the Mortal Plain without allies as I would be dead. We have to accept Abraham's challenge. We have to go.

I'd never expected to have to cast myself as the voice of moderation, but since Lugh didn't seem to be taking on the role, I was the only other choice.

"I can't just show up at some derelict building at midnight with no backup," I said. "That would be like hanging a raw steak around my neck and strolling through the lion exhibit at the zoo."

Abraham thinks you're only human. We can use that to our advantage.

"Yeah, great idea. Have you been with me these last three days? You feel everything I feel, right? Do you want another three days of that? Or worse?"

Of course not. His voice took on a dry tone in my mind. *Never before you became my host had I experienced any human illness. Reading it in someone's memory isn't quite the same as experiencing it myself. I could do without it. However, I think in this case, we'll just have to risk it.*

"Okay, so we turn Abraham's ambush against him. You take control, surprise the shit out of him, and hope you can take him down without killing his host. Then we exorcize him and send him back to the Demon Realm and he knows I'm possessed. We've been trying to avoid that, remember?"

If he were after you because he was part of Dougal's conspiracy, then I'd be worried. But he's not politically motivated. He's just after revenge. If he finds out you're possessed, he won't know there's any special significance to it. He might think you've got spectacularly bad luck...

"He'd be right," I muttered.

...but I seriously doubt that the general population of demons has any idea that Dougal's making a try for the throne. As far as they know, I'm doing a stint on the Mortal Plain, and my brother is filling in for me while I'm gone. Only his inner circle and mine know he intends to make sure I never return. And trust me when I say that there's no chance Abraham is part of Dougal's inner circle. A demon that unstable—and that single-mindedly bent on revenge— would be of no use to my brother.

"So you're telling me your people don't even know there's a war on?"

Right. Because there is no war, at least not yet. A conspiracy, yes. An attempted coup, yes. But not a war. The power of the demon throne travels from a king to his successor, and there is no way to usurp it. Dougal can't get his hands on the power unless I die or abdicate, so open warfare would be meaningless.

Even in the worst-case scenario, if Abraham somehow knows there's been an attempt to seize the throne, and that you were once my host, and that you're not supposed to be hosting me anymore, when he returns to the Demon Realm, it will be as a criminal, a killer. Imagine what would happen if a convicted murderer in the U.S. started blathering to the authorities that there was a conspiracy to overthrow the President and he knew where the leader of the conspiracy was hiding. Who would listen to him?

I felt a little better about the plan now, but I still wasn't exactly liking it. "Okay, so we probably won't blow your cover if we succeed. But what if I show up at the warehouse and Abraham just shoots me in the head from a distance? You're tough, but you can't survive a bullet wound to the head."

He's not going to kill you, Lugh said with a certainty that surprised me.

"Why do you say that?"

Do you think he'd go through all this elaborate work just to go for a quick kill and put you out of your misery? The evidence suggests he would find that...unsatisfying.

Not as unsatisfying as *I* would find it! "You know, we do know someone who can survive a shot to the head. *Two* someones, in fact." I'd seen Saul's current host survive two shots to the head when his previous demon was in residence, and Raphael's host supposedly had the same abilities.

And as soon as Abraham caught sight of Saul or Raphael, one of the people on that list would be dead. If he found he couldn't kill whoever we sent after him, he'd just retreat and try someone else.

I was running out of arguments, though the prospect of walking into a trap and crossing my fingers in hopes Lugh and I could turn the tables on Abraham didn't exactly light my fire.

What else can we do? Lugh asked.

"Call in the troops and have a major powwow session. Maybe if we all put our heads together, we'll come up with something better.

Morgan, think about it a minute. What's going to happen if we tell the council that we want to face Abraham alone? Even if they can't think of a better option?

"It's not like they can stop you! You're the king. What you say goes."

He laughed at that. *I would trust my authority over my people in almost any situation. This isn't one of them. As my advisors, they would feel justified disobeying me if they thought my safety was at stake.*

"They've let us do dangerous things before when you've ordered them to."

Not quite like this, though.

And he was right. The human members of the council would certainly object, but they wouldn't be able to stop him. However, if Raphael and Saul and Adam—and this was the only time I could imagine the three of them being in agreement about something—all ganged up on him, then we wouldn't be going anywhere.

So we didn't dare ask for a second opinion, or even for backup. Only the thought of Abraham picking off everyone around me one by one was enough to convince me to go along with Lugh's plan.

Chapter **28**

Saul did not return to the apartment, which was a relief. I was feeling much better, but I'd have to fake a relapse and take to my bed if he were around, because even though he didn't know me as well as the other members of Lugh's council, he was bound to notice that something was up.

My appetite had been severely put off by Abraham's little love note, but I forced myself to eat another heaping bowl of chicken soup for dinner. The headache and queasiness were gone, but I was still weak, and I didn't think starving myself was a good idea.

Per Lugh's suggestion, I took another nap in the early evening, conserving what little strength I had for tonight's festivities. I was starting to feel that if I never fell asleep again, it would be too soon, but that didn't stop me from conking out the moment I lay down. Probably Lugh's influence, but I decided not to make a big deal out of it.

A major case of cold feet hit me around eleven, and I had to reread Abraham's note several times to remind myself of why I had to do something that seemed patently stupid, even to me. God, I was so sick of being caught between the proverbial rock and a hard place, which is where I seemed to spend most of my life these days. But despite the cold feet, I called a cab to pick me up at eleven-thirty.

At eleven twenty-five, I knew I couldn't delay it any longer. It was time to go. Feeling a bit morbid, I grabbed the note from Abraham and scribbled on the back, "If I don't come back, please tell Brian I love him, and I'm sorry I was such a rotten girlfriend." Someone would find it eventually and know what had happened to me.

If I'd thought of it earlier, I'd have written something more eloquent, but now there was no time. I left the note on the dining room table, then took a deep breath and headed out.

The cab arrived on time, which was a nice surprise. I gave the driver an address near the building where I was to meet Abraham. He gave me a funny look—it wasn't exactly a good place for a woman to hang out at any time, much less late at night—but he wasn't enough of a Good Samaritan to try to talk me out of it.

I walked the last couple of blocks, wanting to get a look at my destination before I arrived. The building was much like I expected it—a large brick monstrosity with boarded-up windows and colorful graffiti scrawled across every flat surface. It had probably been some kind of a warehouse in its heyday. The door had been forced open, the frame flapping loose. I couldn't see any light inside, but I felt sure Abraham was there, with whatever nasty surprise he had in store for me.

I looked all around me, checking to make sure no one was watching. I needn't have bothered. The street was deserted, and while there were plenty of cars going by, they were all on the opposite side of the river. Although I didn't think Abraham was going to make this so easy for me, I armed my Taser and held it out before me. I swallowed what I hoped was the last of my fear and pushed open the door.

It was pitch-dark inside, and I wished I'd thought to bring a flashlight. If the windows hadn't been boarded up, I might at least have had some moonlight to work with, but no such luck. Abraham could jump me, and I wouldn't see him coming until it was way too late.

My pulse kicked up as adrenaline surged through my system, anxious for me to fight or flee.

"Drop the Taser, or this will get ugly fast," said an unfamiliar woman's voice from somewhere deep inside the darkness.

Whoever she was couldn't possibly see the Taser. It was too damn dark in here. My heart sank a bit. So dark that even the tiny indicator lights on the Taser glowed like beacons.

"Don't make me tell you again," the woman said.

I considered firing in the general direction from which the voice came, but then I heard a plaintive whimper. The woman wasn't alone, and if she had a hostage, I didn't dare shoot.

You'd best drop it, Lugh advised. *We want Abraham to think we're helpless anyway.*

I'd rather look *helpless than* be *helpless,* I quipped, but I knew he was right. Gritting my teeth against my reluctance, I dropped the Taser.

A match suddenly glowed in the darkness, and that little light seemed so blindingly bright that, for a moment, I still couldn't see. Then, as my eyes adjusted to the darkness, I took in the scene around me.

I'd been thinking of this building as a warehouse, and had expected wide open spaces. What I got instead was a long, dark corridor punctuated at regular intervals by padlocked doors. At the far end of the corridor, one of the doors was open, and a figure lounged in the doorway.

It was a woman, no doubt Abraham's current host, but I didn't know her. Maybe about thirty years old, reasonably pretty, except for the feral flicker in her eyes. Or maybe that was just the reflected light of the candle she held—in the hand that *wasn't* holding a gun, that is.

"Who the hell are you?" I demanded, as if I didn't know.

"If you really have to ask, then my answer would be meaningless," she responded.

There was another whimper, and Abraham's mystery host glanced into the room behind the open door. She apparently liked what she saw, because she smiled as she turned back to me.

"Come on in," she said. "See what I have planned for this evening's entertainment. Move slowly, though. Sudden moves will have severe consequences. And stay where I can see you."

My hands itching for the Taser, I started to walk toward her. She backed up as I approached, keeping a substantial distance between us while making sure neither one of us lost sight of the other. Sweat trickled down the small of my back, though I wasn't particularly hot.

You want to take over now, Lugh? I asked.

Not yet. I want to leave you in control as long as possible. Maybe that will make you less sick in the aftermath.

I wasn't holding my breath on that one, but since I preferred being in control anyway, I didn't argue.

Slowly, I crept forward as Abraham backed up, until I was finally able to see what awaited me in the room beyond. I'm not sure what I expected, but it certainly wasn't what I got.

Another woman I didn't know lay on the floor at the opposite end of the room. Pixie-cut blond hair framed a heart-shaped face, which was streaked with runny mascara. She was the source of all the little whimpers, though she barely seemed to be conscious. I could see no obvious wounds, but that didn't mean she wasn't seriously hurt.

"Who is that?" I asked Abraham.

"That is Jessica Miles. You know, Jordan Maguire's ex?"

I nodded to indicate that I recognized the name. "What is she doing here? And what's wrong with her?"

I wasn't entirely surprised that he ignored my questions. "Tell me, have you figured out why I'm unhappy with you yet?" He frowned theatrically. "You *have* figured out that I'm a demon, right?"

"Yeah," I said. "That part's pretty clear. And you're pissed at me because Jordan Maguire didn't burn."

He nodded. Or should I say "she"? It was rather confusing. I decided since demons usually adopt their hosts' names that I would think of my enemy as "she" for the time being.

"Very good. I had no idea whether you were smart enough to put the pieces together or not. How nice not to have to draw you a picture."

I tried taking a cautious step closer, but her eyes narrowed, and her finger flexed on the trigger. I froze, and she smiled.

"To make a long story short," she said, "Jessica here helped me frame my good friend Jordan for hitting her. She's a wicked, wicked person. A murderer. And a stone-cold bitch."

"None of that clarifies why she's here."

"Patience, patience. You've fucked up everything I've tried to do, and if I want to take my own sweet time explaining how the game will end, then it's my prerogative." She looked at me expectantly.

If she thought I'd argue, she had another think coming. I knew crazy when I saw it, and it was staring me right in the face. Reasoning with a crazy person seemed like more effort than it was worth. I made a zipping-my-mouth gesture and waited.

Her lips tugged downward in an almost petulant expression. Jessica took that moment to issue another whimper. She made what appeared to be a feeble attempt to get up, but she collapsed almost immediately.

Abraham smiled. "To answer your question about what's wrong with our dear friend Jessica, she's drugged to the gills. Frankly, I'm surprised she's conscious. I thought I'd have to wake her up for the grand finale."

What the hell was this psycho up to *now*?

Abraham moved a little closer to Jessica, and the light of the candle glinted off something on the floor. A kitchen knife. Not one of those big-ass chef's knifes, but not a tiny little paring knife, either. I'm no expert in the kitchen, but I decided this was probably a utility knife.

Abraham put the candle down on the floor. It was a fat pillar type, so it didn't need any kind of holder. The gun didn't waver in its aim.

"I've wiped it clean of prints," Abraham said, then stood and kicked the knife across the floor toward me. Her smile became even more vicious. "Pick it up!"

The knife came to a stop against the wall, a little bit to my left. Unfortunately, I was beginning to see where this was leading, and I didn't like it one bit.

I swallowed hard, though I made no move toward

the knife. "You failed to frame me for the last two murders, but this time..." I couldn't finish my own sentence.

Abraham laughed, having a jolly old time contemplating murder and mayhem. "This time, it won't be a frame. This time, you'll be guilty as hell. Now pick up the fucking knife."

Any ideas? I asked Lugh.

Maybe it was just my imagination, but his voice in my head sounded tense and strained. *Do as she says. As long as she's got that gun on us, we can't afford not to. Maybe once she thinks we're doing what she wants, she'll relax her guard a bit and give me an opportunity.*

Too many maybes! But, as he said, we had no choice but to obey as long as she had that gun pointed at my head.

Moving slowly, in case she had an itchy trigger finger, I retrieved the knife. It looked lethally sharp.

While I bent over to pick up the knife, Abraham knelt by Jessica's feet and grabbed her ankle. Her aim didn't waver the whole time.

"When I tell you to," she said, "you're going to very, very slowly come closer. I'll want you to come kneel by her head." She shook Jessica's ankle, hard. "Come on, honey, stay awake for this. You don't want to sleep through your own gruesome murder, now do you?"

Jessica sobbed and made a feeble attempt to free her ankle from Abraham's grip. Abraham continued to smile up at me, savoring every moment.

"That knife I gave you is a little short for the job," Abraham continued. "It'll take quite a few stabs before she finally gives up the ghost." She held up Jessica's ankle. "I'll make sure she doesn't go anywhere, but she'll probably find she has some fight left in her when you start stabbing her. It'll be a shame if she gets your skin cells under her fingernails." Her laugh was maniacal. Almost over the top, really. Nothing like being trapped in a dark room with a B-movie horror psycho holding a gun to your head.

"Come on over," Abraham invited when the laughter died. "Slowly."

I swallowed hard and stayed put. "What if I refuse?" I asked, just to make sure I fully understood the situation.

Another psycho-cackle. "Then we all go our separate ways, and every person on that list I gave you dies."

"You won't just shoot me in the head?"

She snorted. "Way too quick and easy."

"So you don't actually need that gun." Hey, a girl can hope, right?

"It's to discourage you from trying anything heroic," Abraham explained.

It was my turn to snort, though it probably sounded pretty forced and phony. "Like you're in any danger from me!"

"I like to be cautious. For all I know, you have another Taser on you. And don't get any funny ideas about sacrificing yourself by forcing me to shoot. If I have to kill you, then you'll have cheated me of my revenge yet again, and I'll be forced to take it out on your loved ones. I have nothing else to live for, after all. Now get your ass over here and get to work."

I swallowed hard and shook my head. "What did Maguire's demon do to you that's worth all this mayhem?"

"You're stalling, and I have no patience for it. Move!"

I started edging forward, my mind working frantically. *Lugh, I don't know what to do!*

Just keep following her orders.

A shiver ran up and down my spine as an ugly suspicion hit me. *Tell me we're not actually going to kill her.*

That may be the only way to get Abraham relaxed enough for me to take him by surprise.

But—

Remember, as far as Jessica knows, she caused Maguire's demon to be executed in a fit of jealousy. This is not an inappropriate punishment.

Oh, so now you're going all Old Testament on me, are you?

I guess my subconscious desire not to be sick as a dog for the foreseeable future had helped me resurrect at least some of my mental barriers, because I actually felt it when Lugh tried to take over. Reflexively, I fought him.

"Get over here!" Abraham barked. "If I have to tell you again, then I'll go to Plan B, which you've already indicated you don't like."

Moving while fighting to keep Lugh out of control was almost impossible. However, in my already weakened state, keeping Lugh out was *entirely* impossible. Between one step and the next, my free will was taken from me.

I understood Lugh's point. In a rational, logical way, I knew he was right, and we had to kill Jessica Miles if that's what it took. It might be our only chance to stop Abraham—our only chance that he might lower the gun, or at least waver in his aim so that if he shot us, it wasn't in the head. Lugh could heal most gunshot wounds, and with the element of surprise on our side, he was likely to be able to overpower Abraham even wounded.

No matter how logical it was, I couldn't bear the idea of killing someone in cold blood.

I'm doing it, not you, Lugh reminded me, but that didn't make me feel any better about it.

Lugh continued to follow Abraham's orders and knelt by Jessica's head. She took a weird, awkward swing at him. Maybe she was hoping to knock the knife out of his hand, but she hit the wrong arm. Her nails managed to dig in, though, conveniently getting my skin under them as further evidence that I was her murderer.

"To answer your earlier question," Abraham said, looking a little wild-eyed, "Brennus and I were rivals in love—several times, actually—and I never came out the winner."

"I can't imagine why," Lugh mumbled.

"Shut up!" Abraham snarled, and the gun wavered slightly. But not enough—and based on the madness in his eyes, we were out of time.

"I'm sorry, Jessica," Lugh said, and his knife arm started to swing down toward her back.

A bunch of things happened at once then. There was the distinctive sound of a Taser pop, coming from the hallway outside. Abraham's body jerked spastically. Losing his grip both on the gun and on Jessica's ankle, he crumpled into a heap. And Lugh, with his demon-quick reflexes, managed to arrest his swing just short of Jessica's back.

Lugh turned toward the doorway, where Barbie was ejecting the spent Taser cartridge. She smiled at us, though her eyes were a little too wide, and her hands were shaking.

"Whew," she said. "That was close."

"What are you doing here?" Lugh asked.

Let me back in, I demanded.

And how will you explain to Barbie why you're fine one moment and puking your guts out the next?

Argh, he had a point there. I hoped the amount of

time he remained in control didn't contribute too much to the misery level I'd suffer when I was back in the driver's seat.

Barbie shrugged, trying to look casual. She almost succeeded, too. "It was nice of you to leave that note with all the details sitting on your dining room table. Made it real easy for me to find you."

Behind me, Jessica was breathing hard, like she'd just run a marathon, but Lugh didn't seem too interested in her panic attack, or whatever it was. Instead, he said exactly what I was thinking.

"You were in my apartment? How? And *why?*"

Barbie, looking smug, came farther into the room, though she kept a healthy distance between herself and the temporarily disabled demon.

"I'm a private investigator," Barbie reminded me. "About eighty percent of my job is convincing people to do things or tell me things they're not supposed to. Saul's staying at my place tonight and he needed an overnight bag. He's still pissed about something you said to him, and didn't want to run into you, so I agreed to go for him. The gentleman at the front desk of your building was very accommodating."

Jessica's harsh breaths were now even louder and faster, punctuated with little growling sounds that sounded more like anger than fear or pain. Barbie came closer.

"Hey, is she all right?" she asked.

Suddenly, Jessica's leg kicked out, catching Barbie right in the shin. I heard the sickening crunch of breaking bone only seconds before Barbie screamed in pain.

And then Jessica was on me, punching, kicking, and clawing. For just a moment, Lugh and I both failed to recognize what was going on. Long enough for Jessica to lift me off my feet and toss me into the wall.

Lugh kept me from feeling any pain, but even *he* had the wind knocked out of him, and by the time he'd recovered, Jessica was on him again. But, of course, it wasn't Jessica, it was Abraham.

Lugh managed to evade the punch that Jessica threw at his face. Which was a damn good thing, since that punch left a sizeable hole in the wall. Lugh threw both arms around Jessica, trying to pin her arms while dragging her to the floor beneath him. He was making at least a token effort not to kill Abraham's current human host, but he'd underestimated Abraham's strength.

Abraham broke Lugh's grip, and I felt Lugh's shock as we were once again airborne, heading for a wall. Lugh managed a patently nonhuman maneuver, executing a complicated twist and somersault in the air so that he managed to land on his feet instead of slamming into the wall.

Jessica's mouth dropped open. "What the fuck?" she screamed, and I could see the mingled glows of madness and a demonic essence in her eyes. "You were *exorcized*!"

Lugh grinned at her, and I got the sick impression that he was rather enjoying himself. "Surprise!" he said, then charged Jessica again.

This time, he and Jessica hit the wall together. I was surprised it didn't give way under the ferocious impact. Chunks of plaster rained down on us, but neither demon paid any attention. When they rolled free, locked together in mortal combat, Lugh was on top. He reached for Jessica's throat, possibly meaning to try to break her neck, but he was once again surprised when she managed a tremendous burst of strength and flipped them both over.

As king of the demons, Lugh was necessarily one of the strongest among them all, but it seemed Abraham was able to hold his own.

Though my mind still resided within my body, there was a distinct separation between the two, seeing as how I had no control whatsoever. Nor, in this particular situation, did I have any *desire* to have control, because I would be dead in five seconds flat if I didn't have Lugh's demon strength.

Because I wasn't driving, I was able to pay more attention to our peripheral vision than Lugh was. I'm sure he saw Barbie out of the corner of his eye, but his gaze didn't even flick in her direction, his entire concentration focused on Jessica/Abraham. *I*, on the other hand, could see Barbie, her back propped against the wall, her face contorted with pain, loading a fresh cartridge into the Taser.

Abraham mirrored Lugh's last move, going for his throat. Instead of trying to turn the tables again, Lugh grabbed for Abraham's wrists, trying to hold him off. Which I suspected meant he was aware of Barbie after all—he was making sure Abraham stayed on top where he made an easier target.

The Taser popped again, the probes latching on and pumping fifty thousand volts into Jessica's system. Powerful though he might be, Abraham reacted to that Taser shot just like any other demon: He lost control of his host's body and went completely limp.

Chapter 29

Lugh pushed Jessica's body to the side and sat up while I tried to figure out exactly what had happened. The unknown woman, Abraham's host, had let go of Jessica's ankle before Barbie Tasered her. When she'd collapsed, I'd been *sure* she wasn't in contact with Jessica. So how the hell had Abraham ended up in Jessica?

He was in Jessica the whole time, Lugh said, and I knew he was right. Jessica had seemed a little... weird. Particularly when she swung at Lugh as if trying to knock the knife away. Yeah, she was supposed to be drugged out of her mind, but she'd still managed to gouge out some skin for evidence. Not a coincidence.

But if Abraham had been in Jessica all along, who was the woman with the gun? Whoever she was, she still lay in a heap on the floor, but her body was wracked with sobs.

"Now that I saved both your ass and your soul," Barbie said, "do you think you're ready to level with me?"

Lugh turned to her, though we were both keeping

a careful eye on the two Taser victims, just in case. Even in the light of the single candle, I could see the sweat that coated Barbie's face. Her eyes were squinched almost shut with pain, and her cheekbones stood out in stark relief.

I mentally reviewed everything Barbie had seen and heard, and it was not good news. She'd probably have been able to explain away the inexplicable quickness that had stopped me from stabbing Jessica, but not the strength it had taken for me to throw Jessica across the room, nor the midair acrobatics that had kept me from hitting the wall when Jessica threw me.

We're screwed, I said to Lugh.

"I'll get back to you in a moment," Lugh said to Barbie. He grabbed my cell phone and quickly called Adam.

"What?" Adam said when he answered, sounding groggy and grumpy.

"I need your help, immediately," he said, then rattled off the address. "Get here yesterday."

Adam was instantly awake. "What's going on?"

"Too much to explain. Just get down here. And get Raphael down here, too. We may need his inventive storytelling abilities."

Adam must have realized he was speaking to Lugh, not me. If it had been me barking orders at him like that, he'd have balked. Instead, he hung up with a promise to be here ASAP.

"What, no ambulance?" Barbie asked.

"Not yet. We're going to need Adam to be a bit creative about what happened here, so we need him here before anyone else."

Her gaze was shrewd. "Because you need to hide that you're somehow still possessed."

"Among other things."

"Don't worry," she said. "I won't tell anyone."

Lugh looked back and forth between the two Tasered women, and Barbie said, "Oh."

He crossed the room to her, squatting by her side and dropping his voice to the softest of whispers. "Morgan will explain everything later," he said.

I will?

"For now, just know that she and I don't have the typical demon/host relationship."

Are you sure about this? I asked.

Yes, was his succinct reply.

"When Adam arrives and my strength is no longer required," he continued, "I will put Morgan back in control. She will no doubt become violently ill again, but that can't be helped. Please contain your curiosity for now, and go along with whatever story Adam and Raphael—that's Tommy Brewster's demon—come up with." He held out his hand for her to shake. "Deal?"

She managed a smile, though pain was written across her face. "I'd do just about anything to find out the real story behind all this. I'm just *dying* of curiosity." She shook Lugh's hand, and her palm was clammy with sweat. "If it's all right with you, I'm going to pass out now." And true to her word, her eyelids fluttered, and she slumped to the side. Lugh lowered her gently to the floor.

Then he took the Taser and gave Abraham another jolt, just to make sure he was down for the count. I suggested the unknown woman could use another jolt herself, despite the fact that she was curled up in fetal position and crying.

She wouldn't have enough control to curl up and cry if she were a demon, Lugh reminded me. As usual, he was right.

Adam arrived in less than fifteen minutes. Lugh quickly took him aside and told him the whole story.

Raphael arrived only a couple minutes later, and while Adam shared the story with him, Lugh drove my body over to a corner and sat down.

Are you ready? he asked.

God, no. The idea of going through another three days or more of the hellish sickness was almost enough to make me leave Lugh in control for the rest of my life. Well, no, not really, but you know what I mean.

Then Lugh shifted control back to me, and I was so violently ill I had no idea who said what to who or what exactly happened afterward.

I have only the haziest of memories of the next few days. I know I was in the hospital—The Healing Circle. You've got to love the irony. And I know that an exorcist was brought in to the hospital to examine my aura. But I was mercifully unaware of whatever tests may have been performed on me in an effort to figure out why I was so damn sick. All things considered, I was probably a lot less miserable staying in the hospital than I had been when I'd stayed home. After all, they have *way* better drugs.

I had visitors every day, although I was rarely clearheaded enough to know the difference between dreams and reality. The first time that I woke up and was actually coherent, it was Adam who sat at my bedside. I might have been touched that he cared, only he was really there just to fill me in on the official story about the showdown at the warehouse so I wouldn't say anything to contradict it.

Apparently, everything had gone down approximately as I remembered it, only it was Tommy Brewster who'd gotten into the nasty fight with the possessed Jessica. He'd come with me to meet

Abraham because I was ill, and he'd defended me against the attack, the stress of which had somehow made my illness ten times worse. Jessica had, of course, disputed the story, but since all the other witnesses—even the mystery woman—corroborated it, and since the examination by the exorcist had proven I wasn't possessed, her claims were dismissed.

I listened to Adam's version of what happened and decided that even with my meager lying skills, I could pull it off. It was close enough to the truth not to make me squirm too badly. But what I really wanted to know was who the hell the woman with the gun had been. Luckily, Adam was in an expansive mood and was happy to tell me.

"Her name is Susan Harvey," he said. "She's an actress. A pretty good one, too, with aspirations of Broadway. She's also a single mom, and Abraham kidnapped her son. She was ordered to put on the show of a lifetime, and if she failed to convince you, then she'd never see her son again. Ms. Harvey was contrite enough that she needed little persuasion to remember things the way we wanted her to."

I remembered the nearly hysterical look in her eyes when Lugh had been about to stab Jessica. At the time, I'd interpreted it as Abraham's excitement at seeing his revenge come to fruition, but the truth was it was unadulterated horror. Despite the fact that she'd held a gun to my head, I felt sorry for her.

"Is her son okay?" I asked, my voice weak and raspy from disuse.

Adam's lips tightened with displeasure. "For the most part. Jessica had tied him up in her basement. She hadn't exactly been gentle with him, and she hadn't bothered to feed him or give him any water while she held him, but the doctors say he'll make a full recovery."

I shuddered, thinking that, with Abraham's callous disregard for human life, the boy was lucky to be alive. Certainly he wouldn't have survived once his mother had completed her mission. Nor would his mother, for that matter. I remembered how "Abraham" had held onto Jessica's ankle, supposedly to keep her from getting away. I should have realized how strange that was at the time, seeing as Jessica was pretending to be so out of it she could barely move, much less make a run for it. If Lugh had gone through with it and stabbed Jessica, Abraham would have used that physical contact to transfer into Susan.

"Jessica had a child, too!" I gasped as I suddenly remembered.

Adam nodded. "But luckily she was visiting her grandparents for the week, so Jessica didn't have to deal with her." Because we both knew exactly how she would have dealt with such an inconvenience.

And now for the biggest question of all. "I assume Jessica was exorcized while I was out of it?" I shouldn't have cared what happened to her. After all, she was a killer herself, or at least she thought she was. But no matter what the human host was like, I couldn't help feeling sympathy for someone who'd had Abraham rampaging around in her head. "Is she one of the lucky ones?"

Adam's face was hard, his expression stony. "Three different exorcists tried to cast Abraham out, but he was too strong for them."

Horror stabbed through me. "Oh, no."

His lips tipped into a smile, but his face retained that feeling of hardness. "It was poetic justice, Morgan. The only exorcist in the country—possibly even in the world—who could have cast him out is under suspension by the U.S. Exorcism Board because of the lawsuit Abraham himself put into motion."

"*Was* poetic justice?"

He nodded. "Yeah. He was executed this morning at around eight, when the third exorcist failed to cast him out."

"And so was Jessica," I murmured, feeling cold.

Adam shrugged. "I can't get too worked up about that," he said. "She was no innocent bystander."

Even though I saw his point, even though she'd kinda had it coming, in an Old Testament, eye-for-an-eye way, I still wished I'd been available to do the exorcism myself. I hated the idea of *anyone* being incinerated to destroy a demon.

My eyes slid closed, and I realized I had used up my meager strength. "I'm going to go back to sleep now." Maybe when I woke up, things would look brighter.

I had the vague feeling that Adam stayed at my side until I fell asleep, but that was probably just my imagination.

I managed to fight my way out of the hospital the next day, against medical advice. Although I was feeling much better, my doctor still wanted me to stay for observation, because she had no idea what was wrong with me. She never would, either.

Dominic picked me up at the hospital to take me home, but since it was around lunchtime, and I was eating again, he took me to his and Adam's place instead so he could set me up with some nourishing Italian food. Adam wasn't home.

"It's just leftovers," Dominic said apologetically as he seated me at the kitchen table.

"After you were nice enough to come pick me up *and* to feed me, I can hardly complain about leftovers. Especially not if *you* made them."

As usual, the praise made him blush. I lavished more on him when he served me the most delicious stuffed shells I'd ever eaten. I almost cried in gratitude when he put together a care package to take home with me.

When I say I almost cried, I mean it literally. Now that the crisis was over, the emotions I'd been holding at bay with a vengeance were eroding away my shields. I felt like there was an aching hole in my chest where Brian had once been. Even when I tried to summon some anger to bolster my defenses, I failed miserably. I couldn't blame him for finally giving up on me. I just wished with all my being that he hadn't. Or that I could go back in time and *force* myself to open up to him, to tell him the truth. To *trust* him, because he was right, and I'd often withheld my trust even when I knew in my heart he deserved it.

"Do you realize you've been staring off into space for almost ten minutes?" Dominic asked, startling me out of my reverie.

I blinked, then glanced at my watch. However, since I hadn't thought to check the time when I spaced out, it didn't do much good. "You're shitting me."

He smiled and shook his head. "Nope. Do you want to tell me what's wrong?"

I can't count how many times in my life I've answered the "what's wrong" question with "nothing," even when the sky was falling. I almost did the same now by sheer reflex, but the words died in my throat.

"I need help trying to figure out how to win Brian back," I blurted, and I don't know who was more surprised, me or Dom.

He blinked at me like I had to be an imposter. "What kind of drugs do they have you on?"

I tried to laugh, but it was a pathetic effort. "If

desperation is a drug, then I'm overdosing on it." I swallowed the lump in my throat. "I love him too much to give up on us yet, but I don't have a clue what to do."

Dom looked at me long and hard. I couldn't read the expression on his usually open book of a face. "I'm pretty sure I know what the problem is between you, but will you put it into words for me anyway?"

It was so unlike me to talk about my feelings that I almost wondered if I'd been brainwashed or put under hypnosis. But I kept talking anyway. "The problem is that I have major trust issues, and I've given Brian every reason to believe I don't trust him to look out for me, to look out for himself, to make the right decisions..." My eyes blurred with tears. What an unholy mess I'd made of everything!

"So to have a hope to win him back, you're going to have to prove that you trust him after all."

"Just like that, huh? How can I prove it? I tried promising him I'd—"

Dominic cut me off, meeting my eyes and capturing me with an intense gaze. "Ask yourself why you're asking *me* how to win Brian back."

"Because you're the only one I know who wouldn't laugh at me, or patronize me, or tell me I was reaping what I sowed."

He shook his head. "That's not it, Morgan," he said in a gently chiding voice.

"What do you mean? Of course that's it!"

"I'm not going to do all the work for you. If you can't dig the real reason out of your subconscious, then I can't help you."

I swallowed the next denial that wanted to spring to my lips. I had a funny feeling a part of me knew exactly what Dom was talking about—a part of me that wasn't always on speaking terms with my conscious mind. A part of me I wasn't sure I was willing, or even *able* to acknowledge. A part of me that had some inkling of what gesture I could make to symbolize my trust.

Despite the sudden panic that screamed through me, I started putting the pieces of my own thoughts together. Brian had dropped me for my lack of trust. The only way I could hope to get him back was by proving that I did trust him. And the person I was asking advice from was the M half of an S&M relationship, a man who routinely made himself completely helpless before his lover and *liked* it.

"Oh shit," I said in a near whisper as the tumblers in my mind lined up and the safe opened.

Dominic smiled. "I believe you're beginning to get the picture."

My only response was a loud gulp of fear. Brian and I had danced around the edges of some fairly kinky sex—thanks to Lugh giving Brian some pointers—but what I was thinking of now wasn't dancing around the edge anymore.

"When you submit to someone you trust completely," Dominic said softly, still smiling, "you open yourself up more fully than you can possibly imagine. Every part of you becomes vulnerable. It's not just an act of the body. You're opening up your emotions, the very essence of yourself." The smile turned a bit sheepish. "Of course, I'm speaking specifically of myself. Not everyone experiences it the same way."

I took a slow, deep breath and tried to push my panic out when I released it. "But if I'm looking for a metaphorical way to symbolize my trust..."

"Only if you think Brian is open to it," Dom hedged. "It's possible he'd be too weirded out to even realize there's a message, much less understand it."

But instinct told me he wouldn't be weirded out.

He'd shown no hint of discomfort when things had gotten a bit kinky between us—hell, he'd been a lot more comfortable about it than *I* was—and he'd clearly enjoyed himself.

"He'd get the message," I said. Assuming I was willing to deliver said message, and he was willing to receive it.

Dom nodded. "I can't guarantee it will be enough," he reminded me. "But it would say a hell of a lot more than a bunch of words ever could."

I had to agree with him there. I cleared my throat. "So what would I, uh, do?"

There was what I could only describe as an evil glint in Dominic's eye.

"One of the reasons falling in love can be so scary is that you're basically giving the other person your heart, along with all the weapons he needs to destroy it. You're giving him the means to hurt you terribly, and trusting him not to do it even though you have no tangible guarantee. So, think about how you can symbolize that to Brian."

I squirmed. "I have no experience with this S&M stuff." My face burned. If you'd asked me a couple of weeks ago if there was a chance in hell I'd ever have a conversation like this, I'd have laughed.

Dom shook his head. "This isn't really about SM. SM is about the giving and receiving of pleasure, just in unconventional ways. You can work out a lot of trust issues during SM play, but it's still about pleasure for everyone involved. I'm not sure you're ready to do it for pleasure yet."

I bristled. "What do you mean, *yet*?"

His smile was both placid and disgustingly knowing. "You know how some of the most vehement homophobes sometimes turn out to be gays who've refused to come out of the closet?"

My cheeks were so hot I feared I might spontaneously combust. The harder I tried not to, the more I found myself thinking about the fantasies Lugh had created for me—and about some of my more...adventurous sexual forays with Brian. I decided my wisest course of action was to pretend I hadn't heard what Dom had just said.

"This asking-an-expert-for-help thing isn't working too well," I muttered.

"If you want my advice on how to dip your toes into the BDSM pool, I'm happy to help. But if you're just looking to make a grand symbolic gesture, then I think the ideas have to come from you or the gesture loses a lot of its power. That doesn't mean I can't help out—it just means I can't tell you what you should do."

Dom's words resonated somehow, and I knew he was right. This was my gesture to make. The idea had to come from me.

My heart fluttered erratically in my chest as an idea began to form. Dom had described falling in love as giving the other person the means to hurt you and trusting them not to. And that was just what I was going to do.

I dug my courage out of hiding and met Dom's eyes. "I'd like you to pack me up another care package, if you don't mind. I don't want to know what's in it, but it shouldn't be wimpy stuff." I'm not sure there *is* such a thing as wimpy S&M gear, but that's beside the point. "I'll take it to Brian's, and if he doesn't slam the door in my face, I'll give him carte blanche to use whatever's in the package."

For the first time, Dom looked dubious. "I'm not sure—"

"Brian wouldn't hurt me. Even if you put something awful in the package, he wouldn't use it. In fact, you *should* put something awful in there."

Dom bit his lip. "Are you sure you don't want to—"

I shook my head. "No. I don't want to know." I forced a seriously nervous smile. "It's a demonstration of blind trust."

He was silent for so long I thought for sure he was going to refuse.

"I can always go buy the crap, but you know I can't afford it. I'll do it if I have to, but—"

"All right, all right. At least if I choose the toys, I'll know it's the good stuff."

I let out a sigh of relief. "Thanks, Dom."

He grimaced. "I hope you'll still be thanking me later." He pushed away from the table.

"Don't wimp out on me, okay?"

He met my eyes steadily. "I won't," he promised, and I knew it was the truth.

Chapter **30**

I've faced a lynch mob that tried to burn me at the stake; a sociopathic demon who had every intention of torturing and then killing me; and a psycho demon who wanted to make the entire rest of my life a living hell. And yet I swear I was more frightened now, as I stood outside Brian's door with Dominic's "care package" at my feet, than I'd ever been in the face of true physical danger.

It had taken me more than three hours to get ready, as I'd considered and discarded about thirty different outfits, and at least another hour to nerve myself up to set foot outside my own apartment. Not that anyone would know how embarrassing my outfit was, since I'd covered all the sexy stuff with a mundane khaki shirtdress. No, the only sign that there was anything out of the ordinary was the pair of fuck-me pumps that had me teetering slightly with every step.

Everything I was wearing was brand-new, purchased specially for this occasion. The only reason it had taken me so long to get dressed was because I tried so many times to chicken out of my selections.

But hell, if I was going to do this at all, I was going to do this right. If that meant adding a dash of humiliation to the experience, then so be it.

The people in Brian's building know me by sight, and there was no sign they knew we had broken up. When I asked the front desk clerk not to call up to Brian's apartment to let him know I was coming, he smiled at me and gave me a conspiratorial wink. It was almost enough to make me flee in terror, but once again I gave myself a mental kick in the ass.

Now there was only one thing left to do. I took a deep breath, wiped my sweaty palms on my dress, and rang the doorbell.

It was always possible I was getting myself all worked up for nothing. Maybe Brian would open the door, see me standing there, and shut it again without saying another word. Or I might tell him what I had in mind, and he would laugh at me. But in all honesty, that wasn't how I expected this to go.

My heart was going at about a thousand beats per minute. When Brian opened the door, my heart went for a thousand and one.

The fact that he didn't slam the door was both a relief and a source of terror. He cocked his head to one side, taking in my outfit from head to toe. His eyebrows arched when he saw the shoes, and he looked even more taken aback when he saw the suitcase that contained the "toys," as Dominic called them.

"May I come in?" I asked in a scratchy whisper.

I would have liked to look sexy for Brian, but all I could manage right now was not to look too much like a deer in the headlights. He couldn't possibly miss how nervous I was.

"This ought to be interesting," he murmured, a wry smile on his lips, as he opened the door wide enough to let me in.

I gulped. Step one was successfully completed: he hadn't slammed the door in my face. As a bonus, he didn't even look at me like I was the last person on earth he wanted to see. I hesitated only a moment before picking up the suitcase and going inside. Then I kinda ran out of steam and stood there in the entryway wondering how the hell to begin.

Brian came to stand in front of me, his arms crossed over his chest. "I have to admit, I'm insanely curious as to what you're doing here and what's in that mysterious suitcase," he told me. He finished up with, "Nice shoes, by the way."

I stiffened my spine to the best of my abilities, then met Brian's eyes. "I'm here to beg you to take me back," I said.

His eyes widened at that. I wasn't one to beg, and he knew it. But after that moment of surprise, I could see him starting to shut down, closing his heart to me. I hurried on before he could finish that process.

"The reason you dumped me is because I've given you every reason to believe I don't fully trust you. But the truth is, it's not *you* I don't trust, it's *me*. I can't get over the feeling that you're just too damn good for me, and I've spent most of the time we've been together tensed and ready for the moment you'd wise up to what a lousy catch I was." I took a deep, steadying breath. Not that it helped a whole lot. "I came here tonight to prove to you that I *do* trust you, with all my heart."

Brian licked his lips and looked thoughtful. At least he'd stopped shutting down on me. His eyes flicked to the suitcase, then back to me. "I'm listening," he said cautiously, his tone clearly saying he was making no promises.

I began to unbutton my dress, pointing at the suitcase with a jerk of my chin. "Dominic calls that a 'care package.' I don't know exactly what's in it, but I know it contains what he and Adam consider 'toys,' if you know what I mean."

I had the dress unbuttoned all the way to my waist by now, giving Brian tantalizing glimpses of my black peekaboo bra and the gold belly chain. I paused for half a second, but he seemed in no hurry to interrupt me, so I soldiered on.

"You know what an utter control freak I am," I said, then swallowed hard. "But for tonight, and tonight only, I'm going to put all the power in your hands. Anything that's in that case, you can use on me and I won't object. *Anything*. I know you'd never harm me, even if you're pissed as hell at me. So I know I'm safe taking my hands off the wheel for a while." Even if the very thought made me break out in a cold sweat.

I let the dress drop to the floor. My cheeks burned, and my mouth was parched. Brian had seen me naked hundreds of times, but I felt ever so much more vulnerable this time. Almost *more* naked than when I wasn't wearing anything.

Aside from the peekaboo bra, the belly chain, and the fuck-me pumps, I was also wearing a flimsy black lace thong, a garter belt, and black stockings. I didn't know if this was anything like an outfit a truly submissive person would wear, but I did know it was sexy as hell. Or totally ridiculous-looking, depending on your point of view.

From the look on Brian's face, I'd say he thought "sexy as hell." His eyes had darkened, and there was a noticeable flush in his cheeks. And yes, his pants were looking a bit tight. No matter how angry or disgusted he might be with me, I still lit his fire.

Brian tore his eyes away from my body to look me

straight in the eye. "Is the offer still on the table if I tell you there's no chance in hell I'll take you back?"

I flinched. I couldn't help it. I almost lost my courage completely, but I managed to dig it up from somewhere and meet his eyes once more. I was here to prove how much I trusted him. Brian would never put me through this if he wasn't planning to take me back. I'd have loved for him to tell me that straight out, but I suppose that would have violated the spirit of things.

"Yes," I said, and I could see the effect that single word had on him.

His Adam's apple bobbed as he swallowed hard. Then he grinned, a wolfish expression I'd never seen on his face before. "Let's see what's in the case of goodies, then."

Brian picked up the suitcase and headed for his bedroom. I was lucky I didn't fall over as I followed him with my shaky knees and my insanely high heels. He plunked the suitcase on the bed, then turned down the dimmer to bring the lights to a more atmospheric level.

Nervously, I came to stand beside him as he unzipped the suitcase. I was actually holding my breath when he flipped the top open. But there was nothing to see—yet—except for a length of black velvet that was tucked around the suitcase's contents, and an envelope with Brian's name on it and the words "for your eyes only" underlined.

"Why do I have a feeling I'm going to want to kill Dominic when this is all over?" I muttered under my breath.

Brian gave a huff of laughter as he picked up the envelope. "Go stand on the other side of the bed," he ordered. "I don't want you reading over my shoulder."

I tottered my way over, holding the bedpost to

help my shaky balance. It seemed to take Brian about three hours to read whatever it was Dominic had written, and the expressions on his face as he read it sparked both curiosity and terror in me.

Brian was grinning evilly when he finally looked up at me. "It's mostly an explanation of what everything is and how to use it. I guess he thought I might find some of them a mystery."

I raised an eyebrow. "And would you?"

He laughed. "Yeah. I'm afraid in this arena, I'm a babe in the woods."

"That makes two of us."

"I can't believe you actually talked to Dominic about this. Wish I'd been a fly on the wall for *that* conversation."

The fire in my cheeks burned higher. "Just another indication of how serious I am."

Brian flipped the black velvet out of the way, but in the low light and from across the bed, I couldn't see into the case well enough to identify anything other than a bunch of lumps. To clarify things for me, Brian lifted each item out of the case one by one, laying them on the bedspread for my inspection. I was really, *really* glad I had the bedpost to hold onto, because Dominic had taken me at my word—and then some.

At first, the items Brian laid out were easy to identify and no more intimidating than I'd expected. Black velvet ties; lengths of silky-looking rope; fur-lined cuffs; a blindfold; a—gulp—ball gag.

Then came some of the scarier items I'd expected. An oblong paddle, punctuated by scary-looking studs; something that looked like a short whip but with lots of thongs; a riding crop; dildoes in a variety of sizes and shapes.

After that, I had trouble figuring out what the hell you were supposed to do with the objects Brian continued to lay out on the bedspread. Lots of little clips and clamps and bars and strings and springs. Something that looked like a miniature pizza-cutter with teeth. A black leather glove with lots of prickly metal barbs on the fingers. And a long, fluffy feather, of all things!

I thought the case was completely empty when Brian looked up across the bed and met my eyes again. There was a warning in his eyes, and he held my gaze as he reached into the case and pulled out one last item. An item I knew all too well: the hellish whip Adam had used to tear my back to shreds.

I swayed, and for half a second, I thought I was actually going to faint. I gripped the bedpost with all the strength in my body and bit down on the inside of my cheek until I tasted blood. There was a challenge in Brian's stare, and I knew he was waiting for me to tell him to put that particular item back in the case. I also knew there was no chance he'd ever use it on me. The only reason it was in that case was as a challenge to my will and commitment. A challenge I was determined to meet.

When I didn't balk or otherwise object, I saw a hint of what might have been approval in Brian's eyes. Then he rubbed his hands together like a cartoon villain. I might have laughed if I weren't scared shitless. I held my breath as he slowly perused all the items on the bed, then reached for the blindfold.

I can do this, I told myself as Brian stalked around the bed toward me. My every instinct urged me to flee, but I stayed put.

"You know you're courting disaster if you expect me to move in these heels while wearing a blindfold," I said with a nervous laugh. "Maybe I'd better lie down first."

He didn't answer, moving behind me and sliding

the blindfold down over my eyes. It was thick and heavily padded, the padding conforming to the shape of my face so that no hint of light seeped through. Brian adjusted the elastic band behind my head, then slid one hand slowly down the length of my spine. Goose bumps immediately peppered my skin, and I shivered. I tried to tell myself that I wasn't really blindfolded, that I was just in a very dark room. I wasn't convinced.

I expected Brian to lay me down on the bed—the image I had in my mind was of being tied, spread-eagled, to the four posts. Instead, he put his arm around my shoulders and guided me around toward the back of the bed. I kept hold of the bedpost, because even with his arm around me, I felt weak and disoriented, and I didn't want to fall and break my leg. He turned me so that my back was to the room, then let go.

He must have made a special effort to move quietly, because I couldn't hear a thing, and I had no idea where he was. For all I knew, he'd left the room and I was just standing there like an idiot waiting for the ax to fall. But no, I was pretty sure he was picking out the next "toy." I tried not to imagine just what he might select, or why he'd positioned me with my back—or perhaps more importantly, my backside—to the room.

I jumped and let out a choked scream when his hand landed on my shoulder again. I hadn't heard the faintest sound of his approach. He laughed at me, and I summoned a little surge of indignation.

"Let's change places and see if *you* don't get a bit jumpy in this position," I grumbled at him.

"I'm the only one allowed to do any talking," he informed me, his lips inches from my ear. I could feel the heat of his body against my back.

I opened my mouth for a snappy comeback, but

before I managed to say anything, Brian shoved something into my mouth. I realized instantly that it was the ball gag, and my veins were suddenly flooded with enough adrenaline to jump-start a semi. For the first time, I let go of the bedpost, my arms flailing with the surge of panic.

Brian put his arm around my waist, balancing me when my sudden move almost toppled me. He made no effort to trap my arms, and when the worst of the panic faded, I realized all I had to do was spit the damn ball out and yank off the blindfold if I was ready to call it quits. I shuddered and pressed into the heat of Brian's body, calming myself by inches. The straps that were meant to fasten the gag behind my head hung loose, the ends tickling my collarbone.

"I like the idea of you not being able to talk back," Brian murmured in my ear. "But when you're ready to wave the white flag, you can let me know by dropping the ball."

Yes, I was nervous, uncomfortable, even scared. But I was still *me,* and I bristled at his use of the word "when." So I let my fingers do the talking. Only one finger, actually. He made a tsking sound, and I tensed, waiting for him to do something S&M-like, like spank me or pinch me. But he didn't.

He moved away again, but my senses had adjusted a bit to my blindness, so I heard the faint whisper of his feet brushing the carpet, and I heard him when he came back. Even so, I jumped a bit when his hand circled my left wrist. Then it wasn't his hand circling my wrist, it was something decadently soft—the fur-lined cuffs, I gathered. I hadn't taken a real close look at them, but from the sensations, I gathered they closed with buckles. He put first one, then the other on me, but they didn't seem to be attached to anything. Yet.

"Are they comfortable?" he asked. "Nod if they're okay, shake your head if they're too tight."

I flexed my hands and wiggled my fingers. The cuffs felt like soft, furry bracelets, snug, but not uncomfortably so. I took a deep breath through my nose and nodded.

There was a strange whispering sound I couldn't identify, and then Brian was lifting my left arm up toward the bedpost. Even when he let go, I couldn't lower my arm, and I realized the sound I heard was probably one of those lengths of silky rope being attached to the cuff and then tied to the bedpost. My heart fluttered, and I swallowed awkwardly, the gag making the latter difficult.

When Brian started lifting my right arm, I felt another surge of panic. This was it. Once he'd secured that arm, I would have no defenses left, no reassurance that I could remove the blindfold myself. I would be completely dependent on Brian to free me, helpless to stop him from doing anything he wanted. Even now, I'm amazed that I found the will and the strength to let him do it.

He smoothed his cheek up and down my neck, his stubble abrading the sensitive skin there. "Remember, you can always drop the ball, and everything stops."

This was a test of my trust and of my resolve. If I dropped the ball, I failed the test. Period. I bit down on the ball between my teeth. I had no intention of failing.

Once again, I heard the whisper of Brian's feet on the carpet. Even with the gag in my mouth, I managed a little groan of discontent when he turned on his CD player. He put in something mellow and classical, but it was just enough to mask the sound of his footsteps, as I'm sure he intended.

Time got a little wonky on me, my senses completely out of whack. I have no clue how long I stood there, my entire body tense enough to make my muscles quiver, waiting to see what Brian would do next, and *when* he would do it. That wait was pure agony. I *knew* that he wasn't going to hurt me, at least not in any but the most minor of ways. He was too gentle a soul to be really brutal with me, no matter how vigorous he wished this test to be. But bound, gagged, blindfolded, and helpless, I couldn't help letting my imagination run away with me.

I was strung so tight after waiting I don't know how long for something to happen that I actually jumped and shrieked at the feel of the feather caressing my ass. The gag kept the shriek from being terribly loud, but Brian certainly heard it. His laugh told me he was enjoying himself despite my misery.

The tip of the feather tickled first one cheek, then the other, then followed the line of my thong downward. I squirmed at the sensation, my skin twitching at the tickle that was at once sensual and annoying. It was probably a good thing for Brian I was gagged, because I don't think he'd have wanted to hear what I thought of him at that moment.

The feather started tickling the insides of my thighs, and I squirmed some more. Brian chuckled softly, and I wondered if it would violate the spirit of things if I were to aim a kick backward. He hadn't, after all, bound my legs. I managed to restrain the impulse, even as the tickling drove me mad.

I wasn't exactly relaxed now that Brian was tickling me to death with the damn feather, but I wasn't braced for pain as I had been during the excruciating wait. Which made the sudden smack of his hand against my ass all the more startling. He didn't hit me hard, the blow more like the kind of playful smack you'd give a lover who'd just teased you about something. But in the context, it was a shock to my system, and I gasped as if it had been brutal.

He followed up with more strokes of the feather, easing the faint sting. He repeated the process several more times, waiting until the tickle of the feather was driving me so crazy I forgot to brace against the spank. I jumped and squealed every time, only belatedly realizing that he hadn't really hurt me.

Somewhere along the line, I recognized the similarity between this situation and the erotic dream Lugh had created for me, but I was way too tense for this to be erotic. Of course, it also wasn't a dream.

When the tickle of the feather finally ended, I was momentarily relieved even as my cheeks clenched in anticipation. The relief dissolved into anxiety when nothing happened, and I realized that once again I had no idea where Brian was. Had he gone to pick out another "toy"? Was he standing there staring at me, watching me squirm and loving every minute of it? Hell, for all I knew, he'd gone out to watch a ball game on TV! For the record, being blindfolded sucks!

Once again, my sense of time got seriously distorted as I waited in nervous anticipation for whatever was to come next. My jaw muscles were getting tired from the gag—I felt like I'd been sitting in the dentist's chair while someone kept telling me to "open wide" for an hour. And I was more than ready to lose the fuck-me pumps that were forcing all of my weight onto the balls of my feet—and not, so far at least, getting me fucked.

I was surreptitiously trying to wiggle my ankles around to restore circulation to my toes when a new tickle made me jump for the millionth time. Was it possible to run out of adrenaline? Because it seemed like I should have done so by now.

At first, I didn't know what was causing the tickle.

It was something bigger and more diffuse than the feather, and Brian was dragging it up the side of my body. I had to stifle a laugh, because my sides are super ticklish. Then I started going over in my mind the items Dominic had put in the care package, and recognition shivered through me. This was the multi-thonged whip.

Nope, definitely not out of adrenaline. I started breathing hard, and I forgot all about the discomfort of the gag and the shoes. I did *not* want Brian to hit me with this thing! He was dragging it over my back right now, the long suede thongs paradoxically soft against my skin. I let out a little whimper.

"Remember," Brian said, "you can always drop the ball."

My jaws tightened reflexively on the ball. I was not going to chicken out now. I'd survived the hell that Adam had put me through; if I could survive that, it seemed almost silly to be afraid of anything that Brian might do.

He teased me a bit more with the whip, swinging it lightly so that the thongs brushed over my ass, letting me think about what it would feel like if he really did haul back and hit me with it. But of course, he didn't.

Brian let out a dramatic sigh. "Considering some of the crap you've pulled in the last couple of months, the idea of tanning your ass with this thing has some serious appeal. However, Dominic's note says I'd need to practice before using it, so I guess I'm SOL."

My heart bled for him. Really.

"Of course," he continued, "I could just use my hand. I bet I can manage that without any practice at all."

There was a long, pregnant pause. I imagined he was watching the ball very carefully, waiting to see if

I'd drop it. I certainly didn't want him to spank me, but if that was what it took to convince him to give me another chance, then I'd take it willingly. Which didn't mean I wasn't relieved as hell when he let out a regretful little sigh that told me he wasn't going to do it.

"Unfortunately, I don't think I have the patience for it right now," he said, and I didn't immediately know what he meant.

I groaned in relief when he removed the gag. My jaw muscles screamed in protest as I closed my mouth, but I was really glad to be able to swallow normally again.

Brian freed first my right hand, then my left from the bedposts. It was only then that I realized my shoulders had been getting pretty tired of being stretched out like that.

I figured he'd take the blindfold off next, but he didn't. Instead, he took my hands and pulled them behind my back. Apparently, those fur-lined cuffs could be connected together. I guess this wasn't over yet, after all.

He turned me around to face him, and I came very close to doing a not-so-graceful nosedive into the floor. Brian steadied me with his hands.

"Maybe we'd better get you off your feet before one of us ends up in the emergency room," he said, and though he wasn't laughing, I could hear the smile in his voice.

By "off your feet" he meant "on your knees," a fact I was able to divine without any further prompting from him. He kept his hands on me the whole way down, making sure I didn't topple over. I heard the jingle of his belt buckle, then the rasp of his zipper. I sucked in my cheeks and flexed my jaw a bit, hoping I'd be able to manage a good blow job after spending however long that had been with the ball gag in my mouth.

"Open wide," Brian commanded, and there was still that smile in his voice. I was kind of glad for the blindfold all of a sudden, because I didn't much want to see how much he'd been enjoying himself— although I guessed I was about to get some pretty concrete evidence in my mouth.

I love giving Brian blow jobs. His pleasure in it is downright contagious. But after everything that had gone between us lately, I couldn't just swallow him without a word of affection, especially not when I was kneeling at his feet, blindfolded and with my hands tied behind my back.

"I love you," I murmured, and to my surprise, tears sprang into my eyes behind the blindfold.

Brian's hands caressed my hair, then slid down to gently cup my cheeks. The tenderness of the touch brought even more tears to my eyes.

"I love you, too," he said, then pushed the blind-fold up and out of the way.

I got a quick glimpse of his rampant arousal before he fell to his knees in front of me and seized my mouth for a hard, passionate kiss. I opened wide for him, all right, my mouth, my heart, my soul. Kissing me all the time, he fumbled at the cuffs that bound my hands and managed to get them off by feel.

As far as I had noticed, nothing he'd done to me while I was bound had aroused me in the slightest. And yet now, only moments after he'd freed me, I was desperate to have him inside me. Luckily, he seemed to feel the same way.

Who needs a bed when you've got a perfectly good floor available? Before I knew it, Brian had rolled me under himself, away from the bed. My thong panties were flimsy enough that he was able to rip them off with one quick jerk. And then he was making love to me, his strokes hard, and masterful, and perfect. I wrapped my arms and legs around him, tears falling unheeded from my eyes as I clung with everything I had.

Afterward, Brian rolled to the side, pulling me with him. He was still buried inside me, and I pressed as close to him as was humanly possible.

"Don't ever leave me again," I said as I pressed my lips to his chest and tasted the salt of his sweat. "Of all the bad things that have happened to me, that was the worst."

He squeezed me even tighter, so hard I practically couldn't breathe. "I didn't like it so much, either. It seems like whatever either one of us does, we always end up back together. Maybe the universe is trying to tell us something."

"Maybe so," I agreed, raising my head so I could meet his eyes. And maybe, just this once, I would actually listen to what the universe was saying.

Later, when we were both recovered enough to stand and were both feeling a little awkward and shy with each other, Brian showed me the "instructions" Dominic had written him:

If you've gone along with Morgan's plan enough to get to this note, then I presume you're planning to go through with it. Let me give you some friendly advice about the toys in this case. First, if you don't know what it is, don't even think about using it. Second, if you don't know how to use it properly, don't even think about using it. (Hint: You don't know how to use the crop, the flogger, or the paddle, even if you

*think you do.) Third, make sure Morgan always
has a way to signal she wants to stop, and respect the signal if she gives it. And last but not
least, if you ignore my advice, I'm going to come
over there personally and kick your ass! Don't
think because I'm gay I can't do it. Respect and
treasure the power she's putting in your hands,
and don't abuse it.*

My eyes misted with tears when I read it. Brian
slipped his arms around me from behind and pulled
me close to his heat.

"Dominic's a pretty cool guy," he said softly into
my ear.

I nodded and sniffled, then turned in Brian's arms
so I could lay my head against his shoulder as I held
him tight. "So are you," I whispered, then raised my
head to look into his eyes. God, I loved him! I was
sure tonight's encounter was little more than a patch
on our wounded relationship, but a patch was a step
in the right direction, and I vowed that I was going to
do everything I could to put all the pieces of us back
together.

Brian lowered his head, his lips brushing softly
against mine. Returning his kiss, I closed my eyes and
let Dominic's note flutter to the floor.

Epilogue

A week after I'd left the hospital, my lawyer finally convinced Jordan Maguire Sr. to drop the lawsuit. Without any outside forces to whip him into a frenzy, it seemed Maguire just didn't have the will to persecute me. I suspect in his heart of hearts, he knew I wasn't really at fault, but it's not a theory I'll ever be able to confirm.

Saul now had an official identity, having magically become Saul Davidson, a twenty-eight-year-old native of Southern California who had been a legal, registered demon host for five years. He even had all the paperwork to prove it. I wondered if somewhere in a courthouse in California there existed a falsified video of Saul's registration process. I decided I didn't want to know.

And then there was Barbie.

I'd avoided her as much as I could, not being anxious to fulfill Lugh's promise. Truthfully, though, I knew it had to be done. Barbie had seen and heard far too much, and with her inquisitive mind, she'd be able to put together enough facts to come up with some uncomfortable conclusions, even if those conclusions were all wrong. Raphael contended we'd be better off killing her and hiding the body, but I think he was just saying that to goad Saul.

To make sure everyone was on board and fully aware of Lugh's wishes, I called together the entire council before I invited Barbie to my apartment for the long-awaited explanation. She was, of course, on crutches, her leg broken in two places from Abraham's brutal kick. Not coincidentally, she ended up sitting next to Saul when I called the meeting to order.

I told Barbie the whole, long, intricate story of Lugh's banishment to the Mortal Plain and the danger Dougal represented to the human race. Others chimed in occasionally with extra details and clarifications. Barbie had to be surprised by what she was hearing, but she mostly hid the surprise well, only the occasional widening of her eyes betraying her shock.

I didn't exactly *invite* her to join Lugh's council—council membership was more of a command performance than a choice—but I couched it as delicately as I could.

"I know being part of the council will sometimes interfere with your paying job," I said—it sure as hell interfered with mine, even when I wasn't suspended. The U.S. Exorcism Board moves with all the speed of your average bureaucracy, which meant they still hadn't lifted my suspension, even though the lawsuit had fizzled. "But we'll do whatever we can to make sure Blair is taken care of."

Barbie's eyes widened hugely and she gasped. "Oh! So *you're* the one who set up that trust."

"Huh?" I said, looking around at the other members of the council and seeing similarly blank expressions.

Barbie frowned. "The anonymous trust? The one

that came out of nowhere to fund Blair's stay at The Healing Circle?"

Still no signs of recognition from anyone as we all looked at one another and shrugged or shook our heads.

"But it *has* to be you guys," Barbie insisted. "I couldn't even come up with a far-fetched guess who it could be before you told me everything. Why would anyone else give a damn about Blair's care? No one ever has before now."

We each took a turn saying something to the effect of "it wasn't me," leaving Barbie looking flummoxed and perhaps even a little frustrated.

Conversation flowed around me, full of theories and conjecture, but I stayed out of it. There were only two people sitting in this circle who had the means to set up Blair's care: Adam and Raphael. The rest of us were pretty much broke. If Adam had set up the trust, there would be no reason for him not to admit it. But then, there wasn't really any reason for *Raphael* not to admit it, either. Of course, it didn't really seem like the kind of thing Raphael would do. A philanthropist he was not! But, like Barbie, I had a hard time believing the money could have come from anyone but a member of this council.

I met Raphael's eyes from across the circle. His expression was studiously blank, but he broke off the stare quickly, and my conviction strengthened. When the rest of the council members filed out one by one— or two by two, in the case of Adam and Dom and Saul and Barbie—I grabbed Raphael's arm and made him stay behind. Brian gave me a raised eyebrow, and I mouthed "later" at him. He accepted that without comment.

"So what's the story?" I asked when Raphael and I were alone.

"What story?" he asked, sounding genuinely baffled. But then, Raphael was one hell of a good liar.

"The trust fund?"

He shook his head. "I had nothing to do with that."

"Bullshit."

He laughed. "Usually, you're accusing me of the most heinous acts you can imagine. Why on earth would you suddenly start suspecting me of doing something...nice?" He grimaced when he said the word, as if it were distasteful.

"Instinct."

"It wasn't me."

"Why don't you want anyone to know?"

It looked like there was another denial on his lips, but he stopped himself and sighed. "Let's pretend for a moment that it *was* me. What would be the first thing everyone on the council would think if I took credit for it?"

I nodded, getting it. "Gee, I wonder what's in it for you?"

His lips thinned in displeasure, but he had to know he'd earned his reputation. "Right." He sighed again, the muscles in his face relaxing slightly. "There's nothing I can do to make the rest of you think better of me. But I'd like to believe that I'm not quite the embodiment of evil you all think I am. So if I were to make a gesture like setting up a trust for Blair's care and then not take credit for it, it would be to prove to *myself* that I have redeeming qualities. But if I took credit for it, it would be just one more way I'm trying to make myself look better to the rest of you, and I'm back to being an irredeemably selfish bastard. So, it wasn't me. End of story."

It was still almost impossible not to doubt Raphael's motive. He probably could have deduced that I'd figure out it had to be him and that I'd call him on it. That would allow him to take credit for his charitable act while still pretending not to. The way his mind twisted and turned, it was hard to know what to make of his gesture.

I think he actually meant well this time, Lugh said. I was pretty sure my subconscious barriers were gone for good, because I wasn't particularly stressed right this moment, but I could still hear him.

I thought Raphael was finally going to leave, but I wasn't that lucky.

"I was going to bring this up during the meeting," he said, "but I figured I should give Lugh the heads-up before I shot my mouth off. We're in a stronger position now than we have been since Lugh first was summoned to the Mortal Plain. Dougal and his supporters haven't been able to find him. He's set up his court with people he trusts. And no one's trying to kill, frame, or otherwise persecute you at the moment."

"That we know of," I mumbled.

Raphael ignored me. "We've had no choice but to continually play defense so far. But eventually, we're going to have to go on the offensive. Dougal can afford to wait us out, so we can't just sit back and twiddle our thumbs forever."

He could have put that more tactfully, but I knew he was right. Problem was, I hadn't a clue how to go about going on the offensive.

"What do you suggest?" I asked. "It's not like we can go to the Demon Realm after him—even if you or Lugh could kill him there, which I gather you can't. And we've already established that he's not going to conveniently show up on the Mortal Plain where we *can* kill him."

"Not at the moment. It would be a highly unnecessary risk, and Dougal doesn't take unnecessary risks. So we have to find a way to make it a *necessary* risk."

"And have you got an idea how we can manage that?"

Raphael frowned. "Not yet. But I'm working on it, and you and Lugh should, too."

He's lying, Lugh whispered in my mind. *He has an idea. He just doesn't like it and is hoping we'll come up with something he likes better.*

When you accuse Raphael of lying, you're right at least fifty percent of the time, so I believed Lugh. Trouble was, Raphael would stick to his lies like superglue until confronted with irrefutable evidence.

"You *sure* you don't have any ideas?" I prompted, but it was a halfhearted attempt at best. I'd have dropped dead on the spot if Raphael had suddenly admitted he really did have an idea.

"Of course I don't," he responded with his trademark sincerity. Anyone who didn't know him well enough would be convinced he was the soul of honesty. "What possible reason could I have for not telling you if I did?"

"Good question."

Raphael gave me a look of pure disgust. "I swear, you'd think I was lying if I said water was wet! I don't know why I bother talking to you at all." He turned on his heel and headed for the door.

Was this a real fit of pique? Or was this an attempt to deflect the question?

"Raphael!" I called, on the off chance he was really upset and didn't deserve the suspicion.

"What?" he asked, turning to me with a snarl.

"You did a really good thing, arranging for Blair's care. Thank you."

His Adam's apple bobbed, and for the life of me I

couldn't recognize the expression on his face. He turned away without another word, slamming the door behind him.

"Think he'll tell us what he has in mind?" I asked Lugh.

He might not need to. I'm afraid prolonged contact with him and his Machiavellian ways has had an unsavory effect on me.

I couldn't feel Lugh's emotions like he could feel mine, but there was a world of tension in his phantom voice. "What exactly does that mean?"

Lugh didn't answer, which was probably just as well. If whatever conclusion the Brothers Grimm had come to made them both so uneasy, I didn't want to know about it. Maybe if I was a good little exorcist-cum-demon-host, I'd never have to. Ignorance is bliss and all that.

Somehow, I didn't think there was a whole lot of bliss in my future.

About the Author

Jenna Black is your typical writer. Which means she's an "experience junkie." She got her BA in physical anthropology and French from Duke University. Once upon a time, she dreamed she would be the next Jane Goodall, camping in the bush making fabulous discoveries about primate behavior. Then, during her senior year at Duke, she did some actual research in the field and made this shocking discovery: Primates spend something like 80 percent of their time doing such exciting things as sleeping and eating. Concluding that this discovery was her life's work in the field of primatology, she then moved on to such varied pastimes as grooming dogs and writing technical documentation. Visit her on the web at www.JennaBlack.com.

And don't think the action stops here:
It's all fun and games until someone dies in

THE DEVIL'S PLAYGROUND

The latest book in the Morgan Kingsley series

by
Jenna Black

No one ever wants to serve in Hell...

*The Seven Deadlies, a demon club in
Philadelphia, has always catered to the most
attractive and desirable hosts. Recently, though,
more and more of the lower dregs of society have
been showing up with demons of their own—in
alarming numbers. Morgan is sure that Dougal is
behind this, but isn't sure why.*

*Is Dougal building an army to snatch the throne
of the demons from Lugh?*

*If there's one person who can get to the bottom of
this, it's Morgan Kingsley, but caught between her
mortal lover Brian and the demon she lusts for,
Lugh, it's going to take everything she has to keep
her head—and heart—in the game.*